**Also available from JN Welsh
and Carina Press**

In Harmony
In Rhythm

Also available from JN Welsh

Gigolo All the Way

Sea Breeze Seductions Series

Before We Say Goodbye
Bitter Sweet
Moonshine and Mistletoe

IN TUNE

—

JN WELSH

carina
press

carina
press®

Recycling programs
for this product may
not exist in your area.

ISBN-13: 978-1-335-89590-5

In Tune

First published in 2018. This edition published in 2024.

Copyright © 2018 by Jennifer N Welsh

For questions and comments about the quality of this book,
please contact us at CustomerService@Harlequin.com.

® is a trademark of Harlequin Enterprises ULC.

Carina Press
22 Adelaide St. West, 41st Floor
Toronto, Ontario M5H 4E3, Canada
www.CarinaPress.com

Printed in U.S.A.

To my loving family and amazing friends,
who give new meaning to the word *support*.
I love you and thank you for
never letting me give up.

Chapter One

If Leona Sable had known how this day was going to turn out, she would have stayed in bed, nestled against her boyfriend pillow with the covers pulled over her head.

How the fuck did I get here? A conversation with her boss and mentor, Abraham Wallace, that started with "The client only wants you" and ended with "Meet me at the Metro Hotel this evening at seven and be dressed for a night out." That's how.

Ever since that conversation a few short hours ago, Leona had been collecting intel on Electronic Dance Music DJ Luke "The Musical Prophet" Anderson.

Had Abe not looked so stressed and hell-bent on acquiring said potential client, she'd still be in hiding, paper pushing due diligence forms.

Leona sat in the hairdresser's chair in Midtown Manhattan. Her tight corkscrew curls dripped wet onto the towel draped over her shoulders, while she pressed the cell phone to her ear.

"Dale, sweetie, you're telling me that Luke's manager left his tour? Just like that? Why?" Leona strained to hear above the light music playing in the salon.

Dale, her fabulous, long-time source swam in the

know while others simply dipped their toe into the pool. "Allegedly, there was a mash-up of problems. Money issues and fraternization," he whispered into the phone.

Leona wasn't a gossip but she sometimes had to play the role of one to get the information she needed.

"They were dating? Was it serious?"

"Who knows in this industry? But I will say that hearts were broken. And…"

Leona couldn't believe the next words that came out of Dale's mouth, and neither would Abe when she briefed him. "No!"

"Yes, but you won't find a lick about it in the rags. The family is wealthy and adamant about her privacy. They keep paying out."

"Then why would she do that?"

"I don't know, girl. Money got these people like… whoa!"

"Stop." Leona laughed, assessing her milk chocolate brown image in the mirror. "Thanks, D. You gave me a lot to work with. I appreciate it."

"Listen, love. Please don't ever go underground again. I need my concert tickets."

"I promise." Leona hung up.

Her hairdresser started to work. "Let me get started on your twists."

"Change of plan, Kim. Geisha bun. Sleek and sexy."

Kim stilled with wide-toothed comb in hand. "You haven't had that style in a while. Does this mean you're back?"

Kim's excitement surprised her. "No." Leona's raised voice carried above the music.

"Okay, okay. Just asking." Kim's grin reflected in the mirror.

Leona surveyed the room and tapped her left ear-lobe. "The last thing I need is that rumor getting out."

Kim readied her tools—complete with blow-dryer and brush—for Leona's hair. "Maybe after tonight it won't be a rumor."

For the past year, Leona had stayed out of the spot-light. Lately, she had to admit that the administrative role Abe allowed her to perform was a snore fest, and she'd thought about waging a comeback and once again doing the work she loved. Though she was an experienced personal manager, with production and tour experience, the entertainment industry was fickle and would make her pay for her absence. More importantly, a nagging question remained.

Am I ready?

Leona checked her messages and returned a call to Tracy Ruiz, one of the resident lawyers at Wallace Entertainment. "Hey, Tracy. Got anything on Mr. Wonderful?"

"He doesn't have any priors, but there have been some disturbances of the peace. Mr. Anderson has had a string of episodes involving angry outbursts, but no one was hurt. Only a couple of scuffles here and there."

"This just gets more interesting by the hour. Okay, Tracy. Thanks."

What the hell did Abe got me into? A client with a shady business past and anger management issues... Seriously? A shiver scuttled up her back and her shoulders shimmied in release. *Just get him in the door, Leo, and you'll be done.*

Kim took a brief break from pulling at Leona's kinky curls. "You cold, girl?"

"Oh, no, I'm good. Just some old ghosts trying to bully me."

Kim patted her shoulders.

Leona was tempted to contact Luke's family members for more information, but her experience with her ex-boyfriend gave her pause. The media craziness had adversely affected the Sable family. And though she only sought information—it was a line she was unwilling to cross.

With her hair completed, Leona thanked Kim and headed home. In her walk-in closet, Leona chose her outfit while she listened to one of Luke's interviews. He mentioned a fondness for animal crackers and she chuckled. "And not just any kind either." She loved researching potential clients. Sometimes their quirks and preferences were predictable, other times quite unexpected.

Her phone rang. She picked up when she saw it was Abe.

"Leo? I'm on my way to the hotel. What'd you find out, darlin'?" he asked. Though from Scottish and Spanish stock, Abe had been born and raised in North Carolina. He used the touch of Southern twang in his voice to sweet-talk anyone into doing his bidding.

"He's very into his fans. In fact, that's why this guy is all over the place and not just in the States." She put Abe on speaker and scrolled through some notes on her phone. "Yeah, Brazil, Australia, United Arab Emirates… Yikes. The list of worldwide appearances goes on for pages. What a treacherous schedule."

"Hard worker. What else?"

"He's passionate about his music and active on all social media outlets. We like passion."

"We?"

"Wallace Entertainment," Leona clarified. "People have nice things to say about him. But, Abe? There's a bit of controversy around his last management. His ex-manager stole some astronomical amount of money from him and—"

"That's an unfounded rumor. We need him, Leo."

There's that desperation again. "I get that you want him, but…"

"No, Leo. The company needs him."

"The company? Okay, Abe. What's really going on here?"

Abe was silent. "I'm in a cab, coming up on 14th Street. We'll talk later. See you in a bit."

"Abe…" she called to a dead line. *Damn it. What the hell?* She breathed deep.

She dressed in snug off-white leather bootleg pants and a fitted black shirt with capped sleeves. Sexy black lace accented the top of the shirt—from above her bust to her neck—and covered her back. It was the perfect day-to-night outfit, yet still professional. Too much time had passed since her life required such attire. The outfit felt foreign at first, until the old familiar part of her began to stir.

A sheer off-white shawl draped over her shoulders allowed the light material to pop off of her brown skin. Black peep-toe booties added four inches to her five-foot-four frame. She quickly evaluated her image in the mirror and extended her arm to the reflection, as if offering a handshake to see how her outfit moved. She hadn't done that in years. *You're nervous.* She wiggled her shoulders. *Shake it off. This is old hat, Leo.*

She didn't know what situation awaited her at the Metro Hotel but she was as ready as she'd ever be.

Chapter Two

Pockets of fans gathered outside the hotel with cameras and signs ranging from *I love you, Luke* to *Disciple of The Musical Prophet*. Leona passed them and glided through the sliding doors, heading for the concierge desk.

"Hi—" she glanced at the man's name tag "—Sam. Leona Sable. Rooftop bar. Anderson party." The economy of words allowed her to catch her breath. Construction had turned her bright idea to take the subway into delays that had her booking it to the hotel. She hated being late.

The young concierge smoothed his pressed suit. "Ah yes, Miss Sable. You're expected. Identification, please." His moves were slow and deliberate.

Leona fished for her license and handed it to him.

Sam reviewed and returned the card. "Mr. Wallace has arrived. Mr. Anderson and his agent are guests of the hotel and await your arrival. You'll need this." He handed her a black hotel room key along with some instructions. "The key expires in two hours."

Leona evaluated the shiny metallic card, flipping it over between her middle and index finger. "Thanks."

She rounded the corner toward the elevators, regarding the beautiful black-and-white contrasts of the modern and artistic décor. Splashes of red and purple from fresh tulips brought life to the area.

In the elevator, she adjusted her clothing, pressed the heel of her palm against her forehead to pat away perspiration, and dabbed on tinted lip-gloss.

Leona thought she knew Abe's motivation for the meeting, but their last conversation had inserted a pressure element. Abe needed to sign The Musical Prophet and Abe never *needed* anything. Perhaps the company's money issues were worse than the water cooler talk had implied. Guilt rose within her. She pushed it down and straightened her slumping posture. *Focus, Sable.*

The elevator doors opened to a small corridor that led to the rooftop bar. The cool air was more brisk at this elevation. The Empire State Building loomed deceptively close enough to touch, and the Tower lights blazed signature white. The endless light pink and burnt orange colors of dusk surrounded the building and city skyline with the promise of night. *I love my city.* "Empire State of Mind" by Jay-Z and Alicia Keys played in her head.

When Abe spotted her, he waved her over. He was about five foot eleven, a powerhouse of a man, and stood taller among the handful of shorter folks in the bar.

"Leo, I'm glad you could join us," Abe said when she stood by his side. "And early as usual."

"I'm never late." *Thank goodness that damn train ride didn't ruin my record.*

Abe shot her a sideways glance. "Which I'm sure you obsessed about the whole way here." He spoke under his breath.

"Shh-shh."

Abe really did know her well. She turned her attention to the man before her, who bore no resemblance to DJ Luke but was familiar to her. Tom "Boombox" Mills's hipster-style gray suit was highly tailored and close fitting, accompanied by a crisp, white shirt and violet-colored tie. Black-rimmed glasses matched his black hair, and a five o'clock shadow grew on his chin and cheeks. He held an old-fashioned glass filled with ice and amber liquid.

"Boombox, right?" She shook his hand and thought he was attractive in a detail-oriented kind of way. "Leona Sable. Please call me Leo."

"It's nice to finally meet you, Leo. The industry knows me as Boombox, but you can call me Tommy." His warm brown eyes smiled at her.

"A pleasure, Tommy." Leona knitted her fingers together.

"Abe and I were just discussing the success you've had with well-known clients. Impressive." Tommy sipped his drink.

"Thank you for the compliment."

Grapevine had it that Boombox's exclusive client list was a short five. She wondered why he and DJ Luke needed her.

Leona scanned the small deserted bar. Faint ambient music played, further emptying the space. Even the quiet movements of the bartender spoke of loneliness. Leona was anxious to meet Luke and add some realness to the larger-than-life artist Abe had inflated the DJ to be. "I don't see Mr. Anderson."

"He'll join us momentarily." Tommy swirled the liquid and the ice rattled against the glass. "I wanted to familiarize you both with Luke's present situation and the way he likes to do business."

Abe drained the remains of his highball glass. "Tommy has informed me that because Luke is playing at Aurora Nightclub tonight, he only has a short amount of time to meet with us. Tommy works out of California, something you two have in common."

"In common?" Tommy raised an eyebrow.

"I worked in LA for two years before returning to New York." Leona's fingers itched to play with her hair, and she wished she, too, had a drink. "No one ever remembers because most of my success has been here in the city."

"That's good to know," Tommy noted.

"Tommy's negotiating the terms of Luke's residency, so the event and his performance tonight are important." Abe's speech carried with it the scent of cranberries layered with the tinge of vodka.

"Nice." Leona adjusted her shawl as the chilled rooftop wind blew through her thin barrier. "Can we?" She referenced a modern lava-rock fire pit. The yellow and orange flames danced over the charcoal gray pebbles, beckoning her closer with their inviting heat.

"Sure." Tommy followed.

Abe trailed behind.

They sat on the java-colored rattan love seat with white cushions that matched her outfit. The railing and deck glass allowed for an ample view of the city lights.

"Having a residency with consistent monthly appearances is a good sign that he's in demand. Any reason why he didn't choose Las Vegas? It's a hot spot for DJ residencies." If Leona were Luke's manager, securing a spot in Vegas would be one of her top priorities.

"Good observation. Right now, Luke likes the vibe in New York and Atlantic City, but Vegas is on his radar," Tommy clarified.

"I'm going to refresh my drink. Would you like something, Leo?" Abe inched toward the bar.

Leona would have loved red wine or whisky, but she wore white. To avoid the possibility of a crimson or rusty stain on her clothing she made the safer choice. "A white wine spritzer, please. Thanks."

"You got it." Abe left to get their drinks.

Leona was familiar with this chess game.

"Leo? Luke's talented and one of the front-runners in EDM. As you can tell by the fans waiting outside the hotel to get a glimpse of him, he's also popular. He's approaching a level many DJs aspire to, but he needs real management. It's what's held him back for years. I can get the gigs and appearances, but he needs a champion to propel him forward."

"Abe is the best in the business, so you'll be well taken care of." Leona tried to remain a queen protected by the knights instead of a pawn being sacrificed for the king. Check.

"Funny, he said the same thing about you." Tommy sipped his drink. "Listen, I'm sure Abe is great, but your work is respected throughout the industry. The success you had managing Ramsey is epic. The way you not only grew his fan base, but also his net worth, is the bar everyone tries to achieve to this day. It's the reason I suggested Wallace Entertainment to Luke."

"I see." *Respected?* Sure, she had an impressive resume, but after the way her ex-boyfriend and client, Paul Reese, had bad-mouthed her and Wallace Entertainment—claiming to the media that she caused loss of revenue and engaged in fraudulent transactions when they broke up—Leona wasn't sure *respected* was the word anyone would use to describe her reputation. That was just the tip of the iceberg. Before the shit hit the fan, one might have even hailed that her work with Paul was the best of her career.

Abe returned and handed Leona a glass. "Here you go."

Leona took a long awaited swig of her spritzer. The oaky wine added flavor more than any real potency.

"Before we continue, let me explain Luke's management preferences, so that there are no misunderstandings." Tommy again brought the glass to his lips.

Leona raised an eyebrow and peeked over at Abe. She pulled her shoulders back and puffed her chest, ready for whatever Tommy was about to share, when a man zoomed up to them. His swift movement startled her.

"Luke," Tommy called and they all rose to greet him.

Luke was well over six feet, olive-skinned, and muscular with short dark brown hair. He was now the tallest man in their party. He wore a short-sleeved green tee shirt that partially exposed a random pattern of thick, black, curving, inviting lines on his forearm that merged together into an intricate tribal tattoo. His dark blue jeans fitted snug against his strong thighs and he sported a pair of trendy black sneakers with white soles.

"Hey, Tommy, sorry I'm late." He put a hand on Tommy's shoulder and leaned close to his ear. "I've been trying to put my set together, but I've gotten three calls so far telling me sound check is in an hour. Shouldn't they be calling you instead of me? Anyway,

I need flash drives to back up my music. I'm starving, too, so let's get something to eat after this."

The relaxed and friendly exchange between the two men made her smile. They interacted like genuine friends. Her first impression was that she liked Luke. He was easygoing with his agent, even though this was an important night for him.

"All right, man. I'll get it all straightened out." Tommy turned to Leona and Abe. "Luke, I'd like you to meet Leona Sable and Abraham Wallace from Wallace Entertainment."

Luke shook Abe's hand. "Pleasure to work with you, Mr. Wallace."

The rooftop breeze carried Luke's fragrance. A combination of musk, sandalwood, and patchouli hung in the air.

"Mmm." Leona's entire body melted into relaxation as if she had just snuggled under a warm duvet in the middle of winter. *Whoa.* Her potent response to Luke and his scent was unexpected.

Luke did a double take when he saw her. His green-gray eyes evaluated her and lingered a moment on her lips. "Leona Sable." He stretched his hand out. "I apologize. We don't have much time because of my performance tonight."

The Internet didn't prepare me well for this yummy-smelling hottie. Not at all.

Though a blush warmed her cheeks, she grasped his hand firmly, and shook it with a businesslike nod. "Hello, Luke. It's nice to meet you. Please call me Leo."

"Leo? Your name sounds familiar."

Shouldn't the person's name you requested a meet-

ing with sound familiar? You're cute, but maybe not so smart. "I'm—"

"That's because Leo does stellar work." Abe stretched his hand out to Luke. "Her reputation precedes her."

Luke turned back to Leona and twisted the soul patch of hair beneath his lower lip. "Who did you last manage, Leo?"

Leona couldn't help but notice Tommy's disposition change from confident to anxious. Since she'd assumed they already knew what went down last year, she hadn't thought about how to answer that question, and opted for honesty.

"I've had success with a few clients. I haven't managed in a year, but my last clients were Ramsey Fox and Paul Reese."

Luke's eyes narrowed and recognition spread across his features. His hand shot out and clutched Tommy's lapel. "I trusted you to handle my management and you set me up with Paul Reese's manager? Are you trying to fuck up the progress we've made?"

Instinct surged through Leona and she backed up. *What the hell just happened?*

Has Luke come in contact with Paul's lies?

Tommy placed a hand on Luke's chest to stop his exit. "We need to secure your management so you can focus on the music. I'll take care of everything else, but we need Wallace Entertainment." Tommy set his glass down and took a superhero stance, pushing back his jacket and placing his fists on his hips.

Luke squared his shoulders. "All right. He stays, but she goes."

"Excuse me? Didn't you request this meeting?" *I was running for this jerk?*

Luke faced her, his eyes changing from warm attentive green to angry gray. "I no longer work with female managers. Tommy knows this." Luke dragged his attention to Tommy.

Leona felt her inner Queen Bey stir and the lyrics to "Run the World (Girls)" almost had her doing choreography. "What did you say?"

"Luke, you seemed more open to the idea before. I'm asking you to reconsider," Tommy reasoned.

"That was before I realized she's Reese's ex. I don't need that drama and negative shit around me. I have my share."

Paul Reese strikes again.

Leona attempted to salvage her dignity. "I don't know what you've heard, but—"

"I've heard enough." Luke glared at her as if she caused all his problems. Beyond offended, she was confused.

"What does my being Paul's ex-girlfriend have to do with anything?" Leona braced herself for Luke to recant Paul's gossip. But instead Luke honed in on her personal relationship. It wasn't entirely strange but perplexing.

Tommy stood squarely between them.

"Okay, everyone, just calm down." Tommy's even tone interrupted before she could get an answer.

Leona eyeballed Luke although she spoke to Tommy. "I suspect these are the preferences you were talking about? Fine with me." She pivoted to walk away. Her explanations about Paul ran out long ago. She was done trying to convince people of her worth.

"Hang on, I need Leo here." Abe stopped her by the shoulders and turned her around.

"Luke, think of all you want to accomplish this year. Leo can make this happen." Tommy's voice was low and hard with encrypted meaning.

"Leo?" Abe's stressed expression urged her to stay. *What did you get me into, old man?*

Luke paced and rubbed his head as if to soothe his anger.

"Think about your success. The rest is bullshit, man," Tommy emphasized to Luke.

Luke crossed his arms and once again brought one hand up to brush his thumb against the hair below his lower lip. "Okay, Tommy. I'll consider it, but first I want to see what she's got. She fails and she's out."

"What?" Leona squawked.

"The show tonight isn't sold out yet," Luke informed. "If Miss Sable promises me a sellout show and a five percent increase in VIP tickets, then I'll consider it."

"Luke, the show is in three hours. That's impossible," Tommy countered.

"I know." Luke gloated at her potential failure. "If she's the best in the business, I want her to prove it."

Leona craned her neck at Abe. "What the fuck?" she mouthed.

"Gentlemen. Give us a minute." Abe moved Leona to a private area by the bar.

"This isn't happening. I thought maybe I could orchestrate a comeback with an artist like Luke. Believe me. It crossed my mind, but he is a misogynistic jerk."

"I need you to do this, Leo."

"Why? Tell me fast because I'm out of here unless there's a really good reason for me to torture myself with this nightmare situation." The air was in cool contrast to Leona's boiling anger.

"Damn it. This isn't how I wanted to tell you." Abe rubbed his face. "The company is in the red."

Leona's fears about Wallace Entertainment were true. "But we've been in trouble before and have made it out okay."

"We're barely able to keep up with the monthly expenses and payroll. If I don't find a way to fix this fast, we're going under."

Though in an open space, Leona felt the oppression of everything around her closing in. "How long?"

"Six months, maybe longer with layoffs," Abe delivered.

"Nice one, Abe." Leona returned a wry smile in disbelief until she saw his solemn expression. "You're serious?"

Abe's chest deflated. "Yes." He was a proud man. This couldn't have been easy for him, but his timing was shitty.

"You're dropping this on me now? Why didn't you just tell me the whole story earlier?"

"I promise to tell you everything, darlin', but right now we can't let Luke walk away. Do this for me."

Leona wanted to pull her hair out but it was inaccessible in the tight bun. With Abe's news, her temples pulsated and heat warmed her ears. She had so many questions, but most of all she was pissed that she'd been backed into a corner. She pinched a tranquilizer point on her ear and her stomach churned with guilt and nervous energy. The last year had been tumultuous with the Paul scandal and she wondered how much of the company's troubles had resulted from what happened.

"Leo?" Abe called.

Though she struggled between bolting and getting Abe his contract, Leona knew in her heart that she would do whatever was necessary to get Luke to sign with Wallace Entertainment and help save the company. She was good at this. Even if Luke believed the rumors, she owed it to herself to prove him wrong.

Sonofabitch! "Fine." She stormed back to Luke and Tommy with Abe trailing behind her. "I'll do it."

"What?" Luke's raised eyebrows and contemptuous tone hit her ego where it hurt.

She finished her drink, wishing she'd ordered the whiskey after all. "I'll do it. And I'll guarantee you'll get the residency at Aurora."

Luke inhaled. "Guarantee? How?"

"Because Tommy is going to promise the owners a sold-out show and a five percent increase in VIP tickets. He's also going to guarantee a ten percent increase in revenue, as well as increased media coverage."

"I can't promise that." Tommy gave a nervous chuckle.

"Leo can," Abe announced.

Her heart raced and she tried to slow the rapid angry movement of her chest. *This is how I'm coming back?* "I'll make it happen. Just have the contracts ready."

Tommy folded his arms. "How are you going to do that? That's my reputation on the line."

Leona watched the pair of them, doubt written all over their faces. "Mine, too."

"You want us to believe you can pull this off by eleven tonight?" Luke's wicked snicker infuriated her.

"You wanted me to prove what I can do. I'm showing you." Leona had to stop her neck from snapping with attitude.

"You're a promoter *and* an agent now?" Sarcasm decorated Luke's words.

She didn't want to get into a back-and-forth with him but she couldn't resist letting him know he wasn't dealing with an amateur. "If you must know, I started my career in marketing, specializing in promotions and public relations. Like Tommy, I'm a licensed talent agent in the state of California where I practiced for a few years. My legal background is sound. I don't like negotiating contracts, but I could successfully do that tonight for you, as well. No offense, Tommy. So—" Leona slicked her hair up into her bun even though not a hair was out of place. "Are we agreed?"

Luke showered her with doubt. "Agreed."

Leona opened her cell and started dialing. "We'll see you at Aurora tonight. The contract will be locked in before Luke leaves the stage."

"You're making big promises, Leo," Tommy warned.

"Ones I intend to keep. By the way, there's an electronics store two blocks from here. You can get flash drives there." Leona pulled out a box of animal crackers and tossed it to Luke. "I heard these were your favorite. Hopefully, it'll take the edge off. Let's go, Abe. We've got work to do."

As she rounded the corner to the elevator, she glanced back to see Luke's stunned face as he stared at the box of animal crackers.

Animal crackers. Luke had to admit Leona Sable did her homework. He tore into the box and popped a few in his mouth, watching as she disappeared into the elevator.

"That wasn't necessary," Tommy reprimanded.

"Did you know she was Reese's ex?"

Tommy adjusted his glasses. "I did, but she's not Paul."

Luke popped a few more animal crackers into his mouth. The familiar aroma and taste calmed him. "Birds of a feather flock together."

"Apparently, she didn't want to flock his way or they'd still be together. You could give her some credit."

"Oh, I gave her a lot of credit or I would have walked out." Luke frowned at his friend. "If she's going to manage me, she'll have to do a hell of a lot better than Poison Ivy."

Ivy Nichols, his former personal manager, hadn't been mentioned in conversation for some time. The mess she'd made of his career was the gift that kept on giving, and how he'd come to need someone like Leona in the first place. The money Ivy stole from him was just a bonus.

Tommy tilted his head. "You're actually going to compare Leona Sable to Ivy Nichols? The manager that dropped you like a sack of hot potatoes?"

That comparison, and Leona's association with that weasel Paul Reese, had caused Luke to lose his temper. He'd worked hard to keep his emotions in check over the last six months, but things weren't going well. For a thirty-six-year-old DJ who hammered away at his goals, he was fairly popular, but he still hadn't achieved the level of success he wanted.

This has to be my year.

"I've asked almost everyone we know for recommendations. They all say she's the real deal."

"But had I known she was Reese's ex I would have asked for a different recommendation."

"Reese fucked up your album, but you fixed it and now you're ready to tour."

"He fucked more than my album." Luke crossed his arms and stroked his chin with the back of his hand. One meeting with Leona Sable and all his demons stood in line to kick him in the balls.

"You have to let that shit go, man." Tommy patted him on the shoulder.

He wasn't ready to let it go. Album sales were down even though his fan base grew daily, and he wasn't sure if he delivered the quality music his fans had come to love him for. At a time when he should be reaping the benefits of all his hard work, he felt like he was starting from the bottom.

"Do you think she'll deliver?" Luke stretched the tightness around his neck.

"Not in three hours, but she'll bust her ass trying. Did you see that look in her eyes?" Tommy gave a low whistle.

"Determined and beautiful all at the same time. She wants to prove me wrong so bad. Good luck with that."

Leona knew how to leave a great first impression. The animal crackers were a nice touch, but images of her full lips and her ass in white leather lingered.

"Will you still let her manage you if she doesn't pull it off?"

Luke was silent.

"Ivy nearly destroyed everything you worked for. We

need a miracle worker. Leo can clean this up." Tommy reached for the box of crackers.

Luke evaded the man's attempt to dip into the box. "Stop reminding me."

He would have preferred a man or a less attractive female manager, because when he met Leona, he couldn't take his eyes off her. The last thing he wanted to do was sample Paul Reese's leftovers, but from her creamy brown skin to her luscious breasts, he could see temptation becoming a problem.

"Don't even think about it," Tommy growled.

"What?" Luke tilted his head back and sprinkled the crumbled remnants of the box into his mouth.

"Hey, man, I spent the last six months bringing you back from some pretty dark places and less than gentlemanly behavior. Need I mention your temper? Stay on the wagon."

Luke chuckled. "Let's go." He pondered his friend's words. Leona was a temptation to be reckoned with and as far as the proverbial wagon was concerned, he could see himself hopping off.

Chapter Three

"Leo, I—"

"Not now, Abe. I want to hear everything. Trust me, I do, but we have bigger problems. I have to make good on these promises I just made and I don't know how the hell I'm going to do that right now."

"Darlin'—"

"Let me think." She didn't want to hiss at him because Abe wasn't only having a bad day, but a bad year. Nonetheless, she had to do some major problem solving and she couldn't do that with him chattering in her ear.

While she shared a cab with Abe to their Midtown Manhattan office, the ideas started to flow. She created an online event for Luke's performance and invited everyone she knew, including tastemakers and other influencers who she had great relationships with in the past. She spread the word on all her social media accounts and promised autographs and photos with Luke to the first fifty people and VIP guests who bought a ticket through her invitation. Then she hit her contacts list. Starting with *A*, Leona called or texted her industry connections one after the other with fingers of fury.

She hadn't contacted these people in over a year

and with Paul's lies floating through the airwaves, she wasn't sure they would be responsive.

"Leona is creatively stifling and her marketing is one-dimensional. Wallace Entertainment is robbing their artists of millions," Paul had spewed in an interview that not only played on all the network entertainment shows, but in print media, as well as online outlets. None of his claims had compared to what he'd done.

Leona sighed and scrolled on her phone. Next on her list was Ramelda Manikas, entertainment guru and celebrity publicist.

"Hi, Ramelda? It's Leo."

"Leo? Leona Sable? I thought you left New York. You've been off the grid for…"

"… A year. I know. I took a little time off." Leona tried to sound cheerful.

"You know, darling, time off kills careers." Ramelda's Greek accent and entitled tone emanated through the receiver. "It's been rumored that you have, well…lost your touch." Ramelda had been Leona's go-to person for attracting media attention to her events. Ramelda's deep and international network consisted of legendary artists, entertainment powerhouses, tastemakers, and "celebutants."

Leona swallowed her anger. Paul's rumors had spread like wildfire, but she wasn't going to let it stop her. "I need a favor, Ramelda. I have an event tonight for a hot EDM DJ who is blowing up the scene. Do you think you could spread the word?"

"Darling, I'd love to, but—"

"Ramelda, we're old friends, aren't we?" Leona regarded the city through the cab window as it whizzed across town.

"Of course, darling, however—"

"Old friends help one another, don't they? Like giving access to exclusive bachelorette parties or the many times you got page six information before it leaked."

Ramelda sighed. "Okay, I'll see what I can do. When is the event?"

"It's at eleven, the artist goes on at midnight." Leona held her breath.

"Tonight?" The woman's incredulous tone had even Leona clutching her pearls.

"Yes."

"Darling, that's an aggressive deadline. I can't promise you anything, but I'll try to help you out."

It was all Leona could ask for. "Thank you so much. I'm sending you the information right now."

"Get yourself back together, darling. We miss you. I can do more for you when you come back with some recent success and that fire I love."

"I will." Leona almost sighed the words. "I really appreciate it."

They hung up and Leona recalled a time when an event was the place to be, as long as her artists were attached. But things had changed.

"So?" Abe scanned the screen of his phone and used his thumb to scroll down a page.

"She'll see what she can do."

"And the press?"

Leona plucked her earlobe. "Can you reach out? I'm sure they'll be there to cover it and we need them. I just…let me focus on this."

Abe side-eyed her.

"I'm fine," she assured him.

Abe put his hands on hers. "Just do what you do best and you'll come out on top."

In the past, she could double the figures she gave to Tommy, even under such a tight deadline. She had talked a good game but any success tonight would take some begging and potentially buying VIP bottle service herself.

Leona forwarded the event details to Tommy, including the autograph and photo op giveaways after Luke's performance. Her role, past getting more people and media to the club, was unclear since Luke hadn't yet signed with Wallace Entertainment. She just hoped Tommy would inform the owners and security of the accommodations needed to manage the additional backstage traffic.

When they arrived at the office, Leona was on several calls at once, redeeming favors, bargaining with promoters, and creating a last-minute frenzy for Luke's performance. In between calls, Abe leaned against the edge of her desk. He looked uncomfortable and not as strong as he normally was in these situations.

"I know you're thinking about bailing after tonight, but I want you to manage him."

"A foot in the door. Get the contract signed. That's what you said. Now you want me to manage an artist that doesn't even want me?" Leona reached for the phone to make another call, but Abe stayed her hand.

"You're going to deliver tonight, even if it's less than what you quoted. He's going to want you because of what you will be able to accomplish in so little time. This will be big for us if he signs. We'll be associated with a DJ that is going to explode this year under the right management—*our* management."

Here we go. "What happened, Abe? How did the company get to this point where we have to rely on one difficult client as our savior?"

Abe hesitated to deliver the news, yet looked relieved at the opportunity to share the information. "A perfect storm, really. When Paul changed management, he was vocal about you and the company. The publicity hit us hard. You've been out for over a year and I tried to keep us afloat and work with the other managers and agents. Some stayed and others fled for greener pastures. Sure, that cut down overhead but taxed our agents, and rent in the Big City ain't cheap. We just couldn't acquire new talent or keep up with the demands of our current clients. The entertainment landscape has changed. We weren't able to pull in the kind of revenue we needed."

Her shoulders slumped. "Why didn't you tell me, Abe? I would've done whatever you asked."

He massaged his eyebrows. "That's exactly why I didn't tell you. I wanted you to come back when you were ready and after you faced all your demons."

"Only one demon," Leona returned. "You still should have told me."

"I'm telling you now." Abe shoved his hands into his pockets.

She swallowed the lump in her throat. "This is my fault. I'm sorry I let you down." The tightness in her neck from the overwhelming guilt constricted her words. She blinked back tears that rimmed her lower lids as the sting of grief over her breakup with Paul surfaced. Her private lovers' quarrel with her ex became a public circus. Her effort to separate what happened then from what was happening now failed. Leona had kept the comments about their relationship diplomatic and tasteful, but Paul's determination to destroy her reputation, both on a personal and professional level, pushed her into seclusion. She was ashamed that she'd chosen going into hiding over protecting the company.

"No, darlin'. Things happen. Sometimes they don't work out, but we have an opportunity with Luke. If his tour is successful, the revenue we'll recoup will get us out of the red and we can start recovering. He needs us as much as we need him. I wouldn't trust this with anyone but you."

Leona wiped her eyes and with it the remorse that threatened to swell out of containment. "Which part of that horrific scene did you not witness? You're getting old, Abe, but…"

"Watch it, young lady," Abe warned with a grin.

"I'm kidding but not really." Leona swiveled around in her chair. "Did you see how he flipped when I mentioned managing Paul? He either hates women, just me, or the rumors got to him."

"He couldn't stop staring at you. No man who does that hates women. I don't know what his angle is, but what I saw was chemistry. You both did what you're good at."

Leona smirked at his vague delivery. "Which is?"

"You were managing and he was being a challenging artist."

"Optimistic. But don't you mean difficult artist?"

"No, challenging." Abe patted her shoulder. "Rise to the challenge."

She sighed.

"His agent likes you. That'll help."

"Hmmm." Leona wasn't too convinced that factor would be helpful at all.

"Will you do it, Leo?"

Abe had given her a start at Wallace Entertainment and over the years had mentored her and supported her career. Now she'd help him and the company they both loved. She could be Luke's personal manager and work closely with Tommy on deals while Luke toured, and communicate with the tour manager she'd eventually assign to make him successful. Their interactions would be limited.

That's fine by me. "Yes." She stood up and moved closer to him. "I won't let you down, Abe."

"You never have." He hugged her and then held her by the shoulders. "First order of business is to go and see The Musical Prophet perform tonight at Aurora Nightclub. Tommy put you on the guest list."

"You're not coming with me? Gee, Abe, just throw me under the bus. You saw him with me earlier and you're going to send me into the lion's den solo? With friends like you, who needs enemies?"

"Take your outrageous British friend with you," he suggested. "She'll help you lick your wounds. Just get him to agree to sign with us."

"Okay."

Abe grabbed his leather case by the carry handle and headed toward the door. "Oh, and, Leo?"

"Yeah?"

"Welcome back."

"Go fly a kite, Abe." Leona returned to her contact list. "Now where was I? Ah yes. *R.*"

Chapter Four

The line outside Aurora Nightclub in the Meatpacking District trailed around the block. Club-goers ranging from hipsters and ravers to yuppies and indie rockers awaited approval by the bouncer. The pounding of the bass, from the music inside, reverberated against the brick building.

Leona glanced at her phone. The time read half past eleven. The clock was ticking. Tiny goose bumps formed on her skin from the cool night air and the implications of tonight's potential success.

"This is mad, Leo," Isabelle Fisher said, in a heavy English accent. Though she could be heard at normal volume, she shouted in excitement and surveyed the line.

Izzy was stunning in her fitted, off-the-shoulder, mid-thigh-length, steel gray dress and red five-inch pumps. Her sandy brown hair with blond highlights flowed down her back intermittently covering a hummingbird tattoo they both shared on their shoulders.

"Excellent work, girl." Izzy beamed, her smooth, fair skin sun-kissed from her recent vacation to South Beach.

Leona had picked her best friend up in a cab from

her apartment, so she could give her the details behind tonight's activities. "Thanks, but this might not be enough." There seemed to be an extra boost in patronage, but it wasn't what Leona expected, was used to delivering, or what she had promised.

"I'm sure it's fine." Izzy adjusted her hair. "I'm glad you're back at it."

Leona wasn't quite ready to be back at it, but Abe had pulled her in, dropped the bomb on her about the company, and then split. "We should go in."

As they strutted toward the entrance, they received catcalls and low whistles from some of the men and women in line. One inebriated man grabbed Izzy's arm. Beautiful though she was, Izzy grew up as a scrappy West Londoner who, unfortunately for this poor fellow, happened to be a little wild. Leona almost felt bad for him when Izzy all but tackled him, punishing him for his aggressive gesture.

"Why are you touching me?" Her hair flew around her before it settled back into perfect place.

Leona muffled a laugh and dragged Izzy away by the arm. "Drop it, Izzy."

Once her friend was back on track, Leona checked her phone. There was still no word from Tommy on Luke's residency. She needed to get inside and get an update.

She and Izzy approached the VIP guest entrance where red velvet theater rope cordoned off the area. Leona acknowledged anyone she knew from her social connections but didn't linger long.

When it was their turn for evaluation, Izzy did the honors by flicking her hair at the tall bouncer. His bald head complemented his large frame, and muscles bulged through his black suit.

"Hello, love. We're on the guest list."

The bouncer gave Izzy a quick once-over then returned to the roster he carted in his hand. "Name?"

"Leo Sable," came Leona's official "I'm all about business" delivery as opposed to the "I'm VIP" one Izzy supplied.

The man perused his list. "You have an additional guest, Miss Sable. Will you be waiting for anyone else?"

"No. It's just us tonight." Leona searched his suit for a name tag. "What's your name, by the way?"

"They call me Diesel."

"Cool." Leona smiled. "Thanks, Diesel."

"She'll never forget your name, love," Izzy called back to him.

Diesel nodded and continued with his gatekeeper duties.

Fitted with their VIP wristbands, they entered the club, cover charge–free, and headed through a dimly lit corridor. The music grew louder, enticing them further into the club. Hues of pink, orange, and purple moved in dreamy swirls against the black walls, and gave the illusion of being in the center of an aurora.

Leona spun around as she wandered through the colorful, foggy path. "If inside is this impressive, then I've found my new favorite place."

"This is hot." Izzy sauntered through, taking careful steps in her heels.

The hall opened up into a main ballroom with chandeliers. On the black walls hung huge vintage framed images of the atmospheric phenomena against starlit skies. The two women were immediately hit by the music as it filled every inch of the club and swallowed them into an alternate reality.

The stage at the far end showcased a DJ who played popular music to warm up the crowd for Luke. A large dance floor covered most of the space and the bar circled the perimeter. Bottle service areas were roped off and decorated with velvet ottomans in dark colors, and illuminated glass tables glowed in interchanging shades of neon pink, blue, and yellow—also mimicking an aurora.

"We've stepped into Wonderland," Izzy said. "I'm surprised that neither one of us has been here before."

"It opened last year when I was off the grid. It's amazing."

Izzy hugged her as she jumped up and down, elated by the club. "This is going to be bloody awesome."

"Your feet are going to kill you." Leona knew Izzy would be bellyaching later about the price of pain for beauty.

"I took ibuprofen earlier. I should be good." Izzy headed toward the bar. "Drinks?"

"Yes, please," Leona agreed, her head bopped to the music pumping through the speakers.

"Oh my gosh. If I were high or tripping, I'd be in heaven. The energy in here is sick." Izzy rested her midsection against the bar.

Leona would keep this place in mind for any future club events. She noticed the chilled temperature. Even though the place was filling up, not enough bodies yet packed the space. She prayed the clubbers awaiting entry would help her make good on her promises.

Izzy batted her eyelashes at the bartender. She flipped her hair to reveal the smooth round cap of her shoulder as she ordered rum and cola for herself and then turned to Leona. "What do you want?"

Leona also rested her torso against the bar. "A white wine spritzer," she yelled to the bartender who nodded.

"Boring, Leo. Are you serious?" Izzy's sophisticated pose collapsed into an unrefined lean against the bar.

"I'm wearing white, plus I have to be on point for whatever this guy throws at me tonight."

The bartender quickly made their drinks and placed them on the bar. Leona handed him her credit card. "I got it."

"On the house." He bit his lip and pointed at Izzy.

Izzy's flirtatious currency strikes again. "Of course it is." Leona picked up her drink.

Izzy puckered and gave the bartender a contactless kiss. "Thanks." She then turned to Leona. "What time does DJ Luke come on?"

"He should be on after this guy." Leona sipped her drink. "Hey, let me go find out what's happening with the contract. Do you want to hang out here or go sit down in VIP?"

"I'll hang out here. Do your thing." Izzy batted her eyes at the young and cute bartender. "I have company."

"Easy, tigress," Leo chided.

Izzy teased the bartender with her bare shoulder. "I'm just having a little fun."

"I'll be back." Leona searched for her would-be client and his agent.

As she took the small jaunt toward the stage via the perimeter, she checked off the items on her mental checklist of promises made to Luke and Tommy. The fans were excited to see The Musical Prophet, but she couldn't get a good feel as to whether or not Aurora was sold out. There weren't any vacant tables in the VIP section, and servers were bringing bottle after bottle of alcohol, which was a good sign.

The closer Leona got to the stage, the more buff men in black uniforms materialized to secure the artist. One stopped her from entering backstage.

"Leona Sable for Boombox."

What a difference a year made. It had been a long time since she'd been stopped from entering all access. She stood by one of the speakers and waited for Tommy.

"Leo." Tommy grabbed her arm through the sea of security guards. "Let her through."

Tommy ushered her backstage and gave Leona an all access pass to wear around her neck. Luke was nowhere in sight.

The space was draped in black faux velvet curtains to partition the different areas and to keep out the peering eyes of the crowd.

"So?" Leona asked.

"First, thank you for all of this. It's pretty crowded out there," Tommy began, and an implied *but* hung in the air. "The show didn't sell out. There's still about a hundred tickets unsold, but the good news is that the VIPs came out and there's definitely increased media coverage. In my opinion you over-delivered given the tight deadline."

Leona chewed the inside of her lip. "How about his residency?"

Tommy's face brightened. "The lawyers agreed to the terms I negotiated and the contract is signed. Luke hasn't even hit the stage yet. He's now the resident DJ for Aurora Nightclub. We'll make the announcement tomorrow morning."

Leona didn't quite exhale. "Nice. Congratulations." She dreaded the answer to her question. "And Luke? What has he decided?"

Luke *had* to agree to sign with Wallace Entertainment. Or else all she had tried to do for him tonight would be for nothing. On the inside, she was fidgety and nervous, yet she showed poise and held her breath as she awaited Tommy's answer.

"I've spoken with him and he's changed his mind. He wants Wallace Entertainment to take over all management responsibilities. He wants you, Leo. With some conditions, of course."

Leona exhaled. *Wait. Conditions?* She raised her eyebrows at Tommy. "What conditions, exactly?"

"We can discuss them when we meet with everyone."

Leona grimaced.

"I know you and Luke got off to a rough start. He's not a bad guy. He just—" Tommy broke off. "He's had some difficulties with his past management."

Leona didn't speak, hoping Tommy might reveal more than what she already knew. When he spoke to her about Luke, she noticed he often cherry-picked his words.

"So, will you manage him, Leo?" Tommy raised his eyebrows in question.

Leona paused as if giving it some consideration, but knew she no longer had the option of saying no. "Yes."

Tommy looked as relieved as she felt. "Great. Luke is about to go onstage. Why don't you watch the show from here?"

"I'm here with someone, so I'm going to watch it from the floor. It'll also give me a better sense of the fan experience. I'll come back after the show and we can secure time to finalize everything."

"Okay." Disappointment touched Tommy's face then disappeared just as fast. "Enjoy the show."

"I will, thanks." The two shared a brief handshake before she left.

The crowd chanted Luke's name and Leona was excited to see what all the hype was about. Getting through the now packed club seemed impossible, but Izzy held their small space at the bar like a wild boar guarding her piglets.

"How'd it go?"

"We didn't meet all the demands, but he wants us to manage him. Abe will be happy." Leona set the glass on the bar.

"Are you happy?" Izzy probed, swaying to the music.

A male voice came over the speakers and announced The Musical Prophet.

"We'll talk later." Leona knew the chances of she or Izzy returning to this conversation were slim to none.

Luke appeared on the stage and jumped up and down to incite the crowd, obviously pumped to play. He had changed into a short-sleeved, white button-down shirt that defined his muscular physique. He glowed under the black light against the darkness of the club. An ember of affection kindled in her chest, leaving her breathless.

Damn if that man isn't fine. She fought against the impulse to celebrate this beautiful specimen of a man. Especially when his doubt and abrupt hostility toward her still stung.

Luke took charge of the equipment and put the headphones around his neck and over one ear. Even from a distance, Leona glimpsed the tattooed artwork on his forearm, and her hand itched to touch him.

Leona peeked at Izzy, whose eyes were wide with excitement, confirming triggered pheromones.

The extravagant light show displayed Luke's name in brilliant graphics. The go-go dancers on either side of the stage gyrated, shimmied, and shook with energy. The crowd was electric with appreciation. Vocals from the song echoed through the speakers and the crowd went wild.

"This is mental," Izzy yelled.

Leona strained to see Luke's figure through the sea of smartphones primed to capture him on video. Club staff threw LED light-up foam glow sticks into the crowd. The rainbow of colors flickered at different speeds, adding ambience to the venue and fun for the fans.

The vocals faded to silence and the fullness of the song blared through the speakers. Bass enveloped the crowd, taking them higher until the entire club bounced in unison.

A spotlight illuminated the steel scaffolding above the stage. Scantily clad female dancers in fishnet stockings, platform heels, and bustier tops entertained the crowd. Additional dancers catwalked across the platform in costumes ranging from silver spandex jumpsuits to red mop curl wigs.

"What a fantastic circus." Leona was awed and inspired to move to Luke's music. Like all the other fans, she danced like she never wanted his set to end. The cool club turned into a sauna of sweaty, perfumed bodies and stale alcohol that wetted the textured finish of the PVC tiled flooring.

The consistent thump of the beat and velvety bass kissed an uplifting melody—all of which provided the soundtrack for the night.

Leona now understood why the fans dubbed him The Musical Prophet. She danced carefree, and in this tiny slice of time, was happy.

Happy. Leona hadn't used that word in a long time. She'd spent the better part of the last year just trying to keep her emotions stable and retrieve that strength she could count on.

"He's so good, Leo," Izzy said, breaking her trance.

Leona may have issues with the man, but she fell in love with his music. This wasn't a typical DJ set of popular music. This three-hour marathon of original produced songs and creative remixes left club-goers, including her and Izzy, drained.

When the show ended, they rested against the bar with sweat glistening their faces.

Izzy's hair curled at the temples. "I need to touch up my makeup, right?"

Leona nodded. "If I didn't wear black lace, you'd see my sweaty pits from across the room."

"Outstanding." Izzy gave Leona a high five and then turned to order another drink.

"He was good." Leona refrained from overpraising Luke because he was still a jerk, just one who made amazing music.

"You sound surprised, love." Izzy twisted her hair up and fanned her neck.

"I guess it was more emotional for the fans than I expected." Leona tried to sound unaffected.

"For the fans? How about for us? I'm mad for him."

"Like I said. He was good," Leona admitted, but Izzy eyed her until she folded. "Okay. I'm a fan."

Another DJ replaced Luke to play more popular music and the crowd started to thin out.

Izzy sat on a barstool and crossed her legs. "I'm completely knackered, but if Luke played another song, I would get off my ass to dance. Like that rave at club L'Essence in Paris."

"I'll always remember Paris." Leona tumbled onto Izzy, gathering her friend into a hug. "We've been dancing for hours."

"My feet are killing me, but I don't care." Izzy rubbed her calves. "I can't wait to see him up close and personal."

Convinced that Luke hadn't changed much since their rooftop meeting, Leona hoped he at least met Izzy's expectations.

When she and Izzy arrived backstage, the first thing she noticed was the mess of people. Leona couldn't tell the difference between the dancers, media, VIP guests, and other random individuals. In the middle of it all was Luke, who focused on two half-dressed women, while Tommy spoke to a well-dressed man that Leona guessed might be the club owner.

"What a disaster," she whispered.

When Leona had informed Tommy of the necessary accommodations for VIP guests and fans, she assumed some sort of process for getting fans in and out would be in place. Her mistake. From what she could see, none existed.

She scanned the room as if she were a computer processing data. Her mind cried out for organization and began applying order to the chaotic scene.

"Uh-oh." Izzy plugged her ears with her fingers and backed away. "Go easy on them, love."

Leona loaded a bunch of air into her lungs. "Everybody out!" Her voice filled the room and she marched over to two gentlemen in black. She reloaded. "Security. I want everyone out. Now. I need VIP guests roped off outside. We're going to funnel people in, about five at a time, and out the other way. I'll inform you when. I want all media in the backroom, just there." She pointed in a general direction. "Luke will come in for interviews momentarily."

Security didn't question her command. She searched the room for Tommy and called to him.

Tommy rushed over. "Wow, Leo. Where's the fire?"

"Do you know all these people?" She didn't wait for an answer. "We have to do this a better way. I need you to get Luke to do his media interviews, so the VIP guests and fans get some time with him. It's the only way to get people in and out of here fast. Right now, this mob situation puts Luke in a dangerous position."

There was rustling through the crowd and Leona saw Luke approach. From her position his head floated toward them like it's own entity.

"What the hell are you doing?" Luke growled.

"I'm managing," she growled back. "Don't worry. You'll be back with the ladies soon enough. Like I fulfilled my promises to you, I'm doing the same for the fans who paid extra to meet you."

Luke's eyes narrowed at her. "You didn't quite fulfill your promises, did you? The show didn't sell out."

She sighed. "I did my best under the circumstances. Now, do you want to argue with me or make your fans happy?"

The anxious fans were herded outside of the backstage area. Fans complaining for an explanation buzzed as a metal gate, reinforced by two security men, blocked any reentry.

Luke's hard expression softened. "Okay. What do you need me to do?"

"Interviews…just there." She pointed in the general direction.

Tommy guided Luke away to do his interviews.

"You're welcome," Leona muttered. She called in three more security guards and rattled off additional instructions.

Izzy came out of hiding and stood by her side.

"This may take a while," Leona stated.

"He's right cute, Leo." Izzy fluffed her hair.

"He's a pain in the ass."

Fifteen minutes later, backstage was functioning like a well-oiled machine. Now that Luke wanted Wallace Entertainment to manage him, Leona's name would be attached to the event. Even if the night didn't have the type of success she had been known for, she wanted it to be representative of her professionalism.

Leona's work was quick and calm. All instructions for Luke went to Tommy, since her artist chose to challenge her every time she approached him with a task. Luke wasn't her first difficult client but he seemed reluctant to let her help him.

With all the moving and excited bodies, the temperature in the stuffy backstage felt like humid wetlands. Leona opted to ditch the sheer shawl and handed it to Izzy.

Tommy and Luke approached.

"Uhh… I need to get Luke back to the hotel. He has

a post-show chat with the fans." Though Tommy spoke directly to her, she couldn't help but notice Luke ogling the tight black lace of her mock halter-top.

"What time is the chat and when do you need to leave?" Leona peeked down, even though no watch adorned her wrist.

"The chat is at four." Tommy hesitated. "So I need to get him out of here in about twenty minutes."

Luke didn't speak, but continued to appraise her.

Leona crossed her arms over her chest. "You're joking."

Tommy adjusted his glasses. "I'm afraid not."

Leona massaged her forehead and tried to think. "Well, can he do it from here?"

"No. The camera crews are setting up at the hotel so that we can do a live feed to Luke's video channel. The episode is supposed to be more intimate."

The media interviews were done and most of the fans had gotten their time with Luke, but he wasn't finished. Tommy had just put a wrench into the well-oiled machine.

Leona accessed her deepest thoughts, trying to figure out how to make things go faster, when a photographer began snapping pictures of her talking to Luke and Tommy. Her reflex response had her arm raised in an instant to hide her face, and within seconds she scurried behind Luke.

Luke peered at her over his shoulder. "What are you doing?"

"They should focus on you." She hated having her picture taken, especially after the events of the past year.

Luke evaluated her with curiosity.

Leona again focused on working out a solution. "I need you to get through the rest of this fast. No disappointed fans. Let's make sure everyone leaves satisfied tonight."

Izzy sauntered over. Her red porno pumps led the way. "Still camera shy, love?" her friend inquired with lightheartedness, but gave her arm a squeeze and smiled over the concern etched on her face.

"Hey," Leona said to her and gave Izzy a non-verbal "I'm okay." Leona then turned back to the two men, who were more interested in the gorgeous Brit than anything Leona had to say. "Right." Leona pursed her lips. "Luke Anderson, Tom Mills, this is Isabelle Fisher. Owner, fashion writer, and blogger for *Trendzy Magazine*."

Tommy nearly fought Luke to shake Izzy's hand. "You can call me Tommy."

This was the typical reaction to her friend. Izzy shook Tommy's hand and then Luke's.

"It's nice to meet you, both. Luke, your set was exceptional. However, you could have worn a more festive shirt. I'd like to style you for my magazine."

Leave it to Izzy to insult, compliment, and network all at the same time.

"You'll have to speak with my manager." Luke gave Izzy a brief smile.

Oh, I'm your manager now?

Luke seemed less spellbound with her friend than most men, and Leona was strangely relieved.

Izzy adjusted her hair over her shoulder, further hypnotizing Tommy, whose wandering eyes lingered on her naked shoulder and "come play with me" breasts.

"I'll confirm with Leo, then." Izzy displayed all of

her perfect pearly teeth. "See? He's not so difficult after all, Leo."

Leona wanted to cork Izzy's mouth like a wine bottle. "Luke has a lot to do, Izzy. We really need to get back to work." Leona was thankful the dim lighting hid her embarrassment.

"Of course, love. I'll mingle." Izzy gave one last flick of her hair and departed.

Tommy was completely engaged with Izzy's rear end as it sashayed away.

"Tommy?" She waved her fingers in front of him.

Luke bit back a laugh as he, too, witnessed Tommy's adoration of Izzy's ass.

Tommy snapped his head back to Leona. "Yes?" His cheeks reddened and he cleared his throat.

Humor shined in Luke's eyes.

That was different. "You guys finish up. I'll alert security to the changes."

"Sounds good," Tommy agreed and left.

Leona attempted to follow Tommy's lead when Luke blocked her path.

"Difficult, huh?"

Shit. She searched for a glimmer of the humor they'd shared only moments ago, but none existed. "I call it like I see it."

Luke leaned in close and his enticing fragrance confused her. "If you think I'm difficult now, you haven't seen anything yet. That's a promise." He strode away without waiting for a response.

Leona stomped toward security. "Thanks, Izzy."

Chapter Five

"Let me be clear. We're seeking complete management representation for Luke, including both talent and tour." Patrick Beckham, Luke's lawyer, explained the situation to Leona's team in a late-afternoon contract meeting. "We previously worked with Luke's former personal manager, Ivy Nichols, and Ted Kimmel, a freelance tour manager who organized Luke's four-month summer tour."

Tommy nodded in agreement. "Most of the groundwork is done, but we only have a month before the tour kicks off. The appearances are secured, but the logistics need to be managed."

Luke pressed his back against the office chair as if restraining himself from speaking. Leona wondered what he really thought about this setup and not just what his team presented. He had dressed up for the occasion in a blue button-down shirt that hugged his defined shoulders and biceps. He finished off his ensemble with a dark gray tie and his signature dark blue jeans and white-soled sneakers. She was drawn to the increased level of sexy brought on by the small change in Luke's attire. And though Leona focused on Tommy and Patrick, images of Luke's ass from when he'd first arrived at the office distracted her.

"That's not a problem. Leo has experience with tour management, so we don't have to seek a freelance tour manager. You get a two for one deal. Leo can easily take over the reins," Abe suggested, snapping her back to the meeting.

"Good, because it was our expectation that Leo would take over as tour manager and perform a combined role for Luke. The contract we'll be negotiating today already reflects that," Patrick said.

Leona did a double take at Abe. "You want me to do what?"

Luke leaned forward in his chair. Even when he was poised for an argument, he was a bona fide heartthrob. "Is there a problem?"

"Not at all." Abe's confident delivery forced her to focus.

"Absolutely," Leona contradicted. Luke's musky fragrance wafted toward her. *You smell good enough to eat, but I will not be fooled.* "I assumed that Luke needed a personal manager and that I'd be working with my team and Tommy to help Luke with operations that fit into his long-term career plans. It wasn't my understanding that I would be going on tour. This changes things."

Abe's head whipped around and Leona felt the weight of his eyes on her. "How so?"

"I can't do all the deals, branding and merchandising aspects and be the tour manager at the same time. That's not realistic." Leona leaned back in her chair.

Abe cleared his throat. "Leona can handle a little extra in addition to the work for the tour. However, I'll handle any overflow." Though Abe addressed the table, he arched a Southern brow at her. Abe knew that not only could she simultaneously be a personal and tour manager but that she could do elements of the jobs of everyone else in the room.

"There is also the matter of time," Leona persisted. "The details are based on another tour manager's due diligence. I can't rely on that alone. I have to review everything, which is like doing it over." If this Ted Kimmel was a tour manager worth his salt, his name would be familiar to her and it wasn't.

"I think you'll find there is a foundation, Leo," Tommy announced.

"Maybe you're right, but I don't work that way. I can't trust that someone else did a thorough job."

"Control freak," Luke muttered under his breath.

The insult rolled off Leona. She had long been immune to such digs. It was, however, her turn to enlighten Luke that he wasn't dealing with a thin-skinned novice. "I'm curious, Luke. This Ted guy left you in the lurch. Why did he leave? Did it have something to do with your former manager, Ivy Nichols?"

The atmosphere in the room changed dramatically and Luke's team shifted in their seats.

Anger spread across Luke's face and his green-gray eyes burned steel gray with fury—all of it directed at her. "That's not your concern. You would do well to focus your energy on managing my tour, Miss Sable."

Leona was getting tired of Luke's not so veiled irritation toward her. "Please, call me Leo," she said with forced cheer. "If we're going to work together, then I should be briefed on what has occurred."

Tommy put his hand up. "Leave it alone, Leo." His

expression confirmed this was something more than a management issue. This was personal.

"Okay." Surprised by Tommy's gesture, Leona put this one in the file cabinet for re-visitation along with the information she had learned when researching Luke. Based on how the mere mention of Ivy amped everyone's emotions, there had to be much more to the story.

"So…" Abe's words didn't quite cut the tension in the room, but they did draw everyone's focus from Luke and Leona's standoff. "Leo, I will make sure you have every resource, including Tracy." Abe tilted his head toward the woman sitting across from him.

Tracy Ruiz was the best lawyer Wallace Entertainment had on retainer and Leona loved working with her. Regardless of the support she'd receive, Leona was none too thrilled to pack up and go on tour with Luke and his attitude.

"Abe, why don't you do the tour and I'll do all other management aspects. It may work out better that way. Plus, you know I can't leave Peaches." She might be antagonizing the situation, but she had to make one last-ditch effort to extricate herself from going on tour with Luke. She could help Luke, Abe, and the company right here at home.

"Leo." Abe's voice took on a tone of tried patience. He was right to be annoyed. Taking over Luke's tour wasn't an unreasonable request. In fact, it made the most sense.

Asking Abe to go on tour, on the other hand, was not only ludicrous because of his responsibilities to the company, but also a bad idea. He hadn't run a tour in seven years.

"Who's Peaches?" Tommy's eyebrows raised in intrigue.

Both Leona and Abe were silent.

Abe cleared his throat. "Her Platy fish."

Leona exaggerated a wink at Tommy. At least she attempted to lighten the mood.

Tommy's chest rumbled in humor.

Patrick and Tracy sniggered.

The comedy fairy, however, passed over Luke, who intertwined his fingers and placed them on the table. His movements were as restless as a pot about to boil over.

"We're putting my tour in *her* hands?" Luke scoffed so loud it nearly blew her out of her seat.

Tracy and Patrick exchanged glances.

Tommy frowned at his client. "She was joking."

"Luke, I'm not your tour manager until we actually sign." Leona gestured in the air with a pen.

Tommy interjected, but Abe stopped him. "Let them work it out."

"Considering your reputation, I'm amazed you lack the seriousness I need in a manager. Tour or otherwise." Luke's knuckles whitened and he was motionless.

"Because I made a joke? If you hadn't noticed, Luke, we don't quite get along. Part of my job is to allocate resources appropriately. This includes myself. Being on tour together, though an apparent mandate by your team and one that on paper makes sense, may not be the best solution. Forgive me for trying to lighten the mood."

The room was as still as a post.

"I don't need you to lighten the mood. I just want to get through this meeting," Luke seethed.

"You're a DJ. You play happy music. Why are you so

angry? I only met you a few days ago and despite your attitude, I'm still willing to help you."

An array of emotions played on Luke's face and color returned to his knuckles. "Look, no one likes these negotiations. The quicker we get through it, the less painful it will be."

"I like this part." Leona's plastic smile dared Luke to say something negative.

Patrick rustled his papers. "Shall we get to the contract and the list of conditions?" He pulled out a few additional documents from his briefcase. "Your legal team sent over a redline agreement adjusting for our boilerplate, but this addendum outlines additional conditions from Luke. Failure to adhere to these conditions renders the contract null and void. Though you'll be paid for services rendered up till that point."

Patrick handed out copies and Leona read the document to herself.

i. *Tour management must be handled solely by Leona Sable, who will accompany the artist to every on and off tour appearance, including but not limited to concerts, club/lounge, awards, marketing and publicity events and any other occasion where said artist is scheduled to perform and/or interact with media and fans within the terms of the contract.*

He hates me, yet he needs me so close? She'd accepted this assignment with the assumption that she'd be Luke's personal manager and be able to keep some distance from the DJ. Now apparently she would have to be glued to his fine ass and his *miserabldom.* Yeah, no.

ii. *Wallace Entertainment and Leona Sable guarantee sellout performances at the largest concert venues in both Los Angeles and New York. Wallace Entertainment also guarantees to secure a Las Vegas residency at the new premier Xcelsior Hotel.*

Guarantee? Really? Cameras were sure to pop out any minute now and tell her this was all a prank. Even if she did accept this agreement she'd clobber it with revisions. Buh-bye.

iii. *Tour manager Leona Sable is strictly prohibited from any intimate relations with staff or fans while on the tour (excluding spouse or committed partner) at any tour hotel, transport, or venue.*

What the actual fuck! Heat radiated from Leona and she pressed on her ear. She observed Tommy, who loosened his tie as his cheeks reddened.

Luke nestled in his chair and watched her.

Leona consumed a breath so deep it shuddered upon exhale. Her heartbeat thudded in her chest and she chewed the inside of her lower lip to stop herself from letting fly every profane word she had in her vocabulary. She picked up a pen in one hand and twirled it with acrobatic agility around her fingers.

"I can't agree to this." Leona's voice was low with strained control that commanded everyone's attention.

"To which part?" Patrick readied a pen.

"Any of it." Leona's lips quivered as she enunciated each word.

Tracy interjected. "I have to agree. Some of the conditions put the onus solely on Leo and could potentially ruin Wallace Entertainment's reputation and financial support to its other interests. There may also be a women's rights issue, here."

The men across from her stared at each other.

"My client has the right to his preferences, and to request all of these conditions," Patrick stated.

Abe put a hand on Leona's clenched fist.

Leona expected to see disappointment and anger on Abe's face, but his eyes shot lasers of disdain at the men before him.

"We're open to discussion." Tommy's voice of reason came through. "What are your concerns, Leo?"

"Besides the fact that the first condition binds me to Luke's hip, it also impedes me from doing my job. As tour manager, I have to be everywhere. Now I have to be his shadow for one-off performances, as well? Publicity? Marketing? Do you want a successful tour or a buddy?"

"You've proven you can be creative. I'm sure you can use your skills to satisfy this condition," Luke argued.

"I suggest it say, *unless the tour manager is unable to do so because it is in the best interest of the artist and/or the tour.*"

Patrick scribbled on the document. "That's reasonable. Luke, would you agree?"

Luke squinted at her. "Slight correction to, *it is agreed upon between the artist and tour manager that it is in the best interest of the artist*, et cetera."

Leona rolled her eyes so hard it hurt.

"Leo?" Patrick awaited any additional changes.

"Agreed," both Leona and Abe responded.

Leona knitted her brows at Abe, and then concentrated on the bane of her existence. "Luke, other than obvious monetary reasons for the second condition, why do you want to sell out the biggest venues in New York and LA?"

Luke seemed taken aback by the question, but recovered. "Because it's never been done by a DJ before."

Leona liked his answer. It confirmed his passion and ambition, but she had a feeling there might be more to that goal than he let on.

"That's a team effort. Everyone in this room, and many others, are a part of the team. We all need to put some skin in the game. If the language reflects that I'll *make best efforts to secure sellout performances and secure a Las Vegas residency at a premier hotel*, then I have no doubt that together we can make it happen."

Patrick smiled and made notes. "Luke?"

"Why not specify the Xcelsior?" Luke's eyes stayed on Leona.

"Because there might be a better premier hotel," she offered, as if it was the most obvious answer.

"Agreed." For the first time Luke's eyes weren't filled with some version of fury. If she didn't know any better she would have sworn he appreciated her response.

"Ms. Ruiz and I can work on the correct language." Patrick swallowed and expelled so much air it fanned at the papers he held. "And we're down to the final condition."

"I want that last condition out. We don't work in an industry where anyone needs to dictate to me where or who I can fu…" Leona paused. "…who I am sleeping with."

All eyes in the room focused on her.

Abe wiped his face with his hand. "Leo?"

"No!" Leona's exclamation echoed against the conference room walls and the force with which her fists hit the table was aggressive, but this condition crossed the line. She breathed to steady herself but the action only proved to soften her voice to an almost threatening tone. "We can send an all staff about fraternizing, but no one will prohibit me from getting laid should I so choose. That's beyond idiotic."

Patrick shifted in his seat. "This condition is non-negotiable, Leo. Luke and I have spoken extensively on the language. I can't make any further changes."

"Non-negotiable? Patrick, I don't want you to change it. I want it out. Period."

Luke rubbed his finger over his lower lip. "Do you lack that much sexual restraint, Leona?"

She smirked. She hadn't had sex in over a year. She was pretty sure she had more sexual restraint than he had in his pinky toe. "That's not the point. The truth is you're the real control freak for wanting to dictate whether or not I, alone—" Leona pressed her palm hard against her chest "—have sex while on tour. It's exclusive and archaic."

"The condition stays." Luke's delivery was so low Leona had to strain to hear him.

"Then someone else can manage your tour." Leona was up and out of her seat in seconds.

Abe addressed the room. "Give us a few minutes, please." He motioned for her and Tracy to follow him out of the room.

Before they even closed the door, Leona began.

"A morality clause! Take me off the tour. Better yet, get someone else and Luke can dick around with them.

This is humiliating." But the thought of putting someone else in Luke's line of fire didn't thrill her.

"Are you done?" His parental question irritated her already fried nerves.

"No," she said. "I'm not a whore that needs to be controlled by a contract. I don't give a shit what anyone says, this condition is not legal."

"Abe, I have to advise against this. It could have adverse effects on future dealings with this client." Tracy was all business with her delivery and Leona was grateful that one of them kept it together.

"Tracy—" Abe pinched the bridge of his nose "—I'm going to ask you to be really lax with this one. If we can protect our interests another way, then we'll do that, but this is a deal we can't afford to go sour."

Tracy sighed. "You don't employ me to be lax, Abe."

Abe pressed his palms together. "Please."

"So long as my objections have been noted," Tracy said.

Abe turned to Leona. "Pride aside, Leo, can you adhere to the conditions?"

"Of course, but—"

"Then, agree to them. When the tour is over and successful, we'll have won."

Leona was still shaking her head and resisted the urge to worry her earlobe. Abe took her hand to stop her from pacing.

"Darlin', I know I'm asking you to surrender quite a bit here but I need your help."

Leona groaned. When things had gone south with Paul, Abe had not only given her the time off she needed to recover but had exerted some influence with the legitimate press to release articles to help her reputation. "Abe."

"I'm begging you, Leo. Do you need me to get on bended knee, darlin'?"

Leona thought long and hard about that one. When Abe actually started to go down, she stopped him. "Oh, get up, old man."

Tracy snickered.

"You'll agree to the conditions?" Abe asked.

She nodded.

"Thank you, darlin'. I knew I could count on you." Abe then faced Tracy. "Not a word of this to anyone, Ms. Ruiz."

Clearly, Abe understood what he was asking of her, but defeat still slumped her shoulders. Even worse, she felt handled by Luke and shackled to a situation that would only go from bad to worse. "You have to admit that someone who has to put a condition in an addendum that bans his tour manager from having sex has some deep-seated issues."

"It's an unconventional request, but you're surviving now, aren't you, darlin'?"

Leona blushed. "Not that it's anyone's business."

Tracy chortled.

Abe patted her shoulder. "Let's close this out."

The trio reconvened with Luke and team.

Leona avoided Luke. She refrained from spitting a snarky comment his way and focused on conceding to don a chastity belt to appease the DJ. "I'll agree to the last condition—" she stopped and tapped her pen to her lips "—but only if the condition also applies to Luke."

Everyone in the room, except Leona, froze in place. Neither a breath was released, nor a word spoken. The room was so quiet she heard the sound of the vent humming overhead for the first time since the meeting started.

Sunshine broke through Tracy's steel visage and she began to write extensive notes. "I can have those papers drawn up right away. As you said earlier, Patrick, my client also has a right to her conditions and preferences."

"That's not happening," Luke said.

Leona sat more erect in her seat. "No sexual restraint, Mr. Anderson? It's only about four months."

"Luke?" Patrick awaited Luke's final answer.

Luke read the conditions and when he raised his head, Leona was prepared to meet his contempt, but he appeared relaxed, even nonchalant.

"Agreed," he declared with a slanted smile.

Tommy and Luke exchanged glances.

Leona wouldn't have noticed had Tommy's face not displayed such disapproval. Something was up, but she couldn't figure out what.

"Well done, everyone. All we need to do is sign and then we can all move on to the next phase," Patrick announced, and then chatted with Tracy.

"Leo, I have a packet of information for you. I also forwarded some electronic documents and emails. We can discuss it further when you're up to speed," Tommy said.

"We'll schedule something before you head out." Leona didn't feel quite victorious, but she felt better now that Luke had to abide by one of the conditions. "This is going to be a great tour."

She rested her chin in her palm. Poor Peaches would have to be subjected to Aunt Izzy for four months.

Chapter Six

Luke crammed into the backseat of a New York City yellow cab with Tommy and Patrick. He was glad the contract negotiations were over. Leona had reacted better to the conditions than he expected, but she still put up one hell of a fight. With Patrick's help, he'd protected himself on all levels, and it had almost worked.

"Don't think that I don't know what you're doing," Tommy said to him. "Patrick, why did you let him put that condition in there?"

Patrick shrugged his shoulders. "He has his reasons and he pays me."

Luke leaned forward in his seat to see Tommy cleaning his glasses on his jacket before putting them on again.

"It's very unlike you to agree so quickly, especially given this condition," Tommy noted.

"I don't know what you're talking about." Luke tried to restrain the curl of his lips.

"All right, but you're playing with fire and her name is Leona Sable."

Luke pushed a button to roll down the window. They stopped at a traffic light where two teenage girls stood to cross the street. He was about to respond to Tommy when high-pitched screams all but shattered his eardrum.

"Look! It's Prophet!" one of the girls yelled before rushing over to the taxi.

"Ladies." Luke doubted his greeting was audible through their excitement.

The younger of the two girls rummaged through her bag and pulled out a pen. "Can you sign this for me?" She thrust the pen and a crumpled fashion magazine at him.

"Sure." He autographed the magazine and returned it and the pen to the girl.

"DJ Luke will be on tour this summer, so make sure you get your tickets," Tommy called to the girls.

"Oh my God I can't wait for your tour. Thank you, thank you." The girl squealed, clutching the autograph to her chest.

"Anytime," Luke said.

"Here, sign my arm." The other girl's high pitch pierced his eardrum.

He was about to ask Patrick or Tommy for a sheet of paper, but the car started to roll, so Luke signed his name on her arm.

The girls, giddy with happiness, continued to thank him.

"I'll see you at the concert. Be safe." He waved to them as the car continued to its destination.

"Like I was saying." Tommy returned to his previous point. "You're going to have to deal with Leo. You can make it easy or painful. You can't have it both ways. I suggest you try to talk to her and smooth things over when we're back here next week."

"She's smart. Quick." Luke had expected Leona to complain about the conditions, but she'd surprised him, and everyone else, when she flipped the last one on him.

"Yeah, and you better be prepared for when she figures out what you both just agreed to," Tommy warned.

"I second that." Patrick chuckled.

"You, too, Patty?"

"Yup."

"Noted." Luke stroked the hair above his chin, twisting it between his thumb and index finger. He should proceed with caution when it came to Leona, but when he was in the same room with her, his emotions were erratic. Perhaps, he should try to talk to her. His empty stomach growled as if to complain about the thought.

"Let me buy you guys some dinner."

Stuffed from a three-course lunch at an Italian place and carrying an armful of vinyl from a vintage record place, Luke arrived at the hotel and took the elevator to his suite. He enjoyed New York, but longed for the coast where he could surf. Once on tour, he'd be going nonstop. He'd need to talk to Tommy and Leona about scheduling some time off between tour dates.

When he entered the room, Luke noticed it smelled like him—musky with hints of spice. His sister had gifted him the fragrance a few years ago. The room sensed his movements and overhead recessed ceiling lights illuminated from dim to bright. The cleanliness of the blue walls and the white and brown furniture reminded him of the modern yet homey style of his house in San Francisco.

The lavish penthouse suite came with many hi-tech capabilities, one of which was some funky but impressive remote-controlled experience with the shower and Jacuzzi. After Ivy, he had tried to sex away her memory and would have made full use of this special feature with a willing participant. Things were different now. He was better.

He had to work but hadn't connected with his sister since he'd gotten to New York. Once he was overseas, the time zone differences would make it harder to get in touch with her. He climbed into bed with his computer and his phone, crossed his legs at the ankles, and dialed Santa Monica.

His sister's landline rang twice and he hoped he'd get a chance to sing a message. "Hello," a girl child's voice came through the phone.

Luke skinned his teeth at the sound of his niece. "Hi, Em. How are you, chipmunk?"

"Uncle Luke," Emily sang his name. "Where are you?"

"I'm in New York."

"I mishu."

Emily's statement tugged at his heartstrings. "I miss you, too."

"Are you coming over?" Emily asked. A commotion on the line commenced. "Stop, Ryan," she commanded to her younger brother.

"I want to speak to him, too," his nephew whined in the background.

As he listened to Emily and Ryan argue, Luke couldn't help but laugh.

"Em? Let Ryan say hello." His suggestion fell upon deaf ears when the phone banged against something hard and echoed through the receiver. He knew the two were fighting.

"Hi, Uncle Luke," Ryan shouted.

Luke had to hold the phone away from his ear in order to understand Ryan's greeting. "Hey, buddy. You guys behaving?"

"Yes." Ryan copied his sister. "Are you coming over?"

"Not today, but I hope to be there soon."

More rustling and muffled yelling commenced before his sister's voice registered.

"Hello?" Jane's breathless question sounded as loud as Ryan's greeting.

"It's me."

"Luke? Sorry about that. I was cooking. I figured I'd let the machine pick up, but my kids had other plans."

"When are you going to get rid of that thing? You have a cell."

"Uhh…never. I need it out here when cell service is wonky. Plus the kids love to hear the messages, especially your messages," Jane said. "How are you?"

"Good." He stretched.

"You sound tired," Jane remarked.

"Thanks." His sister's honesty wasn't a new experience. "I just wanted to check on you guys."

"We're okay. How's New York? I saw online that Aurora was a hit. There's a picture of you and this woman. Leona Sable. I thought you were done with that awful behavior, Luke." Jane scoffed.

"She's my new tour manager." Luke explained the story to his sister, including the moment Leona hid behind him to avoid being photographed.

"Oh." Her tone was less accusatory. "I thought you didn't want to hire a woman since—" she paused "—well, because of what happened. I thought you'd give yourself some time."

"I was initially against it, but she's the best in the business. Tommy trusts her."

"Do you?"

"She has the skills to do the job." Luke trusted

Tommy, and Leona's client success couldn't be denied. In the short time that he'd known Leona, she'd already done a better job than Ivy.

He'd met Ivy at an after-party with a bunch of industry folks, and their one-night stand had turned into a yearlong relationship. He'd been eager to help her when she wanted to get out of her family's shadow and build something of her own. He was stupid to offer himself and his career. Ivy had proven to be an opportunist and when a better opportunity came her way, she'd left him and his heart behind.

"Luke? You didn't answer the question," Jane persisted, jolting him back from the past.

"Let's just say I've taken some precautions to ensure she delivers." He didn't know Leona well enough to trust her. Her history with Paul didn't help situations either.

"What things?"

His sister was no less a brat than when they were kids. "Don't worry about it."

"Hmm. She's gorgeous," Jane offered.

"For someone who reamed me out for my past behavior, you're quick to point out that my new tour manager is gorgeous."

"Well, she is. Are things going well with her so far?"

He was silent.

"Luke?"

"Everything's fine, Jane." The truth was things weren't fine. He was touring in a month. Even though he'd signed with the best manager referred to him, things were in disarray.

"See, whenever you say that, I know something's up. Spill the beans, mister."

Luke paused and contemplated how much of the truth he should deliver to his sister. "She's Paul Reese's ex."

"No way!"

"Yes."

"Someone dated that con artist? Why am I surprised when—?"

"Yup."

"There is so much I want to ask you, but I have to finish dinner before my kids starve and Aaron gets home. Just—" she paused "—don't make her pay for it. Okay?"

"What's that supposed to mean?" Defensiveness drove each thud his heart made against his chest.

"I'm sure those precautions you put in place for her to do her job have everything to do with both Ivy and Paul, am I right?"

"What if they did?"

"Just because Paul was an awful producer who wasted your time and money, and stole your manager, doesn't mean Leona has any of the same poor qualities or intentions."

"You're forgetting the worst part, Jane."

Jane sighed into the phone. "I feel for you, Luke, but you have to move on and judge this Leona woman on her own merits. She probably got screwed, too."

Luke considered his sister's words. He had been hard on Leona, but he assured himself it was for the best. If he could keep a little anger for her, perhaps he could control the ever-growing urge to touch her. "I'll try to video chat with you guys later this week."

"Sounds good."

"Hey? How're Mom and Dad?" Luke asked.

"They're doing well. I know you're busy but you

should check in more often. Make sure they see you when you do this tour."

The guilt hit him hard. "I'll try."

"Just not today? They love you and are proud of you. What else do you need?"

"Jane." His firm tone urged her to cease her line of questioning. What he needed was to succeed. But even he wasn't sure how much success would be enough.

His sister sighed. "I'll tell the kids goodbye for you. Love you."

"Love you, too." Luke hung up.

He opened his computer and logged onto a few sites. The activity was what he needed to take his mind off his conversation with Jane.

He started creating his set list for the Brazil performance and put a message out to the fans on social media to request their favorite tracks. Luke's first hit song, "Get Up and Move for Me," was always the number one request. He had remixed the original song so many times over the years to give it a fresh sound.

"Bringing it back ol' skool style, guys." He knew the fans would go nuts once he played the original. They loved it as much as he did. As the melody of the song played, nostalgia filled him. *How long has it been? Ten...maybe twelve years?* The lyrics were affirmations from a motivational speaker. They infused him with good feelings and kept him moving forward. All because two girls had danced for him.

After college, he had spent time in Europe as a roadie for the Lexionic Twins, two brothers from Belgium who played electro house and techno. In the early hours of the morning after the twins had closed out a rave in Paris, they let him deejay.

Two girls had fallen asleep on one of the couches while the club staff at L'Essence cleaned up. He'd seen them dancing all night, barely stopping for a drink. Though the club had cleared out, his goal had been to get everyone up and moving to the music. As soon as he played his first selection, the girls came out of their slumber. Soon they were up and dancing as if they had never stopped. One of them blew him kisses. By the time he finished his set, everyone, including the club staff, was dancing.

Whenever he had been ready to give up on his musical aspirations, he remembered that night and it got him through the tough times. The experience inspired the song "Get Up and Move for Me."

Riding on the wave of good vibes from the memory, Luke read through his social media feeds and noted the fan requests. He created a playlist and worked on it for a bit before saving the draft.

His packed schedule and recent meeting with Leona had drained him. In the morning he'd be on a plane to Brazil. Next week, he would be back in New York for his residency and to meet with Leona's team.

She had almost outfoxed him earlier. "Leona Sable." He rested his head against the headboard and smiled.

"A month?" Leona's team questioned. Individual grumblings of time constraints, impossible task completion, and legal tie-ups followed.

Leona had to inspire them. "The good news is there's some foundation. Let's make sure what's required is in place, fill in the gaps to cover ourselves, and keep it moving."

She received several nods, which was a positive sign.

"We have a decent budget, so if there's a serious problem we can throw funds at, then let's do it. We want happy and safe fans. At every event, I want disciples of The Musical Prophet and brand ambassadors singing our praises."

Sebastian Louis rubbed his palms together in motivation. "Hallelujah."

Sebastian, her superstar marketer, loved a challenge and was a favorite at Wallace Entertainment for publicizing even the most minor celebrity like an icon. He'd also handle vendor management for the tour.

"Do we have authorization to make final decisions on our respective areas, Leo? Given the tight deadline, it will totally tie us up if everything needs to be approved by you," Sara Reynolds inquired.

In the past, Sara and Leona had their disagreements over project decisions, but their creative chemistry was off the charts. When it came to venue logistics, whatever Leona envisioned, Sara could materialize. She was a tenacious scheduler and could organize travel and accommodations blindfolded.

"I trust you guys. You've proven yourselves to me in the past. That's why you're on this team. This is a collaborative effort. All I need is consistent status updates. You know how I like it. We have meet and greet with DJ Luke this afternoon. I have every confidence that together we are going to blow our client's mind and pull off a great tour."

"Great." Tracy made notes in her smartphone. With all the due diligence requirements, Leona needed someone with a thorough understanding of every liability possible, as well as ways to navigate around them. There was no one better than Tracy. She wouldn't be on tour but she would be Leona's legal eyes and ears.

The excitement grew among her team members.

Sebastian nudged Leona. "We're really glad you're back. It's been too long."

Sara pushed back her blond locks. "Yeah, Sebz and I really missed you."

"Aww, you guys. You're my rock stars." Leona hugged Sebastian.

"So, is Luke as cool as the Internet portrays him?" Sebastian inquired.

Before she could stop herself, Leona frowned. Her shoulders tightened and rose up to her ears. She and Tracy exchanged glances.

"Oh boy." Sara clasped her forehead.

"It's nothing." Leona attempted to sequester her opinions about Luke.

Sebastian rubbed his hands over his face and through his brown hair. "We know that face all too well."

"Meet him and form your own opinions. This is going to be great." Deep down inside Leo wasn't so sure.

That evening, when Leona went home, she let her hair down and relaxed with a glass of Shiraz. Her team had met Luke, and Leona had been impressed by and grateful for how friendly, charming, and motivational he was with them.

"He's awesome," Sara had said to her.

"Yeah, Leo. You're right. This is going to be a great tour," had been Sebastian's remarks.

Tracy, however, had been more circumspect. "Don't forget the conditions and stay on your toes."

Leona had given Tracy a curt nod. "Got it."

Now in her apartment, Leona tried to decompress. When she met with Luke, she always wanted to be buttoned up. To keep from playing with her hair, she tucked it away, a trick she'd learned early in her career.

Leona decided it was time to break the news about the tour to Peaches. Even worse, the orange fish, with black spotted tail, would be in the care of Aunt Izzy, who had a tendency to forget feeding times.

Leona almost pressed her face against the fish tank. "I'll do my best to make sure she doesn't kill you, girl."

She opened her satellite radio app and searched for Luke's station, surprised by how much she looked forward to hearing his music again. He wasn't just a DJ with multiple albums, who had written and produced music. He was an artist and talented poet with profound and deep lyrics. He even sang on a few tracks with other artists and musicians.

Leona readied herself for a hot shower. Her hair was still nicely blown out, but in order for it to stay that way she had to make sure to protect it from moisture. She tucked her locks into a shower cap when her doorbell rang. She threw on her robe and tied it sloppily.

Leona went to the intercom. "Who is it?"

"It's…me," a garbled male voice barked through the speaker.

"Abe? Is that you?" More deep garbled sounds came through the speaker. She couldn't make out the voice but it sounded like Abe. Who else would it be? The media hadn't stalked her in about nine months, so she assumed she was safe, and her brother was out of town. "Okay, I'll buzz you up." She pressed the button and made a note to talk with her landlord about the dangers of the jacked up intercom.

Abe had a knack for interrupting her whenever she was about to get into an activity. Leona hadn't had any time with him after the meeting so maybe he wanted to discuss some things.

Moments later came a knock on her door. When she opened it, she froze.

"You're not Abe."

Chapter Seven

"No, I'm not."

Mortified, with shower cap, no makeup, and robe on, Leona was still getting over the shock of Luke in her doorframe. The green and brown button-down plaid shirt he wore was rolled up to the elbow and not only formed to his fit physique but highlighted the green in his eyes. He could have been wearing a paper bag and he would still ooze of sex appeal.

"Are you going to let me in or just stand there?"

"Umm, sure." She let him in. Behind him, her hand went to the shower cap in the hopes she'd taken it off, but as the plastic crinkled under her fingers, her hopes were dashed. She snatched the shower cap off and her hair tumbled out, landing just above her elbows.

Luke faced her to speak but hesitated. Instead, he reared back and fixated on her hair.

"What?" Leona's mouth went dry and she wondered if she had grown some new appendage since she left the bathroom.

"That wasn't smart. I could have been a killer or worse." Luke's jaw tightened and his eyes trailed the length of her body, settling on her exposed legs. After a moment, his eyes scanned up to her breasts before locking in on her eyes.

"My intercom's kind of broken." The tension in her shoulders returned and she clutched at her robe. She closed the door. "You can have a seat in the living room. I'll just change." Leona hurried to her bedroom.

She was too exposed and needed armor quick. She was angry and aroused and pissed at herself for feeling both. *What the hell is he doing here? Whatever you do, don't bring up that contract.*

She dressed, tied her hair in a tight ponytail, and was back in her living room within minutes. Luke sat comfortably on her couch, waiting.

"The infamous Peaches, I presume?" Luke pointed to the fish bowl atop a bookshelf.

"In the filet."

He grunted his affirmation, then tilted his head in recognition. "You're playing my music."

She was happy for the change in subject. "I like to be educated about my clients."

"Do you like it?" His genuine eagerness slowed her movements.

"Yes. I do."

Relief relaxed Luke's features, and she was surprised by the effect of her opinion. "Would you like something to drink?"

"No, thank you." Luke did a double take and his eyes rested on the silver beam. "Is that a stripper pole?"

Leona's ears warmed and, despite her brown skin, were likely as red as the roof on Peaches's little fish pagoda. This was the reason not everyone was invited into her home. The last thing she needed was Luke having the impression she was some sex freak entertaining men in her living room with a strip tease. She didn't want to explain that the best strength-training workout she ever experienced was from doing the swings and flips on the silver pole.

Leona sat opposite Luke. "It is. So, what are you doing here? How do you even know where I live?"

Luke pulled his eyes away from the pole to again focus on her. "I can be resourceful, too."

"I see." She folded her hands and waited.

"This tour means a lot to me. The fans have been begging for a tour like this. For me, their experience is the number one priority."

"Okay." Leona wondered what bomb Luke was about to drop.

He leaned forward in his seat. "I wanted to run some ideas by you."

"I'm listening."

"Some of my fans are aspiring DJs. I want to give them a chance to compete for an opening act at my shows."

"A contest?"

"Yeah. We have forty dates, so we can do forty spots."

Leona mulled it over. "I wouldn't suggest forty spots, though the number does have marketing potential. You want to sell out some big venues. I suggest reserving those spots for more familiar artists and DJs at the bigger shows. That will help boost attendance. However, we can see about the smaller venues and other types of pre-show entertainment."

Luke nodded in agreement. "Good point. Give me an example."

Leona thought he might be testing her but it didn't matter. She was an idea-generating, example-giving machine. "At some of your concerts, we could set up a small secondary stage for the runner-ups by the vendors or even at the entrance as people come in. Our team will be stretched, but I know just the contractor to set this up. For the major winners who perform on the main stage before you, they can submit video and a demo of their set. We need to pick aspiring DJs who are good and can overcome stage fright, as well as invite runner-ups in case someone completely flakes. Losing it in front of twenty to ninety thousand fans could get ugly. Do you want to judge the entries or do you have judges in mind?"

Luke's hand went to the hair on his chin. It was a posture Leona named his pensive pose. "Yes to all," he said at length. "I have a list of people who would be great judges but I'd like to make the final call."

"Shoot me an email on the judges and I'll get the team on it," Leona proposed. This was her first real conversation with Luke that didn't involve an outburst of some sort and it was a refreshing change. "Was there something else?"

Luke scratched his head. "When this tour starts, things are going to get crazy. I need to get back to California. I'm a big surfer. If we can arrange it so that I have maximum time there during the break, that'd be great."

"Of course." Like her, he was banned from sex on tour. In addition to surfing, he no doubt wanted the freedom to get his fill. "I'll go over the schedule with Tommy and organize it."

Luke looked her up and down. "What's your relationship with Abe?"

"Relationship? He's my boss. My mentor."

He raised an eyebrow. "I bet."

Leona frowned. "What's that supposed to mean?"

"Come on, Leona. You opened the door half naked."

She choked at the implication. "Why is that your concern? My personal life is none of your business." She stood and crossed her arms.

Luke did the same, towering over her. "You didn't deny it."

Leona forced herself to keep her anger in check. "Was there anything else?"

"If not Abe, then who? Are you back with Paul?" he asked.

"Whoa. Paul?" Leona's heartbeat pounded against her rib cage and her voice climbed an octave. "You don't know shit about my history with that man."

"I know more than you think," Luke said.

Leona tilted her head back to see him. "Something you read on the Internet, no doubt. It doesn't matter. It's not your business."

"Why don't you just answer the question? Confirm or deny it."

She was so close to him their bodies touched and she pointed at his face, which was a blur from their proximity. "I don't have to discuss my relationship, past, present, or future, with you or anyone." Each time her chest inflated her breasts grazed his torso.

"Leona." His face softened and his lids lowered to her lips before his mouth covered hers.

Her hand went to his neck and she pulled him so hard his lips crushed hers. She responded to the feral passionate charge his lips sent through her body and whimpered a cry laced with the desire for more.

His tongue tussled with hers and his taste was drugging. His hand went to her ponytail and yanked the tie free, and the relaxed feel on her scalp made her lean into him as his hand messed her hair. She was about to climb him when he abruptly let her go.

Neither one of them spoke; they just stood there breathing. Reality brought her back to the room hard and fast. She'd just kissed Luke. She'd kissed her client. *Oh my God, no.*

"That—" Luke started, but she didn't want to hear.

"That will never happen again." She stomped toward the door. She opened it, fanning her hand to hasten his exit. "Good night."

Luke shook his head and lumbered out. He turned to say something to her, but Leona shut the door in his face.

That didn't go as planned. Luke hailed a cab.

"Where to?" the cabdriver asked.

"The Metro Hotel."

He had wanted to smooth things over with Leona. Once on the road, they needed to work together. Things started out okay, but why he pushed her about her relationships was beyond him.

Who am I kidding? He wanted to know who, if anyone, occupied her bed. When she didn't come forth with the information he deliberately touched a tender nerve. Paul Reese.

Leona made him pay for it, too. She was fire when she unleashed her anger, and even more beautiful. And that hair? He couldn't stop himself from kissing her full lips and twisting his fingers in that thick mane. His dick still twitched and he released a few buttons on his shirt.

Leona was off-limits, and not only because of the contract they signed.

His phone vibrated in his pocket. Tommy. His agent was no doubt anxious to hear how things went with Leona. He picked up.

Tommy bypassed all salutations. "How'd it go?"

Luke stretched. "Great."

"That bad, huh?"

"It wasn't as bad as you think. We had a moment where things were going well." They had, and the way they collaborated was effortless.

"But?"

"Forget about it, man."

"You lost your temper, didn't you? No, let me guess, you started asking her questions you had no business asking." Tommy knew him too well and though he yelled, Luke knew Tommy only had his best interest in mind. "Which would you rather have? A friend or an enemy?"

Luke scratched his head. "I hear you, man." Tommy was right, but when he got around Leona his feelings were in competition and even he didn't know which would win out—anger and stress, or exhilaration and optimism. All he knew was that he needed to keep his distance and not ever think about kissing her again.

"It's cool." He arrived at the hotel and fished for his wallet to pay the cabbie.

"It better be cool, Luke. The time is fast approaching where Leo will be all you've got."

Chapter Eight

Leona climbed out of the subway and walked to her parents' house in the Park Slope section of Brooklyn. As she approached, she witnessed her brother, Mitchell, maneuvering a heavy hot water tank.

Mitchell stopped fussing with the object when he saw her. "Hey, little squirrel."

"Whaddup, Mitch-match?" Leona embraced his large frame and lifted to her toes to kiss his cheek.

"The parents have me moving shit as usual."

She laughed. "That's what they bred your ass for."

Taking after her father, Mitchell stood just around six feet. He had a little weight on him, making him an intimidating force.

He peeked into her goody-filled bag. "What'd you bring?"

"Chocolate hazelnut bread pudding."

He touched the pan. "Oh dip, it's still warm. I can't wait for dinner to be over." Mitchell rubbed his hands over his belly and did a little dance.

"I know, right?" Leona joined him. "Let me get it inside before it doesn't make it."

Upon entering the house, she was hit with the delicious, savory fragrance of seasoned food. The combination of thyme, sage, and onions that her mother used when roasting always took her back to her childhood. Her stomach reacted with a growl and her taste buds began to salivate.

"Mom?"

"In here, dear," June Sable's melodic words carried from the back. Moments later, her mother's short, full figure entered the kitchen.

Leona bent to kiss her cheek. "I see you got Mitch-match on slave duty."

"Don't say that." Her mother frowned and the lines creased her cherubic face.

"I'm teasing, Mom," Leona assured. "Where's my father?"

"In his chair. Where else?"

Leona put the bag of goodies on the kitchen table. She found her father, Samuel Sable, in the living room. He rested in a brown La-Z-Boy with a cup of tea sitting on a side table next to him.

"Hey, Dad."

"Sweetheart." He greeted her, excitement in his outstretched arms.

Leona embraced him and kissed his cheek. "What are you watching?"

"The news." He made a kissing noise even though his lips didn't reach her cheek. "I'm always checking things out."

A pang of remorse hit her heart. Her dad had often watched the news but when she and Paul had broken up, he patrolled the channels to keep up with Paul's rants about her.

"Things lookin' good, Dad?"

"A-OK on the home front." He gave the thumbs-up.

Leona was relieved. She'd boycotted any screens having the potential to deliver Paul's nonsense. "I brought bread pudding."

"Oh. I'm sure that will be wonderful."

"You know it, Papa Bear," Leona said. "I'm going to help Moms with the cookin'."

"Okay, dear." He again monitored the television screen.

She returned to the kitchen to find her mother stirring a pot.

"Where's Isabelle?" her mother asked.

"She's finishing something for the magazine. She'll be here soon." Leona took over for her mother and stirred the pot.

"This will be our last Sunday dinner for a while since you'll be going on that tour."

She gave her mother a quick hug around the shoulders. "I'll be back during the break."

Sunday dinner with her family had been her anchor after her rocky breakup. Paul had never attended these dinners so she didn't associate her parents' home and Sunday dinner with his absence.

"How are things with that young man? The DJ. You're working well together?" *Not like that Paul fellow* was implied.

The truth was she and Luke's working relationship was more grueling than Navy SEAL boot camp, and ever since they'd kissed she'd been even more on edge. "Things are manageable for now, but enough about me, Mom. How are you?"

"I had my physical and the doctor says I could stand to lose a little weight. So, I started walking in the park every morning with Mrs. Murray from next door."

"That's great. You should bring Daddy along."

Her mother scoffed. "Your father? Walk in the park?"

The thought of her father walking in the park was a stretch, but she suggested it anyway. "He needs to be more active, too."

"Yes. You're right."

"What's for dinner besides this gravy I'm stirring?" Leona lifted the spoon to check the consistency.

"Pot roast, mashed potatoes, macaroni and cheese, green bean casserole, and salad."

Leona wished it were time for dinner already. "Mitch-match must have done cartwheels."

Noise from the front entrance disrupted their conversation.

"Hello, Sables." Izzy's bustling energy further lifted the mood in the kitchen. She kissed Leona's mother. "Sorry I'm late."

"That's okay, dear. I'm just happy you could make it to Leona's last Sunday dinner."

Leona rolled her eyes. "You make it sound like you'll never see me again."

"I know, sweetheart, but… Mitchell Sable!" Her mother's raised voice made everyone turn to look. "You get those filthy hands out of that pot, right now."

Mitchell jumped and clanked the pot closed. "Jeez, Mom." He left to wash up.

Leona and Izzy giggled.

"You girls set the table and then relax with a glass of wine. We'll eat in about ten minutes."

Leona and Izzy grabbed items along their way to set the table.

"We need to get started on two bottles straight away. One for you and one for me." Izzy peeked to make sure Leona's mother wasn't listening.

"I heard that," her mother called.

"Sonic hearing, that one. So, is DJ Luke still a handsome devil?" Izzy's eyebrows dashed up and down several times.

"*Devil* is the key word." Leona slid a bottle of red wine out from the nearby wine rack.

"He can't be that bad." Izzy opened a cabinet and reached for a few dinner glasses, placing them on the table.

Leona worked on the bottle, the sound of the cork popping. "I don't know what the deal is. Sometimes his behavior is fine, and then other times he acts like I'm the root of all his problems in life."

"You said things went weird after you mentioned your past clients. Do you think he has issues with one of them?"

Leona poured wine for them. "Paul, for sure. He brought him up in a conversation. The way he pressed me about him pissed me right the fuck off." Leona's voice muted as she cursed and conveniently omitted their kiss even though the very thought raised her skin temperature.

"What did he ask you?"

"If we were back together. Like I'd ever go back to that asshole." Leona cringed.

"Leona?" Her mother's warning tone came from the distance.

"Sorry, Mom."

Izzy sipped on her wine. "Really, Leo? You have no idea why a good-looking bloke is asking you if you're still in a relationship with another good-looking bloke?"

"It's more than that. It was the accusatory way he asked the questions." Leona swallowed a gulp of sweet Shiraz. "This would be better slightly chilled."

"Give us a bit of ice."

"Classy." Leona frowned at the request. She stuffed the wine in an ice bucket, grabbed a few cubes, and plunked them in Izzy's glass.

"Luke's a guy. Sounds like he's feeling out the situation." Izzy swirled her glass, the ruby liquid sloshing to the rim.

"He's my client. I just want to do a good job." She was in a high stakes situation and needed success with this tour regardless of Luke's behavior or absurd conditions. Leona had also omitted the details about the addendum for fear that Izzy would lose her shit and seek Luke out.

"You're amazing, Leo. You'll win him over."

"Dinner is ready, everyone," her mother called.

Mitchell wandered into the dining area a few seconds later. "I'm ready to eat."

They gathered around the dining room table as her mother said grace and then sat down to their family meal. Leona relished the banter between her parents and buffoonery between her, Mitchell, and Izzy.

Soon, she and Izzy readied themselves to leave. Leona had work to do for the tour and packing to start.

Her brother hugged her goodbye. "The bread pudding was a hit, little squirrel."

"Thanks, Mitch-match."

"Always a pleasure, Sables." Izzy kissed everyone as she made her way to the door.

"You be safe, sweetheart, and use your relaxation techniques when things get challenging." Her mother held both her hands. "Show them how we Sables get the job done."

"I will, Mom." Leona embraced her parents and hoped it wouldn't be too long before she was able to spend time with them again. "Love you guys."

Chapter Nine

Opening day of the tour in Hartford, Connecticut, arrived. The last month had been grueling, but Leona and her team had pulled it all together. During that time, Leona communicated with Luke via Tommy and Abe unless necessary, so neither one of them had an opportunity to further damage their already strained relationship.

Forty tour dates in four months were planned, not including Luke's residency at Aurora and other one-off performances. Everything was set for the opener and Leona was a positive drill sergeant, keeping everyone on their toes and the machine well oiled.

An hour before showtime, roadies and technicians buzzed around the chaotic venue with focus and purpose. Leona sidestepped equipment and venue security to check on her artist. She searched the usual places, but Luke was MIA.

"Has anyone seen Luke?"

"Not for a while, no," said one of the crewmembers as he moved speakers and wires.

Leona went behind the stage to a false addition. Inside was cool and dark, housing dressing rooms for Luke and the dancers, as well as an area for the media.

She was about to abandon her search when she saw the soft glow of light. She followed the light and found Luke in a corner with headphones on, a computer on his lap, and a few USB flash drives by his side. He snacked on animal crackers and bobbed his head to the music.

Leona's approach was tentative and she readied herself for battle. Music drifted from his headphones and no matter how gently she tried to engage him, she would startle him.

Luke's body jerked when he spotted her.

The big bad wolf is scared.

He fumbled with his headphones. "What's up?"

Leona hated doing this, but making sure he had everything he needed, even moral support, was her job.

"I've been looking for you. As your tour manager, it's a good idea for me to know where you are."

"You found me." His full-body shrug made it clear the interruption was unwelcomed.

Leona sighed. "Do you need anything? Food? Drink? Whatever you need to be comfortable, I'll make sure you have it."

"I'm good. My rider has my preferences."

"Right. Well, you'll do great tonight." She needed to flee the confining space. *At least I tried.*

"Leona?"

"Yes?"

Luke fell into his pensive pose. "Something I may not have mentioned is that when I come offstage, I'm pretty wiped out. I normally like to have a banana and a Gatorade until I can get something more to eat."

She made a mental note. "Okay. I'll make sure to have those for you. Anything else?"

"I'll be drenched, so a fresh shirt."

The image of his drenched shirt clinging to his sculpted body flashed in her mind's eye. "You got it. I'll update your rider, as well." She waited.

"That's all." Luke moved to put his headphones on. Leona made her exit.

"Thank you," was his faint expression to her back.

She stopped short and pivoted at the genuine gratitude in his words. His focus returned to the computer.

"You're welcome."

She left before either of them said anything more to ruin the moment.

Back at the stage, the crowd poured into the venue. The bright neon colors and glittering clothing matched the anticipation of the fans. One of the contest winners provided pre-concert tunes as shirtless boys, and girls in flower bras, flooded the stage.

Minutes before his performance, Luke wiggled his limbs to get loose. Leona argued with her body. *I cannot react to him.* But his hypnotizing eyes and athletic build delivered undeniable swag no matter what he did. He was welcoming and cheerful with everyone around him. He laughed easily with Tommy, who stood close by, and the crew.

Luke's eyes landed on her and she gave him two thumbs up accompanied by a bright expression. His smile faded.

Leona's breath caught in her throat. *Ice cold.* "Well, he's not scowling. That's an improvement," she mumbled to herself. She continued to appear positive even though there was a pinch on her heart.

Luke was announced and ran up the stairs to the stage. The packed park erupted into cheers when they saw him. The outdoor event lucked out with cool air and no rain in sight. As darkness descended, the night called for something magical.

Luke's music teased through the speakers and the crowd screamed in anticipation. He sang the vocals with his fans and they loved it. Leona had seen him play at Aurora, but this was another level and she was again entranced into the world of happiness he created. On this enchanted night, among tens of thousands of fans, everyone felt like one unified entity.

"Wow."

Tommy leaned over and yelled into her ear. "Amazing, isn't it?"

Leona curtly nodded, attempting to appear unaffected. But in that moment she understood. She and her team needed to bottle this experience and feed it to the masses to get Luke to the level he sought to achieve. The level he deserved as an artist. She got that nervous, heart-racing feeling that happened just before she embarked upon accomplishing a big, hairy, scary, exciting, and absolutely audacious goal.

Oh boy.

When the show was over, Leona waited at the foot of the stairs with Luke's requested items. She brainstormed ideas like a machine, not to mention she was still entranced from the show. But she reminded herself about the work ahead of her.

"Great show, Luke." She handed him the fruit and drink and then ushered him to his dressing room. "We're on the move," she mumbled into a walkie-talkie.

As they hurried to Luke's dressing room, he scarfed down both snacks before trashing the remains.

Before he was behind closed doors he undressed. The first thing she noticed was the smooth skin of his torso.

His raised arms accentuated the lean, well-defined muscle of his abdomen, side, and back. She knew how each of them felt against her hands and body.

Leona tried to avert her gaze but his physique was having none of that. The tattoo that normally peeked out of his shirt on his forearm was a much larger sleeve tattoo, snaking up his arm and over his strong shoulder. On his opposite side, more ink spanned the length of his torso, disappearing under his jeans. Leona felt robbed once his shirt came down to cover him again.

Luke caught her open appreciation. The rise and fall of his chest deepened.

"Uhh…" She approached him as nonchalantly as her legs would allow. She was sure the flush of embarrassment displayed on her face. "Are you ready for the press or do you need a minute?" She could smell his familiar musky fragrance and it added further distraction.

Luke shook his head. "I'm good."

She was warm, and pressed the heel of her palm against her forehead.

"Do *you* need a minute, Leona?" He surveyed her face, which only served to increase her discomfort because his effect on her was obvious.

"I…uh…mmm… No."

Leona led Luke down a corridor, wishing she had a cooler response to him. She felt his eyes on her and slowed her hastened speed. "Just this way." She turned to confirm he was following her.

What she didn't expect was to find Luke mere inches away from her. She bumped into his strong form with unintentional force. Unable to regain her balance, Leona began tipping backward. Frantic and seeking something to hold on to, she grabbed at his waist. Luke's hands shot out to clutch her forearms, steadying her. She slammed into him and his warmth coupled with the recent visual of his body set her skin ablaze, and her insides tingled from her navel to her center. Her surroundings faded further into the background and his electric green-gray eyes mesmerized her.

Luke's grip on her forearms tightened, and he hugged her near. "Are you okay?" His eyes settled on her mouth and his face hovered so close she smelled the lemon-lime sports drink on his breath.

She nodded but her tongue lacked life. Being close to him like this atrophied her in place. Luke's head inched even closer and Leona's heart leapt at the thought of his lips anywhere on her. Her mouth parted in wait-ing invitation.

"Leo?"

Leona gasped and fear seized her muscles when she recognized Sara's voice. "Oh my God."

He ran his fingers through his hair and his exhale rang with frustration.

Leona scanned the corridor for her colleague.

"Leo? Leo, pick up." Sara's words were enveloped in electronic static.

Leona almost sank to the floor in relief when she realized Sara's voice emanated from the walkie-talkie on her hip. Leona attempted to clear the fuzziness in her head and fumbled with the equipment. "Leo, here."

"Is Luke on his way to press?"

Leona glanced at the hint of pink in Luke's cheeks as she spoke. "Affirmative. ETA thirty seconds." She affixed the device back in place and attempted to speak.

"Let's go." Luke reached for her as if to usher her

along but then withdrew, shoved his hands into his pockets, and strode past her.

Leona wanted to kick her own ass. Seeing Luke semi-disrobed had put a chink in her armor, and being so close to him disintegrated the entire shield.

When they arrived at the pressroom, Leona handed Luke over to Sebastian, who guided him through the circuit of reporters and photographers.

"The show went well," Tommy said and she lined up between him and Sara.

"Yeah. I'm glad you were here for it," Leona agreed.

"Me, too, but I'm happy to hand over all these management duties to you guys," Tommy confessed.

"I'm sure." Leona gave Tommy a weak smile and her eyes once again found her client.

Luke delivered his interviews, and his professionalism annoyed her. Isn't that what she wanted—a show of unaffected professionalism by her client?

Sara nudged her shoulder. "Everything okay? You look more stressed than usual."

Leona nodded. "How are we doing on time?"

"For day one? Pretty good. We should be done here in an hour and on the road in three." Sara studied her watch.

"Great." *What the hell happened back there? Get it together, Sable, it was one fucking kiss.* Whatever it was, now that they were on tour, by contract it couldn't happen again. Leona sighed heavily. "Or it will end badly."

"What will end badly, Leo?" Tommy asked.

"Did I say that out loud? I was referring to the line of questioning from the reporter." A poor recovery but Tommy seemed to buy it. Leona turned to Sara. "He's almost done. Let's communicate to the team that we're moving him."

Sara had her walkie-talkie in hand. "I'm on it."

"Thanks, everyone. We need to get Luke to Montreal. See you at the next location," Sebastian announced.

Leona gave Sebastian the "okay" sign as he and Luke walked her way.

"Tommy and Luke have some business to finish and will meet us at the bus depot." The words were thick in Leona's mouth.

As Luke's agent, Tommy didn't need to accompany them on tour, but instead worked from his California office on Luke's behalf and communicated remotely with her and Abe. Once they said their goodbyes at the bus depot, Tommy would be heading back to Los Angeles. She and Luke would be buffer-free and no doubt rubbing each other the wrong way.

"I'm heading there now with some of the team. The quicker we can head out the better. Luke needs rest and we need to debrief," Leona added.

Sebastian checked the time on his phone. "Sara and I will finish up here and meet you in an hour."

Tommy and Luke headed toward the exit and Leona couldn't help but ogle his departing figure. Did he question what happened between them? Her concerns escalated when Luke glanced back at her.

Leona waited by the last two buses—Luke's and the one she shared with her team.

"We're all accounted for and ready to go," Sebastian confirmed.

"Great. I haven't seen Luke. Is he on his bus already?" Leona scanned the area.

Sebastian scratched his chin. "I saw Tommy, so I assume he's here but I'll check."

Things were running close to schedule, just the way Leona liked it, but everyone was tired and that was when mistakes happened.

Sebastian ran back with Tommy by his side. "He's not here, Leo."

"What?" Her eyes widened at Tommy. "He's not with you?"

"He had something to take care of and promised me he'd get a cab here," Tommy said.

Sara came over to them. "Are we leaving? What's happening?"

"Luke's not here and we don't know where he is," Sebastian explained.

Leona clenched her fists at her side. "Houdini strikes again."

Chapter Ten

Leona paced and Tommy did the same. If they didn't leave soon, they wouldn't get to Montreal in time for Luke's morning interviews.

Tommy mumbled about possibly missing his flight to Los Angeles and with it, some important meetings. He called Luke's cell phone again.

Leona sent the bus with her team ahead. Luke's bus remained and the smell of exhaust filled her nostrils. Luke's tardiness not only caused a delay in the schedule, but now she had to ride with him for seven long hours to Montreal.

Her phone sounded. Sara had sent her flights out of Hartford in the event Luke didn't show up in time to get to Montreal by bus.

"Is this normal for him?" She felt the gray hairs and another wrinkle appear.

"Not at all. Whatever is keeping him is important."

Leona paced some more, checked her watch, and, like Tommy, dialed Luke's cell phone again. No answer.

"He'll be here, Leo."

"I'm begging you." She pressed her palms together. "Please don't go."

"Luke's a kitty-cat. You just need to learn how to stroke him."

"Isn't it obvious? I'm highly allergic to puss... I mean kitty-cats."

Tommy whipped his head, meeting Leona's winking eye. They shared a laugh.

"Hey, since we have a moment, I've been meaning to ask you about Ivy."

Tommy sobered. "We don't talk about her."

"Who is this 'we' you're referring to, Tommy? It's just me and you here."

Tommy sighed.

"Is there any validity to the rumors? You and Luke are very tight-lipped about what happened. I can respect his privacy about details, but a high-level summary is just professional."

"And you've been given a very high-level summary to do your job." Tommy grasped her hand, which she almost objected to had it not been for the platonic pat that followed. "I like you, Leo, but Luke is my client and my friend. It's a dark past that I worked really hard to bring him back from. Let it rest."

Whoa. There was nothing she understood more than trying to let the past rest. "I just don't want to be the person he takes his anger out on. My name is Leona Sable, not Ivy Nichols."

"I hear you."

Leona appreciated Tommy's loyalty, but she still wanted answers.

At that moment, Luke arrived with two reasons for his tardiness—a blonde woman on his right arm, and her redheaded friend on his left. The women were dressed similarly in purple skinny jeans, heeled sandals, and silver sequined tank tops. Leona questioned whether *women* and *legal* were the right terms for them.

Luke approached and his eyes lingered on the hand connection between her and Tommy.

"He's going to drive me up a fucking wall," Leona fumed through clenched jaws.

"Ow!" Tommy released her hand and pumped blood back into his fingers.

"Sorry." Leona crossed her arms, muttering a quick prayer for self-control.

"Tommy? Leona? Meet Candy and Velvet." Luke's relaxed introductions further infuriated her.

"Wow. This is awesome. It's great to meet you, Leo," Velvet said.

Leona noticed half of Velvet's red hair was shaved and what remained contained platinum blonde highlights. The woman was a striking beauty with her dark skin and model-esque stature. She bubbled with joy and jutted her hand out.

Leona was reluctant to return the gesture. If it weren't for the woman's genuine enthusiasm, she would have declined.

Candy followed. "Yeah. It's an honor." Her blond, short hair was cut with sharp edges and had a blue peek-a-boo streak. Leona was sure Candy was about to hug her, but Candy eagerly shook her hand instead. Leona gave both women a decent salutation before turning back to Luke.

"You're late. We have to go. Now." Leona inched toward the bus.

Luke turned to the women and kissed each of them on the cheek. "It was a pleasure, ladies. Boombox will take care of you from here. I hope to see you in Montreal if it fits your schedule." He released the women to Tommy.

Tommy shook his head and spoke under his breath but loud enough that Leona could hear. "She's pissed at you. This is not the way to hit the road."

"What else is new?" Luke mumbled. "I had to take care of some business."

Leona had had enough and headed to the bus.

"Where are you going?" Luke questioned.

She about-faced. "Do you see another bus here? I'm riding with you." She pointed at him.

"I can't ride with her," Luke said to Tommy, shifted in his stance, and rubbed the back of his neck as if he wanted to take flight.

"Hello? I'm still here." She was certain she'd see aversion on Luke's face, but instead his nervousness was baffling. "I wouldn't have to, had you been on time, so put your big boy shorts on and let's go. Trust me. I'm not thrilled either."

Tommy chuckled, shook Luke's hand, and gave him a pat on the shoulder. "You're on your own. Get on the bus and be on your best behavior."

Luke cursed under his breath, then jutted his head at Candy and Velvet. "I'm thinking west coast tour dates for them."

"Really? Nice, I'll check them out," Tommy responded.

Luke continued to ignore her. "Let me know what you think before I pitch it to my new manag—"

"I'm going to miss you." Leona hugged Tommy goodbye. She didn't care that she interrupted Luke. Tommy had been Luke's interim manager, her go-between with Luke, and her ally. Now he was leaving to go back to LA and his real job as agent and leaving her to endure a long bus ride alone. She spoke close to his ear, inhaling the subtle citrus scent from his hair. "Thanks for everything."

Tommy squeezed her in a bear hug. "You'll be fine. I'll be in touch."

When she released Tommy, she found Luke staring at them with furrowed brows before he stomped toward the bus.

"Okay." Tommy cleared his throat. "Have fun, guys." He left with Candy and Velvet, who both waved with enthusiasm.

Leona mounted the bus and Luke followed behind.

The driver greeted him. "Thanks for joining us, Mr. Anderson. I'm Reggie."

Luke mumbled his apologies.

The lingering smell of oil and fuel was nothing compared to the heavy air that hung between her and Luke. Leona wanted to continue reprimanding Luke for his behavior, but most of all she wanted to ban those women from coming to Montreal. Who the hell were they and why did Tommy have to take care of them?

She sat in the common area, trying to burn the jealousy from her consciousness, and opened her laptop. Her things and her people were on the other bus, so she accomplished what she could. She confirmed Luke's appointments and informed her team about their departure.

Luke stood by the small kitchenette, opposite the common area.

"Do you need something? Are you familiar with your tour bus or do you need a tutorial?" Leona asked.

The bus started to move.

"No, I don't need a tutorial. You're sitting where I work."

Leona's entire body stiffened. The tour bus had a closed off master suite with a queen-size bed. Why couldn't Luke just work in there? Oh, right, his sole purpose was to get under her skin.

She slammed her computer shut and moved to get up.

"Hang on a sec." Luke stopped her.

She settled back into the seat and folded her hands over her computer.

"I see you're upset, and I just wanted to clarify something in case you think that I'm not holding up my part of the conditions."

She tilted her head. "What are you talking about?"

"Candy and Velvet. I'm not...we're not—" he mushed his hands together several times "—together."

"Why should I care?"

"Besides the contract? They're DJs that Boombox is checking out and then he'll pitch it to you, my manager, for the tour," he explained.

"Oh." Jealousy had fucked with her brain cells and her face stung with embarrassment. She squeezed her knitted hands together to keep her hand from flying to her ear.

Luke watched her, his body undisturbed by the moving bus.

"Anything else?"

"Yes." He motioned to where she sat. "I'd like my workspace back now."

A rant sat on the tip of her tongue, but choosing the evasive route, she rose to her feet and picked up her bag. "All yours."

She toddled to one of the lower bunks, slid the curtain back, and climbed into the small space. A light activated when she closed the curtain, and she sat with her legs crossed at the ankles. She tried to shut Luke out and focus on her work, but heavy droplets pooled in her lower lids. Leona blamed the sensitivity on PMS, but knew better. She was tired of being the object of Luke's anger.

Abe was right. Luke doesn't hate women. In fact, she'd witnessed him be easygoing with the female crew and members of her team. He even promoted Candy and Velvet for his tour. He talked about love in his music and when he was interviewed, spoke of wanting his music to bring people together. With her, he was different. Sure, he'd kissed her but that was a mistake on both their parts.

He only hates me.

Even though he battered her ego, she still showed up for him and her body craved him. She blinked the tears dry. The pity party was over. This was about business and saving Wallace Entertainment. When she finished responding to the last few emails, she closed her eyes. Her stomach gurgled and twisted in objection to the movement. In the chaos of searching for Luke, she had forgotten to take her motion sickness medication before getting on the bus. She reached for her bag and searched for the pills. If she took them now she might prevent the symptoms from worsening.

Leona's calm search turned into panic. Her pills weren't there.

"Oh no." Her medication was miles away on her tour bus.

Leona's stomach retched and she jumped out of the bunk. Momentarily tangled in the curtain, she sprinted for the bathroom and made it just in time to throw up

everything she had eaten that day. Her eyes teared and
sickness floated in her belly. The vile smell of undi-
gested nutrition increased her queasiness. She gargled
the sour taste of bile from her mouth and rinsed her
face. She dabbed cold water on her neck and chest. As
the bus continued to move Leona willed her breathing
to slow down and her nausea to cease, but she violently
retched again into the toilet. She hadn't eaten much and
wondered where it all came from.

"Leona?" Luke knocked on the door.

She groaned. Luke was the last person she needed
to see, hear, or interact with. "Yes?"

"Everything okay? You've been in there a long time."

The doorknob started to turn. To Leona's horror,
she'd forgotten to lock the door.

She pushed her body against the door. "Don't come
in here!" *Who does that?* All around her smelled like
throw up and her hair and clothes were messy. "I'll be
out in a few minutes."

Leona rinsed her mouth again and tried to fix her
clothing and hair, but her ashen face and droopy lids
betrayed her. Who was she fooling? She was sick in the
worst way. She sprayed air refresher but the fragrance
only made things worse.

She opened the door and Luke leaned against the
panel opposite the bathroom with arms crossed at his
chest.

He wrinkled his nose and averted his head. Once he
recovered, he regarded her for a moment. "You look ter-
rible and smell even worse."

"Thanks." She passed him and headed to the kitchenette. She opened the refrigerator to see if she could
find some seltzer. This was Luke's bus, stocked with

his preferences. In her experience, musicians usually stocked booze and little else. She was happy to find he had ginger ale.

Luke followed her. "You're sick."

"No shit." Leona sipped the soda.

His form filled the entranceway and he hung on to the railing above him, swaying with the motion of the bus. "Are you pregnant?"

Leona choked on her drink and coughed to clear her throat. "What? Why would I be— No. I'm not." *Asshole.* "It's the bus. The moving."

"Why didn't you take something if you know you get sick?"

"I have medicine. It's on my bus, where I'd be, had you—" Leona snapped, and then tightened the reins on her anger "—had things gone as planned."

"You mean if I wasn't late."

"Bingo." She placed the drink in a cup holder and sat for about thirty seconds before she pushed Luke out of the way and ran to the bathroom.

As Leona retched she cursed Luke. This was his fault. *Jerk.* If he hadn't been late she wouldn't be in a mess of puke. She shuddered at the thought that he might be reveling in her misfortune.

The bus slowed and came to a full stop. She wanted to see what was happening, but she didn't trust her body to behave, remaining hovered over the toilet. They were stopped for a while and the lack of motion helped still her tummy.

Several minutes later, she opened the door.

"Fuck!" Leona jumped at Luke's unexpected presence. "Why are you standing there like that?"

He held a cup of water in one hand and four different motion sickness medications in the other. "Which ones do you take? Are they any of these?" He breathed like he'd been running.

Leona stared at him until her disgruntled belly brought her attention back to the boxes. "That one."

Luke handed her the cup and tossed the other three boxes aside. He tore open the medicine packet and handed her two tablets.

"Take them, Leona," he said when she didn't move.

Luke had never spoken soft and normal to her before. The gray in his eyes often showed irritation, but now the green intensified with genuine concern. She did as he instructed, chasing the tablets with water.

"I need some air." Luke shadowed her. Leona thought his anger was disturbing, but the care he showed unraveled her.

Reggie stood by the driver's seat. "That's right. The air will do you good."

"I hope so, Reggie." When Leona dismounted the bus, she saw they were parked in the lot of a 24-hour drug store. "Thanks for stopping."

"Oh, that Mr. Anderson made me get to a pharmacy for you. Zipped outta here so fast, I barely saw him. Are you feeling any better?"

"A bit, but I'm sure the medicine will kick in soon. You may want to air the bus out though," Leona said to Reggie. Luke leaned like a rock star against the side of the vehicle. A gentle night breeze hit her and the cleaner air improved her health. "Thanks for making him stop and for the medicine."

Luke nodded. "It's the least I could do."

"We should get going. We're way behind schedule. You need to rest and your interview—"

"We'll go when you're better." Luke's authoritative tone stopped any additional questioning.

Leona wasn't sure how far they had traveled, but she could see the stars. She often got lost in the brilliance above and loved being outside of the city so she could see the constellations.

"Glimpsing Leo." She searched the sky to divert her thoughts from the lingering nausea.

"What was that?" Luke asked.

She almost forgot he was there. "The constellation of Leo the Lion. It's kind of my namesake. This time of year it's visible, so I like to look for it." She tilted her head back until it could go no further. "Glimpsing Leo."

"Sounds like a song."

"It does." She regarded him for a moment. "Is that how you come up with your songs? Something sounds like a song and then you go with it or do you have a process?"

"Songs come to me in many ways. Through people, mostly. I'll see, hear, or read something that triggers a feeling. Inspires me. I see stories then retell them with music."

Leona identified with Luke. She had found inspiration in similar ways during her time in the studio with Paul. When Luke conversed about music he came alive.

"You really love music, don't you?" Leona sipped her soda.

"Music means everything to me." He searched the skies, she assumed for her constellation. "I communicate with it. It feeds me. If I couldn't create music, I don't know what I'd do."

Luke kept upping the sexy meter. Now he was sensitive about his passion.

We've got to go. "I think we can get going."

Not only did she need to protect her softening heart, Luke had to be in Montreal in a matter of hours.

He narrowed his eyes at her. "Are you better or are you rushing?"

"Yes," Leona affirmed.

Luke frowned at the ambiguity of her response and she smiled.

She climbed back onto the bus, giving Reggie the thumbs-up. "Fire it up, Reggie."

Leona sat on the bunk bed. The medicine made her drowsy and she knew she would be asleep shortly.

"I'm going to lie down but let me know if you need anything." Leona put her lukewarm soda in a cup holder inside her bunk.

"Take this." He handed her a plastic bag. "Just in case."

The lightheartedness on his face was one she'd seen him give others when he was in good humor. She blushed because he had never directed that warmth toward her. It was gone within seconds.

Leona took the plastic bag from him. "Good night. Thanks again for helping me. You didn't have to."

"You're right. I didn't have to," was Luke's flat response.

Leona flinched. "And we're back," she muttered.

Clearly, Luke needed to hang on to whatever problem he had with her. She was patient and would allow things to organically improve. However, it would only be a matter of time before her patience ran out.

She slid the privacy curtain closed.

"I wanted to," she heard Luke through the partition. She stayed her hand from yanking the curtain back.

Chapter Eleven

Montreal sparkled like a new city in the sunlight while Leona dragged through the corridor of EDMology Radio exhausted, starved, and in need of a shower. Luke and Reggie had stopped to get breakfast, and though she had been hungry, she didn't trust her stomach with food. The lack of sustenance left her sluggish and miserable.

Luke was ushered into a booth and miked for his first interview, and Leona was happy to be reunited with her team.

"You guys made it. We were getting a little worried. How was the ride with Luke?" Sara asked.

"Uneventful." Leona understated her trip to avoid further inquiry. "From now on I want to know where Luke is at all times, even if I have to follow him around myself. If I ask for his whereabouts, I want coordinates."

"I'll put someone on him." Sebastian punched the notes into his phone.

Leona's memory flashed back to that night at Aurora. "Actually, I have someone in mind. I hope he's interested."

"You look—" Sara hesitated. "Unlike yourself. Do you want some coffee?" She pointed to a nearby refreshment table.

"No thanks." Leona spared her team the details of her nightmare with the toilet. "I'm sorry we didn't get a chance to debrief. Any updates?"

"Room assignments are done. Everyone knows the schedule. We stopped at the designated locations for breakfast and the crew is gearing up for tonight's show." Sara looked over to Sebastian to confirm.

Sebastian had been gazing dreamily at Sara since she started speaking. He was usually good at keeping his admiration for Sara somewhat contained. Not today.

Sebastian nodded at Sara and tore his eyes away from the blonde beauty to address Leona. "We've got your back, Leo."

"Thanks, guys. Sebastian, we'll meet at Luke's room this afternoon for his pre-show phone interviews. He has sound check at the venue, and then he's back on-stage. This is the pace we're running with so let's stay on top of everything to keep the momentum going."

"There's a car waiting for you and Luke downstairs, when you're ready," Sara said.

Sebastian pulled out his tablet. "These are the pictures and videos from last night."

"They're great." Leona swiped through the pictures and noted her favorites. Luke really couldn't take a bad photo. His eyes popped and the light loved his skin. And when he smiled, no one was spared his charm. Her chest filled with affection as she scanned the photos. "These are my choices but whatever you decide is fine. Get a few prints for the media package. Let's wait and get a few more recorded performances and then do a medley."

"Done." Sebastian stashed his tablet.

"Call me if you need anything." Her team departed and Leona was left again with Luke.

She wanted to leave and slide between the sheets of a hotel bed with too many pillows and a fluffy duvet but had to stay with her artist. Luke, on the other hand, answered questions about the tour, with refreshed skin and rested eyes.

"Thank goodness," Leona sighed.

Leona had some time before the interview ended and sat in a quiet corner. Her intent was to respond to her messages but she rested her head against the wall and fixated on Luke.

On the bus, he had changed clothes. Black jeans and a short-sleeved button-down white shirt never fit so well on a person. He hadn't shaved and a five o'clock shadow dusted his cheeks and chin. She didn't know if it was pure fatigue or Luke's sexy vibe, but she let herself wonder about how his stubble would feel against her palm.

As Luke spoke, his gaze found her. Normally, she would avoid his eyes but this time she stayed connected. She wasn't sure she was even seeing him anymore. Her eyes glazed over and her heavy eyelids closed.

Leona jolted herself awake and darted up. Targeting the refreshment table, she straggled over to make coffee. She might be playing Russian roulette with her stomach but it was better than falling asleep on the job. She checked on Luke, who had witnessed her dozing. He licked his lips to stifle the half grin from spreading across his face.

"Great." Leona sipped her coffee. Her cheeks warmed and she laughed at her awkward wake-up. *If you can't beat 'em, join 'em.*

The radio station was a bit of a ghost town, which made wrapping up easier. She started her closing remarks with the personnel so she and Luke could depart immediately.

Luke completed the interview, autographed merchandise, and then strolled over to her with swag in his step. "You need a nap."

Leona set her coffee down. "You forget that by contract I have to be here with you. Our team is at the hotel getting ready for tonight."

"You need some rest. We could have agreed on that."

"I'll rest when I get you safely to the hotel. The car is waiting for us downstairs." Her lashes weighted on her eyelids like mini dumbbells and she swayed in her stance.

"Leona?" Luke fortified himself as if to catch her.

She rubbed one eye with the knuckle of her thumb and tried to liven up by shimmying from head to toe. "I'll be fine after a power nap."

Luke frowned at her. "You should eat something."

"I'll order room service." She motioned Luke her way and called the elevator with a press of a button.

They rode the elevator down and shared a car ride to the hotel.

On the trip to their rooms, she was surprised when Luke followed because his suite was a floor above. "Where are you going?"

"To make sure you order room service. I need a healthy tour manager and you look like you'll pass out."

"No, that's not necessary." Leona held her palm up to stop his advance but he sidestepped her.

"You don't even have the energy to argue with me. Save what strength you have left to call for food," he said.

Leona didn't know why he cared. At times, he treated

her like she was the last person on earth he wanted to interact with. Other times his tenderness bowled her over. He unsettled and confused her with all these caregiver demonstrations. Nonetheless, he was right. She often ran on a low tank when she was busy but she had gone past empty. She swiped her room key, the lock release clicking through the vacant hallway. She made a beeline for the menu.

Leona perused the list and then called to order fresh fruit, a spinach omelet, and toast. "Satisfied?" Her mouth was pasty from dehydration, and Luke's presence in the intimate confines of her suite didn't help. She pulled a bottle of water from the minibar and gulped it down.

Luke sat down in a love seat and spread his arms against the back. "I will be when you eat."

"Please go. I need to get a shower and a power nap and you need to prepare for your show."

"Go get your shower, Leona. I'll wait for your food to arrive."

Even her temper fizzled into compliance. "But—"

"The longer you wait, the longer I stay."

She wished she put up a better fight. She yanked on the handle of her luggage. "This is ridiculous," she mumbled under her breath. She placed her suitcase on a desk, unpacked a few items, and stomped to the bathroom.

How the hell is she still standing?

Leona insisted on a shower, but really, even beyond rest she needed to eat.

He cursed himself. Because of his late arrival to the bus depot, she had gotten violently ill. His business with

Candy and Velvet was important. With Tommy leaving
for California, he wanted to get the women set up with
his agent but it could have waited.

Luke was amused by Leona's irritation with the
blonde and redhead. She'd side-eyed the women with
venom and massaged her left ear incessantly. Her response had been telling but he couldn't imagine that
her attraction for him was as potent as his was for her.

A knock on the door interrupted his thoughts. He
opened the door and allowed the attendant to wheel in
a tray of food.

"Over there, please." He dug into his pocket for a few
bills and handed them over. "Thank you."

"You're welcome, sir," the man said and left.

Leona emerged from the bathroom minutes later in
sweatpants and a tee shirt. Her hair was braided in a
side ponytail that lay on her shoulder. He could smell
the scent of coconut and vanilla from her shower. As she
walked about the room, her ass, now unconstrained by
jeans or close fitting pants, jiggled. Luke willed himself to focus on feeding her health, not satisfying her
body. But he couldn't deny Leona Sable's beauty, even
when she was in casual wear.

"Your food's here." He salivated but not for food.

Leona approached him and worried her earlobe—
something she did when she was nervous or irritated.
He was curious as to which one she felt.

She tucked a curly wayward strand of hair behind
her ear but it sprung right back out.

He reached for it and smoothed the soft hair against
her even softer skin. Leona neither backed away nor
startled at his touch and his breath deepened to steady
his racing pulse. *Don't kiss her.* His fingers lingered

a few seconds longer before he once again tucked the piece away.

Her blush was fierce, her swallow visible. "I-I'm going to eat, Luke. You don't have to stay."

He held a seat out for her at the table.

"Oh brother." She sat down and her hand grazed over the spot by her temple where his fingers had been. A couple of forkfuls later, Leona sat back in her seat. "I'm so full."

Luke arched an eyebrow. "Come on, Leona. You only had a few bites."

"I'm satisfied." She pushed the food around on her plate, sighing as if she'd just finished a Thanksgiving meal. She sipped her tea. "Happy now?"

"Yes."

She dropped her fork against the porcelain plate. "So, why aren't you leaving?"

Her question was legitimate. "I know we've gotten off to a rough start." He leaned against the wall and crossed his arms. "My temper... Sometimes I lash out. It's not you."

"You should really work on that because it seems like it's me." Another bite of food disappeared into her mouth.

"You have some associations I'm trying to deal with." He couldn't have downplayed the fact more. He was at war, torn between holding on to his anger about Paul and his increasing desire to know her. He had to let one of them go.

She chewed as if on a wet paper towel. "Associations? Deal with? What are you talking about?"

"Paul Reese." He swore he saw steam coming out of her ears.

Leona filled her lungs and he knew she was about to spit fire. "I thought I was clear that my past with Paul is not your concern. I don't have any association with that man. He ruined my life. I don't know what *you're* dealing with, but I wish you would leave Paul out of any future conversation you have with me."

"I'm not bringing him up to upset you, I'm trying to explain."

"Explain that your hate for me has nothing to do with me? Further making it clear that you should work on that."

"Leona." He wanted to tell her what had happened but every time he tried, the memories tickled his temper to explosion.

"I have to get some sleep, Luke. I ate. I'm fine, okay? I'll see you later for your interviews."

Again, he had upset her. Her point was valid. He didn't know everything that happened between her and Paul, only what was in the media, but she wasn't forthcoming with information any more than he was.

He wanted answers, but Leona needed rest. Now wasn't the right time.

He let himself out. "For what it's worth, you're not the only person whose life Paul ruined."

What the hell did that mean?

If Luke mentioned Paul one more time, she was sure she would dissolve into a puddle of tears. That wasn't a place she wanted to go.

When Luke left, Leona was glad to finally be alone. She needed some space from him to collect her thoughts. She hadn't completely regressed to middle school when he'd tucked her hair behind her ear and his soft, strong hands touched her skin. But he was a hot and cold enigma and she still wasn't sure which version of him was true.

She should rest, but the complications from the previous night put her behind and she needed to stay on top of things.

Just a little bit and then I'll sleep.

They were heading back to the States after their Canadian stops. First on the list was Ohio and then Minnesota. More DJ contest winners would perform in Massachusetts. The tour already had pre-show support from a mix of popular DJs and bands. Had they all arrived at the hotel together, Leona might have had a chance to ask them how things were going. Her team had things under control but she liked to give the tour her personal touch. She had to ensure she didn't spend half her time searching for Luke.

Leona dialed New York. After a few line transfers she was finally connected with the VIP bouncer from Aurora Nightclub. She didn't know if he would be available or interested, but she would give it a try.

"Hi. Diesel?" Leona cradled the hotel phone between her head and shoulder.

"You got him." His powerful voice filled her ear.

"This is Leona Sable. We met the night DJ Luke performed. I'm his tour manager."

"Oh yeah. They call you Leo, right?"

"Yes."

"I saw you in an entertainment piece about The Musical Prophet. It's my job to remember VIP guests. You had an English friend with you."

Leona smiled. *Thank you, Izzy.* "Yes, that's correct."

"She said you'd never forget my name. She was right." He chuckled. "What can I do you for?"

"I have a job for you." Leona explained the situation.

"You want me to babysit him," Diesel stated more than asked.

That sounds horrible. "Well, yes, but I'm hoping it won't always be that way."

"I see." Diesel was quiet for a bit. "Okay, I'm in."

"This is kind of last minute but would you be able to meet us in Cincinnati in two days?" Leona readied alternatives in case his answer was no.

"Not a problem. I've done private work before. Things move fast. I'll work it out," Diesel said.

That's my kind of guy. Now all she had to do was break the news to Luke. "Great. Stay on the line so I can connect you with my colleague, Sara. She'll get you set up."

"Sounds good."

Leona was about to click over to call Sara.

"Oh, and Leo?"

"Yeah?"

"I'm a damn good babysitter."

Leona laughed. She and Diesel would be very good friends.

Luke ran the streets of Cincinnati, cataloguing the landslide of creativity in his head. The last few tour dates had gone off without a hitch and he understood more and more why Leona had come so highly recommended. Not only was Leona efficient with her operations but she also seemed to be in tune to his needs even before he made an inquiry or request.

Back at the hotel, he rubbed his hands together, famished for his post-workout meal. The team leads were having a status meeting and once he finished eating, he quickly showered and headed over, eager to discuss some of the changes to his set for the lighting crew. A large, bulky, familiar-looking dude powered in a few minutes later. The man dressed in black jeans and a black shirt. By the way both Leona and Sara ogled the man, this guy was giving him some competition. He frowned.

Leona motioned the man over to him. "Luke, this is Diesel."

Luke's brain found the connection. "You're the bouncer from Aurora. What's up, man?"

They shook hands.

"Just glad to be a part of your tour. My girl's freaking out about it. She loves your music," Diesel said.

Luke gave Leona a quizzical look. She was up to something. "Thanks, man. I appreciate that."

Both he and Diesel waited for Leona to continue.

"Luke, your tour is popular and as we travel, the excitement of the fans will increase. You're going to need more security in addition to what we already have. Diesel will provide personal protection for you." Leona overdid it on her facial expressions. She was definitely selling him something.

"A bodyguard?" Luke asked. *She thinks I need a babysitter?*

"Yes. Diesel will make sure you get to your destinations on time, and the best part is, he'll always be connected to our team. No one will bother you or question your whereabouts." Leona wandered to the team with her back almost facing him.

Did she just wink? Jeez, it was just the one time. Well,

*there was also the time she was looking for me before
the first show, but I was preparing my set. Okay, twice.*

Sara stifled a giggle and Sebastian stared open-mouthed at Leona as she finessed the situation. Luke
shook his head, sharing his own humorous moment
with her team.

"And—" Leona spun around as if to add a high-lighted feature. He righted his face back to serious.
"Because Diesel is paid by Wallace Entertainment, you
don't have to worry about budget for him or give him
any instructions. He knows exactly what he needs to do
and how to get you to where you need to be."

Luke crossed one arm over his chest and with the
other hand, twisted the patch of hair under his lip.
"Hmm." A smile almost cracked his visage.

She may have been trying to sell him on the idea of
a bodyguard-babysitter, but she was damn cute doing
it. He forced his focus from her swiveling hips back to
her words.

"Diesel will occupy one of the bunks on your tour
bus and his room will be on your floor at the hotels. If
you're going to be somewhere public, he'll accompany
you. Whatever you need. I would feel so much better
knowing you're safe and in good hands. He starts to-night, if you're okay with it." She held her breath and
planted her feet as if for a fight.

But he wasn't going to fight. The start of the tour had
been well received and her decisions so far had benefit-ted him, the team, and the tour. Who was he to stop her
from keeping tabs on him?

Luke smiled but didn't respond right away. "I'm okay
with it."

Leona's eyebrows rose to her hairline. "Really?"

"Really. So long as it doesn't alienate my fans."

Leona frowned. It wasn't the response he was expecting but perhaps his compliance had thrown her. He couldn't fault her for that because it surprised him, too. In fact, their entire exchange during the status meeting had been unlike those in their recent past.

"We'll find the right balance, Luke. I've done this before," Diesel said. "Sometimes you won't even know I'm there."

"Cool." Luke shrugged.

Leona inched over to him and the scent of wild berries and warm jasmine from her fragrance made him lean down further than necessary to hear her. "You're sure you're okay with this?"

"Yup, I'm good." He had a tendency to lose track of time especially when he was working. Maybe it wasn't such a bad idea to have Diesel help him out.

"Okay." Leona clapped her hands. "Excellent. All right, folks, let's give Cincinnati a great show tonight."

Chapter Twelve

Leona fanned herself as she escorted Sara and Sebastian to the airport taxi, but it did nothing to cool her down. The humid Florida weather left her skin clammy. She couldn't believe they were already a month into the tour and about to embark on the southern portion.

"We'll see you and Luke in Nashville." Sebastian held the door open for Sara.

The cool air was heaven and Leona wished she, too, were going to Music City. Since Luke was doing a performance at a Miami club, the owners accommodated both him and Leona with luxury suites at the club hotel. She met with her team at the tour hotel before sending them off to Nashville.

"Where's Diesel? Isn't he riding with you guys?"

"Luke did another pop-up fan visit, so he's running late. He should be down in a minute," Sara said from inside the vehicle.

Leona frowned. One thing she learned about Luke was his spontaneity with surprising the fans in public. She found this endearing yet frustrating, but was thankful for the updates Diesel fed her.

Luke had opted not to have Diesel stay for the one-off performance. Since the club provided security, Diesel could travel to the next location with her team.

"Here he comes." Sebastian pointed to Diesel, who exited a shuttle bus and jogged over with his luggage.

"Hey," Leona greeted.

"Sorry about the wait. The fans didn't want to let Luke leave and he didn't want to let them down," Diesel said to Sebastian, and then turned to Leona. "He's all tucked in with his animal crackers at the club's hotel."

Leona laughed out loud. "Thanks." Diesel was doing great with Luke, so much so that the two had become a friendly pair. He had learned Luke's quirks and preferences and Luke had come to know his. Alas, a bromance was born.

"Hey, Sara," Diesel said.

Leona couldn't mistake the soft inviting intonation in Diesel's greeting.

Sara blushed. "Hey."

When did that happen? Doesn't he have a girlfriend? Leona glanced at Sebastian who returned a weary smile, confirming the sweetness between Diesel and Sara. Leona's heart ached for Sebastian, who had not-so-secretly pined over Sara since they'd met three years ago.

"Umm, okay. You guys be safe." Leona said her goodbyes then retreated back inside the hotel to get some relief from the heat before the next shuttle arrived. She could have easily arranged for a car to pick her up, but the shuttle ride helped slow down her partial free day.

She and Luke didn't have to be at the club until later that night, giving her time to refresh and relax from the intense travel. Over the past month she and Luke had gotten into a rhythm as manager and client. As best as she could she avoided being alone with him for too long, which was easier with close to a hundred roadies, including lighting techs and team members around. But at times there was still a tug of war for control.

Leona had been working on video installments with Sebastian to finalize the montage for Luke's website and social media outlets. Now that they had enough footage, the series of videos was ready.

Leona occupied a conference room down the hall from Luke's room. There was no one else on the penthouse floor so unless it was Luke, she wouldn't be disturbed. She plugged her computer into the large monitor, put on earbuds, and critiqued the images.

As she made minor notes for Sebastian, she reached for the brownie sundae she'd bought from the ice cream parlor. Instead her hand swiped air. She whirled around to find Luke standing behind her, holding her sundae.

She fumbled with the earbuds. "What the…"

"According to Sara you're not supposed to have this. At least, not until you've finished working."

Leona's heart rate settled. "Sara's on her way to Nashville. When did she tell you that?"

"She sent me a text about an hour ago."

"From the plane?" Leona asked.

Luke shrugged then pulled out his phone and read the text. "Leona likes sweets. Please don't let her eat any until she finishes her work. She'll understand."

Leona sniggered at Sara's neuroticism. "I have to approve this so Sebastian can run it. I'm almost done."

Luke peered over her shoulder. "What is that?"

"Footage of you. Now that you've done a few concerts, we can put those clips together for a video series.

They'll be online for the fans and we can use them for marketing ramp-ups to build pre-show excitement."

"Cool." Luke still cupped her treat.

"Don't you have stuff to do for your show tonight?" Leona reached for her bowl.

Luke dodged her hands. "What's the story with this? Why aren't you supposed to have it? Are you dieting or diabetic?" His curious, but mischievous smirk dimpled the space between his brows.

"Just give it to me."

"Answer me first," he said. When she didn't respond he heaped a spoonful of the dessert into his mouth.

"Okay, okay." Leona sighed. "I'm kind of sensitive to sugar. I'll be turned up for a bit, but after I finish eating that bowl of good deliciousness, I'll probably take a nap. Sara calls it my happy sugar coma. That's why she wants me to finish working."

"So, why do you eat it?" He chewed.

"Because I enjoy it. Now, hand it over."

Luke eyed the screen. "Have you finished working?"

"Almost. That's why I'm eating it slowly but it's no good to me if it's all melted, so…" Leona wiggled her fingers at the bowl.

Luke didn't comply. "Can I see how they captured the concerts?"

"Grr." Leona side-eyed the chair next to hers.

Luke sat down and then handed her the bowl.

Glee lifted her cheeks. Once again reunited with the plastic bowl, she readied the spoon with its gooey chocolaty chunks.

"Addict," he accused, humor teasing the corners of his lips. "That shit is way too sweet. Try some berries next time."

"Don't be jealous." Her eyes crossed and drooped

closed as the spoon disappeared into her mouth. "Mmm. It's so good."

With a touch of a smile on his lips, his eyes lingered on her mouth. "Show me."

Leona unplugged the earbuds so Luke could listen to the soundtrack. The video was only about three minutes, but was packed with footage from the concerts, backstage, the tour bus, air travel, and spontaneous interactions with the fans.

"I only have some minor notes. You have some of the best people in the business on this team. Your image is in good hands. They do a great job for you." She shoveled in another liquid bite. Had Luke not been there, she might have taken the bowl with its melted contents to the head, but she refrained.

"We." He focused on the screen. "You should include yourself in that statement."

His kindness was freaking her out so she used the tactic that had been successful over the past month— focus on the work. She set her dessert aside to craft an email about the montage. "Do you have any comments or suggestions?"

Luke shook his head. "No. It's great. Do you mind if I watch it again?"

"Knock yourself out." Leona hit send and clicked to reset the video. "It's all yours."

She moved from the table to the small couch and rested her head against the cushion. The last thing she remembered was Luke bobbing his head to his music in the video.

"She wasn't kidding." Luke stood over Leona's sleeping figure. She neither responded to his voice nor his attempts to shake her awake.

He packed her equipment and collected the other items she had with her. She didn't budge when he hauled her over his shoulder. Wisps of her familiar sweet, floral perfume flooded his nostrils. He secured her against him by the back of her thighs. His palm itched to clasp her rear, but he could successfully transport her to his room without the complimentary cop-a-feel.

The closed curtains darkened his spacious suite and he laid Leona on the white duvet. He held her at the ankles to remove her sandals and then unfastened her bracelet, placing it on the desk.

Once he made her comfortable, he went back to the conference room and retrieved Leona's equipment.

For the past week, Miami had been in a perpetual heat wave and today was no exception. The air-conditioning blew on high yet the humidity still made the atmosphere moist and muggy. He regarded Leona's peaceful figure and recalled how she'd licked the spoon clean after he'd returned her dessert. Had she tasted him? His dick jumped and he forced himself to settle down. He shed his pit-soaked tee shirt and tossed it aside. He kept his shorts on and sat in a corner armchair in case Leona woke up, surprised to be in his bed. She was in his bed and he wasn't?

He stashed the dangerous thought away and opened his laptop in the dark room to work on his set list. Once he had a few tracks lined up, he listened to the song progression in his headphones. Every so often, he observed Leona. Her torso, fitted in a short-sleeved pink shirt, rose and fell with her breathing. Her navy blue knee-length cargo pants covered legs that were elegantly folded into a slight fetal position.

After the initial turbulent start, his tour was running

smoothly. Leona had set a tone of excellence and ran a tight ship. He had learned firsthand why she was the best. With every tour date, the attendance to his shows, his popularity, and his confidence in Leona grew.

He should be happy but his big goals loomed ahead, and with them, accomplishments he hoped would make things better for his family. His chosen career path hadn't come without some casualties. Though his parents and sister had been supportive, explaining to their friends and family members that "Luke was doing his music thing" had always been a pain point. This had to be the year where his success wasn't in doubt.

He'd made the mistake of thinking that Ivy could not only help him achieve his goals but share his life with him, too. His niece and nephew were great and he'd always wanted a family of his own, but when he and Ivy split, the betrayal left him at a deficit—a deficit that lessened each day on tour with Leona. Leona gave him hope that achieving his goals was possible, exciting even, and he had no complaints—none, except for one.

Despite efforts to stay focused on the tour, the more time he spent with Leona, the harder it became to deny his attraction to her. He couldn't get off track, but the fact that they were alone and apart from the rest of the tour roadies hadn't slipped his mind and she was so close—too close.

Leona began to stir.

He sat still and waited.

Leona's eyes cleared and adjusted to the dark room. How did she end up in bed? This wasn't even her bed… or her room. She sat up and rubbed her face.

"Where the fuck am I?" Her heart thudded against her rib cage.

Someone chuckled in response.

"Relax, Leona. You're in my suite."

She directed her attention to the voice in the shadows to find a computer screen illuminating Luke's face. "Why am I here?" Her throat was dry and hoarse from sleep.

"You were knocked out. I wasn't comfortable leaving you in the conference room, so I brought you here," he said.

"Why didn't you wake me?" Leona knew she was impossible to wake after having too much sugar.

"I tried."

"Why didn't you just bring me to my room?"

"A few reasons. I wasn't going to frisk you to find your room key and I had to carry you," he said. "You're only light for about five minutes. My room was closer." The humor in his voice validated that she hadn't dreamt the friendliness they'd shared when she'd showed him his video medley.

"Oh." She tossed a sheepish smile in his general direction because she couldn't fully see him and plucked the hem of her shirt. "Hey, I'm sorry you had to take care of me. I should get going."

"Stay, Leona." Luke's tender command tensed and enticed the muscles in her body, from her big toe all the way to her hairline. "You're already in bed and resting."

Leona jumped out of the bed and attempted to flee the heady trance of his voice. "The last thing either of us needs is a rumor about me doing the walk of shame from your hotel room, especially given your conditions. You never know who's watching." She was unable to locate anything else in the seductive lighting. "Where's my stuff?"

Luke pointed next to him. "Everything is right here."

Of course...right next to him.

Leona almost bumped into a lamp. She needed light and groped for the switch. Squinting from the initial brightness, she refocused to find Luke shirtless and sitting with one leg crossed over his thigh. He shielded his eyes from the light.

Leona hesitated, absorbing Luke's tatted skin and prowess. She'd seen half-naked men before but Luke's effect on her was concerning. Not only was she hotter than doughnut grease, but Luke's words impacted her decisions—like whether to leave or not. She inched closer to the desk where her jewelry was organized and neatly displayed. Her heart leapt in her chest. Luke had gone out of his way to make her comfortable. She peered at him, but didn't ask him the rhetorical questions.

"Thanks." She shifted from one foot to the next, rattled by his care for her and her things. She fastened her bracelet and slid her feet into her shoes, struggling to slow her shallow breaths.

"It's cool, Leona." Luke rose to his feet and laid his computer down on the chair.

She wished he had stayed seated because all he had on was a pair of shorts. The waistband hugged his hips, but the invitation of his chiseled pelvic muscles and the full visual of body art ignited a fire at her core.

"Why aren't you wearing a shirt?" Her accusation fell to a whisper as she reached for her bag.

"The humidity. I keep sweating through everything." His voice dropped to an oozing caramel octave and he stepped so close to her that his size filled her entire vision. "Does it bother you?"

"No, I—I…" The butterflies in her stomach fluttered up, choking her words. She thought of backing away, but her fascination with what might happen next not only transfixed her in place but also had her leaning toward him, summoning him.

Luke responded with blurring speed, seizing her face as he brought her lips to his. The initial connection between them was crushing, amateur and desperate as he devoured her. He opened her mouth and his probing tongue wrestled with hers, deepening the kiss. His heavy nasal breathing hummed over the air conditioner and the warmth and savory taste of him overwhelmed her senses. She had wanted this from the first time they'd met, since the last time they'd kissed.

"Luke," she mumbled against his mouth, and her hands flew to his head, raking through his soft dark brown hair. She tried to separate but the taste of him was more drugging than any sugar she'd indulged.

Her hands had ached to grasp his waist again, ever since day one of the tour when she almost fell in the corridor. She explored the carved muscles there and drew him closer. Luke obliged, aligning his pelvis against her hip. A moan escaped her lips at his hardness. His mouth left hers and traveled to her neck.

"We shouldn't," was her weak protest as Luke planted delicious wet kisses down to the top of her shirt. Her head fell back in lustful submission.

"Yes, we should."

In one motion Luke supported her seat, lifted one of her legs, and spun her onto the mattress. Her ass bounced when it hit the cushioning, and she yelped.

Luke's hand slid under her shirt and over her breast. His touch increasing her already erratic pulse. She lifted slightly and peeled her shirt up and off, tossing the material to the side. He marveled at her black-satin-adorned chest before pressing her backward.

Luke hovered above her but not for long. Leona obeyed the voiceless command, scooting back to lie against the already ruffled duvet. She fought to reconnect with his mouth, punishing his lower lip for leaving with a not too gentle bite. A moaning sigh escaped him and the sound thrilled her.

Sliding her fingers over his perspiring chest, Leona reveled in the feel of his tightening pectoral muscles. She had dreamt about how he would feel and the real thing was better by far. Her hands curved around his waist and down to his muscular ass. He hastily unbuttoned his shorts to give her access to him. She reached inside to feel him and pushed the material down to expose his ass.

"Fuck, Leona."

She didn't have to look to see his hard-on through his shorts. She felt every titanium inch of him against her leg.

Luke wiggled between her legs as they kissed. He propped himself up with one hand while the other traced her cheek, her neck and down further to her breast where he squeezed her through the satin material. His fingers curved over the top of the bra cup rim and yanked downward, revealing her dark, hardened nipple. He teased the sensitive button with his knuckles before he enveloped it in his mouth. Time stopped as the sensation of his hot suckling mouth halted her breathing. Leona's hand flew to his head, encouraging him to continue.

"Luke." Her words were drenched in surrender. She sucked in air as if minutes had passed since she breathed, and with it the spices of his intoxicating fragrance.

Luke worked the button of her pants and his hand slid against her belly and inside her panties. She spread her limbs to allow his fingers access to her center. She writhed under the skill of his caress. Her moans vibrated against his mouth as his kiss fogged her brain.

"You're so wet, Leona." He pulled his finger from her and began to wrestle her pants down.

The separation gave her the time she needed to regain her senses.

Leona scrambled to sit up. "Shit! Luke, I can't. We can't." She maneuvered her leg around him and hustled off the bed. Her pussy screamed, "No! Go back," but she dashed past the desire. She searched for her shirt and gulped in air to clear her head. "Oh my God." She still tasted him and yearned for his kisses. "You're my client. We have an agreement."

Luke moaned facedown into the mattress where she left him. The scrumptious round mound of his butt tempted her like her mother's pot roast. He eventually tucked himself back into his bottoms and positioned himself to sit on the bed. The hardness between his legs creased the material of his shorts.

"Don't worry about the agreement," he said.

She found her shirt and put it on. "What?" She forced her eyes to his. He was way too calm for someone who had been so adamant about banning her from sex. Had he forgotten that the conditions applied to him, too?

"Why would you say that? We signed a legally binding contract preventing us from having sex. The one where—" Leona stopped.

Luke scratched his head and remained silent. Was that guilt dusting his face?

"Wait a minute." Leona mulled over the condition again and again until realization hit her. "That condition doesn't mention the artist like the others do. Staff or fans, yes, but not you."

"That's correct," he said.

Leona crossed her arms as her brain figured out the equation. "So basically, I can have sexual relations with you and you alone, just not on premises or at locations associated with the tour." She scanned the room. "Like here."

"Also correct." His palms rested on the bed to support his weight, unaffected by her epiphany.

"Sonofabitch! You set me up." She was aghast by the manipulation.

"I did no such thing, Leona. You did when you asked that the condition apply to me, too."

"But you knew and chose not to disclose it." Leona grabbed her computer bag from the table. "Why would you do that?"

"I have my reasons for those conditions." Luke dragged himself up.

"You didn't answer the question. Why, Luke?"

He jutted his head to the bed. "Do I really have to answer that?"

She waited, shifting her stance into her hip.

"Because ever since we met all I've wanted to do is touch you."

"But you hated me when you met me."

"No. I hated Paul and your connection to him. I am...
was seconds from shaking the sheets with you."

"You actually say that to people?" Their attraction
was obvious, but he'd deceived her.

"We could see the loophole as an opportunity." Luke
fluttered his eyebrows.

"Opportunity?" Leona gathered her things. "You
know what? You can go shake the sheets alone."

"Leona," Luke called, following her to the door.

"The car will pick us up. Be in the lobby by eleven."
She opened the door and tried to slam it but the safety
slowed its movement, making her exit less dramatic and
pissing her off even more. Luke's amusement chased
her but she didn't turn back.

Chapter Thirteen

Leona slammed her bags on the couch in her suite and attempted to pull her hair out. "Aaarrgh!" How had she let such an important nuance in the addendum slip by? She recalled the meeting when Tommy reacted to Luke's speedy agreement. That was her red flag and she had let it go unchecked.

"Damn it." She paced back and forth. Even now, after finding out about his omission, she wanted him to consume her as he'd done moments before. Her eyes glistened, angry and frustrated from being handled and aroused by the same man who had manipulated her.

Take a breath, girl.

Luke called the loophole an opportunity. The seed of his suggestion grew. He'd admitted his desire to touch her. Perhaps she could have her cake and eat it, too. Why not follow Luke's lead and fulfill her desires with him away from the tour.

"No, no, no, no." She continued to pace. A year had passed since she'd been with a man and she gave herself props for not coming on Luke's bed from a single touch. Her lack of sexual activity might be influencing her current considerations but so was Luke's sorcerous power over her.

She regarded her image in the mirror. "Are you really considering having a fling with him? No. You can't. How do you keep it a secret and out of the grubby hands of the press? What happens on the rest of the tour? What happens if you fall for him? What happens when it's over?" Her voice echoed against the ceramic tiles of the bathroom, cloaking her with reservations.

Izzy's voice popped into her head and yelled, "Calm the fuck down."

"Why did you let your guard down with him? Now look where it's gotten you," Leona scolded her image with desire-glazed pupils.

If her relationship with Paul taught her anything, it was that getting involved with a client had potential catastrophe written all over it. She didn't have any answers to her questions about Luke and there was still so much unresolved between them. All she knew was she craved him more than she had any other man. Caution signs flashed around her.

As she readied herself for Luke's performance, the remembrance of his hands on her rear, how he'd caressed her breasts, and the imprint his fingers left on her insides influenced her wardrobe choice. She slunk into a thin, black, soft-leather backless halter top. The garment was attached to her body by an elegant, jeweled collar and a similar motif clasp at her lower back. The black jeans and peep toe booties with silver studded heels complemented her outfit.

"What are you doing, Leo?" She looked ready for war, but in very sexy battle gear. "So much for being careful."

She wrestled her hair into a neat, side ponytail that hung on her shoulder to soften the style yet still gave off a "badass about business" presentation. She slid on a cluster of silver bracelets, and after she did her makeup, misted her floral perfume.

In the hotel lobby, Leona nestled into one of the white couches, cross-legged, and arms spread out along the top of the furniture. The contrast between her and the couch drew a few lingering stares, double takes, and whistles. The attention was unsettling but the thought of Luke seeing her like this elevated her self-confidence.

He was late and she spotted him sprinting from the direction of the elevator. He wore a white shirt with sleeves rolled up to his elbows, exposing his strong tatted forearms. A black fitted vest outlined the muscles she'd run her palms over, not even an hour ago.

"Oh, come on," Leona mumbled. Luke excited her every sense. His black pants clung to his defined thighs and he topped the outfit off with his signature sneakers with white soles. *And here I thought that I was giving off a sexy vibe.*

His eyes found her and his pace slowed to a stop. His intensity glued her heels to the carpet. Waiting for him to reach her was like waiting to breathe. She finally did when he loomed over her sitting figure.

Luke offered her an outstretched hand, which she accepted with some reluctance and ascended to her feet. "Are you punishing me, Leona?"

"I don't know what you're talking about. The car's waiting."

The Florida weather was hot, but when Luke ran his hand down her arm, she shivered.

"Wow," Luke said as she passed him.

Leona craned her neck to witness his appraisal of her exposed back. She smiled triumphantly and smoothed her hand around her hair but the cluster of bracelets snagged the clasp of her top. She gasped as the material loosened from her chest and the air wisped against her breast.

"Shit." She stood awkwardly with her wrist connected to her neck.

Luke chuckled. "No doubt, karma is paying you back for fucking with me in that outfit."

She spun around to meet Luke's mischievous grin. "A little help, please?"

He stepped behind her and hands went to her neck where he tugged and jostled the tangled bracelets. She relaxed when she was released from the clasp and stretched to increase circulation to her arm.

"Thanks, I—" She stilled and her eyes widened when Luke's hand slid seductively slow down her back. The panties she'd just changed into were drenched again.

"So sexy," he said against her ear.

"Stop." Her low command was vacant and inauthentic.

His hand stopped at her lower back where the other connection to her shirt rested before he spun her to face him and pulled her against him. She neither wanted to pull away from him, nor push him away but they were in the lobby.

Leona pinched his side.

"Ow!" Luke fake-winced. His hands slid down her arms to meet her wrists and he fastened them to his waist. He bent down, stopping inches away from her lips. "People are starting to stare, so make it good."

Neither the concierge, nor the one lone hotel guest at the far end of the lobby, noticed them. *People* barely qualified the vacancy of the space.

"You—" His lips descended on hers.

Leona expected a punishing kiss for pinching him, but his tender lips drugged her into compliance. She gripped his waist and felt him smile when she opened her mouth to receive him.

Damn him.

Luke let go of her hands and grinned down at the arousal she was sure was scripted in cursive all over her face.

Leona glared at him. "You're such an entitled ass."

"If I'm such an entitled ass, then why are you still holding me?"

She cursed and let him go. "If you're done making us the hotel spectacle, we should go."

Luke slipped into his pensive pose. "I'm good." He then extended his hand toward the exit. "Ladies first."

Speeding past him, Leona hurried toward the waiting car.

Luke's performance was an intimate affair. His fans were so close to him that he could touch them over the short partition.

"That was awesome. He played his classics," a fan said as Leona made her way backstage.

The women buzzed around Luke like bees to honey, a scene now familiar to Leona. At every tour event, the women backstage pawed at him in the hopes of landing a VIP ticket to his hotel suite. Could she blame them? Luke's music shot electricity through the hearts of his followers. Infatuation fever came with the territory. He appeared to take it in stride, walking a fine line between rejection and interest.

His popularity was growing and although he loved

the closeness with his fans at these more intimate shows, he had to practice a level of inaccessibility. Leona wondered if any of them would have made it back to his hotel room if he weren't prohibited by contract. That she cared ruffled her feathers.

Leona schmoozed with the owner of the club and the promoter for the event. It was important she and Luke kept a good relationship with them for future performances. However, the promoter she spoke with took "good relationship" to a whole other level.

"He has them eating out of his hands." The promoter inched closer to her and led with his pelvis, putting her on the defense.

The club's security escorted Luke over and his celebrity presence influenced the space to where all eyes were on him.

"Great show, Luke," the promoter said. "Your lovely manager has informed us of your interest in the Xcelsior Hotel in Vegas. That's a great venture." As the man spoke, he targeted Leona's breasts without so much as a veil to his intention.

"Thanks." Luke's jaw tensed and his shoulders squared toward the promoter.

Leona expected gawks and ogles due to her outfit but the way the man's eyes undressed her was straight up creepy.

She crossed her arms over her chest. "Wallace Entertainment has a lot planned for Luke. We're doing a comprehensive package including new residencies. Luke is on target to achieve what no other DJ has done before."

The promoter touched her arm and she backed away, butt first. Luke's head snapped around and his hawk eyes narrowed at the man's hand on her.

The owner tapped Luke's arm and ushered him a few feet away.

"You're a shy one?" The promoter's low-lid gaze searched for a more revealing area of her upper body.

Visions of kneeing the man in the nuts danced in her head, but for the first time tonight she exerted some self-control. "Not at all. I wouldn't want anyone to misinterpret anything. You're more professional than those other grimy promoters who can't control themselves around women."

"I am better than those other promoters, Leo. I have a lot of self-control." The man leaned into her.

Ick. She stepped back and into something solid. When she investigated what blocked her retreat, she found herself face-to-face with Luke's chest. She angled her head up to see him glowering down at the promoter.

"Everything okay here, Leona?" Luke kept his eyes on the man.

"Uhh, yeah," she said, still surprised at how he had materialized.

The promoter widened the space between them. "I know you're booked up with the tour but let's see if we can get you back before the year's out. I'll stay in touch with Leo."

Luke's shirt grazed her arm. "Leona's busy with the tour. All bookings go through Boombox."

"Nice doing business with you." The promoter grabbed her hand.

Leona slid her hand from the man's iron grip to shake hands with the owner. She gave both men a few departing words.

She touched Luke's arm, feeling the tension in him. "It looks like you're all done."

Luke bowed to speak close to her ear. "Yes, and we should go before that outfit of yours causes more problems between me and him." Luke appeared to be seconds away from pouncing on the promoter.

Leona could handle the promoter like she did most overzealous creeps. What she couldn't handle was Luke drawing negative media coverage. She agreed and tugged Luke in the direction of the club exit.

During the ride back to the hotel, Leona guarded her side of the vehicle. Things had gotten weird between her and Luke so fast, and though her insides desired a repeat interlude, her head spun with choices. She welcomed the silence between them and glanced over at Luke. The way he spread out and commanded his space, coupled with his potent manly scent, made her reconsider being with him.

They rode the elevator up and when they arrived at Leona's floor, she hesitated. What was she expecting? What did she want?

"Well, good night. You were great." She opted for the cowardly route and stepped off the elevator. The bell dinged and the doors slid shut, as did the door to her desire. A ball of loss formed in her chest as she walked to her room.

"Leona?" Luke advanced in what felt like slow motion.

"What are you—?" Her mouth was unable to form more words when his warm hand cupped her cheek.

"You didn't give me a chance to say good night."

"Oh," she whispered, dizzy from her now shallow breathing. *This is so wrong.*

He was so close and she wanted him closer. Her hands held his forearms. Luke's mouth moved toward her and his green-gray eyes met hers with a gentle request. She tilted her lips to meet his. *So right.*

His noticeable breathing revealed she wasn't the only one affected and when his mouth tenderly melded with hers, her knees went weak and she drifted into him. Her lips felt deserted as he ended the kiss. "Good night, Leona." He released her.

Luke left her to call the elevator and she stood unmoving in the middle of the corridor watching him. When she didn't go anywhere, Luke's smiling figure returned and rotated her in the direction of her room.

Oh shit. She blinked and craned her neck as the elevator doors opened, like her heart, and Luke disappeared inside.

Sitting on the bed, she pondered Luke's effect on her. She had to think, evaluate and figure out how to steer herself through these new seas.

"Things might get a little rough."

Chapter Fourteen

Leona was grateful for the compacted tour dates because everyone was either busy or passed out from fatigue. In either case, she hoped no one noticed that something had changed between her and her client. She waited with the crew for Luke to arrive for sound check when Abe called.

Leona didn't even allow Abe to get in a greeting. "Hey, I'm doing sound check. Let me call you back."

"This can't wait, Leo."

At Abe's stressed tone, Leona notified the crew she'd be back and found a more private space.

"What's up?"

"I need you on a plane to New Orleans tonight. We have an opportunity to get some good recovery press," came Abe's hushed tone. "I'll have you back in time for the Kansas show."

"Yeah, no. That's not going to work. Things are crazy here. I can't leave. What's this about?"

Abe let out his *big request* sigh.

"Oh no. What are you getting me into?" Leona mentally locked in her rollercoaster harness.

"Paul is working with a client and…"

"No." Leona raised her voice and, though in a pri-

vate area, could have easily been heard by passersby.
"I want nothing to do with it."

"Leo, he's going to show the media we're on friendly
terms again. The artist—"

Click.

She couldn't recall the last time she'd hung up on
Abe. Had she ever? It didn't matter. Paul was working Abe and dragging her along. She pressed hard on
a tranquil pressure point on her ear and took several
deep and long fire breaths she'd acquired from yoga.

Her phone buzzed and she let it go to voice mail.
She wasn't done centering herself and before she even
thought of picking up again, Abe would have to wait
until she re-centered.

On Abe's fifth try she picked up.

"Okay, I deserved that, darlin', but can you hear me
out?" Abe pleaded.

"Go 'head." Leona couldn't believe she was even entertaining the call. Helping Abe with clients was one
thing. Kowtowing to Paul was altogether different.

"Paul is producing an artist who's embarking on a
solo career. The artist wants to work with you."

"Who?" She pressed her palm to a hot forehead.

Abe was silent longer than made sense. "The artist
has chosen not to disclose that information until the
meeting, but Paul assures me he's big time."

"You're dragging me away from Luke's tour and you
don't know?" Leona questioned.

"Reese has the upper hand here, Leo. He mentioned
needing to keep this hush-hush from the media."

"That's BS. Paul doesn't have that kind of discretion."

"Well, he's keeping a tight lid on this one."

"Can I do it remotely with the artist? Without Paul?"

"No, darlin'." Regret laced his words.

She squeezed the phone so hard the equipment creaked. "He's only doing this because it benefits him. If this goes sour, he'll cut us off and flap his gums. I can't go through that again, Abe. You're the face of Wallace Entertainment. You'll have to be enough."

"Neither Paul nor the artist will do it unless you're present. This can further help our cause."

"Don't make me do this." Her heart raced and sickness turned her stomach. Her last falling out with Paul had cost her a year of recovery.

"I've been trying to figure out a way to do this without you, but unless I dress up like an attractive, black woman, I don't see another way." Abe's comic relief did nothing for her nerves. "I promise. I'll protect you from Reese. Will you come out to New Orleans, darlin'?"

Leona bit back tears of frustration. Again, she felt handled. She had said, "no" and it counted for nothing. "Fine."

She was about to respond to Abe when Luke rounded the corner and halted. Leona blinked and blew air to recover. Luke evaluated her for a moment and his chest inflated, loading up to question her.

"The crew's waiting. I'll be there in a minute." Her words stopped any possible inquiry.

Concern etched the corners of his eyes.

"I'm okay," she mouthed.

He lingered a moment longer, nodded, and then departed with hesitant steps.

Shit! "Oh no. He has to release me." Her eyes slid closed.

"What are you going on about, darlin'?" Abe asked.

"The conditions. By contract, Luke has to agree to

let me leave for New Orleans. He has a thing about Paul. Remember?"

"Do you think you can convince him to agree?"

"I don't know." Leona wasn't sure that she could convince Luke to do anything. He either did something or he didn't.

"Well, the artist is flying you privately, so you can get back. Sara has the details. I know you'll do your best to make this work. I have to run."

"But…" Leona started but in typical Abe fashion, he dropped a bomb on her and then split.

Leona returned to sound check. Luke gave the crew his suggestions as he slouched against a speaker. His body called to hers from every angle. As the lights outlined his biceps, she longed to trace his tatted skin.

Luke's one-off performances during this southern portion of the tour had been scheduled close to the tour venues. This conveniently placed them with the team at tour hotels for all performances. As a result, neither she nor Luke, though tempted, technically had an opportunity to finish what they'd started in Florida. That didn't erase the fact that she wanted Luke more than she allowed herself to believe, and she doubted any contract would truly stop them. That man had her open. But she'd been down this road before. Giving in to her feelings for Luke could be disastrous. He was her client. Her conversation with Abe had only reminded her about the destruction her breakup with Paul had had on her career and reputation.

She rushed over to him. "Hey, can I talk to you?"

He studied her with the same concern he'd shown during her phone call with Abe. "Sure."

Once out of earshot, Leona explained the situation

and prayed Luke wouldn't make this any more excru-
ciating.

"You want me to agree to let you go?" Luke asked.

"Yes." Leona was thrown back to grade school and
asking her parents to attend a sleepover.

"No," Luke responded without hesitation. His re-
morseless eyes informed her she was in for a struggle.

"They won't do it otherwise."

Luke shrugged. "Tough shit."

"Is your objection because it's Paul?"

"Facts. Oh, and let's not forget I have a show tonight.
I need my tour manager."

"Sara and Sebastian can manage one night. Tomorrow's a travel day and I'll meet you and the team in
Lawrence." Leona did her best to sound optimistic. Her
team could manage one day without her, but would she
be able to manage one day with Paul?

Luke leaned in close. "Are you hearing me, Leona?
My answer's no. It's not in my best interest. Plus, I know
you don't want to go."

Leona pressed on her ear. *Center. Center.* "It's not
exactly my choice, but it's important."

"You always have a choice."

Funny, it didn't feel that way. "The positive press
will help all of us." She offered a weak benefit but she
was fresh out of ideas to make this impromptu meeting
seem like a good thing.

Luke stretched for five long seconds and rubbed his
reddening face. "Okay."

"You'll agree?"

"Yes," he paused, "but I'm coming with you."

Her eyes widened and her jaw dropped. "What? No,

you can't. You have the Dallas show tonight and need to get to the next location."

"Either I go with you after my show tonight or you don't go at all." Luke's resolute stance made it clear that no matter what she said, he wouldn't budge.

"It's too risky." Her hand flew up to her ear, again.

"No riskier than an MIA tour manager." Luke gathered both her hands in his and stilled her. "That's my final offer."

Shit! "Fine. We'll leave in the morning." So much for choices.

The French Quarter was alive with tourists taking in the sights, and the sound of New Orleans jazz filled the air. Leona sped down the streets toward her destination. Luke trailed behind with his hand in a bag of beignets, wearing a baseball cap to camouflage his identity.

She and Luke arrived at the old French-style building. When they entered, they were greeted by rustic décor. An aged tapestry hung from the wall and luxurious velvet couches, trimmed with gold, sat on antiqued carpeting. The small lounge, before entering the theater, was reminiscent of a burlesque show.

As if on cue, a woman in skimpy burlesque-wear, complete with silver tasseled nipple covers and red garter, greeted them. "Allo, *chéris*! I'm Mademoiselle. Are you here for the show?"

"Yes?" Luke chuckled at her uncertainty.

"Right this way." Mademoiselle, with her creole French accent, sauntered closer to Luke. "You're so handsome."

"Thanks." Luke's whole face smiled.

"Are you two together? How long are you staying in

New Orleans, *mon chéri*?" Mademoiselle pawed Luke's strong shoulders.

"Well…" Luke squatted to sit on the couch.

"Come on." Leona tugged him toward the theater. His laugh tickled the hairs at the back of her neck. She had no idea what to expect having her ex-boyfriend and her current client in the same room. The scenario had her clenching and releasing her fists. Based on previous conversations, Luke and Paul were ingredients that did not make for a good stew.

She stopped Luke before they entered. "Look, you don't have to come in. You can stay out here with Mademoiselle." The thought of him staying outside with a near-naked, aggressive woman didn't thrill her, but it was better than a possible confrontation with Paul or Abe or the artist they were meeting.

"I'm coming in. I'm sure my presence will help speed this along," Luke said.

"Good point." Leona hadn't thought about it that way. "But…behave."

"Oh, I plan to."

Leona's stress level rose at Luke's fight stance.

They entered and Leona's eyes immediately went to Paul, dressed in pressed, brown slacks and a white shirt that popped off his sun-kissed skin. He wore a straw-textured fedora hat with black hatband to finish his signature outfit.

He still looks good.

Next to Paul was Abe, engaged in conversation with a man Leona recognized as Christian Sacks. Christian was part of DJ trio Tres Armadas, the biggest Electronic

Dance Music group on the scene. As far as celebrities in EDM went, Christian was it.

"Way to wail…" Alarmed, Leona ducked as Luke yelled over her head.

"… And wild out," Christian finished as she and Luke approached.

Luke passed her and greeted Christian with a hug.

"What the…" Leona said as she greeted Abe with a kiss on the cheek and nodded briefly to Paul. Her body was electric with nerves.

"I didn't know these two were friends." Abe touched her arm and his hand withdrew as if he'd burned himself on a boiling kettle. "Jeez. Relax, Leo."

She clenched her fists, which cracked her knuckles, slightly improving her disposition.

"I'm okay." Leona whispered the obvious untruth. The last time she was this close to Paul she'd found him, in their apartment, getting his dick wet from a strawberry blonde. When they broke up, his ego had retaliated with lies, even though she'd protected him.

Abe adjusted his suit. "I don't like that he's here any more than you do, but this could work in our favor. Christian Sacks, Leona. Can you believe our luck? And he wants to work with us."

Luke and Christian continued their conversation while Abe and Leona observed.

"So, you're the one beckoning my tour manager? I should kick your ass," Luke threatened and the two men laughed.

"We interrupted your tour?" Christian's strong Dutch accent decorated his words. He tucked his light brown, chin-length hair behind his ear. He turned to Paul. "Did you know that?"

"I like to make things happen." Paul trapped her into an embrace. "Hey, honey."

She wanted to gag, and extricated herself from Paul's arms.

Luke gritted his teeth and followed her as she returned to Abe's side.

"What the hell are you doing here, man?" Christian said to Luke and jutted his head in Paul's direction.

"Ensuring my tour manager gets back in time for my show," Luke said.

The two men shared a nonverbal understanding before Christian glanced over at Leona. "I see why." Christian's low, under breath comment was audible.

"I'm amazed you allowed your artist to break from the tour with an appearance so close, Leo. That's Risk Management 101." Paul's smug remark vexed her.

"Leona didn't *let* me do anything. Seeing as you organized this meeting, knowing she was on tour, seems like a poor choice on your part," Luke delivered with irritable undertones.

Paul went to retort, but Luke's voice boomed through the theater, drowning out any further complaint. "Leona, this is my good friend Christian Sacks. DJ and musical genius."

Come on, Sable. Stay focused. Don't let this get under your skin. Turn on. "*The* Christian Sacks of Tres Armadas?"

Christian stretched his arms out in presentation. "The one and only."

"I only work with the best, Leo." Paul rotated to her, dismissing Luke.

"Right." Leona addressed Paul but kept her attention on Christian. "Pleasure to meet you."

"The pleasure is certainly all mine." Christian enveloped her hand with his. His eyes twinkled.

"So, how can I help you, Christian?" Leona asked.

"I'm launching a solo project. Due to the conflict of interest with Tres Armadas, I needed to seek management. Paul's doing some production on my album, so when he mentioned he could get me an in-person meeting with you and Wallace Entertainment, I jumped on it."

Paul Reese strikes again. Leona wondered if Paul's creativity had come back or if he was stealing tracks from someone else this time around.

"It would be a pleasure to work with you, Christian, but I'm on tour through the rest of the summer with Luke. When does your album drop?"

"The fall, but we'll be releasing a few singles before then. Depending on the Tres Armadas tour schedule, I want to be ready to perform in the New Year," Christian explained.

"Nice. We can continue to talk and work it out. Abe mentioned you had a few tracks you wanted to play for us. Do you mind if Luke stays? I need to ask for artistic confidentiality."

"Yeah, this troublemaker can stay." Christian shoved Luke. "He's featured on two tracks."

"Two of the best tracks," Luke gibed his friend.

"Hey, are those beignets?" Christian reached for the bag.

"Fresh from Café du Monde." Luke gave the beignets to Christian. Their sugary fried fragrance perfumed the air.

"Glad they're not animal crackers." Christian popped a piece of dough in his mouth.

"True story," Luke said.

Leona stared at the two men as if in a surreal daydream. Their jovial exchange displayed their friendship and she enjoyed seeing Luke so normal.

Christian motioned toward a booth on the second tier of the theater and the familiar sound of feedback emitted through the speakers.

"Just a second." Paul seized her elbow. His fingers were like an unwanted insect crawling on her skin.

"Don't touch me." She yanked her elbow free.

"Okay, okay." Paul put his hands up and motioned her to the far end of the theater. Luke's eyes tracked her as Paul attempted to guide her away from the group.

Leona blinked over to Abe for assistance but her boss made no attempt to help. Abe even angled his head in Paul's direction, encouraging her to talk to him. Her heart fell. *So much for that protection he promised.*

"We're on a tight schedule, Paul."

Luke was over to her in a flash. "Hey, we should get started. We have to get back," Luke said to her.

At least someone tried to help her out. "Okay, I—"

"Back up, man, we're talking." Paul's nostrils flared.

Luke tucked her behind him. "She's here for Christian, not you."

"Worried I'll steal her, too," Paul taunted.

Luke clenched and unclenched his fists and a wave of heat emitted from him. "No, she's moved on to bigger and better." He widened his stance. "Much bigger."

Leona's body petrified. Her eyes went back and forth from Paul's tight expression to Luke's icy daggers. *This is so fucked up.* She reanimated and stepped between the two men. "Okay, stop. What do you want, Paul?"

Paul peacocked. "I just want to talk."

Leona pulled Luke toward Abe and Christian. That didn't stop him from glaring over his shoulder at Paul. "Give us a minute, okay? This won't take long."

She marched back to Paul.

"Your pit bull all caged up?"

"Don't refer to him like that. You wanted to talk, so talk."

"You're lookin' good. How have you been?" Paul tried to touch her and she evaded him.

"Great. No thanks to you."

"I miss you, Leo. I think about you and how good we were together. Don't you miss me?"

"Nope," Leona said. Paul's words stirred something in her that she couldn't quite define. She hadn't expected him to lead with feelings of reconciliation. She had to stay on her toes.

She'd forgotten how charismatic he was and the way his sweet talk hid his dark side. It was how he'd wooed her into a relationship, and his bed, despite the rumors. Later in their relationship, she'd been one of the people Paul hurt and destroyed for his career and fame, even as he professed to love her.

Paul continued to lather on the charm but she was well versed in his dark arts.

"Some of the things I said weren't nice—"

"You mean the lies you told. You tried to ruin my career and reputation even after all I've done for you."

"But when you left, I was angry, honey…" Paul reached for her and she backed away.

"Don't call me honey," Leona hissed. The familiar

endearment sounded wrong to her now. "When I left? What a joke? Your ego would actually expect me to stay after that night."

"Don't look at me like that, Leo."

"Like how? Like nothing you've said so far makes any sense? If the shoe fits." Leona eyed their surroundings. "I'm not here for you. Keep your end of the deal. That's the least you could do for Abe. He helped you get to where you are."

"So did you." He grasped her hand. "I want you back, Leo."

Leona peered up into maple brown eyes. She could forgive Paul, but she would never trust him and they'd never be friends, work or otherwise. His behavior repeatedly wounded, and he had cut her too deep. It was only because she'd cared for him once that she didn't tell the world.

"Paul…" she began but stopped when Paul leered at something behind her.

She swiveled around to see Luke and Paul engaged in a stare down that made her seek the sidelines.

"Are you fucking him?" Paul accused.

Leona called upon all of her strength not to hit him. "I was wondering when the real you would finally show up. Thank you for reminding me why I want nothing to do with you." She stomped away and over to Christian, Luke, and Abe.

"Let's hear this album." Anger rippled through her body like a tsunami on Red Bull.

The sour expression on his face catapulted her back to the night at the Metro Hotel, after she'd mentioned Paul was one of her clients.

"What?" she challenged and immediately regretted her tone.

Luke tilted his head and further wrinkled his brows. The warning made her even more miserable.

Leona was thankful when he didn't comment and conceded for the time being. Annoyed that she'd let Paul or Luke influence her professionalism, she tried to give Christian her best smile. "I apologize for the interruptions. I'm all yours." She was betrayed by the spasms in her cheeks.

"Can you handle a third?" Christian asked softly and motioned to Luke and Paul.

His smirk helped relieve some of the stiffness in her shoulders. "A third, a fourth…"

Christian chuckled and Leona was happy for the comic relief.

"Track one," Christian called. Music filled the theater.

If Paul tried to put his hands on Leona one more time, Luke was sure he was going to lose his fucking mind. Seeing his friend and fellow artist did nothing to cool him off. Guilt had riddled him when he found out Christian would be working with Paul on the album.

"Thanks for your time, guys, I really appreciate it," Christian said.

"Glad I could make the connection, Christian. Abe, Leona, we'll be in touch," Paul chimed in.

Leona rolled her eyes and Luke shared her sentiment. Paul had been stewing on the sidelines while the grownups had been working—no doubt plotting his next media tirade or womanizing efforts.

Luke chatted with Christian and kept his eyes on

Paul. Paul returned an equally poisonous glare. If looks could kill, they'd both be obliterated.

"Is that about the past or the present?" Christian asked.

"Both."

"I'm surprised you lasted this long. I heard you signed with Wallace Entertainment but had I known I was interrupting your tour I never would have pushed for this meeting."

"It's cool." Though Luke had history with Paul, his concern for Leona had jumped to the top of his list so fast he'd lost his cool and bickered with his nemesis.

"Ready to go?" she asked him. She'd snapped at him earlier but now offered a less sour tone.

He gave her a curt nod, and then gave Christian some parting advice. "Hey, man. I know you want to work with Paul but be careful. Keep your sound and abandon ship if shit gets weird with production."

"I'm hoping he'll produce one of those chart-blowing hits. It's been a minute but I'd do it for the music," Christian admitted.

Luke was doubtful that Christian would get his wish. "No matter what you do, keep him away from my tracks. I don't want him fucking up my shit. Plus, I have a good feeling about those." One thing Luke knew was music. When Ivy had suggested he work with Paul and change his sound, he'd let their relationship influence him. All that had gotten him was a bag of headaches and an empty bed when Ivy left him to pursue Paul.

Leona and Abe shared a few departing words and then he and Leona headed for the plane to Kansas.

Once on the plane, Leona sank into the cushioned plane seat and her shoulders thawed away from her ears.

"Leona?" Her shoulders inched up again, but he needed to remind her that his name was Luke Anderson and not Paul Reese. "I can appreciate your frustration with this situation. However, if you use that tone with me again, be prepared to get it back in return. Are we clear?"

"Yes." She massaged the chill from her arms and gazed out the window.

"And the next time you get called upon to reunite with your ex—"

"Stop, Luke," she pleaded, her voice small and defeated.

She'd always presented a strong front but the way her voice broke wounded him. He grabbed an airplane blanket from overhead and placed it on her shoulders. She startled at the feel of the soft material on her skin, but then tightened the blanket around her and snuggled into its warmth. Warmth he provided. Not Abe, who had gotten her into this situation, or Paul, who continued to manipulate her.

"Thank you." She hadn't shed any tears that he could see but she rubbed her red eyes.

He returned to his seat across from her and when he thought about everything Paul had done, he gripped the seat arm on either side of him until his knuckles whitened. "Why do you let him handle you like that?"

"Like what?"

"Like he still has some claim on you," he scoffed. "Does he?" He didn't want to believe it because of what was happening between them, but how could he trust her if she had any allegiance to Paul?

"No, he doesn't." The tension in her jaw was visible and he wanted to stroke her cheek. "Paul's good at fooling people and then throwing a tantrum when he doesn't get what he wants."

He scanned her body for any evidence to the contrary. When he was satisfied, he asked, "Why'd you two break up?"

"That's none—" She stopped herself.

The material of the blanket was taut against her fingertips like a shield and she was quiet for what felt like hours.

"Leona," he called. She didn't have to answer but he prayed that she didn't shut down.

She let out a shaky breath as if readying herself for the confession. "While I was promoting him and working my ass off on his behalf he was... H-he was cheating on me, among other things. When we broke up he bad-mouthed me and pretty much lied or told some warped version of the truth. It affected my family. Things got real ugly."

"Hmm. That's a dick move." Luke's eyes widened for a moment before narrowing. He had a feeling there might be more to this story.

"You're not surprised?"

"No," he responded.

She cleared her throat. "Why'd you and Ivy break up?"

"My fiancée cheated on me, too."

"You two were engaged?" Her eyes widened. She tempered her surprise. "I-I'm sorry."

"It's cool, Leona." He should feel shittier after the admission but he didn't. Ivy was his past, but Leona? He stashed his thoughts about the future away.

"Is that why she left your tour? To be with that other guy?"

"Yeah." He omitted the details because Paul had already had her wound up. He didn't want to be responsible for adding any more bad news on her.

Dead air hung between them until at last he spoke.

"I'm sorry about what happened between you and Paul, but…"

Leona waited when he didn't continue. "But?" she prodded.

His entire body sighed. "You don't have to keep letting him hurt you. He's not worth it. You deserve more than a prick like Reese."

"I'm over him…been over him." Her eyes locked with his, no bullshit or curtain of doubt. "I'm just not over me and what I put up with, or all the shit that was left in the aftermath. But I'm working on it." Her lip curled into a half smile and it took all his efforts not to leap out of his seat and kiss the small dimple at the corner of her mouth.

He reached into his bag and pulled out a box of animal crackers. He stared at the box for a moment. He may have needed the soothing treat after the ladder of emotions that were undoing him at the seams but Leona needed it more. "Here." He handed her the box.

Leona gawked at the red container, then back at him. "Luke."

"They'll make you feel better. I promise." The hard expression he was sure had been engraved on his face earlier finally softened.

"Thank you," she said. As she dug into the box and popped a few in her mouth, he was glad to be a part of her comfort and not her turmoil.

"Can we make a deal?"

"Sure." She was way too agreeable, but animal crackers did that to you.

"No more departures from the tour, Leona. Agreed?"

"Agreed."

Chapter Fifteen

Operation: Distract Leona from her conflicting feelings about Luke was in full effect. She even went as far as to have Sara and Sebastian manage Luke's sound check. The two had done a great job filling in for her when she'd been summoned to New Orleans. If he requested her, she adhered to the minimum requirements of the contract, but she kept a physical and emotional distance.

In Colorado, the team prepared for two concerts in addition to a featured photo shoot and interview with *Trendzy Magazine*. With all the recent happenings, Leona had forgotten about Izzy's arrival. Though the timing wasn't ideal, Leona was still delighted her friend was coming out to Denver.

"Hello, love." Izzy's accent was a fresh new sound. She hugged Leona tight.

"I missed you." Leona returned her friend's embrace. "How's Peaches?"

Izzy's face contorted with guilt. "I have a bit of bad news."

Leona froze. "What? She's sick, right?"

"Well, yes, but she's in recovery." Izzy pushed her hair behind her shoulder.

Leona frowned. "Recovery?"

"Yes. See, I changed her water, like you instructed, but I might have put too much of that solution or salt or something. The pet shop guy said I almost boiled her. Anyway, she's fine now. Mitchell's taking care of her while I'm here."

Leona gaped openmouthed at her friend. None of the news put her at ease, especially since her brother's feeding forgetfulness was worse than Izzy's.

"She's absolutely fine. See?" Izzy pulled out her smartphone and showed Leona a short video of Peaches swimming around in her tank.

Leona exhaled. She was a ball of stress and it wasn't only because of Peaches's near death experience. "Okay."

Izzy put her arm around her. "Come on. Let's go eat. I'm starving."

The two women went to a restaurant close to their hotel.

After they ordered, Izzy began her inquisition. "So, how are things going?"

"Great." Leona's avoidance of Luke, since she'd walked *zombified* to her hotel that night in Miami, had turned into a full-on hide-and-seek situation after their brief trip to New Orleans.

"Yeah?" Izzy inspected her cobalt blue painted fingernails.

"I miss New York and the family, but I'm seeing so many more places than any other tour. This is definitely the biggest one."

"And Luke?" Izzy leaned in for a secret. "Anything sizzling with you two yet?"

"Don't," Leona said.

"Why are you blushing? My, Leo, I would think that something's happened."

Leona was silent.

"Something *has* happened, hasn't it?" Izzy's delightful demeanor energized the entire restaurant.

Their food arrived and Leona prayed that eating would silence any further admission and distract Izzy altogether.

"Come with the details." Izzy tapped her fork against her plate.

Leona munched on her salad. "We may have shared a small kiss, but we're on tour so nothing else will happen."

Izzy dropped her fork. "Lies. You both got a taste. It's a snowball effect from here on out. I knew it from the beginning."

"You knew what from the beginning?" Leona asked. Izzy was doing nothing to ease Leona's ever-growing tension.

"You and Luke. You fit somehow. I can't really explain it."

"I'm in New York, he's based in California, and he's my client. It wouldn't work."

"So you're thinking about working it out?"

"No!" Leona said. She shook her head and then lowered her voice. "No."

"Mmm-hmm..." Izzy delivered through pouted lips.

Leona had to get off this topic. "I saw Paul." *Not the best choice.*

She thought it best to give Izzy the consolidated version of how she and Paul came to be in the same room before she heard anything through the grapevine.

"What?" Izzy raised her voice.

"Yeah. He's working with Christian Sacks from Tres Armadas."

"Absolutely amazing. How does he get to work with all these great people? Silly me, it's because of his past hits." Izzy stared at her for a long moment.

Leona shook her head. "Whatever. It's the past."

"He's a fraud. Aargh! I really don't like that guy." Izzy stuffed her mouth with food.

"Anyway, Christian and Luke are good friends, which helped the situation."

"Luke was there? With Paul?" Izzy asked. "The plot thickens. Do tell."

Leona recounted the story. She had tried not to make Luke the topic of conversation but as her and Izzy's chatter navigated back to him, Leona's worries intensified.

"Something is definitely up with those two." Izzy swirled her glass of iced tea. "I'm always impressed by your ability to keep a tight lip, but you let Paul get away with it. Again."

Leona fidgeted with her fork. "You'd prefer I say something so I can be hounded by the press? Again? No way. I'll plead the fifth." Every time she heard someone was working with Paul, the old familiar guilt and anxiety popped to the surface like a buoy that had been held underwater.

"One day, you'll have a reason to speak out, and I want to be up front and center for the show."

Leona hoped Izzy was wrong. That wasn't a display she ever wanted to be on. "Okay, enough about me. How are things with you? I saw the Milan cover. Gorgeous."

"It's my best yet. The success is filling up my already busy calendar but that's not a bad problem to have."

Izzy had started the magazine a few years ago and had only a few subscribers. Now *Trendzy* was not only one of the hottest fashion magazines, it was getting praise from fashion's toughest critics.

"I'm so proud of you, Izzy. You've come such a long way."

"We both have, love." Izzy squeezed Leona's hand.

"So." Leona squinted at her. "Are you dating anyone?"

Izzy glanced at her sideways. "Leona Sable, you're well aware that I don't date."

"I just thought I'd ask. It may change someday when you tire of Boy Toyland." Leona laughed.

"Haha," Izzy joined. "Anyway, I'd much rather hear you tell me what a great kisser Luke is. He is, isn't he?"

"Hey, let's finish up and get you your exclusive." Her deflection was obvious.

"Okay, chicken." Izzy plucked pretend feathers off her.

"Come on." Leona mimicked Izzy's accent.

Leona's team had secured a space in the hotel ballroom for Luke's photo shoot. The space was large enough to accommodate the wardrobe rack, makeup, and changing area for the models, and the staged scenes for the photographs. Izzy's assistants bustled around prepping costumes and doing makeup.

Leona was happy to give Izzy this opportunity with Luke. They had helped each other in their careers whenever possible, but this was the first exclusive Leona was able to offer.

They found Luke and Sara talking by the dressing area. Sara laughed at something he said and her hair swung around her shoulders, and Luke wore a boyish smile on his handsome face. The scene was one she'd seen him share with near everyone who'd worked with him.

"You okay, love?" Izzy's voice grew bubbly. "You've been eyeing him since you walked into the room. My God, Leo, that man is like ice cream. If you don't hurry up and lick him, I will."

Leona nudged Izzy and couldn't help but laugh.

The two approached Sara and Luke.

"Hey, Leo." Sara met them halfway and hugged Izzy. "I haven't seen you in a long time, Isabelle. How are you?"

"I'm well, thanks. And you?" Izzy responded.

"Good." Sara presented the room. "Everything is ready for you to work your magic."

"The ballroom is perfect," Izzy said.

The three of them gathered where Luke sat.

He greeted Izzy. "Nice to see you again."

He was sexy and metropolitan in a fitted bronze, retro suit with black shirt. His shirt, unfastened four buttons deep, revealed part of his defined chest.

Her growing feelings for Luke were the reason she avoided him. The lousy slime Paul left on her in New Orleans had made her withdraw. But Leona had opened up to Luke on the plane and allowed him to crack her emotional armor. She had to get back in control and distancing herself from him had become priority number one. She couldn't, however, deny how drawn she was to Luke. She was starving and he was a brunch buffet.

"Leo?" Sara waved her hand in front of Leona's face. "Hi."

"Huh?" Leona did her best to regulate her reaction back to normal.

Izzy chuckled at her clear distraction from watching Luke.

"Ready to head to the venue? Diesel will be back in about two hours to get Luke to the stadium," Sara explained.

Leona started to make her exit with Sara. "We'll leave you guys to it."

Izzy stopped her. "No way. You've been touring with Luke and can give me your opinion on whether or not I'm doing justice to his image, especially since Sebastian isn't here. You know how my creativity goes wild with a new subject."

Leona was about to complain.

"Do you mind, Luke?" Izzy asked.

Luke locked eyes with Leona and answered Izzy. "I don't mind."

She sunk into his eyes, her breathing visible.

"Brilliant." Izzy went to work.

"Sara, you go on ahead. I'll get to the stadium with Diesel and Luke when we're done here," Leona said.

"Okay." Sara said her goodbyes and was gone.

Izzy set Luke on a plush, off-white couch and positioned her models around him. The women were dressed in provocative, elaborate costumes frequently seen at EDM concerts and festivals.

"Fantastic, Luke. Ladies, an arm around him…legs out to the ends, just so. Relax your shoulders, love."

Luke glanced her way just as a model placed a slender leg over his thigh.

"Give us that scrumptious, sweet, syrupy smile, handsome," Izzy crooned, and Luke's genuine merriment made Leona's knees weak.

The frequent snaps of the camera capturing Luke's

image sounded throughout the ballroom. "Lovely." Izzy adjusted him to shoot his different profiles.

Luke changed twice more before Izzy called for a five-minute break.

"What do you think, so far, Leo?" Izzy pensively held her camera to the side.

Leona's eyes ping-ponged between her friend and Luke. "The couch will make a great cover."

"But?" Izzy raised her eyebrows to encourage Leona to be quick with her response.

Luke also awaited her opinion.

"It's not that he's uncomfortable," Leona said. "But he'll be more relaxed behind the DJ table. It's also how the fans know him best."

Izzy nodded. "See, this is why I need you." She loopy-looped her index finger at Luke. "Go on, love. Do your thing."

As Leona predicted, Luke was a natural behind the DJ table. Now in his signature outfit, he worked the equipment. He played music and danced, as did the models, while Izzy captured it all. He mixed in his song "Get Up and Move for Me," and Leona swayed to the music.

Izzy danced over to her. "Doesn't this sound familiar?"

"Yeah, it's his song." Leona knew she was stating the obvious, but she had been listening to Luke's music for months now. Shouldn't it sound familiar?

Izzy pursed her lips. "No, not like that. Listen. I mean really listen, Leo. The song reminds me of something." She strained to hear meaning in the music.

Leona listened more intently to the lyrics. She grinned as Izzy performed her bouncy dance. Leona recalled a younger image of Isabelle Fisher doing those same moves.

Leona swirled her lightly fisted hands around each other. She and Izzy activated and their smiles widened.

"Paris!" Both women shouted in unison and giggled like the teenagers they were when they first met. They hugged each other and jumped around.

"The rave at L'Essence with the Lexionic Twins." Izzy bobbed her head and waved hands in the air.

Leona moved her shoulders to the beat. "And that DJ at the end. He was so ah-mazing."

"This song could have been about us," Izzy cheered.

They danced like they were the only two in the room.

Luke's unmoving body caught her attention. Normally, he'd bob his head in time to the beat of the music nonstop. Now he held a dazed expression on his face, his mouth agape. At first Leona thought he might be angry but he wasn't angry at all. He was in shock.

Chapter Sixteen

Luke was thrust back to the night almost a decade ago when the Lexionic Twins let him deejay at the end of a rave at club L'Essence in Paris. He had thought of that night countless times, and of the two girls that slept on the couches, spent from dancing. He'd never expected to see them again, let alone that one would be his current tour manager and the other doing an exclusive on him for her magazine.

Leona and Izzy, as girls, had inspired him to keep reaching for his dreams. Leona had blown him a kiss back then. Now, as she danced, his heart swelled. Leona was more than his manager and the woman he wanted. She meant more to him than either of them had realized.

"Holy shit." He still couldn't believe it. Now, if only he knew how to play this.

Diesel arrived and Leona pulled him to dance. The burly man, who he'd become friends with over the past weeks, reluctantly two-stepped with her. When Izzy sandwiched Diesel against Leona, the trio decided it was time to wrap it up.

"That was a blast, Luke. You were lovely. I'll send you lot my final choices for approval." Izzy packed her camera.

"Thanks," Luke managed as he slid his computer into its case.

Leona approached him. "Hey, are you good with the shoot?"

"Yeah. Why do you ask?"

"You look like you saw a ghost or something." Leona gave a nervous laugh.

He'd seen more than a ghost. He saw his past and his present, and wondered if he possibly saw his future, too. "Everything's cool, Leona." He didn't know what else to say. He couldn't just start blathering about their Paris connection.

"You sure?" She hovered. "I mean, I know I've been a little busy, but if there's something on your mind about the shoot or anything, you can tell me. I'll get it straightened out."

He put his hand on her arm and his thumb stroked her exposed shoulder cap. "I'm fine." He left to change. When he was done changing, Luke headed to the stadium with Leona and Diesel.

Leona rested her head against the window. She played with her hands and hummed a tune he couldn't make out. Since New Orleans, she had put more distance between them than after he had almost made love to her in Miami. Yet, the distance did nothing to curb his appetite. Discovering that he'd met her in Paris and the impact she'd had on him and his life only intensified his feelings.

Something hit his foot. Diesel regarded him with a raised eyebrow.

Busted.

Leona turned at his movement. "Everything okay, guys?"

Luke gave her a quick smile. "Yeah. I was just stretching."

She nodded, and again gazed out the window and hummed.

Luke pretended to threaten Diesel with his fist, after his friend caught him studying Leona. His movements screeched to a halt when he recognized the tune Leona had been humming. His song, "Get Up and Move for Me." His fans had sung his songs, so did his friends and family, but hearing the melody coming from her chest dissolved him. He wanted to say so much to her but he failed each time he started.

They arrived at the stadium and split up. Luke readied to perform while Leona worked with the team. In his dressing room, he reviewed his set. A remix of "Get Up and Move for Me" came on and that's when the idea came to him. The timing couldn't be more perfect.

Luke inhaled. He knew what he was going to do.

The next day, during scheduled downtime for the staff and crew, Luke knocked on Leona's hotel room door and waited. He thought about the ten-day tour break coming up. He had plans to visit his sister's place in Santa Monica for a few days, and then travel to his home in San Francisco for the rest of the break. He was taking a chance and rejection would most likely be the outcome, but he had to do something.

Leona opened the door dressed in fitted jean short-shorts and a tank top. "Luke?"

Every muscle, starting with the one between his legs, responded at the sight of her. Though she was short, her legs appeared long and her ass was barely contained by the material. The white tank top gift-wrapped her breasts like a present.

Before she could say anything else, he captured her in his arms and kissed her. Her body stiffened at his initial embrace but then she was warm butter melting against him. Being physical with her felt so natural and he wondered if being confined to the tour contributed to that or if there was more between them. Would what he was about to suggest give him the time he needed to find out? As her hips pressed forward, he thought he might have a chance to persuade her into doing the impossible.

"I have to ask you something," he whispered against her lips, then backed up enough to see her.

Leona didn't speak. Either he had stunned her into silence or she was eager to hear what he had to say. He didn't care which it was, so long as she listened.

"Well, hello there, lover boy." Izzy peered over the back of a small love seat.

"Izzy's here." Leona pursed her lips. "We…uh…we just came back from the pool."

"Hey, Izzy." He didn't care. Izzy was Leona's best friend and probably already knew some details. "Do you mind if I talk to Leona alone for a bit?"

"Not at all." Izzy scrambled up, wearing a light pink bikini top, white shorts, and flip-flops.

Izzy was a good-looking woman, but Leona magnetized him.

"I was just leaving to change out of these wet clothes."

Did Leona swim? Did she share his love for the ocean?

"I'll call you later before I fly out." Izzy hugged Leona then squared to him. "Be great to my Leo, okay?"

He gave her a half smile on her way out and ambled further into Leona's suite, the door closing behind him.

"I want you, Leona, and I know you want me," he said.

"I—I—" she started but he plowed through.

"We have the tour break coming up and I want to invite you to stay with me at my home in San Francisco for part of it. It's only for the last five days of our break, but if you're willing, it would be five days of—"

"Sex." Leona finally spoke.

"I was going to say pleasure, but it's more than that."

"But sex is part of it, no?"

"Yes."

Leona crossed her arms and chewed the inside of her lip.

"I get that we have some unresolved shit that complicates things, so here's the deal. If you agree to come out, we can't bring any of it with us. I'm inviting you, not your baggage."

"My baggage! My baggage?" She side-eyed him up and down.

"Yes. Oh, I have my matching set, too, but it's off-limits for both of us," he said. As far as pasts went, theirs continued to block them like a brick wall and he wanted to experience the Leona that existed beyond the wall.

She tightened her arms. "I don't think—"

"Don't answer right away. Think about it and let me know when we're in New Mexico."

"Luke, you're my client. I—"

Luke held her shoulders. "Just tell me you'll think about it."

Leona was a strong woman who knew what she wanted. If she didn't say no right away, that was a good indication she had thought about being with him and learning more about him, too. If she'd thought about being with him, then maybe she'd eventually say yes.

He waited.

Leona frowned and again chewed the inside of her lip, but he noticed she didn't rub her left ear, which meant he hadn't completely freaked her out.

"Okay. I'll think about it," she said.

He smiled. *Yes!*

In New Mexico, the pending tour break, and planning for the post-break Los Angeles show, had everyone working overtime. Sara and Sebastian would meet Leona in San Francisco to get footage of Luke's one-off performance, and continue to execute the marketing for the LA show. After LA, they would travel to Las Vegas where Tommy, Leona, and Abe would meet with the owners of the Xcelsior Hotel to bid for Luke's residency. The team had to pre-plan for all of it. To say things were busy was an understatement. They were flat out frantic.

Through it all, Leona had to decide whether or not she was going to Luke's during the break. Every time she made a decision, she changed her mind. She had never experienced this level of indecision.

At their tour break dinner, she was ready to give Luke her final answer. This wasn't going to happen. Luke was her client and muddling their professional relationship with sex was the last thing either of them needed.

An opportune moment to deliver the news to him came at their team dinner. She pulled Luke just outside the dining hall and was resolute in her decision. When she gazed up into his green-gray eyes and inhaled his fragrance she was mesmerized by the thought of his hands on her, free to express their desires. His body was so close she could feel his warmth.

"So?" Anticipation creased his forehead.

"I'll go to San Francisco." *That was so NOT the answer I was supposed to give. What the...*

"Are you sure, Leona?"

She shifted from one foot to the other and repeatedly pressed her earlobe. The doubts she had prior to her announcement were now replaced with nervous excitement, and her breathing quickened. She could, and surely should, change her answer, but she didn't want to.

"Yes. I'm sure," she said, the word just passing her lips.

"And you're okay with leaving our baggage for now?"

Leona struggled with this, but she wanted Luke. She was not giving up on getting answers and reminded herself that this agreement was temporary. "For right now, yes."

"How soon can you get to San Francisco?" His happiness surprised her and Leona couldn't help but join him.

"I'm back to New York for an event and to see my family. So Monday at the earliest."

"I'll send the details when you get to New York."

"Shouldn't I book my flight?" Her nerves were high-pitch screaming at her.

"I'll take care of everything, Leona. Just pack."

"But—"

Luke straightened, cutting her off. "I'm going to ask you to give up control this one time. Let me take care of getting you to my home. I got this."

If there was anything that made her feel better it was steering her own ship. Not only had she agreed to this lover's retreat, but she was actually going to let Luke plan their trip?

"I can't believe I'm doing this." Would he be discreet? Oh Lord. What if the sex was bad? What if it was good? What if they couldn't stand each other after a few hours of being alone?

Luke touched her arm. "Get out of your head, Leona."

There was still time to back out but she wanted this time with Luke as much as he did. "I'll wait to hear from you."

"Good girl." Luke snaked his arm around her waist and patted her ass.

Leona lightly hit his arm for chiding her and scoped the hall to make sure no one spied on them. "Watch it."

He laughed and separated from her.

She shook her head. "We should get back." *What the hell did I just get myself into?* Leona didn't know but as she lazed back to where everyone congregated, she smiled.

Back in New York, Leona kissed Peaches's bowl when she saw her fish alive and well.

"I told you she was fine." Izzy stood with hands on hips.

Leona lounged on Izzy's couch. "No more solution overdoses. Okay?"

Izzy scoffed at her. "Like I would make the same mistake twice."

"Uh-huh."

Izzy picked up her clutch. "Thanks for coming tonight. We only need to show our faces for an hour or two and plug the magazine."

"No thanks required. You know I support you in all you do," Leona said.

Leona had a date with Izzy to attend a gallery event for one of New York's premier fashion publications. The event drew people from all industries and was a great networking opportunity.

"I must warn you that the media will be there, but they should all be legit."

Leona nodded. "We're only there to network, right?" She had kept her anxiety mostly under control over the past nine months. "I've been dealing with them for the tour. I'm sure it'll be fine."

"I'm ready." Izzy swung her sandy brown hair behind her. "This dress is gorgeous on you, Leo. White is your color, along with every other color in existence. I'm so jealous. Too bad DJ Luke isn't here to see you. I must send him a photograph."

Leona wore a one shoulder antique white, knee-length chiffon dress with gold sequin embellishment at the shoulder and on the waistline. Her hair was pinned up with a straight side bang that framed her face.

"Thanks." Leona was unable to stop the heat flaming her face. "You look great, too."

"What's that about? That little smirky thing you have going on your face?" Izzy asked as she smoothed over the simple black dress that she wore with strappy red stilettos.

"Nothing. Ready?" Leona tried to get Izzy off her scent but she was a bloodhound and even if she let up now, she'd further inquire later.

"All right, then." Izzy hooked her arm in Leona's. "Let's be off."

The gallery was filled with people from the entertainment industry. Leona strolled in with Izzy and smiled at familiar faces. She received warm greetings from some who mentioned her success with Luke's tour and welcomed her back to the scene. Such a person was Ramelda Manikas.

"Dahhhhrrrliing," came Ramelda's enthusiastic drawl. "You look beautiful and successful." The already tall woman dominated Leona's figure.

"So do you." Leona hugged her, noting Ramelda's sparkling jewelry, tight-hugging red dress, and heels that put Izzy's stilettos to shame. "Thank you again for your help a few months ago. You could have cut me off and you didn't."

"You've already given Isabelle an exclusive with The Musical Prophet." Ramelda flung her tawny hair. "But rumor has it he has some big goals and I want in."

"You bet." Leona knew this give-and-take dance between "friends" in the industry. "I'm sure I can count on you to help us build momentum to ensure it happens."

"Why of course, darling."

They said their "ta-tas" and Ramelda was off to her next networking victim.

"Nonstop, that one." Izzy snagged two glasses of champagne off a nearby tray and handed one to Leona.

A photographer snapped a photo of her and Izzy poised with their glasses.

"You're doing great, love," Izzy encouraged.

They covered the side of the room where the editors were and then made their way to the music folks at the far side of the room.

"Andy," Leona called. She'd been listening to Andrew White's satellite radio show more regularly since the day Abe asked her to help him secure Luke as a Wallace Entertainment artist.

"Hey, pal," Andy said to her. "What's up, Izzy?"

Leona informed him of her newfound pastime. After they exchanged a few more pleasantries she went in for the favor. "I'd love your help with an idea I have for a ramp up. It involves your listeners but will be pretty cool."

"For sure," Andy said. "I'd love to get Prophet on my show when the tour comes to New York."

"Then you're going to love this idea. We'll be in touch."

An hour's worth of power networking later, Leona and Izzy were headed to the rooftop bar for a wrap up drink or two when a voice boomed behind them.

"Well, well, well. If it isn't Leo Sable."

One minute too late. Leona's teeth clenched when she recognized Paul's voice. She faced him and his ego filled the gallery. He escorted an alluring, platinum blonde companion on his arm and his antagonizing tone was different from the sweetness he'd lathered on her in New Orleans.

So much for "I miss you" and "I want you back."

Izzy pulled her closer.

"What's up, Izzy?" Paul snickered like a teenager.

"Go fuck off, asshole," Izzy said.

Paul swallowed as if he tasted the insult. "I'm just saying hello. See, Leo and I are working together, again." He threw the words around as if he were making an official announcement.

"That's not exactly correct," Leona stated as a small crowd started to form. This was the last thing she needed. She smelled alcohol emanating from Paul's pores, which may have contributed to his behavior. *Once an ass...* Paul released his statuesque companion and scuttled over to Leona. He fanned his hand at a cameraman. "Get a picture of us." He went to grab her hand but Leona dodged his grip.

"I told you the last time not to fucking touch me."

"Back up, Paul," Izzy threatened. "Everyone knows how you've bad-mouthed Leo. The last thing she wants is a picture with you. Just walk away."

Paul stumbled backward and into a group of attendees. He righted himself and mimicked Izzy as his companion tried to tug him away, but Paul moved in.

"You know, I thought I made a mistake when I let you go, but you're still not worth it," he spat at her.

Leona had been a victim of, and witness to, his manipulation while they were together and at their last meeting. Still, she was not desensitized to it and was baffled by how night and day he could be. He suggested that he wanted her back in New Orleans, but now she wasn't worth it? She wanted to crawl up inside herself, but she was tired of letting Paul win.

That might have explained why she threw her half-filled glass of champagne into his face.

Gasps from the crowd swelled like a lyrical element in a symphony and Paul shouted as he wiped the wetness from his eyes. He squinted from the stinging alcohol.

"What the fuck, Leo?"

Izzy applauded. "Bravo."

Paul's companion offered him a tissue from her purse, which he hastily snatched. For a split second Leona thought Paul's companion was familiar but her anger had her focused on Paul.

It may not have been smart to get close to Paul, since she'd just wet him with champagne, but she vibrated with anger that blinded her to the possible danger.

She leaned in and hissed at him. "I've played nice and kept my mouth shut, even though you don't deserve it. I even allowed Abe to talk me into helping you save face with Christian. The only reason why you should speak my name again, is to promote Wallace Entertainment. I'm telling you once and for all, Paul. Stay away from me or I'll destroy you." She offered a few parting words to Paul's companion. "Good luck."

"Don't ever threaten me again, Leo." Paul fumed. "Come on, Ivy."

Leona stopped in her tracks. Ivy? Ivy Nichols? Leona pressed her memory for images of the woman. Her hair was different, more blonde than the images Leo had seen from her research, but it was why she looked familiar. And she was with Paul? Back in New Orleans Paul had said something to Luke about "stealing her" and it dawned on Leona that he may not have been talking professionally. When Luke said his fiancée cheated, she'd assumed it was that Ted Kimmel guy, but it was Paul. *Oh my God.*

Leona glanced back to find Paul dragging Ivy away and staring at her departing figure.

"Did I just assault Paul with a glass of champagne?"

"Yes. You. Did. Escape now, to the patio bar. I'll meet you there." Izzy addressed the crowd. "Show's over, everyone."

* * *

Leona rushed to the patio bar. She breathed in the warm night air and tried to calm her beating heart. One arm hugged her middle and her other hand pressed her left ear. She hated losing control, and with Paul of all people. *Inhale one, exhale two. Center. Breathe.* She prayed that the media people at the event didn't moonlight for the gossip rags and that her tiff with Paul didn't make the headlines.

"He better not renege on his deal with Abe," she said to herself. "Let it go. Focus on what you can control." She repeated her mantra several times.

The sound of her phone interrupted her thoughts. Luke's name displayed on the screen and her heart thumped in her chest.

Leona picked up. "Hello?"

"Hey." Luke's voice tickled her ear with anxious excitement that she'd recognized in her own voice. "I sent you an email with your ticket information."

"Whoa. Already?" Leona couldn't keep the smile from spreading across her face.

"Yes." His chuckle was deep and sweet. "That's how much I want you here. I'll see you Monday night."

"Yes, Monday night."

"Hey, you sound different. Stressed, maybe. Everything okay? You're not having second thoughts, are you?"

"No, I'm at a gallery event with Izzy. I'm just waiting for her so we can leave." She hugged the phone. She'd just assaulted Paul, and oh, by the way, Ivy cheated on Luke with her ex-boyfriend and the implications were freaking her out.

"Cool. Well, you ladies have fun."

"And Luke?"

"Yeah?"

"I'm not having second thoughts. I'm looking forward to coming, too."

"We'll see," was his seductive response.

She straight blushed and her clothes smothered her hot skin.

"See you soon, Leona."

"You, too."

"That was brilliant," Izzy's voice bellowed before Leona saw her. "I've been waiting a year for that moment, Leo. I'm so damn proud of you."

Izzy ordered two beers from the bartender.

"I just need him to stay away from me." Leona bypassed the glass the bartender offered and sipped her beer from the bottle.

"And you're feeling all right?" Izzy studied her.

"It took a few moments for me to settle down but, surprisingly, yes. I'm all right." Leona had no doubt that talking to Luke had had some strange calming effect.

Izzy nodded. "Now all you have to do is pull the curtain back on why that awful clown hasn't produced a hit in ages and get your due."

"Are you trying to calm me down or rile me up?"

"A bit of both, I suspect." Izzy swigged her beer.

Leona smirked. "Moving on."

"So you're traveling again on Monday?"

"Yeah. I get to have Sunday dinner with you guys. These last couple of days off has been great. I mean I've been connecting with my team because I love my work, but being back in the city and seeing you and the fam is everything. Traveling will be nice though."

Leona smiled and could feel the corners of her lips tease a smile when she thought of meeting Luke. She didn't want to be nervous but she was.

"What's that about?" Izzy asked.

"What?"

"That thing you're doing with your mouth. You did it earlier, don't think I've forgotten."

Leona went to drink her beer but Izzy guided the bottle back down to the table.

"Out with it, Sable."

Leona felt a flush in her cheeks. This was her best friend, but she still struggled to divulge the information.

Izzy noticed her struggling. "Oh dear. It must be serious."

Leona shut her eyes before blurting out, "I'm going to see Luke in California." She opened one eye to see Izzy's flat reaction to the news. Nothing.

"I know that already. You'll be in San Francisco for one of Luke's separate performance thingies, right?"

"Not like that, Izzy. Alone. Our break is ten days. I'm here for five days." The intention in Leona's words couldn't be missed and brightness illuminated Izzy's face.

"And you'll be there for five," Izzy expelled with soap-operatic flair. She put both elbows on the table and folded her arms. "Oh really? When did this happen? Tell me everything."

Leona filled her in.

"I knew something was up when he landed that smooch on you in Denver."

"We just...oh, I don't know..."

"Get buck wild," Izzy finished, rocking her pelvis.

"Do you have to say it like that?"

"Leo, love of my life, that's what it is. Am I right?"

Leona let out a defeated sigh. "I guess."

"This is juicier than what happened with Paul. You are just winning."

Leona shrugged.

"Do you think you'll really be able to not ask questions about his past? I mean you just saw his ex-manager with Paul. Surely you want to ask him about it? All you two will have is time and each other to spend it with. You, my love, don't put things to rest easily."

"Thanks." Leona frowned.

"Anytime."

Izzy spoke the truth. When Leona wanted to know something, she asked. Tommy had stopped her from pursuing additional information more than once. What would happen with no one around to stop her? What if Luke started his own inquisition and she had nowhere to run?

"What the hell am I thinking? I can't go." Leona plucked her phone from her clutch and dialed Luke's number. The first thing she felt was a hard slap on her hand and the next thing she saw was her phone flying across the low lit bar area.

"Izzy! What the fuck?"

"I'm saving you from yourself. You are going to California, even if I have to put you on the plane."

"But you're right. When I'm in hot pursuit, I don't give up. Why would I agree to try to do something that I am obviously going to fail at achieving?"

"Because failing is better than not trying at all."

Leona was silent for a moment. "I'm a mess. It's been a long time."

"Clearly." Izzy targeted the motion of Leona's hand as she fiddled with her ear.

Leona sighed and folded her hands on the table.

"You're just a little rusty. Once he's naked and in front of you with those eyes, and that body, and those hands, it'll all come back to you." Izzy's accent made the words sound less raunchy.

"Will you stop, please?" Leona couldn't help but enjoy comedy hour with Izzy.

Izzy retrieved her phone, wiping it off with a beer-dampened napkin before handing it to her. "Here you go. All disinfected and everything."

"Great." Leona wrinkled her face and pinched the phone between her index finger and thumb, placing it on the table.

Izzy gave her the thumbs-up.

"This stays between us," Leona warned.

Izzy's face fell flat. "Really?"

Whatever she told Izzy was kept under an ironclad lock and key, but she said it anyway. "I know."

"I can't wait to hear all about it." Izzy raised her beer glass. "To you, my sweetest Leo. To finally getting some."

Leona groaned but raised her bottle and clinked it with Izzy's, nonetheless.

Chapter Seventeen

Leona's plane touched down in San Francisco on Monday night. Her stomach was as tight as the knot on the bright green string that distinguished her luggage from the others. As she exited the airport a man in a suit displayed her initials on a small white board. She worried about Luke's discretion, but so far he had done a stellar job with her arrangements. She hopped into the waiting vehicle while the driver handled her luggage.

As they drove along the coast, she was overwhelmed by the thought of seeing Luke. The sky neared dark but there were still surfers along the white foaming waves. Luke had excitedly mentioned the coast and surfing a few times during the tour, and Leona now imagined him out there gliding over the waves.

The car arrived at a set of wooden gates and the driver buzzed the intercom. Luke's voice transmitted briefly before the locked gates opened. Her heart was pumping so hard it felt lodged in her throat. She was here. This was happening.

As the driver continued, a quaint stucco house with adobe ceramic roofing tiles came into view. Once stopped, Leona got out of the car and the driver wheeled over her luggage.

"Thank you."

"You're welcome, miss."

Large garden windows at ground level welcomed her as they glowed against the night. A few lush, decorative bushes that sprinkled the front provided privacy and rustic landscaping. Before she reached the front door, Luke was out of the house and making his way toward her. The butterflies in her stomach wouldn't quit and her breathing accelerated.

He hugged her for a long moment.

Leona let go of her luggage and held his waist, sinking into the strength of his arms.

Luke breathed her in as he spoke against her ear. "Was the flight okay?"

Leona smiled as his breath tingled her ear. "Yes. Thanks for sending a car."

"My pleasure." Luke finished up with the driver, who bid them good night and departed.

Luke carried her luggage and motioned her to the house. "Come in and let me show you around."

From the outside, the house seemed deceptively small, but inside, the space opened into a modern haven. The living room functioned as the central part of the house and, even without the sun, was bright. The TV was on and Luke quickly shut it off, placing the remote control with his now familiar computer and other music items lying on the couch. A huge picture window overlooked the ocean and another framed the grounds.

"This way." He led her to two separate stairways that led to respective sides of the house. Even with its modern comforts, the house had endless nooks and crannies, giving it a cozy feel.

They arrived at Luke's bedroom and the first thing

Leona noticed, besides his musky fragrance, was a large window on the opposite side of the room with a view of the ocean. The masculine room had light gray walls and black furniture. Large gray rugs lay on dark brown hardwood floors. A gray folded throw sat atop off-white bedding, and white and red pillows decorated the black headboard of a canopy bed. Leona immediately recognized Luke's style.

A colorful mosaic painting of a beach scene hung on the wall facing the bed and, though in contrast with the room, complemented the décor. No matter where you were in the room you were in view of the ocean or its representation.

This man loves the ocean. "This is gorgeous." Leona's eyes continued to scan the bedroom. Some of Luke's items lay on the dresser, but it was neat and clean.

Luke set her luggage down. "There's a bathroom through here."

The adjoining bathroom was white with color coming mostly from the hand towels and decorative marble tiling. Leona was surprised to see *his* and *her* porcelain bowl sinks in the bachelor pad.

"You must be hungry. I made you dinner," he said.

Leona's stomach was so nervous she wasn't sure she could even eat. "You did?"

"Don't sound so stunned." He feigned wounded.

"I didn't… I mean, I'm sure you did a great job." She chewed the inside of her lip and lowered her eyes. "Do you mind if I freshen up?"

"Make yourself at home. Can you find your way back to the kitchen?"

"I think I can manage." She wasn't sure why she would have an issue finding her way.

Luke left and Leona went into the bathroom. As she dried her face, she regarded her image in the over-the-sink wall mirror. "What am I doing?" She sighed. She knew damned well what she was doing and there was no turning back.

Once she was done, she navigated her way through the house. Navigating back to the kitchen wasn't as easy as she thought it would be and now she understood, more fully, Luke's question. Minutes later, she found him in the kitchen.

"Feeling better?" he asked.

"Yeah."

Luke took her hand and led her through a sliding partition to the dining room. He seated her at the table. A bowl of salad and cut Italian bread sat between two place settings.

"Wow. The bread is so fresh I can smell it from here. Do you need any help?"

"Let's see. Do you like wine?"

Leona raised her hand. "Admitted wino, right here."

"Red okay? We're having beef." His face showed concern. "Wait. Do you eat red meat?"

"No. I'm vegetarian." She wore the most serious face she could muster.

"Oh." Luke scratched his head. "Uh...okay."

Luke's concern made it impossible for her to keep a straight face. She finally cracked. "I'm teasing, Luke. You've seen me eat on tour. I eat everything."

"Is that right?"

She straightened at his seductive tone in an effort to keep her guard up at least through dinner. "Red is fine."

Luke smiled, left for a minute, and returned with an open bottle of Chianti. He poured a bit in a glass and swirled it before inspecting the color against a white napkin. He inhaled the liquid's bouquet, then tasted.

"Mmm. You'll like this one," he assured. "Would you mind pouring wine for us?"

"Sure." She cradled the outstretched bottle with both hands and stared at his back as he tended to the food. *Who the hell is this refined, wine tasting guy? Where's The Musical Prophet?*

Luke brought over two plates of lasagna and sat in the chair opposite her.

"A toast." He lifted his glass. "To good wine, great company, and other simple pleasures."

Leona raised her glass. "Cheers." She wanted to gulp down the wine to chill her nerves, but sipped it instead. "You're right. I really like this one." She took a bite of lasagna and the combination of seasoned, herbed meat, cheese, and pasta filled her mouth. "This is delicious."

"It's my mother's recipe." Luke beamed.

Her heart skipped a beat. "Is she the one who taught you how to cook?"

"Yes, and my sister, Jane."

She drank more wine and had a couple more bites of salad. She ogled him enjoying his food. Damn, he even made chewing sexy. She picked at her food, taking heartier sips of wine.

"You have family in New York, right?"

She nodded. "In Brooklyn. Not nouveau gentrified Brooklyn. Real Brooklyn."

"You're not the first Brooklynite to note the difference." He laughed. "Your family must've been happy to see you."

"Yeah. I really miss them when I'm working. Since I haven't managed in over the past year or so, I had time to do things with them."

"Why didn't you manage clients for a year?"

Well, it sure didn't take long for baggage to pop up. Leona tried to shrug away the tightness building in her neck. "That's off-limits, remember?"

"Ahh." He picked up his wine, taking a long sip.

"Let's just say I was riding out a pretty tumultuous storm."

"Paul?" he stated more than asked.

"Bingo."

They sat in silence for a bit. Small talk proved to be a challenge with their agreement to keep their issues on lockdown.

Leona didn't give up. "The lasagna was amazing. You have to thank your mom for me. Let her know you executed the recipe well."

"Maybe one day you can tell her yourself. She'd like you." He slid a forkful of food into his mouth.

Leona cleared her throat, strangely honored at his decisive statement. "What makes you think she'd like me?"

"You're tough. No…" His eyes narrowed as if psychically receiving information. "Resilient. You know what you want, Leona, even if you don't always know exactly how to get it. It's kind of fun watching you figure it out."

"It's cool that she values those traits."

His mouth cleaned the remnants of lasagna off his fork. "Something we both share."

Her pitter-pattering heart was out of control. He was good. Too good.

"Can I ask you something?" She didn't wait for him to respond. "Why do you like those animal crackers?"

Luke wiped his mouth with a napkin and sat back in his chair. "Have you ever looked at them?"

"Not really."

Luke got up and grabbed a box. When he sat back down he emptied a few into his hand. "Check it out."

Leona observed the details of Luke's sculpted tanned hand before she focused on the lion cracker. She had to admit, someone had spent a lot of time giving the tiny cracker extremely realistic detail. "Wow."

"Yeah, wow," he said as if he'd taken part in its artistry.

His features turned pensive and Leona wanted to question him about it but waited.

"When I was younger, my parents went through a bit of a rough patch. They argued a lot. I was a kid, maybe six or seven, and would get upset. I didn't want them to be mad at each other. To calm me down my mother sat with me, assuring me things were okay and that grown-ups argued sometimes. But every once in a while she'd give me a box of these crackers, dangling them in front of me by the white string. Together, we'd marvel at the detail and eat them."

Her heart opened at the tender memory he shared with her. "They're like your Valium."

"Something like that." He finished the last few bites of his meal and touched her hand. "Want to take a walk on the beach when we're done here?"

"That'd be nice."

She was so confused by him. He was the same but different. She had wanted to touch his hair when he told her the story about his mother. She reminded herself to keep things light.

After dinner, she helped Luke clean up even though he insisted she relax in the living room.

She stored the lasagna in the fridge.

"I know you like dessert, so…" He reached into the freezer, pulled out two ice cream cones, and handed one to her.

"I love waffle cones." She peeled off the paper wrapper.

"It's not a brownie sundae, but they're pretty good."

"Thank you." She licked the fudge topping. "Mmm."

Luke tilted his head and ran his tongue over his bottom lip. His hand stroked her cheek and her fingers formed a bracelet around his wrist. He kissed her, his sigh audible. The kiss was gentle and brief but powerful.

"This way," he said.

The feel of Luke's lips was haunting. Leona followed him to a door at the far end of the house. "You can leave your shoes."

She kicked off her shoes before they left the house.

They strolled down a small shadowy pathway to the beach, but Leona felt safe with Luke. They strolled hand in hand in silence for a long time, finishing their cones and dipping their feet into the water.

"I'm glad you're here, Leona." He stopped walking and faced her. He let her hand go to caress her shoulders before wrapping his arms around her.

Leona wanted to flee in fear but craved his touch more. She laid her head on his chest. *Keep talking.*

"Luke? Why don't you call me Leo?"

His hands stroked her back. "Because everyone calls you Leo."

"So?"

"So, I'm not like everyone else. I also think your name is pretty."

The vibrations of his words rumbled against her head. "I see."

She wrapped her arms around his waist. The combination of ocean air and his musky scent was a heady aphrodisiac.

Luke moved his head down to speak close to her ear. "As much as I want you, Leona, I should have you laid out on the sand. But right now, all I want to do is hold you."

Leona's arousal spread through her body and her already fast beating heart accelerated.

They were being kissed by the moonlight and caressed by the sound of the ocean. It had only been a few days since they'd last seen each other, but they needed this time to connect on this new level.

They separated and Leona skipped into the shallow foamy surf that rode onto the sand. "Maybe you need to cool off."

Her intention was to splash Luke with water, but the gentle splash was more like an overturned bucket and he was doused in seconds.

"Oh my gosh." She stared openmouthed at Luke's wet clothing and then erupted in laughter at his surprised expression. "I totally didn't mean to do that."

"Really? Okay." Luke chased her.

Leona yelped and tried to run but he scooped her up and jogged with her into the ocean.

"No! I can't swim."

"It's shallow enough for you to stand. Hold your breath," he instructed.

She shrieked and then held her breath just before she was thrown into the water. She jumped up, drenched, and wiped salt water from her eyes. "It's so cold."

"That's what you get for splashing me." He waded over and pulled her underwater with him. They broke through the surface and Luke whipped water from his head, as opposed to Leona, who sputtered and dried her face with wet hands and clothes.

"Let me take you out a little further," Luke said, catching his breath.

His hands secured her just below her armpits. Instinctively she put her hands on his shoulders. "Will I be able to stand?"

"Nope."

She shook her head and her heart pounded against her rib cage. With each wave that pushed at her the tightness balled in her chest. She instinctively wanted to press her ear but she was too scared to let Luke go. *Breathe, center. Just don't breathe water into your nose or your ass is going down!* She must have looked petrified.

"I won't let anything happen to you." His arms wrapped around her, pulling her closer.

"I know." *I do?*

"How about we try and if it's too much we'll head back?"

She didn't answer right away because land was calling her so loud she couldn't hear her own thoughts.

"Trust me, Leona."

"Okay."

Luke swam out further and she clutched onto him. He didn't take her too far and floated with her in the water as the waves pushed them back toward land.

"See? You're okay." His breaths were short from treading water.

The initially cold water warmed and was as welcoming as Luke's eyes. She leaned in and kissed him. It was the first initiative to intimacy she had taken since her arrival.

Luke returned her kiss and the warmth of his mouth, in contrast to the coolness of the water, was thrilling.

He ended the kiss. "Let's go back."

Luke swam them to shore and when Leona's feet hit the sandy gravel, she rejoiced and they lugged themselves out of the water and trudged to the house.

They laughed as they dashed through the halls, hand in hand, in their wet clothes. Barefoot, Luke slipped and almost fell on the tile but Leona steadied him.

Even as he guided her, she forgot the layout of the house and kept making wrong turns. "I'm so confused." She could barely get the words out as she giggled.

Luke's laughter filled the house. "This way." He hauled her in the right direction.

They reached his bedroom, shivering and breathless. Luke ducked into the bathroom and returned with a towel for them both.

"I'll get a shower downstairs so you can have some privacy. I'll meet you in the living room."

"Okay." She didn't want privacy—she wanted him to stay—but couldn't get herself to ask him if he would. There was a time when her sexual confidence was intact but after Paul, she'd shut down. It wasn't until now that she understood how deeply she was affected.

After her shower, Leona spun around in a strapless bra and matching underwear, unsure of how to dress.

The time was late and though pajamas made sense, they weren't the attire for this scenario.

Lingerie? Sweats? I'm so out of practice.

She settled on the most loungewear thing she had packed. A short green and gold print smock dress with spaghetti straps tied together at the tops of her shoulders. Her hair was beyond help and had shrunk into tight curls by the end of her shower. The best she could do was to moisturize the bouncy strands that now hung around her shoulders and let them air dry. She slipped into flip-flops and made her way downstairs.

Leona neared the living room where music played. When she entered, she found Luke lounging on the couch with his legs welcomingly open in gray sweatpants and a white tee shirt.

"Hi." She approached and saw him take a visible inhale.

"I've seen your hair out before, but never like this."

Leona smoothed one side, but like a sponge, it inflated again. She had no idea if he liked or hated it.

"Come here, beautiful." Luke patted the seat next to him.

She tripped from the weakness in her legs and fell into the seat. "Is that for me?" She referenced the water bottle on the coffee table.

Luke didn't seem to notice her tumble onto the cushion. "Yeah. It's good for you after being in the ocean, but if you want something stronger I can get that for you."

"Water is fine. Thanks."

Luke's hand went to her hair, and then to the back of her neck.

Leona swigged some water before she set it down on the table.

"What are you thinking, Leona?" His slow massage on her neck was distracting and arousing. Her breathing had quickened in just a few seconds.

"How did we get here?" She glanced over at him. Though he smiled, his eyes roved over her, revealing what he craved.

Luke hooked his finger under the string of her dress. "Do you regret your decision to come?" He slid the thin strap down her shoulder.

"No." Leona saw the rise and fall of her own bosom. "I just don't know how we start."

"We've already started."

Chapter Eighteen

When their lips touched, her body quivered as if releasing a year's worth of self-control. She lifted her dress to her waist, straddling him as they sunk into desire. His musk mixed with the sweet pear and lemon perfume of her heavy curls, creating a drugging aroma.

Luke moaned at her gesture and caressed her back as their kiss deepened. His warm, supportive hands dropped down to cup the soft flesh of her rear. His mouth swallowed hers as his arms tightened around her midsection and squeezed.

When she exhaled, he inhaled her hot breath. Luke's hardness poked against the material of his sweatpants and through the barrier of her panties. Her insides had never felt more vacant. The music continued to play in the background, but Leona's only focus was on what Luke was doing to her.

Luke released her mouth, swaddling her into a hug. Though she missed his lips, she welcomed the brief break and laid her chin on his shoulder. His heart thumped against her chest, competing with the pounding of hers. He stroked her back and his hand meandered to the straps of her dress. Leona held her breath in excitement.

Luke tugged at the ties on each strap to undo them. "Is this going too fast for you, Leona?" His hand maneuvered inside the material of her dress and she practically jumped out of her body when he caressed her back.

"No," Leona said. "I climbed on you, remember?"

He gave a light, deep chuckle and grabbed the top of the dress, peeling the material down to her waist.

"Good. Because I really want to fuck you." He whispered the seductive words into her ear and she was heady from the blood rushing through her.

She pressed her hands against his chest, separating from him enough to see the intense desire in his eyes. Her hands went to either side of his face.

"Well, I really want you to fuck me." She grazed his lower lip with her finger.

Luke arched an eyebrow at her bold response.

Leona shrugged. She went to kiss him but he backed away.

"Let me see you." Luke's eyes dropped to her bra-covered breasts.

He had delivered the gentlest of commands and Leona felt compelled to obey. With shaky hands, she reached back and unhooked the undergarment. As she flung it on the couch, Luke's hands massaged her flesh. She moaned at the rightness of his touch. His mouth joined his caress and her breasts rejoiced with hardening nipples.

Her fingers messed his hair, and she drowned in the warm sensation of his mouth as he suckled. His teeth delicately scraped the hardened buds and she threw her head back.

"Luke," she bit out and tightened her grip on his head and neck.

Luke secured his hands under her seat and lifted her.

"Whoa." Leona held on, fastening her legs around his waist.

"I've got you." He carried her the distance to the bedroom.

"For someone who thinks I'm only light for about five minutes, you sure like to pick me up," she whispered against his ear. Her teeth trapped his soft earlobe before teasing it with her tongue.

"Mmm," he moaned, and smacked her ass. "It was the best excuse I had at the time."

"Oh." The light sting of his punishment aroused. She kissed his neck and then his lips before burying her head at the crook of his neck. She moved her hair to the side to prevent it from obstructing his view.

They reached the bedroom and Luke set her down. He dialed down the dimmer switch until the room was a dusky glow and started to undress.

Leona pranced over to the switch and spun it to its highest setting. Luke squinted from the sudden brightness.

Leona shielded her chest with one arm. "I don't want to miss this."

Seduction spread across Luke's face. "Should I do a strip tease or is normal okay for you?"

Leona bit her lip to stifle a smile. "Normal's fine."

"If you get to watch, so do I." He pointed to her shielded breasts.

Leona's hands dropped to her sides and her dress hung at her waist.

He kept his eyes on her as he gathered the material at the bottom of his shirt and stretched it over his head. His movements were slow and determined. His lean, well-defined chest and abdominal muscles were in full view, as was the tribal tattoo snaking up the left side of his body. The artwork spilled onto his belly and crept around to his back. Leona was alive with anticipation at the thought of finally seeing and touching the ink that hid under his sweatpants.

A thin layer of hair feathered his chest and formed a T shape as it extended to his lower abdomen until it disappeared under the cover of his clothes. The chiseled pelvic muscles at his hip guided Leona's eyes down to his hands working on the drawstring of his sweatpants.

Luke untied the drawstring and angled his sweats down at the rim. The material fell to the floor and he stepped out of them. He wore boxer briefs that highlighted the sexiness of his sculpted body and olive skin. His green-gray eyes commanded her to do his bidding.

The protruding outline between his legs motivated her to wiggle out of the dress. Now, in only her lace panties, Leona sashayed over to him.

"Comfortable?" he asked.

Hell no. "Yes."

"Good." Luke pushed her to the bed with force.

Leona squealed as she landed none too gracefully on the bed but exhilarated from the shot of adrenaline.

Luke crawled on top of her and she reached up to cradle his cheek, guiding his face to hers. Passion flared between them and her heart banged against her rib cage. She was in Luke's bed, kissing him, and there was no place else she wanted to be than here with him.

He guided her opened legs wider and nestled between them. Leona collapsed against endless pillows that smelled like him.

Luke pressed his arousal against her and kissed her

deeper. His mouth again left her lips to suck and nibble the flesh of her bosom. He balanced on his knees, grabbed hold of both her legs and heaved her to him. Leona gasped as her butt slammed into his knees and she was spread for his viewing.

Thank goodness I wore nice underwear. Leona hoped he liked the black, high cut, lace panties she chose. Luke eyed the embroidered barrier, indicating it wouldn't be on for much longer.

His hand teased her inner thigh and the triangular indentation of bone and heated flesh that framed her center. His fingers targeted the tender, sensitive folds of skin through the thin layer of her panties. Leona concentrated on his every move.

Luke's thumb found entry inside the moist material and gently massaged the swollen button. The electric sensation spread through her. Her labored breath and her hips wiggled under his touch.

Luke's lips curved upward, satisfied with her reaction. He was adorable even when he was being pompous about his bedroom skills. Affection oozed from her fingertips as she reached for him.

He pulled his ruthless thumb away and descended to capture her lips. As his tongue entered her mouth, his hand crept into the top of her panties and curved until they found the entry point of her pussy. His fingers slipped inside of her and, now lubricated with the honey of her arousal, once again massaged her clit. Leona whimpered and her body jerked in pleasure as Luke's fingers glided over her.

"You're drenched, Leona. Dripping." His voice was heavy and unrecognizable, and his eyes were fixated between her legs as he moved his fingers in and out of her ravenous center.

Leona squirmed and moaned. She had been touched there before but it had been so long and Luke seemed to know exactly what to do to send her soaring. He released her and stood. She delighted at the protrusion of his maleness through his underwear, constricted and angled for entry.

He grabbed hold of her panties at her hip and pulled them down. Leona bridged her hips and he peeled the material over her rump. With her legs in the air Luke stripped her panties off and tossed the lace aside.

Leona sat up, yanked his boxer briefs down to his knees, and gulped at the sight of him. The elusive tattoo swirled and curved down his pelvis, disappearing into the dark hair at the base of his shaft, but beyond the ink, was Luke's size. Leona reprimanded herself for ever considering declining Luke's invitation to come to San Francisco. Seeing Luke in his birthday suit was worth every mile traveled.

Luke's body shook with laughter. "What should I make of that reaction, Leona?"

"It near poked my eye out." She needed humor to calm the growing excitement bubbling inside her.

Luke laughed even harder. "What am I going to do with you?"

Eye level with his bulging cock, Leona wanted nothing more than to pleasure him and have Luke please her in every way possible.

"If you don't know, I have some ideas." She stretched her lips around his hardness. She was tentative at first as she adjusted her jaw, and then claimed him with skilled assurance. Her hands held him at the base where she could feel the soft skin of his sac. He glistened from the slick coating.

Luke's laughter ceased and he sucked in air. "Oh shit." He descended backward onto the bed and pillows. He stopped her long enough to kick off his underwear, and then guided her head back to him.

Leona simpered up at him, kissed over to the left side of his sculpted pelvis, and planted teasing kisses where the rest of his tattoo decorated his skin. The stiffened organ twitched in anticipation of her mouth. Her fingers twirled and played with the hair covering him at the base.

"Leona." His plea motivated her and she decided her name had never sounded better.

Her greedy mouth once again covered his cock. Her tongue pleasured him and her cheek muscles hollowed as she sucked. His taste was like heroin and she was addicted. She savored the salty beginnings of his essence and he continued to harden. His skin smelled of soap and musk. The drugging aroma mixed with the scent of wetness from her mouth on his skin and the fruity fragrance of her hair as it fell on his stomach.

Luke pushed back her hair, his features decorated in strained gratitude. Gratitude was never an expression she had seen on Paul's face. *Fuck! Why did I think of him?* Paul had selfishly taken his pleasure without much consideration for hers. But Luke? He was different. He was with her.

"Your mouth feels so good on me, Leona." Luke's torso heaved at his breath-filled declaration.

As Luke stroked her head, his hissing and moaning made her work harder. She wanted him to only think of her and always remember how she made him feel.

She swallowed him deep, controlling her gag reflex as she sucked and tongued him with one goal in mind— to satisfy him.

His fingers tightened in her hair. "Leona," he called and hauled her off his cock. "Come here." He sat her up and then leaned over to the night table.

Luke pulled out an unopened box of condoms and Leona was happy that the packaging was still sealed. He removed a condom and handed it to her.

"Hold this." He put the box on the night table.

They were on a lovers' getaway and Luke had already given her so many memories from dinner to an impromptu dip in the ocean. Leona wanted to deliver a memory of her own. She tore the wrapper and popped the condom from the casing. She placed the tip in her mouth and collapsed the latex at the tip with her tongue.

Luke began to speak, but stopped to observe her.

She gripped him with one hand and put the other on his defined chest for support. She hatted the condom on the head of his member with her mouth and began to roll the latex down the length of him with her lips. His shaft simultaneously disappeared into her mouth.

Luke caressed her arm up and down and when she was done moved her to straddle him. "I'm going to fuck the shit out of you." He kissed her and lifted her just enough to guide himself inside her.

Leona melted over him, proud of herself for eliciting such a feral response. He was so big and hard and as he slid into her, she gasped and licked her lips.

"Take what you can, Leona." He stroked up her back and down the sides of her arms. He bent his knees slightly to brace her from behind and tilted her backwards with his hand. The other hand was on her hip, urging her to move with him. He wet his thumb in his mouth and fondled the swollen button at her center. He could have easily just taken his own pleasure but Luke was different from any other man she'd been with. He was deliberate in each method he used to please her.

Leona squirmed under his caress and placed her palms on his shins behind her as leverage to lift her body. She trotted up and down and moseyed back and forth as her insides flowered open to house him.

When she was with Paul, he had never taken her to such heights. He could make her come, but it had lacked the intimacy and love she'd always craved. *Love with Luke?*

Luke impacted her emotions so easily and control slipped through her fingers. Fear and doubt seeped into her muscles and she drifted away from the delicious present. Luke's attention was immediate and he hooked his hand around her neck and drew her lips to his.

"Stay with me," he breathed against her lips.

The combination of his words and the way his eyes penetrated her, grounded her to this moment.

Leona couldn't speak so she nodded in response, moaning in a whirlwind of desire as he continued to hit her G-spot. The stimulation from his thumb commanded her to move aggressively against him, making her forget the past, her reservations, and her shield—if only for a little while. Leona wanted more of him inside of her. She pawed at him and encouraged him to go deeper, meeting his hard thrusts every time.

Leona stroked his hand. "Don't stop."

Luke caressed her with more intensity but still gentle enough to stimulate her. She felt the tingling from

In Tune

her G-spot growing as she continued to gallop on top of him.

He was her lifeline and she clasped his tattooed forearm. When that didn't root her, she grabbed at his chest as she rode him at high speed. Luke tightened his grip on her to secure them both for her arrival.

Leona squeezed her eyes shut as her internal muscles suctioned onto him and swallowed him deeper before wildly contracting. She cried out and her sporadic breathing sang through the room as she bucked and trembled against him. He continued to drive into her, stimulating every nerve—branding her and ruining her for all others.

She had experienced pleasure before but the sensations that rocked her now were otherworldly. Leona lost all control and she clutched onto Luke several different ways. No matter which way she held him, she wasn't prepared for her orgasm. The waves washed over her again and again, increasing in their power.

"Leona," Luke called and tried to manage her flailing arms. If someone had walked in on them at that moment, they would have thought they were fighting.

"Luke! Oh God, Luke!" She called his name over and over until she bowed over him. She'd missed this sexual, passionate side of her that she'd suppressed along with the career she loved. Luke had not only kindled her fires again, but also brought her to an explosive eruption.

Her body stiffened, then quivered. She panted and groaned into his shoulder and her fingers dug unforgivingly into him. He still pumped into her and she circled her hips to take every bit of pleasure.

They moved in unison and Luke's hold tightened. He sprung up and wrapped his arms around her waist. His powerful thighs jerked and he shouted out his own intense arrival into her chest. The release of his satisfaction sounded like a beautiful and perfect mating call. She was losing it, but she was happy to be lost as his snug hold on her midsection constricted her breathing.

Leona continued to shake against him as the slightest movement from either of them sent delectable jolts through her.

Luke rubbed her back and as her breathing slowed, her spasms subsided.

"You okay?" he asked.

Leona buried her face in his neck. *What the hell just happened to me?*

"Look at me, Leona."

"I can't. Not yet."

"Why?"

Leona shook her head against his shoulder. She was certain the embarrassment from her first and wild sexual performance with him danced on her face.

He rubbed her back and kissed her collarbone. "Are you hurt at all?"

The concern in his voice forced her to meet his worried expression.

"No, I'm not hurt." But she was rattled by the sexual and emotional nakedness they had just experienced. She eased off of him and he grasped the base of his member to secure the condom. Her stressed joints and exhausted muscles reminded her of their wild exercise.

Luke removed the latex shield and tossed it in the trash bin by the bed. Leona lay next to him, staring at his shining member.

He touched her chin and brought her attention back

to his face. "Though I enjoy you admiring my dick, I'm asking you a serious question. Did I hurt you?"

"I'm fine, Luke. That was just…intense."

"That's an understatement." He went to the bathroom and cleaned himself before returning with a warm washcloth for her. Once back on the bed, he pulled her into his arms.

Leona laid her head on his chest and inhaled his scent. He'd pleasured her far beyond anything she'd ever experienced. She brushed her leg against his, making it clear she wanted more. When Luke kissed her deeply, his tongue playing in her mouth, she wondered if more would ever be enough.

Chapter Nineteen

Leona woke up to hands on her. She forgot where she was until the soreness all over her body reminded her of what had transpired the night before. She rolled over to see Luke with both eyes closed and smiling. His long, thick eyelashes stirred. She continued to watch him and he opened one eye.

She giggled. "You cannot be sleeping."

"I was dreaming about you."

"Yeah, right." Leona sat up to get out of the bed.

Luke pulled her back to him. "I don't think so. I've been waiting hours for you to wake up."

"Hours?"

"Okay, an hour." He flashed a mischievous grin.

"I have to pee." Leona jumped out of bed and grabbed the closest thing to cover herself with, which was Luke's shirt from last night. "I'll be right back."

Luke pouted. "Hurry."

She hopped into the bathroom to do her business. *I can't let him experience this dragon breath.*

She found her toothbrush and tried to be quick. When Luke wandered into the bathroom and planted himself behind her, it was apparent she wasn't moving fast enough.

"Right back, huh?"

Leona brushed her teeth as gracefully as possible, communicating with grunts, exaggerated expressions, and eyebrow lifts. She waved her hand in front of her mouth and shook her head, noting her bad breath.

"I don't care about morning breath." Luke pressed himself against her and touched her arms. "I want you."

That he understood her made her cheese through the brushing.

Luke lifted the shirt above her waist, examining her in the large mirror above the sink. From behind, his hand burrowed between her legs and rubbed her.

Leona held on to the side of the sink and almost choked on the foaming toothpaste. She opened her legs to make room for his hand. He trailed kisses down her neck as he continued to massage her. His fingers entered her and Leona moaned. Her brushing slowed to the tempo of his fingers, sliding in and out of the drenched slit of her pussy.

She spoke to him with the toothbrush in her mouth.

"What was that?" The green in his eyes twinkled brighter.

With lazy lids, Leona hastily rinsed her mouth and toothbrush. She honestly didn't know how she could even function with the way he raised her temperature with his touches.

"What are you waiting for?" Leona now had both hands placed on the sink, desperate for him to fill her. She pushed back on his fingers, nudging them further inside her.

"You feel so good, Leona. I wasn't lying when I said I was dreaming about you. I was dreaming about how soft you feel, here." His fingers slid through the folds of skin. "And here."

Luke massaged her clit and strength left her body. She bent over the counter to keep from falling. At that moment, Luke could have asked her to jump off a building and she would have thought it was a brilliant idea. His touch was magic and she was charmed.

Luke removed his hand and Leona glanced over her shoulder to see Luke stiff to capacity and condom readied.

When the hell did he put that on?

She was glad she didn't have to force the conversation or ask him every time about contraception. She relaxed and prepared herself for the ride.

Luke sunk into her and Leona's knees buckled from his stiffness against her internal walls. His one arm wound around her midsection. He held her as he burrowed into her from behind. He slid his other hand down her stomach and between her legs to again caress the delicate inner folds of her center.

She moaned and gripped even tighter to the sides of the sink. The spearmint smell from the toothpaste tickled her nose, along with Luke's strong male scent as his temperature rose.

He continued to meet her gaze in the mirror. He squeezed her breasts through the tee shirt and then his hands traveled under for skin-to-skin contact.

Leona moaned and her arousal skyrocketed when his fingers pinched her hard and tender nipples.

Luke tugged roughly at the shirt. "Get rid of it, Leona."

Without hesitation she shed the shirt and reached

behind for him. The reflection of their naked bodies as they pleased each other only heightened her arousal.

Luke began to pull out.

"Don't. Please," Leona pleaded through the mirror.

Luke teased her opening with the tip of his member and Leona thought he would deny her, but he plunged inside her and pumped relentlessly. She called out as the beginnings of her arrival burned her insides.

"You're close." Luke spoke close to her ear, most of his words decorated in short heavy breaths. "I can see it all over that beautiful face."

She observed herself and shame bloomed in her chest as if she'd been caught spying on someone else. She lowered her eyes.

"Look, Leona," Luke whispered in her ear. He nibbled and sucked on her earlobe. "See how fucking hot you are."

At his seductive order, she forced her eyes to her image. Leona had never seen herself like this—a voyeur to her own experience.

His words coupled with the sensations growing within her. Witnessing her own pleasure pushed her over the edge, and she groaned as orgasmic vibrations rocked her. "Yes!" she cried.

One hand held the sink and the other grabbed Luke from behind begging him to increase the speed and power of everything that he was doing.

Luke obliged her with quicker flicks of his fingers at her core and the pumping action of his hips. He followed with his own thunderous coming as Leona trembled against him.

She turned on the sink and splashed water on her neck and between her breasts.

Luke laughed.

To her surprise, Luke hardened again inside her. *He's a freakin' machine.*

She splashed him with water.

Laughter rumbled in his chest. He left her insides unoccupied and she heard the snap of the latex that sheathed him. He tugged her toward the bed where last night's magic happened, discarding the condom on the way.

"I can't get enough of you."

Leona shimmied onto the bed. Luke again readied himself for her and was inside the slick confines of her center again.

Leona surrendered to his need and the wild bliss of being filled by him again. Luke was by no means a selfish lover, but she knew from the feverish flush on his face that this time was for him. He took everything she gave him, and when his orgasm all but pushed her off the bed, he clutched her in his arms. Even in his heightened state, he wouldn't let her fall.

"Shit, Leona." He blinked rapidly as if trying to regain focused vision.

Leona's insides ached and her muscles were fatigued. She wanted to sleep even though she just woke up. She closed her eyes, her breathing shallow.

Luke withdrew and gave her thigh a playful slap. "You need food."

Leona opened her eyes. "Lasagna?"

"No." He chuckled and trapped her in his arms. "I have something better."

She kissed his chest before resting her head against it and listened as his quick heartbeat started to slow. Like her, he was sweaty and weak, but his embrace was no less blissful. He squeezed her tighter and kissed her temple.

"If we don't get out of this bed, I can't guarantee you'll walk again." His words vibrated against her head.

"Yes, I notice you have quite the appetite." She rubbed her feet against his calf.

"Me? You're the enchantress keeping me worked up." He kissed her lips.

They stayed in bed a while longer before Luke got up. "I'll be back." He jogged downstairs and in a few minutes returned with some fresh fruit for her.

"Aww…thanks." Leona leaned over the bowl to kiss him.

"I put on a pot of coffee in case you wanted some but I'm taking you into town for breakfast."

"Okay." She noticed Luke wasn't eating. "You're not going to have any?"

He shook his head. "I'm going to catch some waves while the getting is good. I'll have some after I surf. I don't want to cramp up. Want to come watch?"

"Hell yeah," she said.

"Cool, then let's go."

Luke cleaned himself up before he put on a gray and black wetsuit with an orange symbol on the front.

"Sexy. You're all rippled and everything." Leona's commentary made him chuckle. Though she made light of his figure, Luke's body had some magnetic hold on her and she was in a constant state of heat.

"Let's go before I sprain myself getting hard in this seal suit." He bowed down to bite the flesh on her rump.

She laughed and kicked her feet, amazed by how quickly things had changed between them. Teasing and laughing with him was as natural as fucking him.

She finally hopped out of bed. "You go on ahead. I'll meet you out there."

Luke pivoted several times before finally leaving.

Leona flung herself back on the bed. "Oh my gosh."

Luke was the best lover she had ever had. His stamina was inhuman and even though they had already experienced several intimate sessions, she couldn't get enough of him either.

Keep it in perspective.

The warning didn't do much since Luke had just consumed her with pleasure. Being with him forced her to turn off and when thoughts of the tour and the repercussions of these few days popped up she pushed them down.

Leona showered and dressed, Luke's hands a ghostly imprint with every move she made. Their intimacy elevated so fast her head spun but it was no comparison to how her emotions responded to his care, his stories, and the memories they'd created since her arrival.

Leona snagged a bottle of water from the fridge for Luke and brought it, and a cup of coffee, with her to the beach.

She found the sandy route and continued until she spotted a few surfers way out in the ocean, certain one of them was Luke.

He'd been out there for about an hour now. He loved the water and had made it a point to tell her to schedule a significant break in the tour to be in California. He must have needed this.

Luke rode the wave for about eight or ten seconds before he "wiped out." "Oooh!" Leona laughed at his awkward tumble underwater.

He disappeared from view. When his head broke

through the surface of the water and he shook his hair, Leona exhaled and her shoulders eased back to neutral.

"Whoa."

Soon, Luke glided in on his board, and paddled toward the beach. Once on land, he tucked his board under his arm and ran to her.

I'm in an episode of Baywatch.

Leona hopped off the rock as elegantly as possible so as not to dirty her white jeans. She put her hand up and gave him a high five. "That was cool." She wanted to kiss him, but hesitated.

"Thanks." Luke hooked his free arm around her waist and kissed her with ocean-seasoned lips.

"This wetsuit is getting very uncomfortable." Luke mumbled against her lips.

"Yeah?" She continued to kiss him.

"Yes." Luke pulled her closer.

"Well, I have just the thing for that."

"Oh yeah?"

"Mmm-hmm." Leona grabbed the water and gave it to him.

Luke laughed out loud and nearby seagulls squawked at the disturbance.

"You said you love the water. I aim to please." She cheesed. "I thought you'd be thirsty."

Luke downed half of the bottle. "Thanks."

"See? I've got you covered." She grabbed her coffee mug and they strolled along the beach to the house.

"I'd love to teach you how to surf. It's a travesty you don't swim." He swigged more water. "I could teach you."

"Many have tried and failed." Leona recalled her near drowning experience when her brother Mitchell decided that all she needed was to be thrown into the deep end.

Luke glinted at her. "I'll teach you one day." There was sureness to his statement.

Leona's stomach growled.

He stopped short. "What the hell was that?"

She blushed and rubbed her stomach. "I'm hungry from all that…our…activity."

"Then let's get you fed because we haven't even gotten started yet, Leona."

Her bare feet stumbled in the sand and she almost spilled coffee on her turquoise tank top.

Luke chuckled. "C'mon. I know a place."

They arrived at the house and Luke left her briefly to secure his surfboard in the garage, and then peeled out of his wetsuit. Leona's eyes stalked his naked body, taking in the lethal combination of his powerful thighs and tight, muscular ass. She reminisced about how his strong chest rippled against her torso. Then, the vision of him was gone as he dashed to the bedroom to shower and dress.

While Luke got ready, Leona checked her phone for emails and messages to make sure that social media for Luke remained active. She saw he had posted something early in the morning.

"Feeling inspired. New music coming soon." She didn't read into the message and was happy that even with her presence, he was communicating with the fans as usual.

A few emails needed her response, but no emergencies. *Thank God, nothing about the gallery surfaced.* She didn't want to keep scanning and taint her time with Luke so she shut it down. Luke had his one-off performance in a few days and their time would be over.

You just got here. Stop, before you freak out and leave.

"Ready?" He returned and interrupted her thoughts.

Luke was dressed in tan cargo pants, a gray V-neck tee shirt and a faded brown cap. He wore a black woven leather bracelet on his wrist. His scent drifted over and she wanted to gorge on every part of him.

"Yeah. Let me grab my bag."

"You don't need it," Luke called to her as she jogged up the stairs to the bedroom.

"I always need it." She was back in an instant.

She followed him to the garage, a part of the house she hadn't seen yet.

Luke set the alarm before he closed the door. The filthiest pickup Leona had ever seen greeted them.

"Sorry about the truck. It's really for off-roading and surfing in some remote areas. I rarely clean it, but I should have at least rinsed it off." Luke guided her around to a Land Rover that shined like new with a dark gray exterior. He opened her door for her and Leona climbed into the plush elegance of the vehicle.

As he mounted the SUV, the car waddled with his movements.

"All buckled up?"

"Buckled." Temped to fiddle with all the gadgetry in the vehicle, Leona shook her head. "Boys and their toys."

"Yup." Luke started the ignition and the car roared to life. "And you know what the best part about this toy is?"

"Do tell."

Luke turned the stereo on and up. "The speakers." His boyish grin spread to his ears and he bobbed his head to the music.

She flipped him the sign of the horns and stuck out her tongue as the bass vibrated around her. "Nice."

He opened the garage door with the press of a button and they were on their way.

On the drive into town, Luke pointed out a few landmarks and promised to show her more after they ate. He parked in an eclectic area with tattooed pedestrians and a cool, communal vibe. Whenever Leona had been to San Francisco she was working. It was nice to experience the scenery carefree.

"I love it here." Leona mused at the graffiti art, the colored houses, and the shops.

Luke intertwined his fingers with hers as they crossed the street.

"This is the Haight-Ashbury part of San Fran. It's my favorite part of town. There's a place I go called The Naked Café. They're a bar slash restaurant slash club. Basically, it's an everything kind of place."

Leona was an admitted people watcher and here, the melding sea of bohemian and hippie culture mixed with the rawness of the city streets. She felt welcomed even among strangers and tourists. Strangers and tourists with cameras aimed at graffiti on buildings and in her direction.

Photographers. Paparazzi. Leona came to her senses. She and Luke promenaded. In public. Together.

She chewed the inside of her lip. "We're really exposed here, Luke. I wouldn't advise this. I—I…" Leona scouted for media. The whirling motion made her dizzy and she swayed in her stance. They shouldn't be here. *She* shouldn't be here. Unprotected like this, they were fodder for the media.

"It's cool, Leona. I blend." He pulled a baseball cap out from one of his cargo pants pockets and fitted it on his head. He continued onward against her objections until he noticed she wasn't moving.

"Hey." Luke repeated a few times and squeezed her hands in his but she withdrew.

"This is a bad idea." She continued to search her surroundings.

"What are you looking for, Leona?"

"Paparazzi. They hide everywhere—parking lots, behind your parents' car, your bathroom. They're relentless."

"Come inside." Luke led her into a small sunlit foyer before the main dining area of the restaurant. He rubbed her shoulders. "Breathe."

She inhaled a heaving breath and as she let it out, her chest ached. She anchored on Luke and chugged a bit more air until her paranoia ceased. The anxiety had been the catalyst for her yearlong hiatus. She had been managing it with breathing and hadn't had frequent attacks anymore, but she was still susceptible to the occasional freak-out.

"I'm sorry," Leona whispered. Despite the cap Luke wore, the sunlight streaming into the foyer found his face and she saw the stress lines around his mouth.

"It's okay, baby." Luke's soothing strokes ran up and down her arms. "I know how sadistic the media can be."

They'd had such an amazing morning and she didn't want to ruin their time together. "I didn't mean to lose it like—"

The part of her brain that produced words came to a screeching halt when Luke lifted his hand up to massage her left ear. The tenderness in his strokes made her eyes water.

"Is this okay?"

She nodded.

"What else can I do? Tell me what you need. We can go back. Whatever you need, baby."

Her breathing decelerated and deepened. "Just give me a minute." Her hand went to his forearm. "Don't stop."

"I won't."

People entered and exited the restaurant but she focused on Luke as he did on her.

"I'm better," she announced. The ball in her chest dissolved and her stomach growled. "I'm really hungry."

Luke smiled, yet stress lines continued to crease his face. "That, I can help with."

The Naked Café was lively, but not packed. Its open beach feel with rustic wood walls and nautical memorabilia on the wall was a treat, even post-mini-meltdown.

"Wait here. I'll get us some seats." Luke dashed to the bar and greeted the bartender.

A sharp, loud whistle cracked the humming chatter in the room. "Bobby," the bartender called and pointed to Luke. Luke said something else to the bartender, who handed him a glass of orange juice.

A very tanned, and heavily bearded man in a black tee shirt and khaki shorts greeted and hugged Luke.

She smiled at the greeting between the two men.

Luke chatted with the man and they both glanced in her direction. Luke motioned her over.

"Bobby, this is Leona Sable."

The man was shorter than Luke and wore a charcoal cap atop his uncombed, dirty blond hair. He was fit, yet old enough to house quite a bit of gray hair in his beard.

"Nice to meet you, Leona." Bobby gathered her into a gentle hug.

Leona stiffened, taken aback by the kindness in his hug, and wondered if Luke had mentioned her meltdown. It didn't matter since the nurturing embrace reminded her of her father, easing her worries.

"You, too. Please, call me Leo." She peered up at Bobby and could tell the man spent a lot of time in the sun.

"Welcome to The Naked Café." Bobby ran a hand over his beard. "Me and this guy go way back."

Luke handed her the glass of orange juice he'd been holding. Her post-meltdown headache started to needle over her left eye. She took a long sip.

"When I first started out," Luke said, "I was broke, with just some turntables and records. Bobby fed me, sheltered me, and let me play here. He was the one that introduced me to surfing."

Leona's heart warmed at their familial relationship. "It must be pretty incredible to see how popular he is now?"

"Oh yeah, but he's still the same, grounded boy." Bobby slapped Luke loudly on the back.

Luke winced and Leona delighted in their horseplay.

"Well, let's get you guys a spot. I hear you're starving, Leo," Bobby said.

"Yes." She nudged Luke.

Bobby seated them outside and the cool air aided in her recovery.

"Thanks, man." Luke seated her.

"My pleasure. I gotta get back but Taylor and Kim will be by with beverage service and your food in a little bit."

Luke stopped him. "I know you're busy, but come by and sit with us for a little bit before we go."

"Yes. I want to hear some embarrassing Luke stories." Leona flickered her eyebrows at Bobby.

"Only the clean ones." He winked. "Enjoy your meal."

Luke studied her as he sat. "You good?" he asked when Bobby was out of earshot.

"Yeah, I mean, my head hurts a little but this OJ is giving me life." She drank some more.

Luke continued his inspection.

"I'm okay. Really." She played with her hands. "Thanks for helping."

Luke's chest inflated with questions but she was glad that he didn't push for answers. "I went ahead and ordered for us," he announced.

"What did you order?" Leona scooted her chair closer to him.

"Breakfast."

Perplexed, Leona persisted. "Yeah, but what?"

"No clue," was Luke's innocent response.

Leona shook her head.

Luke adjusted his hat to the back so she could see his face. "I'm not being funny. Check out the menu."

She picked up the menu and true to Luke's words the menu read "Breakfast Food" under "Breakfast," and the same format continued for lunch and dinner. There were no further descriptions under the headers, just the prices.

"What the...?"

"Told ya. It's kind of an adventure to eat here."

Leona went back to the menu and read the statement on top. "We cook what seems like a good idea for the day. Everything is organic, delicious, and good for you. We promise. So, if you have allergies or specific dietary restrictions, this may not be the place for you to eat. We get it! We have a great bar. So, come have a drink with us, even if you can't eat with us." Leona laughed. "Seriously? That's so unlike a Californian place."

"The menu's been like that ever since Bobby opened the place over twenty years ago." Luke stole the menu from her hands.

"I'm excited to see what they bring out."

Two servers arrived moments later with a variety of food on their trays. It was like having a buffet at their table.

"So, here's how this works." The young man's spikey dark brown Mohawk remained a gelled sculpture atop his head. "Take whatever you want. Don't worry. We have lots more cooking. Think of me as your own personal server. I'll provide you with whatever you desire."

Leona raised her eyebrows. She couldn't miss the double meaning in the young man's words. His blue eyes lingered on her.

"Hey," Luke called to Mohawk guy.

Leona jumped at Luke's volume. Her eyes shifted between the two males and she stifled a laugh.

"Sorry." Mohawk guy's lips twisted to one side.

"This guy loves the ladies." Luke shook his head. "She's with me."

The young lady laughed and focused on her service. "I have all the yummy bread kind of food, like toast, hash browns, and pancakes. It can get overwhelming, so if you can't make a decision, we'll be back."

"Oh, I know what I want." Leona began taking food off both trays.

"That's her 'I love food' dance." Luke referred to her twirling arms as he piled food onto his plate.

"We'll be back." Mohawk guy's eyes again lingered on Leona.

"I'm right here, man." Luke's voice boomed at the young man.

"He's harmless." Leona giggled. "And cute."

"I'm going to give him an ass whupping if he keeps it up. I know where he lives."

She giggled. "Come on. Let's eat."

Leona was so famished she ate quicker than usual, inhaling bites of her eggs and hash browns.

"It's so good," she said in between savory sweet bites of bacon and pancakes.

The young servers arrived with beverage service. They navigated around the restaurant, never missing a single person, and socialized like they were feeding friends.

"That's amazing." Leona watched them move.

Luke swallowed his food. "What?"

"How they never bump into each other with this moving buffet." Leona ate more of her food.

"Yeah, it took me a while to figure it out."

Leona didn't want to tell him she already knew how it worked.

"Let me guess, you just did."

She nodded. "They're moving in overlapping figure eights."

"It took me much longer," Luke grumbled.

"I like to solve puzzles. You know, figure things out." She blushed. She must have sounded like a geek. "Dorky, huh?"

"I think that's cool." He chewed his food.

Her blood sugar started to level out and though she continued to eat, her movements slowed. "I love this place."

"Bobby makes this place awesome. Before my sister moved out here, he was the closest thing to family I had."

"He has a welcoming spirit. It's good to have people like that in your life."

"He's made a lot of friends over the years. We keep coming back."

Luke hadn't just brought her anywhere. He'd brought her to a place that was special to him and his family.

"Are you close with your family?" she asked, sipping her coffee.

"Yeah. I see my sister, Jane, regularly. She and her husband come out to my shows when they can."

"And your parents? Do you see them often?"

Luke wiped his mouth, pausing a bit longer. "Not so much."

He didn't say much more and Leona wondered if they had a falling out.

"Are you close with them, too?" She should have stopped her inquisition, but she was close with her family and was curious about his.

"I love my parents very much, Leona. We just... I have some things to work on before I see them again."

"How long has it been since you've seen them?" *Leona Sable. Stop.*

He sighed and shifted in his seat. "It's been a while. Almost two years."

Leona would have understood if he snapped at her. She had a hard time letting things go even when it was an obvious sore spot.

"They must miss you. I'm sure you miss them, too."

"Yeah, I do. I hope to see them again soon. Maybe when the tour hits Chicago."

Chicago was his hometown. That would be a great opportunity for a reunion.

Luke finished his food and then reached for her plate and swapped it with his empty one.

"Hey. I'm eating that." She reached for the plate but Luke moved it away from her.

Luke continued to eat from her plate. "Hardly."

Leona clucked her tongue and its loud noise drew Luke's attention. She ignored him and pinched a piece of pancake from the plate, and then popped it in her mouth.

"Careful. I have big plans for that mouth."

Leona choked on her food. "Oh my gosh." She searched for eavesdroppers.

"Don't get shy on me, now." He scooted his chair even closer.

"I'm not shy. I'm modest. There's a difference." The heat in her cheeks told a different story.

Luke rubbed his leg against hers under the table. "Trust me. I know." His eyebrows flitted and amusement curled the corners of his mouth.

Bobby came back to sit with them and she was grateful. Her flushed face needed to cool down.

"Get a room, people." Bobby didn't miss a beat. "Glad to see you finally brought a lady friend here."

"What do you mean, Bobby?" Leona's interest went from zero to ten.

"Nothing." Luke attempted to quiet Bobby.

"Luke's never brought a woman here to see us, not even that Ivy woman you were…"

"Bobby!"

Leona's ears perked at Luke's volume.

"Bring it down." Bobby's paternal tone instantly changed Luke's disposition.

"Sorry." Luke shifted in his seat, but seemed to relax.

"Everything okay, guys?" Leona sat so erect she grew a few inches.

"We're good, Leo. Just a misunderstanding between old friends, right, Luke?" Bobby stroked his beard as he studied Luke, but once again appeared to be in good humor.

"Right." Luke's restless movements suggested otherwise.

Leona wasn't about to be the only one left out of this saucepot full of drama. "What's this about Ivy?"

"We had an agreement, Leona."

"You knew that wasn't going to last long, right?"

Luke's entire face frowned and he reddened through his tanned skin. "I—"

"You haven't told her?" Bobby laced his fingers and placed them on his belly.

Leona wanted to cool Luke's growing temper but she craved answers more. "Tell me what?"

"How that witch robbed his ass," Bobby volunteered and Leona appreciated the man even more. He didn't mess around.

"Rob me? She fucked me from every angle." Luke's anger was tinged with the pain of betrayal Leona knew all too well. Her throat was dry as sawdust, but she didn't relent.

"How?" Her hand capped Luke's balled up fist and she released a shaky breath when he didn't recoil from her touch.

"She was skimming money from my shows. By the time I found out, she'd pilfered close to a million dollars."

"Oh my God," Leona gasped. "Over how long a period?"

"Six months," Luke mumbled.

Six months! "B-but your accountant…your bank statements?"

Luke went rigid. "She handled all of it."

Leona recalled her conversation with Dale, her informant when she was researching Luke. Dale had mentioned that Ivy stole money from Luke, but a million dollars wasn't chump change.

"You trusted her. With everything?" She squeezed Luke's hand and saw sadness soften the angry lines at the corners of his mouth.

"Even his music," Bobby added. "I'm no genius but even I knew you didn't need to change your sound."

"Your music? How'd she do that?" Leona was appalled that anyone, much less Luke's manager and fiancée, would ever suggest he change his sound.

Luke and Bobby again shared an unspoken exchange. There was a chill of dead air before Luke responded. "I'm done rehashing this."

"But—"

"I'm serious." Luke's tone silenced both her and Bobby.

"Okay, okay." Leona bit her lip. The fifteen seconds of quiet at the table felt like hours.

Bobby gave his beard long meditative brushes before finally speaking.

"So, what story should I start with first? The one about Luke streaking most of downtown San Francisco might be a good tale to tell."

"Oh man." Luke leaned back in his chair and scrubbed his face.

And just like that, the conversation about Ivy and her wrongdoings was over.

Whatever else Ivy had done had wounded Luke deeply. His fiancée had betrayed him on so many levels and Leona had been paying the price. Leona wanted to show him she was different, that she cared and most of all that he could trust her.

She leaned forward and flowed with their tempo. "Yes, please."

Luke and Leona spent the day visiting some of the sights of San Francisco. She'd enjoyed the comical retelling of surfing and party stories with Bobby but her nosy alter ego screamed for details. She indulged Luke and his mini tour commentary of his city.

On their drive back to the house, she couldn't contain it any longer.

"Luke?"

"I'm sorry I was crabby with you, earlier."

She covered his hand with hers. "Apology accepted. I'm sorry if I pushed." She hoped he would tell her more, but he focused on the road.

Luke side-eyed her and sighed. "That you can't ask me about what happened at the café is killing you, isn't it?"

Leona blinked at his intuition. She could have asked

him anything. That she'd witnessed him anger so easily from the mere mention of Ivy must have been on his mind, too. "Yes."

"Just like not asking you more about your anxiety attack is burning a hole in my tongue."

Leona bit her lip. "It wasn't a full attack. It was just a little paranoia. I'm okay now." And there it was—their pesky baggage, noisily shooting around the conveyer belt of their lover's retreat.

Luke navigated the vehicle and was silent for a long time.

"It's just that the media really did a number on me and my family when I broke up with Paul. They were everywhere, even in my parents' home. I was..." She choked. "There were times I was afraid of my own freakin' shadow. When the attacks started, Abe suggested I take some time off to get them under control. You know, stay out of the public eye for a bit and, well, before long, a year had passed."

She knew she was breaking the rules but perhaps if she offered an olive branch, he would, too.

"I'm sorry they hounded you. No doubt because Paul fed the media enough to keep things going." His knuckles whitened as he gripped the steering wheel. "I didn't want to bring our turmoil to this getaway. I wanted us to feel safe, here together. Bobby didn't know Ivy was off-limits. I've changed my life, and moving here to San Francisco is a part of it. It's a new beginning in a sense, after all the shit that went down with Ivy—the money, the cheating, my album, and the tour. To recoup what was lost. Can you be okay with that explanation, for now?"

"But I... There's so much... I have a hard time...

What about…" Each time she tried to say something, an internal retort was on the tip of her tongue.

He did a double take over at her several times.

She sighed heavily. "Yes."

"You're like a computer on the fritz." Luke laughed.

Leona knocked his arm playfully.

"Easy, or no dessert for you," he warned, but a touch of a smile still graced his lips.

"Dessert?" Visions of petits fours danced in her head.

"Yes. Later."

Dessert was a distraction, and the past was again tucked away. Though she was curious, Leona would respect his explanation—for now.

When they arrived at the house, Leona and Luke both agreed to catch up on work. She communicated with her team via email so they, too, could enjoy a much-needed break. Luke also busied himself on his computer and music floated from his headphones. So much had transpired between them and they'd catapulted to another level. The more time they spent together, the more invested in him she became.

Later that evening, as Leona plugged away on her computer, Luke offered her a small plate of leftover lasagna. Brunch at Bobby's had been filling, but that was hours ago so she was happy for the portion.

After dinner, Luke disappeared and she pulled up her emails regarding the San Francisco one-off performance. Sara and Sebastian would be arriving in town soon and Sebastian needed footage of the show. The team still needed to brief for Los Angeles. Their marketing blitz for the show had been nonstop. Though ticket sales were up, and with the conditions of the addendum looming over her head, Los Angeles wasn't sold out. Leona emailed marketing with additional instructions she hoped would help boost ticket sales.

When she finished her work she went upstairs for a quick shower. She towel-dried her hair and moisturized her strands, combing and styling them with her fingers. Again, confusion plagued her as to what to wear while in the house with Luke.

It's time to put your big girl panties on. "Literally."

Leona's "big girl panties" weren't big at all. In fact, if they were any smaller, they'd be nonexistent. The pink satin and black lace nighty with matching underwear barely covered her. She liked to walk through Luke's house barefoot and fastened black and silver embroidered barefoot sandals around her middle toes and ankles. She regarded herself in the mirror and her eyes widened.

"What did you expect from pink satin and black lace?" She hoped he liked it and the thought made her giddy.

Leona donned a black matching robe and tied it shut before searching for Luke. She descended the stairs and at first didn't see any sign of him.

Luke reappeared from wherever he was, shirtless and in boxers. He stopped short when he saw her.

Chapter Twenty

Luke stopped in his tracks and reined himself in to keep from pouncing on Leona.

"You're like a present." *That I want to rip the wrapping off of and...*

"I think that's the idea." She blushed.

Luke barely heard her. Her modesty made him want her even more. He longed to see what lay under the robe. With determined steps, he approached her and slipped the satin sash between his fingers. "May I?"

Leona spread her arms wide. "You may."

Luke untied the sash and opened the robe. The garment clung to her body and accentuated her breasts, lifting them so high he couldn't miss them if he tried.

"I like." He breathed in the scent of crisp raspberry and sensuous wild rose that decorated her skin. He retied the sash, and then stepped back. He had a long way to go before he was once again buried inside her enchanted pussy and pleasing her again. "Ready for dessert?"

Leona clasped his outstretched hand. "Yes, please."

He knew she was an addict for sweets and the thought of dessert excited her. He brought her over to the table where a rounded traditional silver platter and dome cover greeted them.

Leona clapped her hands and did her food dance.

Pretending to be a well-trained butler, Luke put one arm behind his back, and then bent over to remove the cover. "Dessert is served."

"What's this?" Leona asked. A digital music player lay on the serving platter.

Luke stifled a laugh as the delightful expression fell from her face. "I made you a playlist."

"Oh." Leona hesitated, unsure how to react. "Okay."

He was pleased by her confusion. The response was exactly what he'd hoped for. He intertwined his fingers with hers. "Come with me."

He guided her through the house to a door at the far end of the first floor and up a short staircase. He trailed behind to witness the alternating movement of her hips. They reached a door at the end of the hall, and entered into darkness before he turned on the lights.

The first thing that greeted them was a large ceiling-to-floor picture window that garnered most of the wall and overlooked the ocean. The space itself was about eight hundred square feet, with speakers everywhere. Here, he was most comfortable and proud of what he'd created. His equipment and turntables were at the side, and a massive vinyl collection acquired over the years was stacked on shelves. The soundproof enclosed glass area housed two standing microphones that reminded him of the hits he had made since moving into this home from Los Angeles.

"This is your studio," Leona said.

Leona scooted by him and made her way around the room. The pink of her nighty that peeked through the robe was the most colorful thing in the room. As she sauntered to the control station, she ran her fingers along the multitude of buttons.

"Fader… EQ…beat loop…cue…tempo," she recited.

He was impressed. "You know your way around a mixing table."

"It's been a long time since I've been in a studio." She stopped behind the table and pushed back the rolling chair with her legs.

Luke was sure she referenced Paul's studio. Anger boiled in the pit of his stomach. He stomped the feeling down and eliminated thoughts of Paul. Leona was here with him. Right now, she was his.

"Wait. Who am I, Luke?" Her energetic question further colored the space.

Laughter rumbled in his chest as she imitated the movements he performed onstage. "I don't do that."

She smirked at him. "If you took a video of me—" Leona put up her left hand "—and a video of you—" then put up her right hand "—and played them side by side, you'd see a perfect resemblance."

"Nah." He half crossed his arms, and twisted the patch of hair between his lip and chin with one hand.

"Promise."

"Never."

"Whatever." Leona continued touring the studio.

She passed his vinyl collection, which occupied most of the south wall.

"My father still has vinyl in crates. Remember when you had to travel with those?"

"Oh yeah." He shadowed her. "People still use them. There's software out there now to mimic that experience even though the music is digital. I still play, mix, and scratch records. I have my purist moments."

She faced him. "This is impressive, Luke."

"I finally created the studio I wanted. It's all insulated and soundproof. My neighbors aren't too close by, but with these big room speakers, it doesn't hurt." He distracted himself with technical talk to quell his yearning for her.

Next to the records, a couch sat off center to the huge window. Leona dawdled past it to stand fully in front of the window.

Leona craned her neck to him. "Trippy."

"Yeah, it is."

Leona was quiet, eyeing the speakers around the room. "And he shall have music wherever he goes."

"What was that?" Luke asked.

"The line is from an English nursery rhyme called 'Ride a Cock Horse to Banbury Cross.' It reminds me of you, although, in the version of the nursery rhyme, he is actually a she. Anyway, music is always accessible to you in some way."

"Yes." He followed her but left a few feet between them.

"There's something charming about that." Leona moved past the controls and toward the end of the production table.

She spoke like she knew what was in his soul. If she kept talking like that he'd explode before he made it to dessert.

Luke waited.

Between the production controls and the wall of speakers was a large cream-colored furry blanket. At the center, a pair of white headphones lay atop a round silver plate. The headphones were made of white leather, pillow cushioning on the earpieces, and the cord plugged into an amplifier. A knife and fork framed the headphones, on either side, like a place setting.

"What's this?" Leona faced him.

He dwindled the space between them and held her hips. "Dessert." He pressed her back so that her ass met the plush blanket. He untied the strap to her robe, slid the material off her, and tossed it aside. He pushed the silver tray, utensils, and headphones out of the way, and then lifted her to sit on the blanket.

She gasped and gripped his shoulders. "I don't understand…"

He kissed her into silence. "Shh."

He plugged the digital music player he'd presented her with in the kitchen into the equipment. He adjusted a few buttons and tapped on others.

He picked up the headphones before speaking to her. "I want you to listen to me because this is the last time you'll hear my voice for a while."

"Okay," Leona said.

He hung the headphones around his neck, then slid a few additional buttons to enhance the sound. He brought one earpiece to his ears to evaluate the sound level.

"This is your playlist, Leona. You inspired it. It's music that I've created and wanted to share with you. Now the hard part." He placed his hands on the table, trapping her between them. "No matter what happens, do not take these headphones off. Understand?"

After a long moment, she responded. "Yes."

Nervousness thinned her declaration.

"Do you trust me?"

"I trust you." She touched his arm with her delicate fingertips and a shiver ran through him.

Her confidence infused superhuman pride in him.

He put the headphones over her head and ears before adjusting them to the correct fit. The thick cushioning on the earpiece appeared twice as large on her head.

"Can you hear me?" he asked in a normal tone.

"Yup."

He flipped a tiny switch on the side of the headphones.

"Whoa." Her eyes widened. "It's like someone just sealed me into an airtight container."

He tapped her chin. "Can you hear me?" he asked her again.

"What?" Leona tilted an ear at him. "I can't hear you."

Luke gave her the thumbs-up. The noise-cancelling feature was activated and she couldn't hear much outside the headphones. He swiped a piece of paper from a table nearby and turned on the music.

He wrote, "tell me when" on the paper and showed it to her.

Leona's eyes scanned the paper. "Got it." She laughed. "I sound weird."

She was beyond amusing without her sense of hearing. Hell, she was funny in general, something he'd quickly learned and found charming about her. He focused on the sound and increased the volume, eyeing her for confirmation.

Leona pointed up and he advanced the dial a little bit more. She pointed up again and he put his hand over his heart, happy she shared his enthusiasm for a more robust sound.

When he moved the sound to her desired level she gave him the thumbs-up.

He wrote on the paper again. "A girl after my own heart."

Leona shrugged and laughed.

Luke pointed to the headphones and mouthed, "Listen." The kiss he landed on her was deep and thorough. His tongue played in her mouth and the familiar sweetness of her was like liquor inebriating him under her influence. He loved the way she opened to him and knew that whatever he wanted from her, she would give him. He brought his hands to her breast and squeezed. He pulled away from her, ending the kiss abruptly. He stepped away from her and crossed toward the studio door.

Whatever you want from me, Leona, is yours.

Gone.

Leona sat alone, listening to the music. She went to remove the headphones, but Luke's instructions stopped her. Instead, she focused on the song filling her ears and the ethereal vocals overlaying the melody.

The headphones must have been professional ones because she could hear every element in the music, from the heavy bass to the titillating breakdowns. The lyrics were in true Musical Prophet form and spoke of dreams, love, and union. They brought unexpected sentiment to her. Luke had put his feelings into the arrangement and the song was beautiful. The music coupled with the knowledge that Luke made this playlist for her only fueled her desire for him and her fear. This retreat was supposed to be five days of carnal pleasure and if she wasn't careful, she'd take Luke's emotional music too much to heart. She was about to go down the rabbit hole of despair when the lights went out.

Leona was in darkness, her only company the music in her ears and the moonlight coming from the window. And then, candlelight flickered in various corners of the room until it was aglow.

"Luke?" she whispered and waited, but he didn't appear.

She jumped at the sensation of hands curving over her shoulders and screamed so loud, she heard her muffled cry over the music and through the noise cancelling headphones. Her heart beat hard and fast. She whipped around to confirm Luke was indeed the boogeyman in the dark. She followed the pressure of his hands and lay back. Again, she was absent his touch.

He reappeared and postured before her. Leona propped herself up on her elbows and forearms, peering over the two mounds of her breasts that partially obstructed her view. The soft blanket provided cushioning under her.

Her heart raced. She watched Luke caress her legs and thighs with gentle strokes, moving upward to grab hold of her nighty. Leona shifted from one side to the other, tilting her hips so he could slide the material up over her hips and expose her belly. He ran his hand over her satin-and-lace panties, giving her the okay sign. That he appreciated the intimates she chose thrilled her and she made a mental note that he liked satin underwear. The song mixed in with another selection that started out quiet, then grew into a slow house rhythm, mirroring the growing fire Luke ignited in her.

Luke grabbed hold of the waistband of her panties and his fingers eased the garment down. She again lifted her hips and he slid the panties down her legs and off, dropping them on the floor.

Low and out of her sight, Luke's lips traced her ankles and his hand cradled her calf. She inhaled at the unexpected touch. His surprising kisses traveled upward to her knees and outer thighs. He spread her legs and she was frantic with expectation. Her pussy ached, making her hope his kisses landed there. Luke's hands massaged her outer thighs and his head moved to her inner thigh where he kissed, licked, and nibbled the soft skin inches away from her center.

Leona's knee jerked and she saw the obvious rise and fall of her heaving chest as she watched his head move over her lower body. She inhaled and Luke's fragrance blended with the scent of candle wax and warmed metal from the DJ equipment.

She felt the heat, vibration, and movement from his mouth against her skin as he spoke, but she couldn't hear him. She strained to touch his head. "What?" Her breathless question resounded in her inner ear.

Luke again reached for the paper and picked up the marker again. He scribbled with speed, then showed it to her.

"You smell so good," Leona read out loud, and the butterflies fluttered everywhere in her body.

Luke tossed the marker and paper over his shoulder and freed himself from his boxers.

Leona's breathing quickened further when she saw his evident arousal aimed right at her. Luke's eyes were transfixed on her as he massaged her legs. He glided his hand in between her thighs and he petted the thin strip of hair at her center. She squirmed, inviting him to give her more.

His fingers pushed into her opening and his thumb flickered over her most sensitive spot. Leona fisted the blanket to keep from flying off the table and the intensive glint in his eyes took her higher. His fingers tunneled deeper and upward and Leona let out a syncopated moan.

"Luke." She squirmed under his caress.

He withdrew his fingers and kissed her belly. Her insides screamed for his fingers to return. Luke trailed kisses down to her lower belly and rested just below her pelvis where the mound of her center was fullest.

"Touch me, baby. Please touch me there." The endearment rolled off her tongue as she jutted her pelvis toward him. He had called her baby when she had her panic attack and she didn't complain because she adored hearing his sweetness. Her jerky movements begged him to taste her sweet spot, but by the wicked smile on his face, the torture was far from over.

Luke opened her legs wider and the cool air melded with the hot, inviting juices seeping from her. Luke planted slow and gentle kisses on her hip bone and down the other thigh to her ankle. The tickling touch sent shocks through her. Maybe it was because no one ever touched her ankle, but the way he held her foot and kissed the bone made her soul blossom with affection so deep it almost inspired a tear.

He continued kissing her inner thighs on his way back up, blazing a hot, wet path to her center, and her hips gyrated in excitement. Slight stickiness from moisture left on his hand slid over her leg. She tried to stay still, but her impatience was mounting. She needed more.

"You're driving me crazy." Leona was a note away

from a squeal. She didn't know how she sounded to him, but between the music and the simultaneous sensory deprivation and overload, their intimacy soared to a new height.

His hands reached up to squeeze the soft contours of her breast. He tugged the lace trimming and pulled down, exposing her as she popped out of the material. She rolled her shoulders out of the lace straps. He feathered his fingers over the nipple and squeezed her flesh as he continued to plant kisses on her stomach. Now able to reach him, she seized his hand and bit it in frustration. Luke didn't even flinch as if taking his deserved punishment.

She kissed the mark. "Please, Luke." She guided his hand back to her breast.

Leona hyperventilated with longing and loved every torturous minute. The more time they spent together the more they opened up, and their lovemaking was no different. The lengths he'd gone to create this experience thawed a part of her heart she'd kept cold and hard.

The constriction of her lingerie added to her frustration. She slid her arms out of the straps and pushed at the material. She needed to escape the garment just like she needed to escape the confinement of the past. Now free from the garment, she shoved it down until it fell to the floor, and with it what was left of her inhibitions.

Luke surveyed her body and his strong hands clasped hold of her hips. He made eye contact with her before his head disappeared between her legs and he covered her hot pussy with his mouth. Leona melted and her back arched to receive the pleasure of his lips and tongue. She cried out, gripping and twisting the soft blanket. She writhed under his touch as his fingers separated the swollen folds of skin to give him fuller access to the sensitive gem at her center.

Her moans vibrated in her ear and were simultaneously bizarre yet fascinating. She tried to censor herself but Luke had annihilated her defenses and she was completely undone. He continued his assault on her stimulated nerves, sending shocks through her. Every time she thought she'd experienced ultimate pleasure with him, he skyrocketed her to unimaginable bliss. She punched her ticket and held on for the ride. He lifted each of her legs to rest on his shoulders. Leona quickly crossed her feet at the ankles, locking him to her.

"Luke. Oh shit, Luke," she squealed as her hand went to his head and her fingers raked wildly through his hair.

The vibrations and heat from him moaning between her legs and the tightness of his hands as they gripped her hips threatened to clamshell her legs shut. Leona fought the urge, determined to receive every titillating touch. She wished she could hear his desire, but beyond that she wanted to hear him say this was more than a fling, more than temporary.

"Don't stop. Please, please, don't stop." In her ear, every breath, moan, and plea was amplified. Her sensual singing added to the music. She groaned and panted as her body contorted and stiffened in expectancy of her arrival.

Luke inserted his fingers and the combination of his hand and mouth sent her to heaven, through the constellations, and hanging on the edge of the universe. Her thighs tightened around his head and she curled up as her orgasm arrived mercilessly. Her movements pulled at the headphones wire and simultaneously unplugged them from the amplifier, shifting the earpiece off her head.

The music playing in her ears blasted through the room. Luke startled at the abrupt loudness of the music, but his mouth concentrated on teasing every drop out of her. Bass shook under her ass, intensifying her orgasm, and the blanket was now a swirling mess.

Luke kissed her and Leona smelled herself on him, tasting the essence he'd just enjoyed.

"I need you, Leona." He barked into her ear above the loud music. He lifted her off the blanket and carried her as she continued to buck and shiver. Leona shrieked as her back hit something cold. She was pinned against the window. The view was so expansive that it was as if she were suspended over the waves.

"We'll break it." Leona shivered and panted against his ear.

"No, but we're going to try." He pressed himself hard against her.

"Can people see us?"

Luke kissed and bit her neck. "Do you care?"

She scraped her fingernails down the length of his back. "No." She captured his mouth again, kissing him with abandon.

Luke secured them against the glass and placed one of her legs around his waist.

Leona gasped as he filled her, and bit his lower lip in pleasure. She wrapped her other leg around his waist and used the traction of her back against the glass window for stability. Luke rammed into her like he wanted to erase every other man before him. The unrestrained thrusts were raw and primal.

She clawed at his shoulders and Luke's fingers dug

into the flesh of her buttocks. The chill from the cold glass sailed through her, freezing her nipples into taut nubs. The exquisite pain of Luke's chest smothering her breasts added to the pleasure of each of his forceful thrusts.

Luke's muscles flexed from exercise, and he claimed his prize after expertly eating her out. Their position allowed him to delve deep without hurting her. As her insides opened to him, her soul offered him the pearl that she'd so ardently protected. Her love.

"Yes," Leona moaned and encouraged him to take his pleasure. "Come harder, baby."

He squeezed his eyes shut and hissed, pushing his forehead into her shoulder. She held him tight. He gritted his teeth and his harsh, frequent breathing was familiar to her now. His triumphant shout announced his ultimate satisfaction.

"Oh shit, Leona." He heaved in air as if to stay alive.

Luke clinched her so hard her lungs wheezed. He brought his head to kiss her and she opened her mouth wide to receive his breath and tongue.

Still inside her, he collapsed to the couch, bringing her with him. They stayed there in post-orgasmic sweat and stickiness. Leona never wanted him to soften or slide out of her. She wanted to feel this way forever and never come down from the high. She smoothed his back and head and after a few minutes, Luke again kissed her deeply and caressed her face. He was so tender. Instead of pulling away to bring things back into balance, she allowed his touch to clip the strings of the past.

When they finally separated, Luke lowered the music before he trashed his used, mysteriously appearing, latex.

"How was dessert?"

"Meh." She wandered back to the table and leaned against the blanket.

Luke placed his hands on either side of the table, trapping her. His seeking tongue licked the curve of her neck and his lips followed, planting kisses along her nape.

"The sweat on you tells a different story. Seems I've left a lasting impression."

"Perhaps." She continued acting nonchalant about the fact that Luke just rocked her world, her universe, her everything.

Luke tickled her neck with kisses. "Mmm-hmm."

"All right. Dessert was delicious. The music was beautiful, emotional..." She rubbed his forearms. "Thank you for sharing it like this with me."

Luke was silent and then leaned back. The intensity prompted her to touch his face.

"Luke?" Leona stroked his cheek. "You okay?"

He continued to stare. He inhaled so sharp it cut through any noise in the room. "Yeah. I... Everything's okay." He pulled her against him. She could feel his manhood on her hip. She shivered under the intensity of his eyes and from the coolness of the room on her sweaty skin.

"Come." Luke grabbed the blanket, placed it over her shoulders, and secured it with his arm. "I'm taking you to bed."

They strolled as one through the studio, snuffing the candles on their way out. Once in the bedroom, Luke left a really good impression on her. Several times.

Chapter Twenty-One

Early the next morning, Leona snuggled over to Luke only to find an empty space.

"Luke?" No response. She listened to see if she could pick up his sound from somewhere in the house. Dawn had not yet arrived so she flicked the light switch on the bedside lamp.

A very low and consistent beat thumped, but from where? She lifted her naked body, feeling Luke's imprint all over her, making her hungry for him again.

She couldn't find her nighty and saw Luke's cargo pants and shirt lying on the leather ottoman at the foot of the bed. She put them on, pinching the shorts at the waist to prevent them from sliding down her legs. She tracked the music through the dark house.

Leona's travels led her back to the door of Luke's studio. She squinted at a wall clock.

5:20?

"What in the world is he doing at the butt crack of dawn?"

She gently opened the door to the studio and the loud music bowled her over.

The room really is soundproof.

Leona found Luke sitting naked at the DJ table, bobbing his head. The light from the large computer screen danced on his face. His eyes roved over the images and his hand clicked the mouse frequently.

The start of sunrise gave a picturesque backdrop of technology meeting nature and man in the middle.

She didn't want to interrupt him and retreated. The music lowered.

"Good morning, beautiful." Luke's greeting stopped her.

She almost came in Luke's pants. He was hot even saying a simple good morning. "I didn't mean to interrupt you."

"I've been working for a while. Come here." Luke motioned her to him. "Did I wake you?"

"No. I got up to use the bathroom and you weren't there." In truth, both the bed and her body were vacant without him. "Why are you up so early?"

"I felt inspired. When that happens, I can't sleep. So, I work."

Once she was close enough to him, Luke drew her onto his lap and kissed her.

Leona hooked her arm around his neck.

"You're pretty sexy in my clothes." Luke tugged on the cargo pants.

"Thanks, but I should go back up so you can finish. Your show is tomorrow and I've been a distraction. Plus the tour will be starting and, well..."

Her words had an effect on both of them and the muscles in his back went rigid. After Luke's one-off show, they would be back on tour and back to reality.

"You're a pleasant distraction, Leona." He shook his leg and she swayed. "Hey, something I forgot to mention. My sister is visiting a friend in Santa Rosa, so she'll be stopping by at lunchtime before driving back to Santa Monica. I should get as much as I can get done before she arrives."

"She's coming here? Why didn't you tell me? Should I split for the day or…? I don't want to impose. She probably hasn't seen you in months."

"I spent time at her place last week. She knows who you are. She saw a picture of you in the entertainment section from that night at Aurora a few months back. I would have told you last night but we were kind of busy." He gave her low-lid seduction.

"Kind of." Leona blushed, and evaluated the aftermath of their lovemaking. "We should probably clean this place up. There are clothes everywhere."

"This is true."

"How about I clean up later when I get dressed. You finish working and get ready. We should be ready by lunch. Sound good?"

"You don't have to do that. I normally have someone help me keep the place tidy but I didn't want any interruptions while you were here. I could call her and see if she's available."

"It's not that serious. It'll be quicker if I do it." Leona looked forward to meeting Luke's sister but her arrival was a pin about to needle their blissful bubble. She didn't want to accelerate the interruption with a cleaning service.

Luke started to caress her thighs and she sank into his body. She purred against him, but then his sister's imminent arrival sprung to the surface. With reluctance, she readied herself to leave. As she stood up she forgot to grab hold of the cargo pants and they fell into a puddle at her feet.

Luke lunged toward her.

Leona gathered the pants and yanked them up. "No more playing. Back to work."

She collected the discarded clothes on the floor and the blanket into her arms. "I'm going to catch a few more Z's and then I'll get started."

"Try not to dream about me, Leona."

She scoffed. "You should be so lucky." She almost broke her hip as she gave him a runway walk exit, complete with a 360-degree spin.

Later on, with house in order, Luke found her at the kitchen counter as she scrolled through emails.

"Jane has the codes and keys to the house, but she sometimes rings the bell when I'm here. I wanted to tell you in case she lets herself in." He tied an apron around his waist.

"Oh, okay." Leona nodded and went on guard to expect the unexpected.

"She likes my BBQ, so I'm going to start the grill and get our lunch in order. We'll eat outside." Luke patted her ass before he went on his way. "I'll leave you to it, but come out when you're done."

"I'll be there in a moment." She typed a few more emails, highlighted a few things in her calendar, and confirmed flight times for her team. They would arrive tomorrow and signify the end of this magical time she had with Luke, and though she was ready for the tour to continue, she wasn't so sure she was ready for this to be over. She would have to sit down with Luke at some point and address the schedule for the next few days. Even though Sebastian was managing the marketing blitz for the show, Luke still had phone interviews to ramp up the Los Angeles show on Saturday.

Leona closed her laptop and was about to head outside when the doorbell rang. She called to Luke, but when she peered through the glass patio doors, he was engulfed in smoke, handling a pretty large fire in the charcoal grill.

"I probably shouldn't interrupt that."

Leona opened the front door and the woman who entered couldn't be mistaken for anyone other than Luke's sister. The similar olive skin and attractive features, complete with green eyes, greeted her. The only difference was that Jane's eyes shined green without a hint of another color. Jane dressed in a flowing, black, knee-length skirt and pink top. Her dark, loose curls were cut in an asymmetrical style.

"Hello—"

"Hi, Leona. I'm Jane, Luke's sister." The woman's friendliness was contagious.

"Yes. Nice to meet you, Jane." Leona extended her hand. "Please, call me Leo."

"It's nice to meet you, too." Jane bypassed her hand and embraced her. "We're a hugging family."

Leona was taken aback by the greeting, but returned a lighter version of June's hug.

A woman with waist-long blond hair glided in after Jane, but before Leona could address her, two little ones ran into the house from behind Jane.

"Uncle Luke," the children shouted.

Leona was surprised to see children. Luke had mentioned that Jane was coming. He hadn't mentioned anything about kids or this other woman.

"Those are my children, Emily and Ryan. Is my

brother grilling already? He knows how I like my BBQ." Jane then presented the other woman. "This is my friend Ariel."

Ariel was dressed casually in cut-off jean shorts and a light blue tee shirt. When songs mentioned California girls they meant Ariel.

"Nice to meet you, Ariel." Leona extended her hand.

Ariel's greeting was less warm than Jane's, but still pleasant. "You, too." They shook hands.

"Luke's out back." Leona smelled the faint scent of charcoal and walked with Jane and Ariel into the house.

Jane evaluated her for a moment. "I've heard quite a bit about you from Luke."

Leona frowned. "Is it awful?"

Jane laughed. "Quite the contrary. He's pleased with the tour."

"Good. Our team works really hard to create an awesome fan experience with Luke." Leona caught Jane's smile.

"He also said you would start talking about work if I mentioned the tour."

Leona couldn't help it. She loved her job. "I guess I can get into work pretty easily."

"I'm similar, so no worries." Jane dropped her bag on the kitchen counter and they advanced to the patio.

"Oh yeah?" Jane sure knew a lot about her. Leona, however, was at a disadvantage. "What do you do, Jane?"

"I'm a vintner. We own a family vineyard in Santa Monica."

Leona was intrigued. "Really? That's hard work."

"It's a lot of hard work, but I love it. Luke brought a few cases back with him when he visited us last week. You may have already had some."

The night she'd arrived, Luke had shared a bottle with her. "Yes, we had a Chianti. That was yours?"

"Oh wow. He pulled out the big guns for you."

Leona blushed. "The wine was excellent."

The full aroma of charcoal smoke choked them as they congregated outside.

"Hey." Luke stood under a canopy, slicing avocado into a salad bowl. "I was wondering what was taking you so long. Your rug rats are tearing up the place."

Jane pushed her brother playfully before kissing his cheek.

Leona hadn't been out to the patio and on this sunny, clear day, the cozy patio was a perfect outdoor living space.

Luke dipped into a camouflaged fridge to get something out. It was stocked with food and drinks.

Leona was still awed by the beauty of his property. A large grass area, where the kids played, sat in the distance between the pool and the patio. The pool was protected to keep young children from falling in and appeared quite unused. Luke loved the ocean and most likely preferred to be out on the waves.

"You look great, Ariel." Luke kissed the woman on the cheek. "Traveling is having a very nice effect on you."

"Hi, handsome. That's what good Aegean Sea air will do for you, but I'm glad to be back for a bit before I head to Ibiza." Ariel swung her hair away from the fire and gave Luke a friendly hug.

Leona did a double take at Ariel's words. When the woman arrived with Luke's sister, Leona assumed she was Jane's friend. Intrigued by Ariel's interaction with Luke, Leona wondered how Luke and Ariel had come

to be friends. *Will he and I be friends after this? Will
he let me be his friend outside the bedroom?*

The kids came running up onto the patio.

"Slow down. Uncle Luke is cooking, so be careful."
Jane leashed Ryan by his navy and white striped shirt.
The material ricocheted the little boy into a stationary
position. Once he was still, Jane let him go.

Emily and Ryan stayed close to their mother, curious about the new person to the group.

"This is Leo, Uncle Luke's friend. You guys want
to say hello?"

"Hi." The two children spoke in unison.

The weight of Luke's evaluation was heavy as he
watched their interaction from his cooking station.

Leona liked kids even though she wasn't around
many. "Hi, guys. Emily and Ryan, right?"

They nodded.

"How old are you, Emily?" Leona asked.

Emily played with one of the attached flowers on
her shirt. "Seven."

"And you, Ryan, how old are you?"

Ryan showed Leona five fingers.

"How does she know my name, Mommy?" Ryan
asked Jane.

"Ask her." Jane encouraged her son.

"How do you know my name?" Ryan blinked multiple times from the sun and also from the dark brown
strands that fell into his face.

Leona moved the hair from his brows. "Well, your
mom told me."

Ryan came over to Leona's side and mumbled something low and indecipherable.

"I'm sorry, Ryan, I can't hear you?" Leona leaned in closer to the little boy.

"You're pretty." He spoke loud enough for everyone to hear.

Leona's heart melted. "Thank you, Ryan. You're so sweet."

Luke had a touch of a smile on his lips.

"He's quite the flirt, Leo." Jane laughed and pinched her son's cheek.

"I see." Leona raised her eyebrows. "Good luck. When he gets older, the girls will be calling your house nonstop."

They all laughed.

"Are you and Uncle Luke boyfriend and girlfriend, like Mommy says?" Emily asked as she took Leona's hand.

Both Leona and Luke focused on Jane.

"Em." Jane's cheeks reddened. "My apologies, Leo."

Luke's shoulders shook with mirth.

Leona's cheeks flushed with mortification. "She's just curious. Right, Emily?"

The little girl nodded. "Are you boyfriend girlfriend?"

Ryan giggled at his sister's question.

"Your uncle and I are work friends." Leona's eyes called to Luke's for aid.

Just like a child, one answer spawned additional questions. "Do you kiss him like Aunt Ivy?" Emily was relentless.

Ryan frowned. "Aunt Ivy was a 'meanie.'"

The tension in the air thickened immediately.

"That's enough, Em." Jane's tone blocked the next question. "My kids watch a little too much TV and forget their manners sometimes." She directed the last part of her phrase to the kids.

Leona could feel Luke's stress level from where she was. She didn't know what she and Luke were, much less how to explain it to the young girl. She also hadn't prepared herself for the possibility of Luke's family members conveying their experiences with Ivy.

Luke sighed. "Come here, Em." Emily skipped to his side.

"Leona is very nice. So be nice to her and no more questions about boyfriend, girlfriend, okay?"

"Yes, Uncle Luke." Emily lowered her eyes to once again toy with the flower on her clothing.

Luke bent down to kiss her forehead and sent her back to Jane.

"So, Ariel, what do you do?" Leona asked in an effort to learn more about their family friend.

Ariel rubbernecked at the question. "I'm a chanteuse and songwriter."

Leona noticed Luke and Jane smiling at Ariel's short and mysterious answer. "Do I know you from somewhere?"

"You may be familiar with my vocal signature." Less talkative than Jane, Ariel didn't elaborate much.

Leona cocked her head at Ariel's savant-type responses.

"Let's eat," came Luke's well-timed interruption.

Leona was hungry, so the thought of eating was more attractive than asking questions, but Ariel was a mystery.

They moved out of the sun to the dining table. The kids sat in chairs that were way too big for them and Jane fixed them each a hot dog with corn and salad.

Leona decorated her plate with chicken, sausage, corn on the cob, and salad. Those in her company had healthy appetites, as well, and piled their plates with food. They ate in silence for a bit and chatted about the kids and Ariel's trip.

Leona chewed her sausage, ate a little salad, and drank some of the beer Luke had given to her.

"Isn't it gorgeous here, Leo?" Jane lugged her chair into the sun and let it kiss her face.

"Yes, you can lose time. I've always liked being by the water."

"Water is like the lifeblood of the elements and most powerful to the creatures of earth," Ariel declared.

Leona felt the quizzical expression form on her face. *What the hell is she talking about?*

Jane and Luke exchanged glances, and then busted out laughing.

Ariel smiled at them both.

"Leo, Ariel has a very strange sense of humor. She tries out her lyrics on us to see if it hits a nerve," Jane said. "She's kind of quiet but she comes out with these random verses every so often."

"Oh." Leona relaxed, thankful it wasn't just her and happy to share an inside joke with the trio.

The kids finished eating and were back to playing on the grass.

"Not too much running around, guys. You just ate," Jane yelled as Ryan and Emily headed for the open area.

"I'm going to get some tea and warm up. I assume we are going to start soon?" Ariel's announcement was not only abrupt but also perplexing.

Warming up for what?

"Yeah. Don't worry about that. I got it," Luke said as Ariel picked up her plate.

Ariel complied and went inside to fix her tea.

Ariel's comfort in Luke's home made her slightly

envious. Leona and Luke's relationship was changing, evolving. They were lovers, her soreness could testify to that all day in court. However, she wondered if she'd ever share that level of friendship with him. *And where the hell is she going?*

Before Leona had a chance to ask, Jane touched her arm. "Leo, would you mind keeping an eye on the kids while Luke and I clean up?"

"Well, I can help, too."

Jane put her hand on her arm. "Oh no. You are a guest here. I don't trust them enough to not disappear if left unattended. Luke and I will take care of the mess."

"Are you sure? It's no problem." She wanted to do her part.

"You are helping, Leona. Enjoy that good ocean air." Luke collected the plates for the trash.

"Yes, relax." Jane echoed his sentiment.

As Luke and Jane cleaned up, Leona traipsed down to where the kids were. They were playing a game of tag, so she joined them. Leona suggested "walk tag" for a little bit since they'd recently eaten. When the kids were bored with "walk tag," Leona offered them a walk on the beach.

"We have to hold hands, right?" Emily grabbed Leona's fingers in her small hands.

"Yes. That way we can stay together."

Leona had Ryan on one side and Emily on the other. Sinking their toes into the sand, the kids briefly let her hand go to pick up seashells. She was impressed by how well they behaved.

Emily brought Leona a small clam-shaped seashell. The shell's light color had an iridescent shimmer.

"Wow, that's an amazing one. I can make you a necklace or a bracelet with this one." Leona's closet craft skills made an appearance every so often.

"Yes, please, Leo." Emily bounced like a pogo stick as did her dark curly locks. She was a cute kid with green eyes like her mom. Her skin was fairer which Leona assumed was probably from her dad's side.

"I want one." Ryan tugged Leona's arm.

"Then let's find you one." She pointed and sent Ryan to find a shell he liked.

Being with Luke and his sister's kids made her crave a family of her own.

Mama Sable would love to hear that.

As they returned to the house, Leona shook her head. She needed to slow her roll.

Jane and Luke regarded Leona returning hand in hand with Emily and Ryan.

"She's great with them," Jane said.

"Yeah. They like her, too."

"Luke? Have you ever seen Emily or Ryan hold anyone's hand for that long? You know my kids and their hyperactive tendencies."

Luke chortled. "I guess not."

"Have you given any thought to how this is going to end?"

Luke hadn't thought about ending anything. Since Leona had arrived in San Francisco, his feelings had accelerated more than he'd expected. Sure, fucking her brains out had been top of mind, but he could really talk to her, and she demonstrated time and again that she was in tune with him, physically and emotionally.

Luke hadn't given Jane all the details about why

Leona was staying with him, but he didn't have to. "Not really, no."

"Well, figure it out before someone gets hurt. I like her and so do my kids, which is more than I could ever say for you know who." Jane pursed her lips.

Luke shifted from one foot to the other at the thought of Ivy. There was no love lost between his ex and his family. The last thing he had ever wanted was for anyone to hurt them.

"It's not my intention to hurt Leona."

"I wasn't talking about her." Jane snickered. "I'm talking about you. You're falling in love with her. You can't take your eyes off of her and it's not just about getting your rocks off, brother dear."

He didn't deny it. How could he? He met his sister's knowing gaze.

Jane tilted her head. "I didn't get two kids through immaculate conception."

"Ugh. I don't need that visual, Jane."

Emily ran ahead of Leona and Ryan. "Leo's gonna make me a necklace," she announced, showing off her shell.

"And a bracelet for me." Ryan shadowed his sister.

Leona stood with her hands on her hips. "They're excited. Can you tell?"

"Great, guys," Jane cheered.

"We should go inside. We have work to do," Luke said.

"What work?" Leona followed him inside.

"You'll see."

She touched his arm to stop him. "Hey, I need a few things to make the kids their necklace and bracelet. I'd like to give it to them before they go. If I tell you, can you find them for me?"

"Of course. What do you need?" Luke readied himself for her instruction.

"String, a Phillips head screwdriver…umm, some glue maybe, and scissors." Leona rattled off the items to him.

"Got it. Head to the studio with Jane. I'll meet you there. Ariel is already set up."

"The studio?"

The flush on her face broadcasted their activities from the night before. He may have struggled with his emotions but Leona made him smile.

"Yes. I'll be there in a moment."

He found the jewelry making items she needed. He grabbed some extra art supplies he had for the kids before heading for the studio when Leona's phone chimed. He picked it up to bring it to her and caught a glimpse of the name before it disappeared.

Tracy Ruiz.

Leona had been working and Luke thought it might be an important call related to the tour. When he arrived at the studio, he gave Leona the items she requested.

"You brought me extra stuff. Thanks." Leona beamed up at him. He wanted to kiss her, but with Em asking boyfriend-girlfriend questions, he refrained.

"Oh. Tracy called." He handed her the phone.

"Umm…cool." Leona tapped the phone on her chin as if considering making a call but pocketed the phone instead. "You know what? I'll call her back later." She then went back to the kids.

Ariel was behind the glass and positioned in front of the microphone. Luke plopped into his seat at the production table and flipped a few switches.

Ariel's voice emanated through the speakers as she rehearsed the words to the song.

"Let's make the necklace over here." Emily went over to the table where Luke had set up "dessert" for Leona the night before.

He scratched his scalp and tilted his head at a horrified Leona.

"Hey, Em, why don't you come over here. I think Leona likes being by the window." He was up to no good but she was an easy target.

Leona tilted her head at him. "Really?"

Luke shrugged. "You enjoyed the view quite a bit."

"Hey, guys, let's put everything out on the couch. You can sit on the ends, here." Leona pointed to their respective spots. "I will face you on the chair."

"Okay," Emily and Ryan agreed together.

Leona flipped him the bird behind her back.

Luke loved watching her interact with the kids. It was so different from Ivy's distant and fingertip interactions. Caregiving came naturally to Leona and he could see her with kids of her own. Luke swallowed the dryness in his mouth at the thought of Leona's belly swollen with a child, and forced himself to focus on work before the thought progressed.

"Testing." His voice cracked as he spoke into the microphone. He cleared his throat and with it the idea of Leona pregnant with his child. "Testing, testing. Can you hear me, Ariel?"

"Yup," she responded.

"All set with the tracks?"

"Yup."

"Let's do a practice run and then we'll lay it down."

Chapter Twenty-Two

Ariel's angelic voice drifted through the speakers and lulled everyone into a trance. Leona's eyes dried from widening shock. "She's his voice?"

Jane nodded. "This started out as a one-time thing many years ago when we lived in Chicago. Ariel's talent shined when 'Get Up and Move for Me' was such a hit. Luke uses a few different artists, but she's his most popular songstress."

Leona was honored to be there while Luke created his music with his vocalist. "Does she write the lyrics?"

"Luke does most of the writing. Sometimes she will co-write something with him and he'll give her writing credit, but it's mostly his poetry. Ariel has other song-writing projects," Jane explained. "Can you believe he almost changed his sound working with Paul Reese?"

Leona went rigid. "What?"

"Oh boy." Jane slapped her hand to her mouth. "I thought you knew."

How had she not made the connection sooner? Luke's anger toward Paul over his album and Bobby's reveal was as clear as day.

"I'm sorry Jane, please, excuse me." She turned to

the kids with a happy disposition. "I'll be back, you guys." She left the studio in a hurry.

She found the quiet space where she'd worked earlier and paced a hole in the floor. The guilt she suppressed rose to the surface now that it was personal and had a name and face—Luke's. Why hadn't she figured out on her own that Paul and Luke had worked together? She bit her lip to hold back her tears, but the more she tried, the more her throat strained, choking her.

"Leona?" Luke's soft baritone drew more tears.

Leona hid her face from him. This was not how she ever wanted him to see her. Broken.

He touched her shoulder but she pulled away and hugged herself.

Luke approached from behind and encircled his arms around her waist.

"I just need a minute." She tried to deliver her words in an even tone.

He squeezed her tighter. "I'm here."

Leona inhaled to get herself together. She wiped her chin with the back of her hand. Moments later she faced him.

"Do you want to tell me what's going on?" He stroked her upper arms, warming her skin.

She didn't want to further ruin this time with Luke and his family, especially if it had anything to do with Paul Reese. Seeing her ex so frequently the past month had gotten to her. Being in Luke's studio, while he created music, had profoundly brought back the horrible events of the past. "I spent a lot of time with Paul in his studio, working with him and helping him be a better producer, more creative. I—I gave him everything I had, Luke, and even then it wasn't enough."

Luke wiped her cheek.

"Fuck," Leona bit out. "I didn't want to ruin this." Leona pressed her forehead into his chest. She held her emotions in check by an old, tattered string about to snap. That she let Luke see her vulnerability was already too much.

"Leona."

Her phone chimed in her pocket but she ignored the ringtone.

"Why didn't you tell me Paul fucked up your album? Is that why you hate him so much?"

If Luke hated Paul for that, how would he feel once he found out about the decisions she'd made to keep quiet about Paul?

Luke sighed. "Among other things. I projected that on you in the beginning, but that was before I knew you and who you were. Before this… I was wrong, Leona. Things have changed." He reached for her and she backed up.

Things had changed between them. She was falling so fast for Luke she couldn't catch herself, but she had unintentionally aided in the turmoil surrounding Luke's life and he had no idea. "I've drawn enough of your attention. We should go back in."

Her phone chimed a second time and she checked it to find Tracy calling, again. She picked up.

"Hey, Tracy. What's—"

"I know you're on break, which may explain why I'm the only one courageous enough to call you about this, but the gallery event is online and—"

"Oh no." She rubbed her ear. She'd thrown champagne in Paul's *face*. There was no way he'd let that go.

"Oh yes. Surprisingly, Paul hasn't threatened to sue

for assault or defamation of character, but I wanted to give you a heads-up. We don't want this adversely affecting Luke's tour or the contract agreement."

"That's a joke, right?" Leona was livid and almost dared Paul to sue her.

"Well, you did throw alcohol in his face."

"That'll never happen. Paul knows better and I gave him fair warning." She rubbed her ear.

"What is it, Leona?" Luke was attentive and Leona prayed Tracy didn't hear him.

"Is that—?"

"Do you think it'll keep escalating or can we snuff it?" Leona pressed her index finger against her lip to quiet any further peep out of Luke.

"With Paul involved, I don't know. The media may have had enough of him, but by the coverage it's gotten so far, they still love the earthquakes he causes."

"Great." Leona's anxiety started to float to the surface. First Paul's media tirade, and now Tracy may have picked up on Luke in the background. *How many more ways am I going to get fucked, right now?* She'd only been back two months and the erosion of her reputation was already in progress. "Well, what do you suggest I do?"

"Nothing for now, but just stay alert and keep your eye on it. We'll reconnect in a few days if things don't die down," Tracy said.

"Okay. Thanks, Tracy." They hung up.

"What's happening?" Luke asked.

Leona tapped on her ear. Did she really think she could hide away with Luke without having the drama infiltrate their time together? She'd been selfish and wanted this little slice of heaven with him, because it had to end. Her heartstrings hated the thought. She had to tell him. Once they were back on the road and fully plugged in again, there would be no hiding from what happened with Paul.

"At the gallery event in New York, Paul was there. He was riding me, getting in my face, so I threw champagne in his." She filled Luke in on the details.

"What?" He pulled out his phone and did an online search. He scrolled through a few images and his reaction was not what she'd expected.

"Why are you smiling? This is so not funny, Luke," she admonished.

"It's not so bad seeing Paul get what's coming to him." He tried to suppress his laughter.

"Oh, let me see it." She looked at his phone and her mean mug accompanied an in-action shot of alcohol hitting Paul's squinty-eyed face.

Despite her attempts to be miserable about the situation, she grinned. *I'm smiling?*

Luke approached her and held both her hands. "I know you're worried about the media getting out of control again, but maybe it will just be a small blip and die down."

Leona wasn't so sure, but as Luke wrapped his arms around her, she almost believed him.

"I hope you know that whatever is on your mind, you can always talk to me, Leona."

She had no doubt that Luke would hear her out, but when he did, it would taint every memory they created here in San Francisco.

"Sorry about that, guys." She sat back down in the chair. "You're going to help me, right?"

"Yes." The kids still bounced around and played with high spirits and Leona was thankful her disappearance didn't affect them.

Jane mouthed an apology to her and Leona fanned it off as nothing, but the apology was more impactful than anyone realized.

Luke and Ariel worked on a song and as Leona worked with the kids, Ariel's celestial vocals filled the room.

"I'm coming into the booth," Luke said to Ariel via an intercom. Luke gave Jane a few instructions and she sat in his chair at the DJ table. Luke stepped into the vocal booth with Ariel. He motioned to Jane, who hit a button and the music played. Ariel sang the verses and Luke harmonized with her on the chorus.

Leona studied them in awe. Luke sang on some tracks, but to watch him was an experience of another level. This man was full of surprises.

"We're going to lay this one down with music. Jane?" Luke called.

"Got it." Jane flipped buttons with less skilled hands but got the job done. Leona listened to the different song elements, read the monitor, and jumped in to make some adjustments.

"Hey, you're pretty good at this. Maybe you should take over." Jane eyed her.

Leona shrank inward and again focused on the children. "Nah. You're doing great." She'd been so unguarded with Luke and his family that she'd almost outed herself.

Ariel and Luke finished the song. Luke played it back and the room was filled with The Musical Prophet's signature sound.

Luke pumped his fist, encouraging his niece and nephew as they danced. Leona only stopped staring at Luke, who was even sexier as an attentive uncle, when Jane pulled her up to join them.

The song ended and while he and Ariel worked, Leona, Jane, and the kids soaked up more sun outside and enjoyed dessert.

"Everything okay, Leo?" Jane asked as the kids played in the grass with popsicles in their hands. "I know you were upset earlier. I told Luke what I'd said and…"

"I hope I didn't make you or the kids uncomfortable."

Jane shook her head. "No. I just wanted to help. So did Luke."

"Thank you, Jane."

Jane nodded and watched her children with motherly pride. "Em stands like my father."

Leona evaluated Emily, who admired the necklace they'd made, and recognized the head-on stance the girl had taken when she'd questioned Leona's relationship with her uncle. "Luke stands the same way."

"Right? It's amazing how genetics work."

Leona saw an opportunity to learn a little more about their family. "Do you and Luke get to see your parents often?"

"I see them more often. Luke, not so much."

"Do they get along?" When Jane didn't answer right away, Leona thought it best to back off. "I don't mean to pry."

"Oh no, you're fine." Jane percolated on a response. "Luke is very driven. I think he just didn't plan on music being the source of that drive. He wants to make our parents proud and give them accolades to talk about with our family and their friends, who always ask and compare us to their own children."

Leona was gentle with her next question. "Do your parents put pressure on him?"

"Not at all. At least nothing out of the normal. It's not them. Luke puts pressure on Luke. Like diamond-type pressure. He tried to fit a square peg into a round hole and failed."

"What happened?" Leona asked.

"He loved music more than anything. He always has." Jane shrugged. "He gave up on the whole office grind to 'scratch records' as he would say. I think it would be easier for him to get over if he had some great title in a company, with letters after his name, than to be a DJ." Jane was quiet. "My parents don't give a shit as long as he's happy, but he can't get past the feeling that he let them down, somehow, so he stays away. I think if he hits his goals this summer, he'll be better with them."

Luke's goals were more than just record setting milestones. He was doing this for credibility—for his parents. "I see."

Jane cleared her throat. "If you don't mind me asking, Leo, how do you feel about my brother?"

Jane didn't mince words and Leona was taken aback by the question.

"I don't know," Leona fidgeted with her hands.

"You don't know how you feel about him?"

"I don't know how to answer your question. Things are complicated because I'm his tour manager. We both have some issues that we're trying to sort out. So…"

"But you're here with him, so you must feel something."

Leona didn't answer right away. "I do."

"I know I'm persistent. I just want to see him happy and with someone that deserves him."

Leona was warmed by Jane's love for her brother. "You should want that for him, Jane." Hell, she wanted that for him, too.

"And you, Leo? What do you want?"

Leona thought for a moment. "I want someone who deserves me, too."

Jane smiled. "Fair enough."

Chapter Twenty-Three

After delivering more hugs and kisses than either he or Leona could count, their company departed. Luke pressed his back against the door and relief softened his shoulders. He'd been nervous for Leona to meet his family. When she'd treated Emily and Ryan with unprompted kindness, he'd appreciated the woman she was even more.

"That was fun." She leaned against the wall closest to him. "I really like them and the kids are cute. A handful, but still, they're the cutest."

"They adore you."

"That's because I made them jewelry."

He reached for her hand and knitted his fingers with hers. "It's more than that." He pulled her a little closer.

"What is it?"

"Well, you're the cutest."

She laughed and he wanted to record her and listen to the melody in her voice on repeat.

"How are you feeling? You know, from earlier?" He desired Leona but when she was upset it clawed at something deep inside him and he wanted to do whatever was in his power to ease her pain. That scared the shit out of him the most. More than the way her touch soothed or his insatiable urge to please her both in and out of bed.

"I'm good," she said and squeezed his hand.

Something was bothering her and he had a feeling it wasn't just about the media that had surfaced about her and Paul. He brought her hands to his lips. "Come closer."

She inched toward him with baby steps. Humor mixed with seduction arched her eyebrow. "This good?"

"A little closer, please." He licked his lips. "I got something for you."

She stepped inches from him and he captured her lips in a passionate kiss against the front door.

"Luke," she called his name. Another sound he wanted to capture and add to his growing playlist of *Leona's Greatest Hits*. His free hand slid over her ass and he mashed her against the hard-on he always seemed to have for her. Her hands flew to his head and she matched his passion with her own.

"I want you so much, baby." He peeled her skinny jeans down. The material settled around her ankles and by the way she kicked them off, she wanted him just as much. He spun her around to face the door and attacked his belt buckle and wrestled off his shorts. Within seconds he claimed her from behind.

Leona called out something indecipherable and accepted his unbridled entrance. She was already so wet for him and he enjoyed how she blanketed his dick. The way she swathed his soul and made him believe again. Made him trust her with his heart.

"Oh shit," he hissed. "I have been dying to be inside you. To make you feel good."

Leona was bent over with her torso parallel to the

floor, her palms against the door, and her position excited him. She trusted him to make her feel good. To love her this way.

"Luke." With each wild thrust he lost himself in her. She twisted to observe him, her face decorated with unabashed need. He'd never experienced this level of emotion. He yanked her upright and clasped her chin. He sealed his mouth to hers, kissing her, while he imprinted her insides. He needed to impress this moment into her memory. He wasn't only fucking her but reclaiming what they threatened to lose with all that had happened earlier.

"Tell me how much you love it when I fuck you like this, Leona," he taunted, winded and completely drenched in her pussy.

She stretched her other hand back and reached for him, her movements frantic. He recognized her need for connection because he needed it, too.

"I love…" Leona groaned in pleasure. "You feel so good, Luke. I can feel every inch of you inside me."

She moaned, and he'd never be the same again. She moved her hips in time with his and circled them when he allowed. He gripped her soft flesh and increased his thrusts, his release upon him. The burning sensation in his lower abdomen exploded and he roared his pleasure, filling her hot canal with his seed.

Her hand caressed his thigh and he went weak, relaxing his hold on her luscious curves.

He bent to kiss her back and rubbed her ass and the back of her thigh.

"I'm not done with you, beautiful." Still inside her, he explored the contours of her body. He'd done this so many times since her arrival in San Francisco. He would

know her body even if he touched her blindfolded. He
settled on her breasts, feathering the protruding nipples
through their cover.

"I was hoping you'd say that." Though she leaned
her back into his chest, her body arched toward his ca-
resses. "You can have me any way you want me, baby."

His hand crept to her center where he massaged her
with possessive care. He pulled out of her in one slow
movement, and then spun her around to face him.

"I want all of you, Leona." Luke flattened her back
against the door.

"Please," she said. Her body sloped toward him, her
mouth desperate for his lips, but he kept her pinned as
his finger strummed her clit. She had not yet enjoyed
her own orgasm and he longed to douse the flame he'd
ignited, but he'd fan it a little first. Her mouth beckoned
his and he obliged with teasing tongue.

Her insides still haunted his dick, but he wanted to
please her. She'd felt so good. *I felt her. Skin to skin.*
He stopped kissing her and separated from her. Confusion creased her face.

"Oh shit, Leona. I'm sorry. I'm so sorry." *I'm the worst
asshole.*

"What? Why?"

His shoulders rounded and he folded in on himself.
"I got caught up. Shit. I never do this." Luke scrubbed
his face. "I didn't use a rubber."

Leona exhaled as if she'd been holding her breath.
"Oh."

"Oh?" Luke paced. "Don't you want to murder me?"

A light smile touched her lips. "Why would I want
to do that?"

"You could get pregnant." *She could be pregnant*

with his child. He steadied himself on the wall because the thought of Leona pregnant with his child exhilarated him as much as it terrified him. "You would have my child?"

"Yes." Her delivery was stone and then an array of emotions touched her face but none stayed long enough for him to decode. Then she dipped her head and repressed another smile. "I'm on something."

Relief and disappointment traveled through him. He righted himself before he went any further down that path. He moved in close to her. "And I'm just finding this out?"

Leona shrugged. "I liked that you were doing the right thing without me having to ask."

"Now that I know I can be more spontaneous, don't be surprised if you don't sleep again while you're here. Open." He spread her legs with his knee at the same time she made space for him. He dropped to kneel before her.

He draped one of her legs over his shoulder then buried his head between her thighs. He savored her like a sommelier would a fine vintage. "I love tasting you, Leona. Your scent is so intoxicating." He ate her until she teetered on the edge and finally over.

"Luke!" She trembled as the summit of her pleasure arrived. The shivers layered the tension in her body and within moments she was weak and barely holding herself up.

Leona concentrated on Luke, who evaluated her every movement from below, triggering the dream that maybe this connection between them was more than sex and could last forever. That the past wasn't a barrier but lessons they'd both learned from and could use to love each other.

She never wanted to be without his touch ever again. The thought scared her especially now with her feelings at stake. Her breathing was heavy, as was his. *Holy shit!* She was about to tell this man she loved him.

He held her in an iron grip while his expert tonguing sent uncontrollable twitches to every limb. She snatched a handful of his hair and prayed she wasn't hurting him. He inflamed her body with his searing hot touches. She writhed under him and moaned as she moved her hips in the tiny rotations.

The sensations he forced on her were mind-blowing. She pulled at him, wanting him to continue, and then pushed at him, completely overwhelmed by the assault on her swollen clit and stimulated nerves. The dance was reminiscent of the tug of war with their relationship. Every cell in her feared the definition. Relationship. But as the pressure built quickly within her, she released her trepidation and once again quivered in climactic bliss against the door and Luke. Her legs spasmed from weakness, but Luke continued to hold her.

Leona's screams burst through the house. She was going to pass out from the intensity. "I can't. Luke, I can't." Her labored breath made her gulp in air.

"Last one, baby. I promise." His breath gently fanned her center, blowing, healing both her body and spirit. "Give me one more, Leona."

She wanted to object. If he continued to touch her there, she'd shatter like pressurized glass.

Luke again blew on her, the soft air cooled, but that didn't last long. The heat of his mouth blanketed her and his skilled tongue built the pressure in her again.

Leona thought her nerves were fried, but when the burning of her orgasm fluttered through her again, she was brought to tears that flowed down her cheeks as she moaned and called Luke's name. "No more, Luke. Please. No more," she cried. If sex was ever going to kill her, it was going to be now.

Luke's laughter vibrated between her leg muscles. She was completely spent but still extremely sensitive to his touch. He relaxed his grip and his power sucking became mild licks.

Leona wiggled against him, still experiencing high sensations. She panted and brought her hand to her head in an attempt to catch her breath. She liquefied to the floor.

"I love to watch you come, Leona, and hear you let go." Luke crawled up to her, sat next to her, and put his arm around her. "You can always do that with me, you know. Let go."

Leona sniffled. His double meaning dissolved her into mush. She drew from the strength of his arms. No one had ever said that to her before. "Compliments and cunnilingus." She tilted her head up to kiss his chin.

"Yes." Luke laughed, but then saw the wetness on her cheeks.

The last time she saw similar stress lines on his face was when she'd had a meltdown from being in his studio.

"You, I…" Luke was in bad shape. "Did I hurt you?"

"No. Nothing's wrong. I don't have words to express how wild that was. So…" She wiped her cheek and showed him the wetness on her fingers.

He didn't appear convinced.

Leona laughed. "I'm fine." She gave an exhausted breath. "I need a nap."

"A nap?"

"Yeah, we didn't get to bed until sometime this morning and then we were up at five or something ridiculous. I mean, at least, I was. Did you even sleep?" Leona didn't wait for him to respond. "Anyway, we have been like bunnies since I got here. Let's not forget that your sister, Ariel, and the kids were here and they only just left. It's almost nighttime and you have interviews in a few hours—"

"Uh-huh." Luke followed her story.

"Then, we just did the bunny thing some more."

He laughed at her. "Which we'll do again and again."

"If you don't want me to fall asleep on you tonight, you'll let me take a nap." She nudged him. "Do you want to join me?"

"I'll lie with you, but once you're asleep I'll probably go back to the studio. I don't think I could sleep even if I wanted to."

"I thought my hours were bad. Yours are straight ridiculous. I don't know how you do it." Her leg started to fall asleep. "I don't want to disrupt your routine."

"First of all, you're not disrupting my routine. You *are* my routine. You're my workout and my nutrition plan." He hauled her up with him.

Jeez, he was making her hot again.

"Let's put you to bed, Miss Sable."

They went upstairs to the bedroom carrying their individual pile of clothes, their naked lower halves streaking the hallway.

Leona discarded the remainder of her clothes and

climbed into Luke's bed. She slid under the sheets and waited for him.

Luke undressed and crawled into bed, gathering her in his arms.

"Mmm." Leona relished in his naked body. Had she not been so exhausted, she would have indulged in pleasure with him again. Instead, she enjoyed being held.

"You're like the softest kitten," he said against her ear.

"What woman doesn't like a little cuddle?" Leona nestled into the perfect fit of his torso.

"Good point." Luke squeezed her tighter. "Go to sleep. I'll wake you up later."

"I really liked that song you did with Ariel earlier."

"Which one?" The timber in his voice vibrated against her back.

"The first one." Her palms glided over his forearms.

He started to sing it to her.

She smiled. "Yes, that one. You should play it on the tour when it's ready." She closed her eyes and yawned.

Luke squeezed her again and continued the song as if singing her a lullaby.

Leona's breathing deepened and soon she was fast asleep.

Leona lost count of how many times she and Luke were intimate. Even as she slept, Luke was pleasing, touching, and satisfying her in some way. She savored every minute of it because all good things had to come to an end.

She sat across from Luke as they shared a late lunch the next day. She didn't want to be the bearer of bad news, but she had been tiptoeing around the issue all day. They had to get back to normal. Her lunch tasted like cardboard as she readied herself to speak to him. She pushed her food away.

"I had a good time here with you, Luke."

He met her eyes and he stretched his shoulders back. "I knew this was coming."

"It's what we agreed would happen." Leona chewed the inside of her lip. "In a few hours, I'll be meeting with Sara and Sebastian to get prepped for LA, and then we'll be at your nightclub performance and this will be over." The words were more difficult to get out than she expected.

He chewed his food harder and quicker. "Right."

She took a deep inhale and waited. Nothing. "That's all you're going to say to me?"

"We agreed things would go back to normal when this was over, Leona, just like you said. So let's enjoy it until the end and then it's back to business."

He was right. They had an agreement, but the words were no less painful to hear. *What did I expect? That he'd fall in love with me?* Anything short of going back to the tour in a strictly client–tour manager relationship would cause problems. But how could she go back?

If this was just a fling then why did he trust his sister and Ariel to come to the house, even though their rendezvous was a secret? She had only told Izzy. This was exactly what Luke had promised when he proposed she come out to meet him here. This needed to happen. So what the fuck was her problem?

"Okay, great. I'll start packing. I can stay at a hotel tonight to avoid any questions."

Luke dropped his fork. "Why? We have to fly to LA tomorrow night. It doesn't make sense to split up at this point."

Point taken, but she didn't want to further compli-
cate an emotionally charged situation. "I'll let you know
what I ultimately decide."

Luke nodded.

She waited to see if he would say anything, but he
continued to eat. Anger heated her skin. If he wasn't
going to talk to her, then she wasn't going to just sit
there. She headed to the bedroom to start packing.

Luke's hand shot out to grab her arm. In one motion,
he fastened her onto his lap. She struggled a bit, but he
held her to him.

"Stop, Leona."

She huffed as she tried to get up, but he was stronger. "Let me go, Luke."

His eyes searched for hers but she avoided them. "I
know you want to pretend that you don't give a shit,
but I know you do."

Leona frowned at him. "Me? You're the one who
has said all of two words in this whole conversation."

"What would you like me to say?" His words were
soft against her ear.

"I don't know. Anything." She wanted him to tell her
this wasn't just a fling and that he wanted her in his life.
But even if he did, how could this work? She wanted to
tell him she wanted more, too, and that she was sorry
for what she'd done and how her choices had affected
him, but she couldn't.

"I don't want this to end, Leona. Having you here
with me… I never thought… I don't want to hope for
something that can't be."

Her heart was aching. She had let her feelings get out
of control here, and now she wanted what she couldn't

have. The gallery publicity had shown her that all her hard work could be obliterated in one fell swoop.

"We can't." The words physically hurt, as if they had been torn from her like a plant being ripped from its roots. "There is too much at stake. I'm just coming back. You've seen the gallery gossip. The media will destroy me—us, if they get the chance."

"What if they do?"

"What if they do?" she challenged. "Then it'll be a spectacle. First they'll start on me, and how I'm dating another client. Then they'll bring up Paul's lies and paint me as the bitch ruining his life or worse. Then when I don't give them what they want, they'll infiltrate everything good in my life to try to get it. I can't let them do that again. I can't give them the ammunition."

"You're going to let the media dictate how you live your life? Don't get me wrong, Leona, I get that when they come for you it can get way out of hand, but you don't have to give them control over your happiness."

"That's easy for you to say," she said.

"Is it? When Ivy left my tour and our relationship, the media had a field day creating all kinds of rumors about it until Ivy's family paid them off. Being broadcasted like that hurt me, too, but I kept playing my music, kept interacting with the fans, and held my niece and nephew when I visited my sister. I had to cherish what was good in my life and not focus on what people who didn't know me had to say."

His admission made this even harder. Luke had always had a hard time trusting her. It had pissed her off but she understood. Now he was opening up to her in a way he hadn't before. More than that, he identified with some of what she'd experienced. Some.

Tears sprang to her eyes and she blinked hard and fast to hold them back. "Luke. I'm sorry." She swallowed the thickness of their situation. She buried her head in his shoulder. Her previous bout with the media had handicapped her with anxiety, tortured her friends and family, and deteriorated her work relationships and reputation. Could she risk it all, for Luke?

"Hey. We don't have to make any big decisions right now." Luke pressed his head against hers and relaxed his hold. "The last thing I want to do is spend the rest of our time here arguing."

Leona slid her arms out of his embrace and latched them around his neck, hugging him tight. She didn't want to fight with him or herself. She just wanted to hold him.

Luke cradled her in his arms and caressed her back.

"I'm meeting with Sara and Sebastian at their hotel. I'll come back so we can go to Cosmic City for your show."

"Okay." Luke bent his head and she received his kiss. She didn't know how many kisses she had left because soon they would be cut off from this intimacy.

She had to make every one of them count.

Chapter Twenty-Four

Cosmic City in downtown San Francisco was lit with fans thirsty for Luke's music. He had been quiet ever since their conversation at lunch but Leona thought it was better to have him quiet if it kept him from showing her any affection in public, which was proving to be difficult for them both.

She had separated from him when they arrived at the club, but now, as he was moments away from getting onstage, she checked on her artist.

Luke saw her and crossed his arms, towering over her. "You know this isn't going to work, right?"

"What's not working? Do you need something?" Leona scanned the room to see if something was out of place.

"I'm talking about us, Leona."

She scowled. She had been doing what was necessary to get things back to normal. "You're going to do this to me, now?"

"I'm trying, Leona, but acting like this week never happened is impossible."

"Try harder." She peeped the area for any eavesdroppers.

Luke narrowed his eyes. "It's that easy for you?"

Leona bit her lip. "You know it's not, but discretion is everything. We can't go broadcasting this like Paul—"

"You're seriously going to compare me to Paul Reese right now? That's a fucked up fake out." Every inch of Luke's face frowned.

Exasperated, she explained. "I'm not comparing you. I'm drawing a correlation to the circumstances around this."

Luke scratched his head. "What are you not telling me, Leona? Something's up. I see it every time Paul's name is mentioned."

Her nerves were jittery from the thought of coming clean. What would he do when he found out? If she had ousted Paul as the fraud producer he was when they'd broken up, then the chain of events that had happened to Luke may have been avoided. "You have a performance."

Luke followed her to the backstage entrance. "Then let's talk after."

Leona was reluctant to agree because she hadn't yet figured out what she would say to Luke or how deep she wanted to go. "Fine."

"I'm serious, Leona. No more secrets."

Leona hugged herself. "I heard you."

He moved closer, the glint in his eye her only warning before he kissed her.

She stepped away. "Okay, then. Later."

Luke's presence onstage marked the end of their lover's retreat. The crowd was electric and welcomed him home. Even now, she was unable to rid her thoughts of him touching her and their time together.

He had wanted to talk, but when she told him the truth, would he understand why she couldn't take a chance? They'd have hard times balancing their personal and professional relationship. The distance between her in New York and him in California would strain their intimacy. Eventually things would get ugly and they would break up. She'd have the reputation of dating her clients and again burn professional bridges that she was just starting to rebuild. She had worked hard over the past year to clean her slate.

Now Luke wanted to write all over it. She was sure her feelings for him had far surpassed what he felt for her. But that wasn't even the worst of her worries. What of her secret? Could he forgive her when he found out the truth about Paul and her part in all of it? What if she loved Luke and it wasn't enough? She rolled the tension from her shoulders and summoned her managerial self to the forefront.

Luke was in the zone, playing for about two hours. Things were running smoothly and everyone, from the promoters to the fans, was happy with the show. Leona went backstage to go to the ladies' room.

As she washed her hands, a loud gasp from the crowd carried over the sounds of Luke's music. Whatever had happened wasn't good. She hurried toward the main area of the club. Sara burst through a set of doors, her face paler than normal and creased with worry lines.

Leona's heartbeat quickened and she started to run. "Sara?"

"Oh my God, Leo. He won't come down. He fell but he won't come down!"

Leona tried to apply order to Sara's ramblings but she couldn't understand. "Sara, stop. Breathe. Tell me what happened," she yelled above the music that continued to play.

"Luke did a stage dive. On the surf back in, he tried to climb up to the stage, but he fell and hit his head, really hard, I think. I called for help."

Before Sara finished her sentence, Leona was running to Luke. Sara tried to keep her speed and continued to fill her in.

"He stumbled onstage and I think he's hurt real bad. Diesel tried to get him off the stage but he won't come down."

When Leona got to the stage she saw Luke standing behind the DJ equipment, but he was as still as a post, and his eyes were fixated on one spot. He held himself up with his arms and was inhaling and exhaling as if willing himself to breathe.

Leona raced up the staircase to get Luke and placed a shaky hand on his back. "Luke?"

He turned his head to her, like a creepy doll in a haunted house, his eyes glassy. A thin stream of blood dripped down the side of his face.

She repeated to herself not to freak out. "You have to come down, Luke."

"I have to play for the fans."

He responded to her, which she thought was a good sign, but his lazy blinking added to her worries. She didn't second-guess and thought it better to be safe than sorry.

"We have to check and see how badly you're hurt."

"I can't leave," Luke said.

Leona held his face in her hands. She leaned in and spoke in his ear. "You're bleeding. Please come down, baby. Come on." She pulled Luke and he started to move with her.

With a blood-wet hand, she fanned Sebastian over to help Luke offstage.

EMTs had arrived and Leona and Sebastian delivered Luke right into their hands, while Diesel created space around them. They had a stretcher ready for him.

"I don't need a stretcher, I can walk. See? I'm okay," Luke mumbled to the EMTs.

"Are you feeling dizzy, sir?" one of the EMTs asked.

"Not much," Luke answered too casually for her liking. "I don't need to go to the hospital."

"You're going and that's final." Leona motioned to the EMTs and then called to her team. "I'll go with Luke. Make an announcement. I'll be in touch."

"We got it covered, Leo," Sara said and was off to communicate with the club and corral the fans.

As Leona rode in the ambulance with Luke, she was a bag of nerves. He had hit his head hard enough to cause bleeding.

What if he has serious damage? "Is he going to be okay?" Leona asked one of the EMTs.

"He appears to have a cut, but a doctor needs to check him out to be sure there isn't any further damage."

"You could just ask me, you know?" Luke said to both Leona and the EMT. He reached for her hand. His hands were a little cold and she warmed them with hers.

"I think you would tell me you were fine, even if you weren't." She lifted his hands to her mouth and blew on them. "What happened?"

"I was crowd surfing and I missed my step climbing back onto the stage," he said simply.

All Leona could do was shake her head at him.

They arrived at the emergency entrance and Luke was rushed in.

"You have to wait here, miss," a hospital security guard told her.

"Oh no, I don't." She tried to bypass him.

"The staff needs space to help your boyfriend, miss. Someone will update you as soon as you're able to see him."

As she watched the staff approach Luke through the set of double doors, she alternated between wringing her hands and stroking both ears between her thumb and index fingers. *Dear Lord, please let him be okay.*

Leona was about to lose it by the time a nurse found her and let her know that she could see Luke. They had him in a small room, hooked up to an IV and receiving fluids. Her blood pressure shot up and she leaned against the door.

"It's just a precaution, Leona. I've had to get stitches for my head, but I'm totally fine."

She rushed to his side and gently slid her shaking arms around his neck and kissed him. "You scared the shit out of me. Don't you ever do that to me again."

He nuzzled the bandage-free side of his head against hers. "Is that an order, Miss Sable?"

"Yes." She kissed him again.

A knock sounded on the room door and they separated.

A man in a white lab coat entered. "Mr. Anderson. You're all set. You can leave after your IV is finished. The nurse will take care of it."

"Leona, this is Dr. Vargas." Luke pointed.

"This is the manager you spoke of who won't let

you leave the hospital until I tell her you're fine?" Dr. Vargas teased.

"Yes," Leona confirmed. "Tell me, Doctor. How is he really?"

"He's fine. He has a hard head, that's for sure. He may have been a little disoriented after his fall but he's fine now. Nothing is broken, just some stitches with a little local anesthesia. Once it wears off, it'll hurt. A lot. He may also be sore but he's not complaining. X-rays show no sign of damage. So, I'm sending him home with some pain medication that will also help with any swelling, and a prescription for an antibiotic cream." Dr. Vargas signed a paper on a clipboard and handed it to Luke.

"Can he still perform? He has a show on Friday in LA."

"Sure, but I suggest he take it easy until then." Dr. Vargas quickly examined Luke's eyes with a small light giving him instructions. "You are very lucky, Mr. Anderson. Pay better attention the next time you…what is it…crowd surf?"

"My sentiments exactly. Thank you, Doctor."

Dr. Vargas left and she once again wrapped her arms around Luke.

"See? I'm all good," he whispered in her ear before kissing her earlobe.

"The doctor is right, Luke. You were really lucky. This could have been so much worse. I mean…was it worth it?"

"The stage dive? Every time," he said without missing a beat.

"Wow." *I'm in love with a daredevil.* He squeezed her with the arm not attached to the IV. The way his green eyes shined at her gave her butterflies.

"What?" she asked.

"Nothing." He bit his lip and gave her a sly smile. "I'm ready to blow this joint."

Leona stood up. "Then let's get you home."

Home. A vivid vision of building a home with Leona formed in his head.

In the house, Leona headed to the kitchen and he headed for the bathroom. He had to pee like a racehorse from the fluids. He checked out the gash on his skull. They had shaved the hair just above the right eyebrow and when he tilted his head forward, he inspected the two-inch long wound.

He finished up in the bathroom and toddled into the kitchen, where Leona paced.

"Leona?"

"Yes." Her sharp pivot made her blurry. "Are you hungry?"

The sun had just started to come up. "I'm not feeling up to food right now." He patted his stomach.

Leona moved to the stove. "Some tea? It might be soothing."

Her nervous movements were worse than someone on too much caffeine.

"I'm more tired than anything else." He lazed over to her and collected her into his arms. He was glad she didn't pull away because he needed to hold her.

She squeezed his torso. He knew she cared by the way she'd embraced him at the hospital and now, as she shivered against him. Good idea or not, he could muster up the energy to make love to her if she let him.

"Come to bed with me." He held her hand and steered her toward his bedroom.

"You think you're slick, but I was there when the doctor suggested you take it easy."

"I know."

When they arrived at his bedroom, he pulled her down on the bed with him, unwilling to let her go. "I want to feel you in my arms like this again before we get back on tour."

She touched a finger to his scalp close to his wound.

He saw the stress on her face and moved her hand away from his head and kissed her fingertips.

She was tense when she first lay down, and then her body relaxed as she snuggled into him.

"One last time."

Leona jiggled Luke awake for his morning interviews.

Luke grimaced, holding his head. "Motherfucker!" Dark circles dusted his eyes and his color was still slightly off.

Leona stood by the bed ready with medication and a glass of water in hand. She wanted to take his pain away.

Luke desperately swallowed the pills.

With everything they both had at stake with the tour, she couldn't believe her next words. "We're cancelling the show."

"Huh?" Luke squinted with one eye open. "No way."

Leona buffed her left ear continuously. "You can't perform like this."

"I perform tomorrow. I'll be fine." Luke growled and held her hand as he lay back against the pillows. "Now, please be quiet, baby. Until these meds kick in, any noise sounds like my head is in a fucking ringing tower bell."

She massaged his neck and bent to place a gentle kiss on his forehead. She rubbed light, slow circles on his scalp. Staying last night was already a bad idea. With all that had happened, their chat had dropped lower on the list of priorities. But he was hurt and she couldn't bring herself to leave him.

Once Luke settled back into bed she got with her team. She postponed his morning interviews and made everyone aware of the adjustments she was making to Luke's routine until she was confident he was back to normal.

"How is he, Leo?" Sebastian broke her momentum.

"He's managing a mother of a headache, which is probably why his doctor told him to take it easy today, but he's clear to perform. All we can do is support him as best we can. We'll be driving to LA tonight. Thank you guys so much for being so quick and efficient with this. I read the press release and the news updates are correct, with the exception of the tabloids. Let's keep confirming that no tour dates have been cancelled."

"We got your back, Leo. Are we still going to conference with Tommy later?" Sara asked.

"I'll see if Luke's up to it, but we'll meet regardless."

"We haven't sold out LA yet." Sara's statement with all its meaning hung in the air.

"It's not over. Let's get feet on the ground for our grassroots efforts and blow up social media. We're not in control of the outcome anymore, but we are in control of our own efforts. We have until the first note of the first song to make it happen. So let's go."

"I'm with you, Leo," Sebastian said and Sara agreed.

Leona went over a few more details and then hung

up. She knew Luke would be hungry so she prepared something for him to have when he got up.

She was alone and had nothing but time to think about the what-ifs. Luke felt like a vital organ in her body that she'd soon have to part with. *How can this work? What if I say yes to this?* Leona opened her computer and dug into a few files she'd buried because they reminded her of all that had happened between her and Paul. She was solution oriented, organized, and always tried to cover the bases. Maybe she'd never gotten rid of the files because deep down inside she knew one day she might want to fight. Maybe one day she would need these recorded sessions with Paul and dated images of lyrics and song structure notes in her handwriting. She condensed it all in an email to Tracy Ruiz and typed a message. What can I do with this?

Pressing send had her worrying her earlobe, and her heart raced. All she had done was ask the question but the answer and any action or inaction would rock her world forever.

A half hour later, Luke straggled into the kitchen and sat down at the counter.

Leona watched for any signs that something wasn't right. "How're you feeling?"

"Much better. Those meds are like magic mushrooms."

"I bet," Leona smirked. "Do you feel up to the conference call we have with Tommy later?"

"Yeah. We have LA coming up. This is a big deal." He eyed the food on the table and eased onto one of the stools at the kitchen counter. "Is this for me?"

"It is. Eat what you want and I'll take care of the rest."

"Did you eat?" Luke pointed down at the fresh salad, baked salmon, and fruit smoothie she had made.

"Not yet." In truth the emotional rollercoaster had preoccupied to the point where food was the last thing on her mind.

"Are you going to let me eat alone? Come eat with me."

"Still bossy, huh?" Leona climbed onto the stool next to him and shared food for them both. Was there anything she wouldn't do for this man if he asked her?

Luke gave her that boyish grin that dissolved her into a puddle of mush. He nudged her with his shoulder. "Thanks for everything."

Leona met his hypnotic orbs and nudged him back. "Anytime."

What if?

Chapter Twenty-Five

The effect Luke's accident had on the tour was something Leona and her team could not have foreseen. The
accident had created buzz, and a video of his fall went
viral on social and traditional media outlets. The fans
expressed get well sentiments and shed tears for The
Musical Prophet. They camped out at decoy hotels and
the real hotel. In the end, the team needed to boost
Luke's security.

Candy and Velvet arrived to perform as Luke's opening act. As a much-needed female presence in a male
dominated industry, the duo had been added to the tour.

"We're excited to be here. When we heard about
Luke's accident we thought the concert might be cancelled, but Tommy kept us updated. We're glad Luke's
okay," Candy said.

Leona liked the ambient undertones in their Nuevo
electronic sound so much that she'd downloaded a few
of their mixes and listened to them on the drive to Los
Angeles.

"I'm glad we have this chance to work together given
that our first meeting was cut short. Your sound check
was amazing. You'll do great tonight."

Velvet pushed her half-shaved red hair with platinum

blonde strands over her shoulder. "We were hoping that when we're ready to tour, you'd be our tour manager."

Given the chilled first impression, Leona was somewhat surprised by their interest in her as a manager. "We can definitely discuss it when Luke's tour is over. I think I'd like working with you both. I have to go, but I'll check on you ladies before the show."

She left the giddy duo and found Luke talking with the sound crew. She fell into place next to him as they went through the normal routine.

Sara and Sebastian sprinted toward them. Leona hoped their excitement was a sign of good news.

Sara halted just short of Leona and jumped up and down. "The show is sold out."

Leona's entire body relaxed from a week's worth of anxiety.

Luke pumped a fist. "Yes."

"We were supposed to tell them together," Sebastian grumbled.

"Oh damn. Sorry, Sebz." Sara bit her lip.

Sebastian shook his head in disbelief.

Leona knew the accomplishment meant more to Luke than just selling out the venue. "You made history. That's something to be very proud of."

"*We* made history," Luke corrected.

"Not only is it sold out," Sebastian rushed on, "but we were able to activate the jumbo screen outside because of a permit Leona made us acquire during planning a few months ago. So, the fans that couldn't get tickets can see some portions of the concert outside. With vending that's almost two million in revenue at this location alone."

Luke faced her. "Very cool."

Leona's job was to go above and beyond for her clients, but the way Luke beamed at her made her even more proud of her work. She sent a message to both Tommy and Abe with the news. "One down, two to go. Nice work, guys. We'll make sure to celebrate with the crew. Let's deliver a great show and then get ready for Vegas."

"And in classic Leo form, she's on to the next goal," Sara declared.

Sebastian tilted his head. "Did you expect any less?"

Sara half-smiled. "Never."

Leona studied Luke. "How are you feeling?"

Luke scratched his chin. "I'm good. Just like I was an hour ago."

Leona chewed the inside of her lip. "I know I keep asking, but your work ethic is sick. I'm not sure you'd tell me if you weren't feeling well."

"I'm fine, bab... Leona. Stop worrying." Luke poked her with his elbow.

Sara and Sebastian grinned like sentimental cartoon characters at their exchange.

"Thanks, guys. I'll catch up with you in a bit." Leona again focused on finalizing everything for his set. "Let's get back to work."

When Luke got onstage that night, the roar of the crowd was deafening. Leona was glad he wore earplugs without complaint. The crowd's love was overflowing and as true disciples of The Musical Prophet, Luke's fans would follow him anywhere.

Luke was energized, but by the later part of his show, his movements got smaller. Diesel was close by, as was extra security. Luke spoke to the crowd more, which they loved, and when he mentioned the fans outside, the fans roared so loud Leona thought the building would come down.

At the end of the show Luke did his ceremonial front row pass, shaking as many outreached hands as possible. The fans screamed, cried, and tried to jump over the partition to get to him. Luke had crossed over, with solid footing, into full-on celebrity status. His life, here on out, would never be the same.

Backstage, Luke changed and prepared to meet the press. Leona huddled on the sidelines but kept a close eye on Luke. With the recent surfacing of her picture with Paul she didn't want the focus to be drawn away from Luke so she did what she did best and kept a low profile. Luckily, Luke's fall was still the hot topic. She limited Luke's time with the press so that he could "take it easy some more," which put them ahead of schedule for their Las Vegas departure. Diesel carted Luke off to his bus and things were getting back to normal.

Leona rode with her team to Las Vegas and though she worked on strategy for the Xcelsior meeting, she wanted to let her team leads know about the plans she had for the Epic Stadium in New York. Epic was the largest venue and Leona wanted to not only sell out the stadium but to also shut down the city. She wanted everyone talking about The Musical Prophet.

Creative planning took up most of the trip to Las Vegas, and they were soon pulling into their hotel. The trio was on their way to their rooms when all three of their phones buzzed.

"Interesting." Sebastian noted the synchronicity and reached for his phone. "Must be a media alert."

Leona, too, reached for her phone as hers buzzed

a second time. Both messages were from Tracy. Her heartbeat frequency increased. *What has Paul done now?*

Tracy: We're working on damage control. Let's talk to discuss suggested legal action.

Leona opened the attached image and didn't see Paul, but Luke. Specifically, her and Luke outside of The Naked Café when she'd had her anxiety attack as Luke comforted her.

The headline read: The Musical Prophet Scheduled to Cancel Upcoming Tour to Comfort Wounded Manager Leona Sable.

Leona had to call Luke but she was too busy trying to Zen-out, because her world was over. She didn't have a Wiffle ball bat, so she used her arms to beat the shit out of the mattress in her room until she was exhausted and crying. She had been the biggest fool on the planet to believe that she could somehow have Luke in her life without any messy renderings.

It was bad enough that she had to deal with Paul's media nonsense but now she had to address the intimate photo of her and Luke, as well as damage-control the effect the headline could have on his tour sales, performances, and the goals in the contract. The avalanche just wouldn't quit.

She rubbed her left ear and sniffled. *Breathe. Center.* She tried her mantra. She should go to his room. She inquired with reception to see if Luke had checked in but his bus hadn't arrived yet. *Just call him.* "I'm such a chicken shit."

She was about to call when her phone buzzed. Luke. She took a steadying breath and picked up.

"You okay?" Luke asked before she could get any words out.

"You saw the photo of us," she said, her question more a confirming statement.

"Yeah. Tommy called. Are you all right?" he asked again.

"Yes," she lied, and her small talk deflection was on point. "Is your bus here yet?"

"We're almost there."

"I'm so sorry, Luke. That time was…our time together was special and… This is because of the gallery, Paul thing."

"I'll come by your room."

"No." She wanted nothing more than Luke's strong and warm arms but the exposure of their relationship was causing them pain. "We have to get ready for the Xcelsior meeting. You have to focus on that and be ready to divert any questions. We can't afford to lose this deal."

"Let me come see you, Leona."

"So they can take more pictures?" Her facade cracked. "We'll meet at the atrium outside the conference room as planned."

Luke was quiet and she wasn't sure she wanted to be in his head and privy to his current thoughts. He'd asked her how she was doing but the headline kept floating through her head like a news ticker. *The Musical Prophet to Cancel Tour…*

"We'll talk," she offered. "Please, Luke. Just get ready for the meeting."

"Okay," he said at last.

Leona prepared herself for the meeting and headed downstairs to the atrium. She was nervous to see Luke but when she saw Abraham Wallace she did her best to appear normal.

"Whose bright idea was it to come to the desert in the middle of summer? Jeez! It's like a rotisserie and I'm the chicken."

Leona kissed his sweaty cheek. She was relieved to see he still had some humor given the circumstances.

"Honestly, Abe. I can't believe you have on a full suit. It's summer. In Vegas." She tried to sound light-hearted but her head hurt like hell from the adrenaline and a rock sat in her chest.

Abe continued to loosen buttons and take off layers. "How are you holding up?"

"You saw the media stuff?" She shifted from foot to foot and kept pulling her hand away from her left ear.

"Of you and Paul, and of you and Luke? Yes. I gave Tracy the okay to give the team a heads-up."

Leona cringed. Abe reminded her that her colleagues had seen her and Luke and the exposure made her feel like she'd just streaked the lobby nude.

"But we have bigger problems."

"Moro?"

"Inside information has it that Christian and Paul are having production issues. If that doesn't pan out, that agreement Paul made to offer us good press? Out the window. Paul's been inferring that Luke has some influence on Christian. No doubt part of how the media became interested in Luke, and how this headline about you and Luke came about."

"When did this happen?"

"The rumors have been percolating over the past day or so but when your headline hit…"

Leona rubbed her left ear and her right. It had taken a half hour for her to get herself together enough to show up for the meeting. Now it all resurfaced again with more added on.

Luke and Tommy approached from a side entrance and Leona couldn't help but watch the handsome duo. Sucks that they'd both probably hate her by the time this headline ran its course.

Luke got close, and Leona's eyes widened in horror when he tried to embrace her. She backed up and Luke's hands fisted at his sides.

Tommy broke the awkward silence that hung between the four of them. "Good to see you, Abe." The two men shook hands.

"You, too, Tommy." Abe turned to Luke. "Congratulations on selling out LA. I see things are…on schedule. How are you, Luke?"

"Apparently, I'm cancelling all my shows," Luke responded.

The bitterness in his words strangled her heart.

"Our team is working on having that headline retracted. We'll take legal action, if necessary. Don't worry, Luke," Abe offered when she didn't do her job as manager and put her client's mind at ease.

Tommy cleared his throat. "We should head inside."

Leona slowed Luke down to her pace. "Look, it's obvious you're upset."

"Upset? This media bullshit is threatening to ruin everything—"

"I'll fix it," was all she could get past the constriction in her larynx.

"Leona, I didn't mean—"

"No, it's okay." She plowed through for fear that she'd lose her shit right when she needed to keep it together the most. She summoned all her prowess as manager "We're about to go into this meeting. I need you with me. We have to do this as a team. You ready?"

His face reddened and he straightened. "I'm ready."

She was hurt, but she had to push her emotions aside. She turned "on," determined to get Luke his residency at the Xcelsior Hotel.

He was losing her and there wasn't a damn thing he could do about it. He'd seen how any mention of the media had shut her down. With the most recent head-line broadcasting such an intimate moment, she would hide from him, even though she needed him the way he needed her.

Despite the recent incident, they handled the bid meeting well. His success on the tour and the Los Angeles sellout was enough to have the owners seeing dollar signs. His team did their best to snuff the rumors, and Luke assured the owners that there was "no way in hell I'm cancelling my tour." His popularity would pull in international crowds to the hotel. The Xcelsior owners would inform the team whether or not they got the bid in a few weeks.

"I'm starving. Let's get some lunch." Tommy rubbed his stomach. "I hear the hotel has an excellent restaurant."

Luke started to withdraw. He wanted to talk to Leona and no temptation of food would deter him. Under the circumstances, he didn't call her out directly. "I should get some rest and go over my set for tonight."

Tommy's hangry gaze burned a hole through him. "Luke, it's an hour. Abe's in town. Plus, we should strategize given the recent activity. Let's have lunch."

"He's right," came Leona's solemn agreement, which further irritated him. He reluctantly agreed and stepped in line with Abe toward the restaurant.

Luke vaguely heard the conversation over lunch. Abe and Tommy discussed some legal options and talked about scheduling time with their legal teams to coordinate strategies. All the while he focused on Leona, who, though sporting a tough exterior, was drowning inside.

"Are we in breach of the addendum, given Luke and Leona's rendezvous?"

Luke glared hard at the man. "No."

"I'm just trying to cover all the bases, Luke," Abe clarified.

"For this matter, all anyone needs to know is that the last condition in the addendum doesn't always apply." Luke relaxed his grip on his napkin.

"Ahh. Well, that's a plus. We'll get this train back on the right track. You have my word." Abe forked a sliver of filet mignon into his mouth and Luke hoped it would shut the man up for a few seconds.

"The train has always been on the right track. It's the media that's trying to derail us," Luke said to Leona.

Abe continued through his meal. "And we'll do our best to rein them in. We've learned a lot since our last big media scandal."

Leona winced.

Luke had had enough. He was wrapping this shit up. "Check please."

On their way back to their complimentary rooms at

the hotel, Tommy and Abe split from them and he and Leona shared an elevator ride.

"We have to talk about this." Luke observed her and his heart was sore from the sadness she'd inadvertently allowed through. Her chest heaved. If she cried, he didn't know if he could take that.

"Yes, we do." She didn't complain when he bypassed her room and took her to his, which stressed him out.

"Something to drink?" he asked.

She shook her head.

His heart cantered with uncertainty. "Please sit down, Leona."

"No, this won't take long." She leaned her butt against the desk by the far wall, creating even more distance. "This is what I feared would happen. They found us, exploited us, and on the same front Paul is attacking. Now your tour is coming into question and if we don't stop the bleeding it will impact your ticket sales and your Xcelsior deal."

"Leona—"

"Let me finish, Luke. You don't understand. This will only get worse and you'll hate me. I'm ruining your life." She rubbed her ear. "I have already ruined your life."

He was getting more uncomfortable with this line of conversation with each second that passed. "What are you talking about?"

"Paul."

He fumed. "It always seems to come back to Paul. The only thing I care about is that what he does hurts you."

"Everything that has happened between you and Ivy and your sound is because I didn't speak up sooner."

She let out an even shakier breath than the one before. "People often wonder why Paul hasn't had a hit in over a year." She made the statement and waited for it to settle on Luke.

"That's when you left him. You were, what? His muse?"

The corners of Leona's mouth twitched.

He could feel the intrigue wrinkling his forehead. "Leona? Did you give Paul your ideas?"

Leona's eyes glistened and she shook her head. "I wrote those songs."

A few seconds passed before the information processed. "You? You were the one?"

She nodded. "In the beginning I thought I was helping him. If he needed money, I funded his projects. If he couldn't find his creativity, then I did it for him. In the end, he just used me."

Luke squinted his eyes in disbelief. "Who else knew about this?"

"Izzy, my brother, and more recently Tracy. The only reason I never told Abe was because Paul was on contract with Wallace Entertainment and I didn't want him caught in the middle."

"Leona—"

"Paul knew I was going to leave and had a lot to lose, so he humiliated and ruined me into silence. It worked. Because of my secrecy, you worked with Paul and he messed up your album, and then he stole your fiancée, and she fucked things up for your tour and your finances. If you'd never worked together then maybe things would be different for you. If only I'd said something. I'm so sorry, Luke."

Anger coursed through him and lit his whole body.

"You deserved to know," she whispered.

"You said that most recently, you told Ruiz. Why?"

"Because I wanted to see if I had enough evidence to sue Paul for writing credit and back royalties. She's looking into it."

His palm rested on his hot forehead and he was still trying to digest what she was telling him. Leona had been the hit-maker that he, Christian, and many other artists had been seeking. His mind flew back to how upset she got being in his studio when he was recording Ariel. "Oh, Leona."

"I hope you understand now why we can't be together."

"What? Wait. No, I don't. Things feel supercharged right now because it's fresh." He stared at her like he was meeting a celebrity for the first time but this was his manager, his lover, and even if she didn't know she was, a famous producer. "Leona, what we have—"

"What we have, and this drama right here, will destroy us, Luke. It's destroying us now. When Paul lied and bad-mouthed me throughout our networking circles and my reputation was called into question, my work and career suffered. While he relished in the media circus, my family suffered. My mother almost got into an accident ducking from the paparazzi and my father scrounged the entertainment shows searching for fake news about his daughter. When I was so scared that I couldn't breathe, I suffered, Luke. It's happening again and I can't risk it all to—" Her voice broke. She gulped in air and her shoulders shook in silent sobs.

He moved to caress her shoulders. "You can't risk it all to love me." The words were heavy in his mouth. She had been through more than he could ever fathom,

and though they weren't visible, her scars were deep.
He squeezed her in his arms. Being with him was hurting her too much and he weighed which was worse—
hurting her or being without her. Both killed him.

Chapter Twenty-Six

Leona was sick. Her inconsolable bloodshot eyes were dry and a constant reminder that her separation from Luke was killing her. Alone in her hotel room she paced, lugging her steps on the tan carpet. *But what else can I do?* The tour must go on.

The first week after the incident, and back on tour, Leona was acutely aware of the roadies eyeing her and Luke. Some with sympathetic eyes, others with curiosity, and the rest just doing their jobs. All of them, however, had to adjust to the new changes. Sara and Sebastian, and members of the team, were assigned to accompany Luke at sound check and help him with his pre- and post-stage itinerary. Leona filled in wherever she was needed, so long as she managed Luke from afar. Everywhere Luke was, she wanted to be but couldn't, so every time she saw him, a little piece of her died. Though Luke was physically and emotionally connected to the tour, they were quarantined like biohazard.

Now, alone in Chicago, she awaited her team's return from Japan and prepped for Luke's concert in his hometown. The special out-of-country performance had been scheduled to distract the media and keep them from capturing additional images to support their ludicrous headlines. As a result Leona worked solo. But, the career she loved lacked luster with the events that tarnished not only her reputation, but also the transcendent time she'd had with Luke at his home in San Francisco. Luke's absence added to her misery. They'd spent every moment together in California and the separation made her even sadder.

Izzy called again. She was doing overtime on her best friend duties.

"How are you, my love?"

"Still shitty."

On call number one, Izzy had listened, supported, and consoled. Izzy had even tried to abandon her projects and fly out to be with Leona. However, by call number two, Izzy was reaming her out for letting the media spoil a good thing. Leona wasn't sure what she'd get on call number three.

"Yes, that is to be expected," Izzy said in her ear. "Especially when you're in love."

Leona's heart pounded in her chest. Of course her best friend would know that she was in love. She had never been so wrecked from a breakup. A breakup? She and Luke weren't even dating.

"I know you want to whip me around, Izzy, but every day on tour with him is torture enough. I promise you. If you want me to feel pain, no worries, I'm feeling it."

"I don't want you to feel pain, Leo, my darling friend. I want you to fight for what you want and deserve and not be bullied into…well…this…that you're experiencing now. This doesn't have to be."

"I gotta go. I have work to do." Leona didn't want to hear this.

"Oh no you don't," Izzy shut her down. "Luke is in Japan with your team leads."

Luke *was* in Japan with Sara and Sebastian. Tommy scheduled an out-of-country, one-off performance to help with the strategy of separating her and Luke after Leona had suggested leaving the tour for a little while. Luke had emphatically disagreed, and had even used the contract to stop Leona's exit from the tour.

"How do you know that?"

"Because you were crying to me about it on our last call," Izzy said.

Apparently, on this call, Leona was taking Bitchology with Professor Fisher. "You're such a bitch, Izzy."

"So are you, at least you used to be. You were one of the greats, too. That is, until Paul spoiled you."

"Paul didn't spoil me. The media freaked me the fuck out."

"I love you, Leo. I let you have your cry, but now you need to do what The Musical Prophet says in his song. 'Get Up and Move for Me.'" Izzy stretched her statement like a true emcee.

Leona had enrolled in Cornyomics with Izzy, as well. She laughed. Her first real laugh since everything had gone south.

"You're ridiculous," Leona said. The two of them laughed for a bit.

"I really do have work to do. I'm still running a North American tour but I'll talk to you soon. Thanks for checking on me."

"You're welcome," Izzy said, and made kissing noises into the phone before hanging up.

Leona went back to work, making the necessary calls to her network in New York. One thing she did look forward to, among the chaos, was pulling off the marketing scheme with her team, and the events leading up to Luke's last show at the Epic Stadium. What she envisioned would be epic worthy if the team pulled it off. Luke was still her client, and making him successful meant even more to her now.

She did her best to focus on work, sending and checking emails. A new email from Tommy popped into her inbox about the Xcelsior and Leona hoped it was good news, but the message just asked that she call him.

A night alone in an unfamiliar city without her team, lover, or family? No time like the present. She called Tommy.

"I got your message," Leona said after they exchanged a greeting.

"Yeah. The owners want to meet with us again, but this time they want to see Luke at his residency in New York. They also suggested we bring legal representation."

Leona sat next to her luggage on the bed. "That sounds promising, Tommy. Normally, legal equals contract. Did they give you any indication about why they still haven't made a decision?"

"Not in detail, but from what I interpreted from the conversation, they're questioning his commitment. They like the numbers but they don't want the ego," Tommy relayed.

"That's pretty left field." Leona scoffed. "What gave them the impression he has ego problems?"

He sighed. "Some rumors about his relationship to other big names?"

Christian? Paul? Both? Under the circumstances, Leona thought Luke had pulled it together for the meeting and was professional, even charming at times. She hoped the owners would bypass the rumor mill and just focus on Luke.

"I thought we reassured them in the meeting that Luke was committed to the tour. We'll just have to do whatever's necessary to put them at ease. Luke gets back tomorrow. I'll talk to him." Leona paused. "I have to say, Tommy, this is going to be a busy time for us. Luke has his residency and we're doing the teaser to ramp up for his final show at the Epic Stadium. It's all hands on deck, including yours."

"My hands are your hands. Use them at will," Tommy teased.

She smiled. "You're great. Thanks."

Tommy cleared his throat. "How's everything else going?"

Leona didn't respond immediately. "So far the smaller shows haven't been affected. The team have been spinning the press questions and Sebastian has worked his film magic with trailers that have kept the focus on how great Luke's shows are."

"That's not what I meant."

She was heartbroken and though she wanted to run back into hiding and lick her wounds, she couldn't. "Hey, I have to go, but thanks for the update."

"Leo? I know you and Luke both care for one another, and I'm not telling you what to do, because handling the media is a big headache for everyone. Just... don't give up."

Leona was trying to rebuild the wall around her heart and wasn't about to let Tommy's appeal stall the already slow construction. "Thanks, Tommy. I'll talk to you soon." She hung up the phone before he could say anything else.

The news from Xcelsior raised the stakes for New York.

* * *

Luke sat in first class on a twelve-hour plane ride from
Haneda Airport in Tokyo, Japan, to O'Hare in Chicago,
Illinois. He flew with Sara and Sebastian but something
had been missing the entire trip.

Leona was a thorough and creative tour manager,
with finesse, but it was more than that. He missed her,
and not only the way she moved under him in bed but
her essence, the way her soft hand touched his arm and
the way her eyes beheld him. If he could time travel
back to California and time loop them there, he would.
He longed to experience the Leona she was around his
family and the one that purred when he held her in his
arms. Now their professionalism stood between them
like an impenetrable wall.

He rubbed his face, feeling anxious and caged hun-
dreds of miles away from the woman he loved.

The plane landed in Chicago and Luke rode to the
hotel with Sara and Sebastian. This had been the new
routine for the past few weeks. The Tokyo show had
gone well, and did its job—further separated him and
Leona. He was exhausted and glad to be back in the
States. He toured the sights of his hometown as they
drove through the city streets. The excitement of being
in his hometown, where his DJ roots started, had been
dulled by the events of the past few weeks.

He checked in with Jane and let her know he was
back safely. He had wanted to see his parents while
he was in Chicago, but they were on a cruise. Part of
him was relieved because he hadn't yet achieved all
his goals for the tour, but the other part of him really
missed them.

He snacked on a box of animal crackers left over

from his flight. What he really wanted was to show Leona his hometown and cover all the hot spots with her. Share a deep-dish pizza or take her for a The Turtle Split at Margie's Candies, have her meet his folks, and make out with her at his favorite lookout, but he didn't have those options anymore.

His phone rang and Christian Sacks's voice came through the phone.

"Hey, man," Luke greeted him.

"I'm sorry to bother you, man, but I need a favor. I was wondering if you could help me out with some production."

"What's up?" Luke asked as if he didn't know, but he wanted to hear it from Christian.

"Paul's been stalling and I have to finish my tour dates with Tres Armadas," Christian groaned in his ear. "I don't know, man. Something's funky. Paul just didn't have any ideas and the sound he was coming out with was way different than the vibe he's famous for."

Luke had experienced the same thing when he and Paul had worked together. Only recently had Luke found out that the style he had been enamored with, and the sound that made Paul famous, was really Leona's.

"Sure, man, I can help," Luke said. Of course Paul had been stalling. He wasn't the hit-maker DJs and artists salivated to collaborate with. "I can work on some stuff but let me reach out and see if anyone else is available."

"Thanks, man. I appreciate it." Christian sighed. "Maybe Paul will come through, but if he doesn't, I don't want to be left holding the bag."

Luke wanted to help his friend but more than anything he wanted to help Leona. Paul was celebrated in the music industry for Leona's work. *She* was talented, and famous, even if no one knew it yet. "Do you think you can hold off on production until after my tour?"

Christian hissed. "That's cutting it close, but I can wait for you."

"Not for me." Luke knew he couldn't tell Christian that the producer he was seeking was Leona, but he could tell him something else.

"For who then?" Christian's accent was heavy on his words.

"For the producer you've always wanted."

"You want to be any more cryptic, man?"

Luke chuckled. "Remember what I told you in New Orleans about working with Paul?"

"Yeah?"

"Just trust me on this. Wait."

"You've never let me down." Christian paused for a long moment. "I'll wait."

"Cool," Luke said and ended the call.

He may not be able to be with Leona but he'd damn sure do his part to make sure that Paul never damaged another artist or took credit for Leona's work again.

Luke strutted around in his towel and turned on the TV. He had showered and ordered room service after he got in a quick and necessary, all-types-of-tension-releasing workout. The flight had been comfortable, but he had been sitting for so long that all he wanted to do was stretch his bones.

There was a knock on his hotel room door.

Luke expected room service when he opened the door, but found Leona instead. The sight of her exhilarated him, and he had to stop himself from hauling her into his arms.

"Leona. Come in."

"I shouldn't." She cleared her throat and averted her eyes from his near naked body. "I tried to call, but your phone keeps going to voice mail. How was the show?"

"It went great." He scratched his head to occupy his hands.

"Good." She idled.

"How are you?" he almost whispered.

Her body physically breathed and she gave him a weak smile. "We heard from the Xcelsior. They want to see you in New York when you do your residency at Aurora, so the stakes are high for that performance. We haven't spoken about the marketing scheme, but it's going to be a busy time for all of us."

"Sara and Sebastian gave a me a rundown on the plane. So I know a bit about it."

"Oh. Okay. Umm… That's good." She crossed her arms at the sound of the elevator, and stepped back from him.

Luke inhaled. All he wanted was her with him. *Fuck this!* He was about to reach for her when a loud male voice in the hall cut him off.

"Little squirrel," the deep voice called.

The biggest smile spread across Leona's face. She ran down the hall and Luke witnessed her hop into the arms of a large, good-looking black man. Her legs went around him and she kissed his face.

"Mitch-match! What the hell are you doing here?" Leona asked the man.

Luke didn't care that he was half naked. Who the hell was Mitch-match?

Chapter Twenty-Seven

Luke burned a path right behind Leona until he was in earshot.

"Izzy said you were kind of down. I was going to be out here for business, so I got in touch with Abe and he helped me surprise you. I thought we could have Sunday dinner." The man referenced a bag in his hands.

"You smuggled it here? You're the best. Are you staying at the hotel?" Leona asked excitedly.

Leona's closeness to the man grieved him because he wanted that, no, *needed* that from her.

"Nah, I'm staying at the airport hotel. I fly out after my meeting tomorrow, so I'm in and out, but tonight I'm all yours."

"Yay!" Leona jumped up and down and clapped her hands. He hadn't seen her this alive since California, and though he wished he was the reason for her improved mood, he was just glad she was happy.

"Who the hell is this?" The man pointed at him when Luke approached.

Luke crossed his arms. "Who the hell are you?"

The man protectively tucked Leona behind him. Luke deduced that the man wasn't taller but certainly larger than him, and on a normal day might have kicked his ass. Not today and not if it had anything to do with Leona.

"Easy. Mitch-match, this is The Musical Prophet. My client."

"Oh yeah. The one from the scandal." Mitchell's eyes squinted at him and evaluated Luke's features.

Leona's shoulders slumped a bit. "Luke, this is my brother, Mitchell Sable."

"Your brother?" Had Luke not been so envious of the man, he might have seen the resemblance or even remembered Leona mentioning him during their intimate conversations in San Francisco. Instead he had only seen another man lavish her with affection. Affection he desperately wanted to give her.

"Why's he out here in a towel? Unless…" Mitchell's eyes ping-ponged from his sister and back to his near naked form.

Leona punched her brother's arm. "We were talking in the hallway and—"

"Whatever. Hey, Luke, why don't you join us for Sunday dinner?" Mitchell suggested.

"No-no." Leona shook her head. "Luke just got in from Japan. He's exhausted…"

"I insist," Mitchell said.

"I accept," he RSVP'd to Mitchell.

Leona shifted in her stance, but he wasn't about to miss this opportunity. For what, he didn't yet know, but he followed his gut.

"Great, but you can't come like that." Mitchell side-eyed his sister.

Luke liked Mitchell, now that he knew Mitchell and Leona were related.

"I'll just change."

Back in his suite, Luke cancelled room service, and dressed in jeans and a tee shirt. When he arrived at Leona's room, Mitchell opened the door while Leona readied the food.

"It smells like a country kitchen in here."

"Our mom's cooking. She sent me with loads of food for Leona," Mitchell said. "Pull up a chair, Leo's warming up the last of it."

Luke sat across from Leona at the small table and noticed her relaxed disposition with her brother. She'd been so stressed over the past few weeks, and their relationship had contributed to the bundle.

"Let's bow our heads." Mitchell offered one hand to Luke and another to Leona.

Luke hadn't touched her in so long. An electric jolt pierced through him and his breathing hitched in his chest. She squeezed his fingers, a motion he returned.

"Leona normally makes the best desserts, but seeing as she has no time to be cooking on tour, my mom sent along a little strawberry cobbler."

"Wow. I'll have to thank your mother when I meet her." There was certainty in his words. Based on Leona's sharp glance, he'd surprised her. He had made a similar statement about her meeting his mom when they were at his home. Though things were messy between them he still hoped the statement would one day be true.

She took a few bites of her food. "Mom outdid herself, as usual."

"So." Mitchell jutted his head toward Luke. "What did you do to Reese that has him gunning for you?"

Luke pointed to himself with his thumb to confirm. "Me?"

Leona frowned. "What do you mean, Mitch-match?"

"He's blaming Luke for a sour deal with some Christian Sacks dude and was on one of those gossip TV shows that Dad always watches, talking about Luke having a big ego because he had a sold out show in LA. He's on a rampage, again."

Leona's fingers curled around the end of the table and Luke thought she might actually break it.

"So, Christian fired Paul?"

"Uh…yeah." Mitchell scoffed. "Where have the two of you been?"

In misery.

"I told him to leave me alone. Now he's attacking Luke? After all the problems he's already caused? Why am I surprised?"

"Beats me." Mitchell shrugged.

Luke had asked Christian to wait on producing his album. Though he was relieved for Christian, he hadn't expected him to fire Paul and ergo create more problems for Leona and himself. Now that Christian and Paul's connection was severed, Paul would no doubt continue to behave badly.

Heat lit Luke's face like he'd stuck it in an oven. "I think I had something to do with that. I told Christian to wait for another producer. I didn't think he'd fire Paul."

"Wait, another producer? Who? You? You're on tour."

"No, Leona. You."

"What?" Her voice boomed.

Luke explained Christian's call. "I didn't tell him it was you and I don't know what's happening with Tracy, but I couldn't let Christian experience what happened to me."

Guilt washed over Leona's face and Luke would have preferred her wrath.

"Every time I try to fix things or hide them, it gets worse." She played with the food on her plate.

"Then stop hiding and trying to fix everything by yourself," Luke suggested.

"He's right, little squirrel." Mitchell patted her shoulder. "Perhaps it's time to muscle up and give a little shove back of your own. Show them how we Sables get the job done, or in this case, fight back."

Leona's eyes slid back and forth between him and Mitchell, and then her hand floated to her left ear. She wasn't ready.

Luke exchanged glances with her brother. "What did Paul do to you?"

Leona shook her head at her brother.

"It's okay, Leona." They had no more secrets between them and if he ever hoped to have her in his life again he'd have to be done hiding, too.

He explained to Mitchell that his tour manager and fiancée had cheated on him with Paul, how Paul ruined his album, and how Ivy ultimately left him to be with Paul because he was a successful producer and she saw an opportunity to further her career.

"The stealing money part was just a bonus, I guess," Luke finished.

"So…basically that woman left you for Leona," was Mitchell's mic-drop moment.

Both Luke and Leona gawked at Mitchell and let his reasoning sink in.

Luke laughed first. "Well, yeah."

"Somebody ought to tell her." Mitchell laughed.

"Way to go, Mitchell." Leona shook her head and frowned, yet a smile touched her lips.

"That's some true drama right there." Mitchell leaned

back in his chair and eyed his sister with some unspoken sibling language. "Man. Sorry about that."

"Paul did a number on Leo, too. It's hard to trust people in this industry. You're really lucky to have my sister. You won't find anyone more trustworthy and caring. She's the best at what she does, but she's also the best person I know."

"Mitchell…" Leona faced her brother.

"It's the truth, Leo," Mitchell said.

"So, Mitchell. What do you do?"

"I'm an executive at Schroeder and Emblem Investments. I do my fair bit of travel, but I always make time for family. Especially this one." Mitchell pointed to his sister.

Leona beamed at him.

"So what kind of music do you play, man?" Mitchell forked a bite full of his food.

"EDM. You know, Electronic Dance Music. Mostly house, electro house, some dub-step."

"Oh, that crap you and Izzy listen to." Mitchell hung his head, then sat back in his chair. "I'm a classics guy. Classic rock, classic hip-hop. Classical."

"It's not crap. You just don't get it, Mitch-match," Leona chided her brother.

Luke loved her even more when she defended him, and smiled at the exchange between Leona and her brother. "I dig the classics. I've sampled quite a few songs."

"Hmm." Mitchell didn't seem quite convinced they shared the same taste in music.

"Leona? Why do you call him Mitch-match?"

Leona's love showered her brother as she spoke. "I was about four and Mitchell always had problems wearing matching socks. My mother would always complain about it. I think at one point I thought mismatch was his name. Somehow, I remixed it and started to call him Mitch-match. The name stuck."

Luke laughed as he pictured a four-year old Leona running after her brother.

"Do you have family?" Mitchell asked him.

"Yeah. My parents live here in Chicago, and I have a sister who is married with two kids in California. We're very close."

"They're great." Leona picked at her strawberry cobbler. "Especially the kids."

"Yeah? When did you get to meet them?" Mitchell asked.

Luke could feel the flash of heat emanating from her even from where he sat.

Leona cleared their plates. "In San Francisco."

He could see past her casual delivery. Like him, she replayed every delicious moment of their time at his home.

Mitchell tapped him on the shoulder. "Come on, man. We always help with the cleanup."

When Luke had come to his hometown, he'd expected to see his parents and show Leona around. The last thing he expected was to find himself having Sunday dinner, with a spread provided by Leona's mother, in Leona's hotel with her and her brother.

Luke helped Mitchell, but the jet lag was catching up to him. He needed to get some sleep and be up early and prep for his show. He was about to leave when Mitchell stopped him.

"Hold on, Luke. Let me talk to you privately for a minute."

"Mitchell, Luke has to get going." Leona had over-heard her brother's request and wasn't in favor of the conference.

"Hush, little squirrel," Mitchell instructed his sister, and then motioned to him. "Right this way."

Leona wasn't about to fight with big, strong Mitchell, so Luke would have to hold his own.

"Make it quick, he has to go," she called to her brother.

She went into the kitchenette and put half of the re-maining dessert in its container for Mitchell and the other half on a plate for Luke.

God, she was losing her mind to think about what she was thinking about. Tracy had gotten back to her and they'd had a brief call.

"You have more than enough evidence against Paul. I've already started building a case. Just tell me if you want me to pull the trigger."

What am I going to do? Leona had tried to toughen her heart but the exterior didn't hold up around Luke. Seeing her brother reminded her what was at stake. *How can this work?*

A few minutes later, Luke and Mitchell returned. An aura of testosterone surrounded them. "Everything okay?"

"Yeah," Mitchell answered. "Right, Luke?"

"Sure." Luke shook Mitchell's hand.

"Here." Leona handed Luke the cobbler. "Just keep an eye out heading back to your room."

The implications of Luke being caught leaving her room was visible in his jawline. She hated to give him the reminder.

"Thank you." Luke took the cobbler and moments later he was gone.

Leona sat with Mitchell. "What did you say to him?"

"Wouldn't you like to know?"

Leona regarded her brother with hands on hips.

"Relax. I just said that you're special to a lot of people and that if his intentions are anything other than noble, then he could have problems."

The last thing Leona needed was her brother threatening Luke. These past few weeks, Luke had been through the ringer with her.

"Mitch-match."

"Look here, sometimes a man needs to know that what he wants comes with a heavy price." Mitchell paused. "Leo, meet 'Heavy Price.'" Mitchell pointed to himself.

Leona couldn't help but laugh. "You're so silly."

"That man's got it bad. You can see it in that picture of you two in the news."

Leona's hand flew to her ear at the mention of the picture. She could barely look at herself in such a vulnerable state much less study it.

She shook her head.

He patted her shoulder. "I know you hate being on display. I was there with you when Reese did a number on you but when you feel up to it, take another look at the photo."

"There's nothing more to see."

Mitchell cocked his head to the side. "Keep telling yourself that, little squirrel."

Luke's hometown performance brought the house down and Leona had celebrated him from VIP. With their separation still in effect, the what-ifs again floated through her brain all the way until her head hit the pillow in her hotel room that night.

Leona didn't recall when she'd gone to sleep but she sure as hell jumped out of bed at the continuous rapping on her hotel room door.

"What the fuck?" Hell hath no fury like a sleep deprived Leona Sable. She squinted through the peephole and saw Diesel. Her mind cleared and she yanked the door open.

"Is Luke okay?" Her heart vibrated through her body.

"He's fine, Leo, but I need you to get dressed and come with me, now." Diesel pulled his baseball hat up to see her.

She leaned against the doorframe as adrenaline left her, and flapped her lips. "What? It's 4 AM."

"Please. It's important."

"I don't understand… I mean it's the butt crack of dawn and…" She grumbled and then stopped at her words.

Diesel fluttered his eyebrows with a half smile.

Leona shook her head. "I can't."

"Just put on your clothes and come with me."

Everything in her was saying no, but as she put on her clothes and snuck through the hotel to a back entrance, excitement clashed with practicality and she didn't know what to make of her state of mind. Diesel gave her a baseball hat, as well, and she pulled it low. When they exited through the back, Diesel delivered her into the front seat of a dark blue sedan with heavily tinted windows and closed the door.

"Hi," Luke said.

She buckled her seat belt. "You know this is fucking nuts, right?"

"That I'm stealing you away in the middle of the night? Yup." Luke drove off.

Luke drove the short distance to Lake Shore Drive, stopped at a lookout and killed the lights. He and Leona couldn't see much in the dark except for the city lights shimmering on the water, but it was the smallest memory he could give her here in his hometown.

"We won't stay long," he said. "I just wanted a little time with you. And..." He reached into the backseat and presented her with a dozen cupcakes from Sweet Mandy B's. "We have sweets and scenery."

"No way." She popped off her cap and her hat head was adorable. "I hear these are like...the best."

He watched her, proud of his good deed.

"This is better than a dozen roses. Thank you." Her eyes lit up as she inspected the box.

"You're welcome." He'd wanted to do so much more for her and with her, but instead they'd have to make the most of this short time under the cover of night.

"Your show was really good tonight. The hometown fans really appreciate you. Have you enjoyed being here?"

"It's been okay."

"I'm sorry you didn't get a chance to see your folks," she said.

He shrugged it off. "Maybe next time."

She scanned the perimeter of the vehicle through the windows and doubt wrinkled the corners of her eyes. "Maybe we should go back now."

He wouldn't be deterred. He'd never do anything to

hurt her but beyond making love to her, he missed his manager and his friend. He put his distraction techniques in full gear.

"Leona? I've been meaning to share something with you."

"Sure. What is it?"

"Remember Izzy's photo shoot in Colorado?"

"Yeah?"

"Well, it made me realize something that kind of blew my mind, actually."

She'd rushed him along but his next question slowed her down from lightly interested to one hundred percent intrigued.

"Have you ever been to Paris?" he asked.

She rubbernecked. "Yes, I have. That's where Izzy and I met."

"How about a club called L'Essence, and a rave with the Lexionic Twins?"

Her eyes widened and she shook her head. "Okay, you're officially freaking me out. How do you know that?"

Luke recounted his story about deejaying at that same rave in Paris. Her eyes widened in what he could only perceive as a bit of shock.

"No fucking way. That was you?"

Luke nodded. "That was me."

"Oh my God! Izzy and I went around back to see if we could find out who that DJ was. Who *you* were— but you guys had already left."

"You blew me a kiss."

She slapped her hand over her mouth and spoke through it. "I totally did."

"'Get Up and Move for Me' is about that night."

"Hell no."

"Hell yes." Luke touched her hand.

"When we were dancing at your photo shoot we'd thought that the song could be about us. And it is? Wow." She blinked rapidly at him as if he'd morphed into something else right in front of her eyes. "Izzy is going to flip."

"See, Leona? In that small way, we've been a part of each other's lives." He touched her hand and he could see the speed at which she breathed.

She pulled away and leaned against the car door. "Luke?"

The rejection stung but he tempered his reaction knowing what she battled. "You don't have to say anything, Leona. Just be with me here."

"No, I do," she began. "This is so kind of you and hearing about Paris *is* mind-blowing but this is so dangerous for us. You've done all this to keep the media off our tail but what if someone jumps out right now? We have to stay focused on the tour and your goals."

His tour was *the* talked about event of the summer and he finally got the recognition to sell out stadiums and make history. The spotlight was great for his career. But the more popular he became, the further his popularity forced Leona back into hiding.

Maybe bringing her out here had been a mistake. His hand rested on the key in the ignition.

She gave an audible breath through her nose. "Tracy says I have enough to move forward with my case against Paul," she whispered.

He dropped his hands to his lap and angled toward her. He hadn't realized he'd stopped breathing until he spoke. "How do you feel about that?"

"I'm…" Her tongue tickled the corner of her mouth. "I'm scared."

He knew those words were hard for her to speak out loud. He kept his mouth shut to let her own her statement.

"I don't want to be in front of everyone answering questions about things that I wish would just go away but if I don't do this, then what kind of career am I going to have? I have to trust that the truth about my reputation can coexist and even rival what's said or printed about me. Can it?"

"I think it can. So many people love and respect you, Leona. You don't have to do this alone. They'll help you."

"Will you? If I go forward with this, will you help me?" she asked.

His pulse thudded in his inner ear. "There's nothing I wouldn't do for you."

She swallowed so hard it echoed in the quiet car. "I'd have to tell the team." She hyperventilated as she said the words. "We still have a few weeks to your final show and it's going to be crazy in New York and with the ramp up, Aurora, and the final show. This is such a bad idea."

"But a great idea." He could see her shaking as she clutched the plastic container. "You can do this."

She nodded and plucked a cupcake from the box and bit into it. The city lights glimmered against a tear running a path down her cheek. Her loud sniffle slashed at his heart and his hand tingled with the urge to wipe her tears away.

"I should take you back."

Leona had to do what was best for her career, but

as his blossomed, it clashed with his desire to have Leona in his life. He wondered if he'd ever be able to have them both.

Luke called Diesel to coordinate their return. That morning, he lay in bed wired and wanting Leona in his arms. His goals were important and he'd worked with his lawyer Patrick to ensure that his management upheld their end of the deal. However, his separation from Leona had been devastating for them both. The car ride with Leona had given him hope, even though he didn't know what Leona would ultimately decide to do with her case against Paul. He would be there for her in whatever way she needed him.

Luke picked up the phone and made a call.

"Hey, Patty." Luke inhaled and pulled back his shoulders. "I need you to make some changes."

Chapter Twenty-Eight

In Baltimore, the team packed up for New York and the final leg of Luke's tour. The next few days would be crunched with a week's worth of festivities to publicize the New York events.

The media ramp up featuring Luke's mini teaser concert would kick things off in New York with the afterparty at Luke's residency at Aurora. His contract with the Xcelsior Hotel rode on his performance and guest turnout. Two days later he'd perform his final concert at the Epic Stadium, one of the largest venues in the country, and the tour would be over.

What would happen between them? There were still so many things up in the air and once the tour was over, he'd head back to California and she to her apartment in New York. Wouldn't they?

"Have you seen this itinerary? I won't even have time to take a piss," one of the crewmembers complained. She agreed.

"Stay positive. Greatness comes at a price. We can do this." She spoke loud enough to address the room.

"Sorry, Leo."

"I know I'm stretching you guys, but if we're successful, then everyone wins and will reap the benefits of being associated with the best tour of the summer. So let's get on the road and give New York our best."

Through all the busyness, Leona had to connect with Tracy. Paul had been left unchecked for long enough. When he'd extended his anger to Luke that was the last straw. Now Paul was about to experience "a world of hurt."

Everyone was curious about why Paul hadn't made a hit in over a year, now Leona would tell them. She had taken the higher road and let Paul live the celebrity life with all its fame, but he continued to hound her, smearing her name. She had hoped things would die down and tried not to engage to protect her loved ones, her reputation, her career, and now Luke. All it did was allow Paul and the media to bulldoze her. Well, she was done hiding and letting others manipulate her. This was her decision and would finally put an end to it all.

She thought back to her time in California with Luke and the moment she considered taking legal action against Paul. Deep down inside she'd known that one day she might want to fight. *Fight, Leo.*

She pushed fear aside and called Tracy. "Pull the trigger."

"Done," Tracy said into the phone. "We'll have to schedule a press conference to get ahead of it but we'll make sure to do it while you're here in New York. It's still a good idea to keep a low profile and focus on the tour, but with the events you have planned, you need press attention."

"Okay. I'll do my best." Leona's nerves were sizzling again but she had lost so much over this already. She had let the media run her life and let Paul bully her into this person she didn't recognize. Not anymore.

"I know this wasn't easy, but you've made the right choice," Tracy encouraged. "We'll win."

Tracy's confidence was empowering. "Thanks, Tracy."

Later that day, Leona put in a call to Ramelda Manikas with some exclusive information about Paul that Leona made Ramelda "promise" not to share to any of her network.

"Oh, and I already emailed you some footage. But again, that's just between us," Leona stressed.

"Of course, dahhhrrrlling," Ramelda crooned.

Leona gathered her team including Luke to inform them about what was happening. Her team had been supportive when the picture of her and Luke surfaced and had taken on some of her responsibilities without complaint. She owed it to them to keep them in the loop.

"Tracy will send a press release about it but I wanted you guys to be aware before the shit hits the fan. Paul will be vocal but let's use whatever we can to drive attention to the tour events and performances."

Paul and the press had used her enough in the past. Now it was her turn.

"With the craziness we're about to experience in New York, I'm taking back my normal duties and responsibilities with Luke. You guys will need me at full capacity." She got some positive and excited nods. "As it relates to the Paul situation, refer to the press conference Tracy will set up and the press releases the media will receive. As it relates to me and Luke, keep with the same lines regarding our great working relationship and—" she smiled at Luke "—our friendship."

Sara hugged her first. "It's about time, Leo."

Sebastian followed with a sly smile. "We're going to spin and redirect this so hard they won't see straight."

Leona lavished them both with love and appreciation. "You guys have been great. I mean really amazing. I don't know how the tour would have managed the media without you."

Luke came over. "When's your press conference?"

She hated to tell him. "Tracy is trying to schedule it sometime after Aurora and before your last show. It's our only breathing room, if you want to call it that. This way we can get ahead of it."

"Don't worry about the timing." He held her hand and even though Sara and Sebastian were present, she didn't pull away. "We're doing this together."

Her heart leapt into her throat and all she could do was bobble her head.

New York City had better be ready for them because they were coming in hot.

Leona didn't know why she even slept. She was up at eight and running on three hours of sleep. She was delighted to be in her apartment again, even if only for the short time. By eight thirty, she was on the phone and on the computer communicating with her team. She had to pack some items for the hotel where she'd be staying for the next few days to be closer to the team, Luke, and the events.

By noon, after a coffee and croissant brunch, she was at the radio station to meet Sara and Diesel, who had escorted Luke to the location. Leona thought Sara and Diesel would make an okay couple, but she thought Sebastian was perfect for Sara. Why Sara didn't see that was a mystery. Diesel confirmed he had a girlfriend, even though it was clear his fondness for Sara had grown over the course of the tour. This was not an area where she needed to meddle.

"Hey, guys."

"Hey, Leo," Sara greeted.

"Where's Luke?"

"I'm here." Luke emerged from a small corridor.

When Leona saw him, she nearly came in her pants. He hadn't shaved and wore a black V-neck short-sleeved shirt, gray jeans, and black sneakers. Though he was casual he was sophisticated at the same time.

Leona smelled his spellbinding aroma from where she stood. *Calm your horny ass down.*

"Leona?" Luke came over to her and the corners of his mouth curled upward.

"Hey."

He was so close his form filled her vision. "Do me a favor and stop looking at me like that." The vibrations from the timbre in his seductive tone stimulated every nerve in her body.

She was breathless. "Like what?"

"Like you want me to touch you, which we both know is off-limits, right?" The way his eyes scanned her body and lingered at the area between her legs took a bit of the bite off his comment.

"Yeah," she confirmed but it didn't stop the heat from spreading through her. It was the busiest day of her entire career and she wanted to fuck? It had been weeks since she'd been with Luke and no amount of self-love replaced his arms, his tender kisses, and the way he filled her.

"Leona. Good to see you again." Andy's greeting interrupted her hedonistic thoughts.

Leona made the introductions.

"I see you're surviving the media parade. Sorry about some of that shit. But gotta tell you, pal, the tour still blew up. Your fans are true soldiers, Prophet. NYC is going to be lit with this scavenger hunt teaser concert and Aurora after-party tonight."

"Thanks, man. I appreciate it. I have a great team." Luke's eyes held hers.

"We have a tight schedule today but for now, he's all yours," Leona said and handed Luke over to Andy.

"All right." Andy clapped his hands and rubbed them together. "Let's get ready to unleash mayhem on Gotham."

The scavenger hunt to find his teaser concert was in full swing and Luke was able to catch a lot of the fan activity at the various clubs via a live feed on the Internet. The fans were dressed in neon dancewear and carried signs for him. They showed their excitement to the cameras and sang his songs. Hour after hour their numbers grew and he was overwhelmed by the response.

"Are you guys seeing this? It's fucking awesome," he said to his team as they pulled into the location.

Leona made this happen. The affinity she helped create between the fans and him would have a long lasting impact for all involved.

"Luke, we need you to get ready to play. They're loading up the streets. We want the music playing as they open up the barricade. We're going to catch them as they surround the theater. Diesel is already on the roof to secure that no fans miraculously made it up there." Leona grabbed his arm and guided him toward the staircase to the roof.

Photographers snapped images of them as they

walked through the deafening alley of chaos to get him to the roof of the Roscoe Theater. Leona didn't cover her face or let him go. The death grip she had on his arm, however, stopped the blood flow to his hand. They plowed forward together to the stage sandwiched between Diesel, who trailed a path for them ahead, and additional security. She rubbed her left ear but didn't cower. *Wow how things have changed.* His thoughts flew to that first night they met at Aurora when she literally hid behind him to avoid being photographed. Now she held her head high and continued to amaze him. He knew he probably stared at her like a new puppy but he didn't care.

Luke was about to head up to the roof when he peered over his shoulder at Leona. "A good luck kiss?" He didn't wait and melded his lips to hers.

She responded to him without hesitation. "Go." She pushed him by the butt up the stairs.

From the top of the short old building he saw his fans. People who lived in the area were on the roof and peered out of their windows. There were DJ stations on both sides so he could hop from one side to the other and still be visible to all fans, even if he wasn't facing them. It was genius.

The fans congregated in unfathomable numbers. Luke gave a silent prayer for a good performance, safe fans, and a great time for all. He started to play music and picked up the microphone.

"What's up, guys? Come on down." He waved the fans to him.

The fans screamed and the barricade was removed. They ran down, swarming the building like ants within seconds. Luke jumped up to the beat of the music and laughed, amazed at the sight of them. Though he had played large festivals, he had never experienced something like this before. As the fans danced he was in an elevated state of gratitude.

"Thank you." He pointed up to the sky. "And thank you, Leona."

Leona hugged Sara and Sebastian as they bounced in delight. Tommy and Abe made their way through, as well.

"That was phenomenal! Did you see that? No casualties, lots of vending, happy fans, happy us." Leona clapped her hands together.

Luke exited the roof and Leona squeezed his hot, sweaty, and exhausted body. He was quickly carted off to speak to the fans via a live feed to thank them and plug the concert.

"That was just a little taste. I hope to see all of you at the Epic Stadium this Saturday. We're gonna blow the lid off of New York City," Luke responded when an interviewer asked about how he would top this event.

Izzy finally made it through. During the concert, she and a few other media people were stuck in the crowd and had to wait until the concert was over to enter.

"That was massive." Izzy embraced Leona. "You've outdone yourself, Leo."

Leona was so high from the successful scheme her face ached from smiling. "Everyone is pleased it went well."

Izzy's hair was in a ponytail and swung wildly with her animated speech. "How about you? This is going to make you the most sought after tour manager. Again."

"I'm happy but I'm glad it's over. We still have to get ready for the concert on Saturday, so tomorrow will be all press, everyone will get a tiny break, and then Luke has the Epic Stadium." Leona took a breath. "We have to sell out the show."

"Blah, blah, blah. You will, Leo. After this, they should give you whatever you want." Izzy swung her hair.

"Hey, I don't have a lot of time, but I saw Luke's issue. Nice," Leona said excitedly.

"It's selling like hot cakes with all the stuff that's going on with him, everyone is so jealous that I got the inside scoop. Thank you, my love."

"You're welcome." Leona had never told Izzy about Paris. "Hey, I have something to tell you. You're going to freak, so I'll warn you in advance." She told Izzy that Luke was the DJ they experienced in Paris and how his song "Get Up and Move for Me" was about them.

"You're pulling my big toe?" Izzy's face stayed in a stunned expression for what seemed like minutes. Izzy shook her head out of her daze. "You can't make this shite up."

"Right? I mean, what are the freakin' chances?" She hugged Izzy. "You're coming to Aurora, right? It's a great place to network."

"I wouldn't miss it. I'm so proud of you, Leo," Izzy called to her.

The sentiment hit her deep. "Thanks, girl."

Tommy came over and joined their excited group. "The owners from the Xcelsior have been in touch and they're amped to see Luke at Aurora tonight. This is all the city is talking about. Must say, Leo, this was clever as fuck."

She beamed. "Thanks, let's just hope that it was enough for the owners to see that not signing Luke would be the worst decision they ever made."

Chapter Twenty-Nine

Leona and Luke met Tommy, Abe, and Patrick, Luke's lawyer, at Aurora. Instead of being backstage, she found herself in VIP with the owners of the Xcelsior Hotel. They had to close the deal for Luke's residency. As they socialized with the owners, Leona let Tommy and Abe do most of the talking.

"Luke always delivers a great show. His fan base is global. A location like the Xcelsior, where people are coming from all over the world to enjoy Las Vegas, is great for both our interests," Abe said.

"Well, there are some negative opinions about his ego. We want to work with people who are successful and humble," one owner discussed.

Tommy jumped in. "I'm sorry that you've been fed inaccurate information about Luke. He is a generous artist to his fans and those that work for him."

"Tell us more," another owner said.

Leona was done listening. She needed to give the owners an inside look at the artist they evaluated. "Luke is exceptionally talented, but beyond that music means everything to him. His songs are addictive and emotional. He stays up late to communicate with the fans on social media and on live Internet feeds—answering their questions. Even when he was hurt, he didn't want to leave the stage to go to the hospital because he didn't want to disappoint the fans. I've worked with a lot of clients and I don't know any who would do what he did."

The owners nodded. "He's definitely successful."

"Yes, and an asset. He has values that are aligned with your vision," Tommy added to her statement.

"He's about to perform." Abe pointed to the stage.

Luke appeared onstage and performed with high energy. The crowd was elated to see him. With each song he played, he lifted the fans to higher levels of happiness and excitement.

Leona and her companions in VIP danced to his music.

Luke got on the microphone and spoke to the club. "Thank you guys for the love and energy. I see you. You give me your all every time I come out here and I want to give something back to you. Here's a new one for you tonight. It's called, 'Glimpsing Leo.'"

The crowd went wild.

"What?" Leona's feet were cemented and her eyes widened. "Oh my gosh." She swallowed visibly as all eyes from the men in VIP were on her.

Music boomed through the speakers. Leona recognized the radiant melody from when she and Luke shared "dessert" in his studio in San Francisco. Leona listened to the lyrics. The bass was heavy and the poetic vocals on the track spoke of seeing Leo smile. The song made reference to the zodiac signs and constellations, but glimpsing Leo was light in the dark, magic, and grounding gravity.

Luke had written an amazing song for her and froze her in time. The crowd was into it and enjoyed the new music in his set. He put his hand over his heart as he sang the lyrics out to the crowd and then directly to her.

Her heart filled with gratitude for his gift as if it were the very blood in her veins. She turned from watchful eyes to wipe away tears she couldn't control. So much still hung in the balance from the press conference about Paul to Luke's final show. The ship, though it had dodged quite a few icebergs over the past months, could still go down. The press could still attack. She breathed. *Stop! This is Luke's gift to you. Receive it.*

Even if only for this moment, she danced and lost herself in the experience. Everyone in the club, except Luke, disappeared. Leona blew him a kiss and thought of Paris. This was her Luke and she claimed him.

Tommy spoke close to her ear. "That was some song. It seems that you have finally tamed the not so awful kitty-cat, Leo."

"Allergies are clearing up," she said.

Luke was in the zone and played for a few hours, enlivening the fans with each song and remix. By the end of his performance the owners were having a good time and waving glow sticks—the sight a common one at Luke's shows. The owners finally understood the magnetism of The Musical Prophet and what an impactful presence he had on the industry. Now all they had to do was offer him the Las Vegas residency at the Xcelsior.

When Luke's show ended, the owners met with him.

"We want you for the Xcelsior residency," one of the owners announced.

"It would be an honor." Luke shook hands with each of them.

"Yes." Leona nudged Tommy who smiled down at her.

Leona thought back to their very first meeting at

Wallace Entertainment when she'd wanted to wring Luke's neck. Now she couldn't be more proud of him and how far they'd come.

Soon Luke was being ushered off to do post-show press. On the way out, Luke passed Leona and touched her arm.

"Did you like the song?"

Leona nodded, trying to catch her breath. All he did was touch her and she unraveled. "Yes. I loved it."

Luke's chest inflated and a smiled teased the corners of his mouth. He squeezed her hand before he continued to the press area.

Abe trailed behind her. "That went well. Two objectives met and one to go to fulfill the addendum. Oh, and Ruiz scheduled your press conference for tomorrow afternoon."

"Yeah. She sent me a calendar notification." Leona sighed. It didn't take long for reality to squeeze its way in and remind her that her biggest hurdle was only hours away.

"I'll be there to support you, darlin', but I wish you would have told me about all this back at the beginning."

"Says the man who told me the company was in trouble at the eleventh hour."

Abe grunted. "I guess we both had our reasons."

She nudged him with her arm. "Thanks for supporting me."

Abe grinned. "I'm not even going to ask about the song."

"Good. Don't." Leona feigned a professional demeanor but gave him a tiny smile.

"Well, I'm going to put this old man to bed. Saturday should be groundbreaking." Abe hugged her.

She frowned at him. "Way to put the pressure on."

"Which you work so well under. Great job as usual." He kissed her cheek then departed.

Leona glided over to where they were doing press and stifled a yawn as she watched Luke answer questions.

As the women circled and hovered, Diesel made sure to keep people at a reasonable distance from Luke. Luke targeted a wink her way. The simple gesture was sweet but the effect his smoldering eyes had on her, as they lingered, rattled her lid like boiling water.

Just like most nights, this was another late one. She networked on Luke's behalf and introduced him to people of interest. At one point she hung by the bar in the packed venue. Everyone wanted to congratulate Luke or just be near him. She wanted to be near him, too, but the song had already set off a buzz among the attendees. With her press conference tomorrow, she needed to keep the positive vibes around Luke's tour going as long as possible.

Luke made his way toward her, tempting her with each stride.

"Ready to get out of here?"

Leona stifled yet another yawn. "Yes, please."

She spoke into her walkie-talkie to inform the team of their departure and called for the car. Sara and Sebastian hitched a ride with them back to the hotel. As they all separated to their respective hotel rooms, Leona had a harder time justifying not being in his arms.

Chapter Thirty

Leona jolted out of a restless sleep. Between her longing for Luke and her pending press conference, she'd been up several times during the few morning hours. She dialed room service with repetitive emphasis on coffee. She showered and dressed, her fingers charged with nerves. Her breakfast arrived as she fastened the last button on her coral blouse. Summer in New York was miserable but the city gave them a few spring weather days, allowing Leona to wear close-fitting slacks that stopped at the ankles and strappy gold sandals. She searched for her phone and found it in her clutch while she munched on a piece of toast and sipped lukewarm coffee. Her phone's battery was almost dead, but she saw she had received several calls and quite a few text messages. As she brushed her teeth, she checked the first message from Izzy.

You're on TV.

Leona tilted her head. "Huh?" She checked another one from Tracy.

Where are you? We need to connect.

Another message from Sebastian popped on her screen. The Paul situation is trending. I need you.

"What the hell is going on?" She listened to the first message, which was from Tracy.

"Leona. Paul is on the rampage. We had to move your press conference to noon. We have to give the press something ASAP to counter Paul's tirade and keep this to a tidal wave instead of tsunami."

"Uh-oh." Leona went to check the next message but her phone died. She plugged it in to charge it but thought maybe it was a good thing that she couldn't continue to read the messages because she was legit about to freak the fuck out.

She pinched her fingers together in a mediation pose and breathed. "Today is going to be a day from hell, so *whoosah* into it." She readied a larger bag with what she needed for the day.

There was a knock on her hotel room door. She opened it and Luke and his handsome ass strolled inside. "Good morning, beautiful."

"It's a mad house out there! Paul's been yapping, the team is up in arms, and my phone is dead. I have my press conference at noon now, and…and…" She hadn't intended to greet him with the flurry of chaos. She gulped in one wallop of a breath and exhaled. She ambled over to him, lifted to her toes and kissed his cheek. "I'm sorry. Good morning."

"You look pretty." He touched her cheek. "Ready to go to your press conference? Emmett is downstairs."

"Yes?" She massaged her earlobe.

Luke stroked her shoulder caps. "Remember. Every time you hide, they have something to surprise you with. Tell the truth and take the charge out of it. Take your power back."

Luke's pep talk did little to deflate her tension but she was past the point of no return. "Okay. Let's do it." She grabbed her purse and phone and they left together.

The camera lights were blinding and all she could hear was the sound of cameras snapping off shots as fast as her racing pulse. She breathed, centered, anchored, and did whatever she could do to not flee. Her stomach gurgled and she was sure beads of sweat glistened on her face. At the podium she was alone.

Leona spotted Luke and her team. *No, I'm not alone.*

She cleared her throat. "A few weeks ago I made a legal claim against Paul Reese. The claim was for writing credits and back royalties for six hit songs that Paul produced within the last three years. However, the songs were written and produced by me. I have evidence to support my claim which my legal team will be presenting on my behalf."

"That'll never happen, Leona. You want to take credit for *my* work, now?" Paul's voice boomed and he made his way toward her. Security stopped him.

"Hey, check this out," Sebastian said and showed his phone to one of the press guys. After a while there was a murmur across the room and multiple people were watching something on their phones. Her eyes landed on Luke and his grin reached his brows.

"What's happening?" she asked.

Luke came over to her and showed her his phone, and the exclusive video she'd leaked to Ramelda Manikas played on the screen. The video showed Leona and

Paul in his studio. Leona produced a song, writing and editing lyrics while Paul watched on.

"Oh my gosh." *Don't freak out. This particular varietal of shit was supposed to hit the fan. Thank you, Ramelda. Do not freak out.*

Tracy took over. "Thank you, everyone. You all have the press release. For any additional information or interviews, please contact Wallace Entertainment."

"Let's get you out of here," Luke said, but as they walked toward the side entrance, Paul blocked their path.

Luke seemed to have every intention of plowing through, so she pulled his arm to keep him from colliding with Paul.

"You'll never see a dime," Paul hollered at her around Luke.

Leona felt the charge in Luke's body. She would have loved to see Luke drop Paul but the last thing she needed was for them to fight in front of the cameras. She tucked Luke behind her and addressed Paul.

"It's over. You don't get to dictate what happens or control the conversation anymore. I'm at the table now."

"I have a legal team, too, Leo." Paul reached for her and she swatted his hands away while simultaneously pushing back on Luke, who she knew was itching to get to Paul.

"Trust me. You don't want to do this." She motioned to all the cameras snapping photos of them. A security guard finally reached them and pulled Paul away. Paul hesitated for a moment but then embarrassment came over his angry visage. The rapid sound of lens shutters capturing every emotion.

"This isn't over," Paul mumbled but Leona knew

him well enough to know that he didn't believe his own words.

Luke ushered her out quickly and she was glad that was finally over.

"You should have let me deck him," Luke said once they were on their way to the hotel. He rubbed his knuckles as if they were still thirsty to connect with Paul's face.

"That's the last thing I should have let you do." She faced him. Luke plucked two miniature bottles from his pocket. One whisky and the other was vodka. "Pick your poison."

"Vodka." She'd never welcomed a shot of alcohol more than this moment.

He handed her the drink.

Luke shivered as if a chill ran down his spine. "Has Paul ever touched you in anger, Leona? Have you ever been afraid of him hurting you?" He swallowed the shot of whisky.

"No." She gave him a sheepish smile before she shot the vodka. Her face wrinkled as the potency slid down her throat. "He lost a lot today. So, I'll give him the benefit of the doubt that he wouldn't have tried to physically hurt me."

Luke blew out a shitload of air and fisted his hands so tight they cracked. "Let's pray I never cross paths with him ever again." He put his arm around her shoulder and pulled her to him.

"We have to meet up with the team for your interviews, and we have the vendor dinner tonight, and there's the big concert—"

"We have to work on your workaholic ways. You

just did something big. Give yourself some credit and relax. We'll get to all the rest, eventually."

She eased out of his embrace to face him. "My workaholic ways helped sell out most of your tour, execute a brilliant ramp up—"

"Brilliant?" he asked.

"Yes, brilliant. And what about your Xcelsior—"

"I'm not complaining too hard. I just want you to take a minute to recognize how much you've overcome to give that press conference."

"I do in my own way, I guess," she said. Luke was right but there was still a large milestone ahead of them.

He arched a brow at her.

"Okay, I'll work on it." She leaned her shoulder against the backseat. "I'm glad you were there with me today."

He kissed her temple. "I got you, baby. I always will."

Since their split in Las Vegas, Luke had respected her decisions even though it had caused them both pain. Yet he was there for her while she overcame her biggest challenge. "I know."

"I fucked up, Leona."

His declaration had her sitting more erect in the moving vehicle. "What?"

Luke twisted his soul patch. "I should have told you that I didn't blame you for Paul. I've never blamed you. Paul was the one who pawned your work off as his own. I assumed you'd know I could never blame you."

"I should have spoken out a long time ago. I was sure you'd hate me when you found out." Her pulse hit like typewriter keys against her skin and the stronghold around her emotions slacked. "If you did, my brain would get it but my heart couldn't take that."

"I could never hate you. I love you, Leona." He held her gaze. "You have to know that I love you."

A shaky breath rippled through her like the water rings around a skipping rock. She reached for his hand. "I love you, too, Luke. I have ever since you got me motion sickness meds."

"That long, huh?" He chuckled. "I'll do you one better. That first day you threw me a box of animal crackers."

"This whole time I just kept thinking about one thing. Like an anchor of focus."

He intertwined his fingers with hers. "And what's that? That you were thinking about?"

"You." She peered up at him, her eyes moved from his sparkling green-gray eyes to his mesmeric lips.

Luke captured her mouth with his. Her mouth opened to receive his ravenous tongue. Damn, she missed his taste. She placed her hand on his chest and his heart as it thudded against her palm.

"Fuck, Leona. You can't say things like that to me." He squeezed her breast and fondled the imprint of the nipple that protruded from her blouse. Her hand moved to caress the taut muscles in his arm. His finger curved into the opening of her top, gripping the material, ready to rip. "I've been lost without you…starving for you."

"Not as much as I have." She was breathless and eager for more.

"Miss Sable, Mr. Anderson. We've arrived." The sound of Emmett's voice through the backseat intercom barely broke through the sound barrier of their love cocoon.

Luke cursed, his eyes shadowed with the same longing that robbed her of good sense. Her legs stuck slightly to the leather seats through the thin, close-fitting material of her pants. They separated and Luke grabbed her hand, and dashed with her into the hotel.

Don't rip her clothes off in this fucking elevator. His mantra did nothing to dull the pain of his aching dick against his jeans. Leona melded her body to his and the way her hands ventured to places below his waist didn't help. He did his best to shield her from the elevator security camera as he consumed her. The make out session that commenced lasted the three minutes it took for them to ride up to his suite. His hands shook as he worked his card in the door. He wanted her more than he could withstand.

Inside his suite Leona pulled him to a love seat. He kissed her and left in search for a condom, which was no small feat since he'd only been fucking himself and he didn't need a condom for that.

"Where you goin'?" Her breathless plea nearly ended his search as she shadowed him.

"Condoms," he growled.

"Get over here." Her laugh carried notes of frustration. "I'm on something, remember?"

He hadn't, and was back to her faster than he knew he could move. Her phone buzzed and Leona reached for it in her pocket.

"Oh no you don't."

"You have press. They need you."

"*I* need you." He plopped into the love seat.

His hand shot to her waist and he drew her to his sitting figure. She stood between his legs and regarded him as he lifted her blouse up to reveal her belly. He ran his tongue over her navel and kissed the exposed skin. She trembled at his touch.

"It's been too long since I've tasted you, Leona." His hands slid to unfasten the button on her pants. He tugged the material down to discover that she was panty-less, revealing the mound of her center. His temperature skyrocketed and he wanted out of his clothes.

Leona's fingers combed his hair and tilted his head up. "Luke. We have to go." Her voice was heavy with desire.

He peeled her pants over the bump of her rear and she swayed with each tug before the material passed her knees. He slipped one hand between her legs as he continued to kiss her belly, while the other caressed the flesh of her ass. With her pressed against him and inhaling her scent, she was his again. He had returned home.

"Luke," she whimpered. Constrained by her clothes, she bent her knees outward to accommodate his hand. He felt the weakness in her and supported her every move.

"I've missed you, Leona," he moaned from deep in his chest. He slid his fingers inside her moist center and his mouth descended on her.

Leona let out a cry that pierced his soul. She slumped against him. He grabbed a hold of her waist to keep her from falling and pulled her down. Leona was tangled in her pants and made an awkward fall backward onto the floor. She couldn't help but laugh and neither could he. He tugged off her shoes and pants.

"I want you so much, baby." His mouth continued to assault her clit and her hips bridged upward for more. He came to eye level with her and positioned the tip of his hard cock at her center.

The clanking of his belt garnered her full attention. Leona huffed, stroking his head. "We have to... we should—"

He filled her and her delectable insides surrounded him, drowning him. Her high-pitched squeals of pleasure grew louder, as his slow and hard thrusts pleased her over and over. He needed to consummate their love. He desired her more than food, air, or water. Loving her like this was all that mattered.

"Do we have time now?" he teased against her lips, pumping into her.

"Uh-huh." Her tongue played in his mouth and she devoured him.

Luke slipped one hand between her legs and she melted further into the floor.

"I've been so empty without you inside me. I've missed loving you like this." Leona spoke against his lips and the thought of her tasting her own essence with him brought him closer to the edge.

He increased his speed and her nails dug into his shoulders as her body shook with each of his full-bodied lunges into her.

"Fuck, baby," he hissed against her lips. "I won't last with you saying shit like that to me."

He flipped her on top of him. Her legs straddled him and he gripped her waist to minimize her movements while he jackhammered into her, sending delicious delights through her. Her body jiggled as her pleasure mounted.

"Yes, Luke," she called, as her passion rocked through her and into him. She stiffened and squealed, and her pelvis bucked against him.

His arms circled around her waist and he squeezed

her tightly. He catapulted up and shouted his potent and virile orgasm into her chest. She loved hearing him come.

"I love you so much," she heaved. She held his head and they both shivered from the aftershock of their wild and thirsty lovemaking.

"And I love you, baby. All of you." Luke nuzzled his sweaty forehead against the slick perspiration under her chin.

"No way," Leona said when he hardened again inside her. "We have to go."

A rumble of laughter escaped his chest as he flipped her back onto her back and dragged himself out of her. He swept down to kiss her exposed belly.

"I'll be back." He spoke close to the mound between her legs before he kissed the thin patch of hair there.

Leona was in stitches. "Silly."

He pulled her up and with wide, cowboy-like steps, dragged her to the bathroom where they cleaned up and dressed. His stiff dick led every move and Leona's inability to take her eyes off him wasn't helpful.

"I just need a sec."

Leona smirked before leaving to wait for him in the main room while he finished up.

When he returned, he found her deep in thought by a window overlooking the city. He could only imagine what went through her head. She'd closed a big deal, held a press conference to defend herself, and still had a tour to finish. In the middle of it all was their love for one another, which they both wanted to protect. He loved her and would do anything for her. He believed she would, too. With the pending closeout of the tour, one question remained. How was this going to work?

"Tomorrow's a big day. The Epic Stadium should be a great finale," she said.

"About that, Leona." He joined her. "The tour is ending and being without you just isn't an option anymore. I'll do anything to have you in my life."

"I feel the same, baby." She angled her body to his.

"What do you think about me moving to New York? I've spoken to Patrick and my broker, and I'd be willing to sell the San Francisco house."

Leona gasped. "But you love that house and the ocean."

"I love you more. Building a life with you means more to me than a house. Plus the surf in Rockaway, Long Island, and Jersey ain't half bad." He charmed her with his killer smile.

Leona said nothing for a long time. She knitted her fingers with his, squeezing his hand and stroking his skin.

"Don't sell the house. We fell in love there. Jane and the kids are on the west coast. Your studio? We'll make staying there work, even if only part-time."

"You don't want me to sell the house?" He kissed her forehead.

She shook her head.

"Then I won't sell our house." He tilted her chin up to kiss her lips.

"You know I'm going to marry you, don't you?" His breath hitched in his throat at the thought of being her husband one day.

"Yes." Her eyes glistened but she beamed up at him. "But you'll have to date me first."

Luke laughed. "As you wish."

Epilogue

Luke's moment of truth had arrived. He scanned the computer screen as he made some minor changes to his music. He had set some lofty goals and had the woman he loved. He was confident Leona would love him whether or not they succeeded, but if he didn't achieve this last goal, how would he feel?

There was a knock on the door followed by Diesel's entrance. "Ready?"

"As I'll ever be." Luke headed to the stage with Diesel. On the way, they picked up Tommy and Abe.

Music filled the stadium as the opening act played. The tech guys secured his computer and readied it on the stage. Luke looked for Leona. She normally made sure he was all set, but he knew she was stressed about the numbers.

"It's been a great summer, Luke. I'm sure tonight will be no different. This is your biggest and best tour, yet. You did it, man." Tommy hugged him.

"The offers are rolling in, Luke," Abe chimed. "This was a lucrative partnership for us both. We don't know if you've sold out yet, but it has been a pleasure to work with you. I hope we continue our relationship."

The man was shaky and beads of sweat pimpled his

forehead. Abraham Wallace worked to put on a good face but he was worried. Failure to sell out the Epic Stadium meant the loss of big bucks for Wallace Entertainment. Luke would be nervous, too, if that was his possible fate.

"Thank you," Luke said.

From the corner of his eyes he saw security escorting a group of people, Leona, his sister Jane, her husband Aaron, and…his parents?

They smiled at him as they approached and the emotion rumbled. He had wanted to make his parents proud of him with the work he did this summer.

"Mom?"

"My son." His mother held his face with tears in her eyes. She kissed him several times. "It's so good to see you, honey." She held him tight—almost as tight as he held her.

"I'm so proud of you, boy. We both are. I mean… look at all this." His father hugged them both while Jane sniffled and held on to Aaron.

"Thanks, Dad," was all he could express through the tightness in his chest. "How?"

"Leona arranged for us to come. She thought this moment would be important for you and wanted you to have your family here. All of us." His mother motioned to his tour manager–girlfriend.

"Leona?"

"Yes. She called us when you were in Japan, just before we shipped out for the cruise," his father explained.

Luke spotted Leona with Tommy and Abe.

She had organized this during the stormy events after Las Vegas. "You did this for me?"

Leona nodded and blotted her eyes with a knuckle. "Jane helped."

His mother held his face in her hands. "We've missed seeing you, honey. We love you, Luke. I hope you know we don't want you to be anything other than who you are."

"Screw anyone who thinks otherwise," his father bolstered, his athletic build mirrored his own.

Though he wanted them to be proud of him, they were here to witness him possibly make history if he sold out the Epic Stadium, and that was enough.

Jane and Aaron came over to hug him.

"I have to go check the box office, but I'll be back." Leona inched toward the exit.

Luke grabbed her hand and squeezed it. "Thank you."

"You're welcome. Hold them close. They love you," she whispered and left.

Luke turned back to Jane. "Where are Emily and Ryan?"

"With a sitter at the hotel. We almost brought them, but that would have been the worst idea ever thought up." Jane's eyes widened.

"Without a doubt. We'd actually like to enjoy the show. We could use a date night." Aaron draped an arm over his wife.

Luke laughed, knowing firsthand the manpower needed to care for his niece and nephew. He finally remembered his manners and introduced his family to Abe and Diesel.

A few minutes later, a commotion startled him from his conversation with his family. Leona, flanked by Sara and Sebastian, ran at full speed, shouting something he couldn't make out above the thud of the music.

"We sold out! The show is sold out!" They continued to run before finally stopping in front of him.

Leona tried to catch her breath. "You just sold out the Epic Stadium. You made history. Again. You are the first DJ to sell out the Epic Stadium!" Her octave grew higher and louder with each word. Her delivery of the news made him love her even more.

Abe clapped his hands together. "Yes."

"I didn't doubt you for a minute," Tommy said.

Leona hugged him but he was still immobile from the news.

"I couldn't have done it without you guys in my corner," he somehow stated to the group who he'd seen work their asses off for him. "This is your moment, too."

"You did it, son." His father patted him on the back while his sister and mother hugged him. Aaron shook his hand. He was completely overwhelmed.

"We have to get him to the stage," Leona instructed Diesel then faced him. "Ready, Luke?"

He nodded, still overcome with his family's presence and the news about selling out.

Leona addressed his family. "Security will get you guys to your viewing location and we'll make sure to meet up with you after the show."

"I love you guys." Luke finally found his voice.

He and Leona gave a few parting words to Tommy and they headed to the stage with Diesel.

"Get your ass on that stage and bring the house down," Leona said in his ear.

Luke spun her into his arms and kissed her like it was the first time he'd tasted her. He released her and ran up the stairs. The earsplitting screams from the crowd filled the stadium when they saw him. He picked up the microphone as the beginning of a song played.

"Thank you guys for supporting the tour. This is our last show and because of you and the great team I have, we have made history. They said a DJ couldn't do it, that our music wouldn't last, but we did it. We sold out the Epic Stadium. Together."

The crowd went wild and nearly bowled him over.

Luke absorbed the tens of thousands that filled the stadium.

"Let's make this a night we'll never forget," he howled into the microphone.

The song he played built until the beat dropped and the fans went wild. He was filled with gratitude and love. He had made it. He had done the impossible and he knew that he couldn't have done it without the woman he loved.

Friends and fans of The Musical Prophet attended the wrap party to celebrate their final show. One such person was Christian Sacks.

"There appears to be more than one reason why I am going to need you once you tie up all the post-tour loose ends, Leo." The news about her suing Paul for writing credits and royalties traveled fast.

Leona chewed on her lip. "I've never officially done this, Christian."

"Well, for someone who hasn't officially done this, your track record is decent. You also have me and the perfect tutor over there to help you." He referenced Luke.

"I do, don't I." Leona's eyes showered Luke with adoration.

They discussed managing and also working on his album a little bit more before Christian was pulled away. Luke mingled with his family and everyone wanted time with the man of the hour. Leona imprinted the happy faces to her memory. The company, though not completely out of the woods, was in better standing and Luke's career was flourishing. They had done it.

Later, when everyone started to depart, Leona and Luke rode a car back to the hotel.

"Hey, can we stop at my apartment real quick?" Leona asked.

"Of course, baby." Luke intertwined their fingers.

In her apartment, Luke strolled into the living room and perused Peaches as she whirled around in her tank.

"I think this is well deserved." Leona greeted him with two flutes of champagne.

"Thank you."

They clinked glasses and took a celebratory sip.

Leona held his hand and guided him to her bedroom. "Come with me."

"Oh?"

His sexual energy was electric and engulfed her body like a hand-stitched afghan. "You're so one track minded."

"You do it for me, baby, and I'd want it no other way."

In her bedroom she waited for Luke to see her surprise. "This is for you."

He cocked his head when he saw a dark wood dresser tied in a huge, shiny blue bow, and guffawed. Leona clapped her hands at his reaction. She'd had Izzy set it up for her during the frantic New York events for Luke, and her friend executed the task perfectly.

"Open it," Leona instructed and Luke tore the bow away. He opened each empty drawer and in the last one found a key attached to a retro key chain of a box of animal crackers.

Luke turned to her with a smile that creased his entire face and tapped the key on his palm. "Not only are we officially dating. We're officially living together."

"Yes," she said.

"You're mine, forever." Luke pulled her by the waist against him.

"And you're mine."

Her hands rested on his biceps as he danced with her and sang the words to "Glimpsing Leo."

Glimpsing Leo.
Reflecting constellations to the sun.
Gravity I've come undone.
Out of darkness light and love.
A burning path to her I run.
Come alive. Come feel the love.
She's music and magic, my only one.
Glimpsing Leo.

"The tour is over, Leona. You know what that means?" He started to undo the tie on her blouse.

"What?" she asked and caressed his muscles. She inhaled his familiar scent and closed her eyes.

"I can have intimate relations with you wherever the fuck I want." He planted delicate kisses on her neck. "So you can start getting undressed now."

"I think we already broke that rule," Leona razzed and leaned into his caress.

"Shh. I won't tell if you won't tell."

"Are we negotiating another agreement?"

Luke chuckled and gave her a more thorough kiss as he continued to undress her. "No more agreements, baby."

"Agreed." Leona laughed against his lips.

* * * * *

Acknowledgments

Thank You, God, for this journey and all of Your blessings. Through You all things are possible.

Thanks to my editor Stephanie Doig (and the team at Carina Press) and my agent Sarah Younger (and the team at Nancy Yost Literary Agency). You both gave me the best early Christmas gift ever!

Thank you to my writing partners and groups. I truly and deeply appreciate your valuable time, advice, and talents.

Last, but not least, thanks to my fans and readers. You're the best!

About the Author

JN Welsh is a native New Yorker and natural story-teller. As a young student in school, she was a voracious reader who stole her older sister's romance novels. She graduated to writing entertaining love stories, in the form of long notes passed in class, for her friends. The writer was born.

She writes entertaining, often humorous, and provocative tales about strong, career-driven, multicultural heroines who are looking for love. Her punchy, flowing dialogue and big-city stories are heartwarming and stick to your ribs. When she's not writing she can be found dancing, wine-ing, rooting for her favorite baseball team, and/or indulging in countless guilty pleasures.

To purchase and read more books by JN Welsh please visit JN Welsh's website at www.jnwelsh.com/books.

Follow JN on Social Media:
Twitter: Twitter.com/JN_Welsh
Facebook: Facebook.com/JNWelshBooks
Instagram: Instagram.com/JN_Welsh